LC-4

Gray, A. W. (Albert William)

The man offside.

$18.95

© THE BAKER & TAYLOR CO.

THE MAN

OFFSIDE

A. W. GRAY

THE MAN OFFSIDE

A DUTTON BOOK

DUTTON
Published by the Penguin Group
Penguin Books USA Inc., 375 Hudson Street,
New York, New York 10014, U.S.A.
Penguin Books Ltd, 27 Wrights Lane,
London W8 5TZ, England
Penguin Books Australia Ltd, Ringwood,
Victoria, Australia
Penguin Books Canada Ltd, 2801 John Street,
Markham, Ontario, Canada L3R 1B4
Penguin Books (N.Z.) Ltd, 182-190 Wairau Road,
Auckland 10, New Zealand

Penguin Books Ltd, Registered Offices:
Harmondsworth, Middlesex, England

First published by Dutton, an imprint of New American Library, a division of Penguin
Books USA Inc.
Distributed in Canada by McClelland & Stewart Inc.

First Printing, June, 1991
10 9 8 7 6 5 4 3 2 1

 REGISTERED TRADEMARK—MARCA REGISTRADA

Library of Congress Cataloging in Publication Data

Gray, A. W. (Albert William)
    The man offside / by A.W. Gray.
        p.   cm.
    ISBN 0-525-93310-7
    I. Title.
    PS3557.R2914M36   1991
    813'.54—dc20   90-24941

                                                                              CIP

Printed in the United States of America

Set in New Aster
Designed by Leonard Telesca

PUBLISHER'S NOTE
This is a work of fiction. Names, characters, places, and incidents either are the products
of the author's imagination or are used fictitiously, and any resemblance to actual per-
sons, living or dead, events, or locales is entirely coincidental.

For Martha, my Martha, my life, my love.
Rough roads gettin' behind us.

THE MAN OFFSIDE

ONE

Donna Brendy's eyes weren't quite blue. They weren't quite gray, either. They seemed to change color depending on what she was wearing, which right now was a French-cut one-piece swimsuit that was dove gray bordered by royal blue. They were laughing eyes with little crinkles at the corners, and they narrowed some against the glare created by aqua water shimmering under the kind of buttermilk sky that comes to Texas in late August. And there was some hurt in those eyes that the laugh crinkles couldn't quite hide. I'd helped put some of the hurt there a few years back. I didn't feel really tall about that.

She was seated poolside on a chaise longue made of cedar planks. She crossed one smooth, tanned leg over the other, then uncrossed her legs and recrossed them again, and adjusted the elastic at her hip with a red-nailed finger. She still was squirmy. That hadn't changed.

"I wasn't sure you'd come," she said.

"That makes two of us," I said. "How've you been, Donna?"

"How have I been? Since I've seen you I've been a lot of different ways. It's been nine years, Rick."

It had. The last movie we'd seen together had been *Chinatown*. Elvis had been alive. There wasn't much for me to say

say to that, so I folded my sport coat over my arm and shifted my weight from one foot to the other.

She gestured toward a lawn chair, also cedar, which sat in shade cast by an enormous snow white beach umbrella. I sat down. My collar was damp. I loosened my tie. The knot was damp also.

"I didn't call you on my own," she said.

"You didn't call me, period. How'd you know to get in touch with me through Sweaty Mathis? Bail bondsmen aren't in your circle of friends, or at least they didn't used to be."

There was a round cedar table at her elbow, and on it was a tall frosted glass with a lime wedge impaled on its edge. She picked up the glass and sipped from it. "I was just following instructions. Jack told me who to call—I don't know how Jack knew. He's so panicked."

Asking her to get in touch with me must have been tough on Jack. He would have thought that over for a long time. I said, "He has a good reason to be panicked, from what I've read. Does he know I'm meeting you over here, at the house?"

There was the barest flicker in her gaze. I'd seen that look enough times to know she'd just been thinking about lying, then changed her mind. She said, "I didn't tell him where. He's hoping that we're meeting someplace else, I suppose. He didn't ask."

The back door was a solid nine-iron shot from the edge of the pool. A uniformed maid appeared on the redwood deck and set a tray on the top step. The tray was loaded down with glasses, ice, and throwaway bottles. The window at the maid's back was stained glass. Jack had done well. The maid went inside. The pane in the door caught a flash of light as she closed it.

Donna said, "Wouldn't you rather go inside? You look awfully warm." She still pronounced "inside" like "'insahd."

Her swimsuit was cut away in a diamond pattern from just below her navel up to the point where a thin cloth string held it together between her breasts. She looked pretty warm herself. "It would be cooler," I said.

"Our talk may take awhile. I don't want you passing out

on me." She put one foot on the treated Kool-Deck. "I'll be just a minute. There's a bar in the den, help yourself."

There was a small bathhouse behind the pool, in back of the diving board. She slipped her feet into rubber sandals, went around to the bathhouse, and went inside. I watched her bare, rounded hips disappear, then headed for the house, slinging my coat over my shoulder. A drop of sweat plopped into my eye. I brushed it away.

Three little girls in sunsuits had appeared from the yard outside the pool and surrounded the maid's tray of drinks. One child was clearly in charge, doling out the goodies on the top red brick step.

"Hey. She's got more'n I do," said a freckled redhead with a front tooth missing.

A brunette who had her hair tied into doggy ears made a face and stuck out her tongue at the redhead. "Do not!" the brunette said. "Jacqueline's being fair."

The kiddie in charge was wearing a blue pair of shorts with a white bodice held up by shoulder straps. She took the glasses away from the brunette and the redhead, and held them out to me. "They're even, aren't they, mister?" She had wide, laughing eyes that were a color somewhere between blue and gray. Her hair was thick and hung nearly to her waist. It was a shiny mahogany color. More heredity.

I bent and made a show out of eyeballing first one glass, then the other. Each was about half full of red sparkling punch. "Right on the button," I said.

"See there?" said Jacqueline Brendy. She handed the drinks to the other little girls—who held them side by side and checked up on me—then faced me again. "Aren't you a friend of Daddy's?"

"An old friend. I haven't seen him in awhile."

"He's not home," she said.

I wasn't quite sure how to handle that one. "Oh. Well, I'm an old friend of your mother's, too."

"My daddy's in jail," she said. The other little girls giggled. Jacqueline had used the same tone of voice she'd probably use in saying, "I'm six years old." Which was about how old she was. She led the other girls, each one carrying a glass of punch in both hands, back through the wooden gate into the yard. A fancy swing set, complete with a tent-covered landing at the summit, was visible over the top of the gate. A jungle gym rose to one side of the swing set. I went into the house.

The maid was dusting built-in, hand-carved bookcases in the den. Most of the books in the stacks were classics— Melville, Twain, Dickens—along with a couple of modern works by Michener. Not to my taste, which probably meant that it took some breeding to appreciate them. The maid was a chubby Hispanic, a Mama Rosa type. She stopped what she was doing, gave me a disapproving nod, and left the room.

I made the fifty-foot journey from the back door to the bar. On the way I sidestepped a long, low-slung couch and a Wm R Knabe & Co baby grand piano. The piano was polished and its keys shone like flossed teeth.

Jack's bar was the only thing in the room that I recognized. It was dark-stained wood and sat on short legs that were carved into lion's paws. Jack and I had lugged the thing up from Mexico one spring, placed it in the apartment that we were sharing at the time, and had parties around it. It was one of those things left over from bachelorhood that wives would like to get rid of but know better than to ask. The bar had stood up pretty well, considering some of the parties. I fixed W.L. Wellers over ice in a rock glass.

On the wall behind the bar was an old Cowboy team photo in a silver frame—a good-sized picture, probably thirty by twenty. Jack was in the top row between a grinning Bob Lilly and a scowling Bob Hayes. I squinted and looked for myself in the picture, then noticed the banner hanging over the heads of the players which read, "SUPER BOWL CHAMPS." I gave up the search. They'd traded me to the Rams two years before this picture was taken. Jack's Super Bowl ring was mounted on a small gold atlas, inside a glass case on the bar. I'd always wanted one of those rings.

I strolled around, sipping my sour mash whiskey and acting as though I belonged, enjoying the springy feel of the rich green carpet. Dimitri Vail had done the painting of Jack and Donna that hung over the mantel. She was in snug riding breeches astride a muscular palomino. He was leading the horse, and I thought that the horse looked a whole lot happier about it than Jack did. Donna would have really had to put on the pressure to get Jack to pose for that one. I was admiring the painting when Donna came in.

She'd put on a yellow terry robe that was open at the throat. The opening extended downward far enough that I should have been able to see the string which held the top of her swimsuit together, but the string wasn't there. There was a faint tan line across her breastbone. Her smallish feet were still in rubber sandals, her long, dark hair slightly tousled. "Dimi painted it at the ranch," she said. "Two models actually posed for him, and then he drew our faces in later. You know how Jack is about being still for anything."

"I was wondering about that," I said. "You thirsty?"

"Nothing alcoholic. I can't take liquor during the day. My dizzy spells."

I knew all about Donna's dizzy spells. Nothing really serious, something she'd have to live with. They used to come to her in the afternoon; one in particular I remembered during the year I'd held out until September and Jack had been in training camp at Thousand Oaks, California. I'd revived her and barely gotten her steady on her feet in time to meet Jack's plane. I fixed her ginger ale. We sat on the couch.

"How's he holding up?" I said.

"About as well as you could expect. He's putting up a front, trying to be funny. He says he's kingpin of the cell block. Oh, Rick . . ."

I gave her a handkerchief. She blew her nose and sneezed a little sneeze.

"The paper says he's having a bond hearing," I said. "What, Thursday? Two days from now?"

She nodded. Her eyes were slightly red from crying.

"He's not going to have it easy," I said. "Believe me, I've been through it."

"That might be why he wants to talk to you," she said.

"Might be?"

"I don't really know the reason," she said. She raised her hand Girl Scout fashion. "Honest. Things are happening so fast I can't keep up. All I know is that Jack wants you to talk to his lawyer, then come to see him. After I give you some money."

I absently brushed my thigh, where my total liquid assets lay folded in my pants pocket. Two twenty-dollar bills. "Give me money for what?" I said.

"That's for Fred to tell you. Fred Cassel, he's Jack's lawyer."

I leaned forward, took a slug of the bourbon, and rested my forearms on my thighs. There was an ivory statuette of a stampeding longhorn on the coffee table, and I watched it as I said, "This isn't making any sense, Donna. Me? Give money to me, to talk to a lawyer? Are you sure you've got the right guy? Do you even know what I'm doing for a living these days?"

"I've heard rumors. Aren't you some sort of gambler?"

"Some sort of gambler." I laughed, and hoped that the laugh didn't sound as bitter to Donna as it did to me. "I'm a second-rate runner for some bookmakers, which means that I collect from guys who bet more than they can afford to lose. Oh, yeah, I also do some work for Sweaty Mathis, chasing guys that've skipped out on Sweaty's bonds. None of it's any fun, but it keeps me eating. Or usually it does, not always, which is more than I can say for a lot of the guys I knew in prison. But none of my credentials are anything that're going to help Jack. Not in the fix he's in."

She nervously rubbed her forehead. "I'm telling you all I know."

I'd been angling for her sympathy over what poor little me was doing for a living, but was glad she hadn't taken the bait. I was giving myself all the sympathy that one man could handle. My face muscles relaxed. "If you think that was good," I said, "then you should hear my shower soliloquy. Straight from *Hamlet*. How are you taking all this, Donna?"

She adjusted her position, curling her legs up underneath and sitting on her ankles. The robe parted slightly, revealing fine dark hairs on her inner thigh. She said, "I don't have time to wonder about me. I'm too caught up with how Jacqueline's taking it."

"She's a straight-out young lady."

Donna looked puzzled for just an instant, then her features smoothed. "Oh. She hit you with the jail bit. She's too young, really, for what's happening to sink in. Right now she likes the shock value of telling about it. It's Jack's idea, he says not to hide anything from her. If it was me I'd do it differently."

"You don't have any say-so?" I said.

She smiled helplessly. "Confessions of a rooster-pecked wife. Look, Rick, there isn't any reason for you to believe this, but except for—except for the times I was with you I've been a protected hausfrau. Jack makes all the decisions. All of them."

It was the first time either of us had spoken it aloud. The mention of us—of Donna and me—started some vibes in my temples, and I hoped that the subject didn't come up again. Not right now, anyway. I said, probably too quickly, "Look, it's really none of my business. But this house, plus a ranch yet. Paintings by Dimitri Vail. What's paying for all of this? All Jack's ever told me was that he had an investment company. Investments in what? You don't buy homes in Bent Tree on what Jack made playing football. Maybe at today's wages, but not when Jack and I played. I've got some experience with that."

She wiggled and extended one leg straight out in front of her on the sofa. "You know as much about it as I do. Investments, that's all he's said for years. Oh, he talks some at parties—oil deals, a couple of movies. But you know what? I think he was just trying to impress people with whatall he knew about different things. He's tried so hard to shake the dumb jockstrap image, he's obsessed with it. Do you think . . . ?"

"I don't think anything until I know," I said. "But they're going to try to prove that all of this came from drugs. Cocaine. If they prove it you'll lose it all." The afternoon sun was sinking on the horizon, and a few slanted rays were making outlines on the carpet. She got up and closed some flowered drapes over a window and switched on a lamp. "So? Naked I came into the world," she said.

"None of which explains why anybody wants to see me about it," I said.

"You don't have any idea? Funny, I thought you would."

"Well, Jack and I were tight once upon a time," I said. "And I'd do about anything to help. But I don't have any money, and I'm sure as hell not going to have any clout with the U.S. prosecutor's office. Not with my record."

She strolled thoughtfully to an antique rolltop desk, rolled the top open, and sat down. She picked up a thick brown envelope with a rubber band around it. "I'm supposed to give you this. It's five thousand dollars."

My throat went dry. That morning I'd asked Sweaty Mathis for an advance on my five-hundred-dollar fee for locating a skipped burglar. I'd been looking for the guy for more than a month. Sweaty had laughed. I said, "That's a lot of money just for going to see Jack's lawyer."

"Do you know Fred Cassel?" she said.

"No. Know of him. Jack's got the best, from what I hear."

She slid the rubber band to one side and peeked in the envelope. "There's a card in here with Fred's address and number. He's expecting you this afternoon." She popped the rubber band back into place and held the envelope out to me.

For a couple of seconds I just stood and watched her. A ray of light glistened on her soft lower lip. I knew better than to take the money, of course, just as I'd known better than to do a lot of the things I had done in the past. Donna's looks hadn't changed much; if anything, they'd gotten even better. I thought about an old Harry Chapin tune, about a taxi driver who picks up a long-lost love in the rain.

I took the envelope from Donna and stashed it in the pocket of my sport coat, then went downtown to see Fred Cassel. Harry Chapin would have been proud.

T W O

I stood in Texas Bank Plaza's clear plastic bubble of an elevator car and pressed the button. Sudden increased gravity sank my feet deep into plush carpet, and the people in the lobby shrunk in seconds into scurrying army ants. Down there in the cavernous lobby was a fountain spraying water over an oblong pool. An artsy cluster of stainless steel balls was suspended over the pool, and its green tile bottom was nearly covered in wishing coins. As I rode upward, a kid of about ten, wearing faded jeans, jammed his arm up to his shoulder in the water and came up with a handful of change. Earlier in the day I might've joined him.

An auburn-haired girl who was sharing the elevator with me was carrying a paper shopping bag by cord handles. She wore a red mini that struck her about four inches above round, dimpled knees. The car came to a hair-standing halt on the seventh floor. The girl uttered a tiny "Eek!" and jiggled on her way. I went up two more levels, got off, took two strides down the corridor, and halted in my tracks.

I was face-to-face with a pair of shaggy gray eyebrows, a long nose showing a slight hump in its bridge and a lot of blackheads, and a wizened mouth that seemed about to say either "Hell no" or "Fuck you." The guy looked like Rumpel-stiltskin. At least I'd always thought so.

"Let's see," he said. "Don't I remember you?" He snapped gnarled fingers. "Bannion, that's it. Rick Bannion, used to be one of the football he-men. How's life among the common folk?"

I breathed slowly in order to keep my anger from building. Cracking wise with this solid citizen had cost me five years out of my life, once upon a time. I said politely, "Afternoon, Mr. Aycock."

A round-shouldered man a couple of inches shorter than I was, he was wearing a pale blue suit. He shifted a bulging satchel from one hand to the other and cocked his head to one side. "You wouldn't be on your way to see Fred Cassel now, would you?" he said.

I had the feeling that I ought to lie to him, but was a little afraid to. I said lamely, "Oh, do you know Mr. Cassel?"

"It would figure," he said. "Going to talk about your old buddy, aren't you?"

"I beg your pardon?"

"You beg my pardon? Look, Bannion, let's don't bullshit each other. Seeing what kind of witnesses that Fred's going to call makes me feel better about my own case. We're going to bust your friend Brendy but good. Really strap it on him."

I straightened. Aycock actually flinched, as though he was afraid that I was going to throw a punch at him. I said, "Well, if it's that cut and dried, maybe they'd better just do away with any trial." I'd had just about enough.

All of a sudden Aycock's expression changed. He showed me his version of a sympathetic smile, which looked neither reassuring nor particularly cheerful. He said, "You know, Bannion, in a way it's a shame about you washed-out jock-straps. Get used to life in the fast lane, screwing all those cheerleaders, hey? Then one day the bubble bursts and you can't cope, isn't that it?"

I opened my mouth, then closed it. I couldn't think of anything cute enough to say. Visible past Aycock, two young guys in business suits went down the hall and made a left through swinging glass doors marked "CASSEL AND GRIMES,

ATTORNEYS." In the reception area inside, a brunette was seated at a half-moon-shaped desk, pressing flashing buttons and routing calls.

Aycock said, "You're going to do what you want no matter what I say. But maybe you should think about coming over to our side and testifying. I'll bet you know some things we'd like to know, and we help folks with the good sense to help us." He produced a business card from his breast pocket and handed it to me. "I carry a lot of weight with the parole commission, son," he said.

I read the address and phone number of the U.S. attorney's office, in the Earle Cabell Federal Building on Commerce Street. There was an ash receptacle filled with white sand by the elevator. I retreated, deliberately poked the card down in the sand, and faced Aycock. "You haven't been keeping up with me, Mr. Aycock. I'm off parole, as of last September. You people don't have any hold on me anymore."

His eyes narrowed. He stepped briskly around me and pressed the down button. "Don't bet on it, my boy," he said. "Don't you bet one fucking nickel on it."

Fred Cassel looked like a well-dressed English lit teacher. He was around my height, six-two, and about fifty pounds lighter than I was, with mouse-colored hair receding from a smooth unwrinkled forehead. He wore a navy Brooks Brothers suit with a plum-colored silk bandanna in its breast pocket. Black-rimmed, I'm-smart glasses rode the bridge of his slim nose above a clipped rectangular mustache, sort of like Hitler's. I folded my sport coat across my lap so that the J.C. Penney's label didn't show and crossed my legs.

"I don't like the way that ball bounced," he said. "Jesus Christ, what a time for Aycock to come calling." He was standing before a rolling aluminum server parked in front of his window. The heavy velvet drapes were parted. I was seated on the visitor's side of his desk in a cushioned leather armchair. Seconds ago he'd handed me steaming coffee in a Styrofoam cup. Mine was black. He plunked a second sugar cube into his own and added powdered cream.

"I still don't know what this is all about," I said. "So I

don't know if I should like the way that ball bounced or not, Mr. Cassel."

He carried his coffee around behind his desk and sat down in a high-backed swivel chair. The desk was the size of an eight-seater hot tub. "Dispense with the formalities," he said. "Call me Fred."

"All right, Fred. I still don't know what this is all about."

He removed a file folder from his top drawer and popped it open. "Did you ever see such a pile of shit in your life?" He indicated two cardboard shoeboxes stacked on the carpet in a corner.

"I don't guess I have," I said. "What are they?"

"They're Aycock's excuse for coming by. It's supposed to be copies of the government's evidence against Jack Brendy. Aycock brought them so I wouldn't ask for discovery in pre-trial motions, but I'm not even going to look inside the boxes. It'll be the evidence that Aycock wants me to see, nothing more. Fuck 'em, I'm asking for discovery anyhow. Asshole must think Fred Cassel just got off the boat from the old country."

I sipped at the coffee. It wasn't quite cool enough to drink, so I set it down. "I still don't know what this is all about, Fred." Maybe the third time would be the charm.

"What did Aycock ask you?" he said, scratching his chin. He was reading from a yellow-ruled piece of paper that he'd taken from the file.

"He didn't ask me anything. In a roundabout way he told me he wanted me to be a federal witness."

"He would. So Aycock was the prosecutor on your case, huh? Small world. One thing that's good, he thinks you're up here because you're going to be a witness for the defense. Good, let's keep it that way."

"What *am* I going to be? What's this all about, Fred?" I was determined to be persistent.

"Did Mrs. Brendy give you any money?"

'Yes."

"That's just a down payment. Bannion, how would you like to make . . ." He paused and looked straight at me. "Twenty thousand dollars?"

"The last time somebody asked me a question like that, I wound up going to prison," I said.

"Yeah," he said, "I know. Did five on a ten. Most of it behind the wall in El Reno. The last year or so in the country club, out in Big Spring. You wouldn't talk, you know, cooperate with them?"

I didn't think that question required an answer, so I uncrossed and recrossed my legs.

"I like your style, Bannion. There's too many folks running around spilling their guts to those people. Give me a hundred guys that'll keep their mouths shut and I'll rule the world."

"You've been reading too many novels, Fred. Being a stand-up guy doesn't pay too well. Take it from me."

That drew a small chuckle from him. "But as far as your conversation with Aycock went, he doesn't really know what you're doing up here?"

"No, and neither do I." I squinted to read the name of Cassel's law school in the black-framed diploma on the wall behind him. University of Oklahoma. Boomer Sooner.

He arched an eyebrow. "My sources say you're well connected. That you know a lot of, well, fringe society people."

"Now, Fred. What kind of question is that to ask a guy who did five years in the federal joint and makes his living working for bookies and bail bondsmen? Yeah, I know a few people. So what?"

"And you're known around as a stand-up guy," he said.

"We've already been over that. Yeah, I guess so. Stand-up Stan. But those references don't qualify me for American Express. Quit farting around, what do you want from me?"

He regarded me with the same look a man reserves for a horse turd in the middle of a narrow road; he can't squeeze around the damn thing and can't run over it without getting shit on his tires. Cassel said, "How about Herman Moore, street name Skeezix? Full-time drug dealer, part-time snitch. Lovely fellow."

"It doesn't ring a bell," I said. "I don't run with the druggies. I could have run across him, I don't know."

Cassel shut the folder and laid it carefully on his desk. "Jack Brendy's got a bond hearing on Thursday. Mrs. Brendy's probably told you. Aycock's going to try to get the judge to hold Jack without bond, which brings us to Mr. Skeezix. He's the guy that set Jack up with the feds, and he's going to be their witness at the hearing. The only one, the only guy who dealt directly with Jack. Our problem's pretty simple. The only way I can get bail for my client is if this Skeezix doesn't testify."

I hooked an arm over my chair back. "I'd go slower if I were you, Fred. If you're proposing what I think you are, you can get in some pretty hot tamales. Not to mention me."

Cassel got up and sat on one corner of his desk, gazing out the window. The view wasn't so hot: a couple of factory smokestacks, beyond them some office buildings along Harry Hines Boulevard. Cassel said, "Bannion, I've had you checked. I can trust you. You might turn me down, but you won't do any tattling. It's going to take two guys, as I see it. You've got an old roomie around town, from up at El Reno."

I gave a low whistle. "Bodie Breaux. You been doing a lot of homework, paisano."

"You don't beat the feds playing honest injun," he said. "You should know that from experience."

"Yep. Experience and more experience. And I don't like the idea of going through it again."

"Then you're not interested?" he said.

"In twenty thousand dollars? I didn't say that. I just didn't say that I liked the idea."

"There's more to it," he said.

"I'm not surprised," I said.

"If we make a deal and it goes sour, then it's your baby. One hundred percent. Nothing comes back on me, nothing comes back on Jack Brendy." Cassel turned his face away from the window and looked at me. "After all, twenty thousand dollars ain't exactly peanuts. It's got to buy us some protection."

My throat was dry, even dryer than it had been when Donna offered me the envelope. I fished a Pall Mall from a crumpled pack and lit it with a Bic lighter. I don't smoke that much. I didn't see an ashtray in the office, and didn't know whether Cassel was a no-smoking nut or not. Right then I didn't care. I dragged smoke into my lungs and blew it at the ceiling.

"Tell you what, Fred," I said. "Let's make it thirty thousand."

THREE

Prisoners in the Lew Sterrett Justice Center live in a fish-bowl. There aren't any bars. One wall of each cell is inch-thick transparent plastic and the lights are always on. It's a clean, modern jail, with fully automated control centers on each floor where guards sit and throw levers that open and close sliding doors and cause the lights to brighten and dim. Dallas County thoughtfully located the center on Trinity River lowland acreage a mile or so west of downtown, away from the tumult and the hubbub. It's a quiet neighborhood. The people inside Lew Sterrett don't like it there.

I stood in the sign-in line behind a black woman who weighed close to three hundred pounds, and who was wearing a faded print dress. She had a little boy by the hand. He looked to be around Jacqueline Brendy's age, and as his mother signed the register he stuck out his tongue at me. In a few years he'd probably be sticking knives in people. After the kid and his mom had moved on, I stepped up to the counter, entered Jack's name and cell-block number on the register, and scribbled out my signature.

The registration deputy was a pudgy kid in a light blue short-sleeve uniform shirt with the county emblem high on his bicep. The emblem was a gold shield encircled clockwise

by the words "INTEGRITY" and "DEPENDABILITY." He spun
the register around to where he could read it and said, "You
used to play for the Cowboys."

I shuffled my feet. "That was a ways back. You must be a
real fan. Not too many folks remember offensive linemen."

"When I was a kid I could call off the roster and give you
everybody's number," he said. "I played hookey the year you
guys played the 'Niners for the NFC Championship. You had
the best team, man, what, three interceptions? Still would
have won the game if . . ." His gaze lowered.

"If I hadn't jumped offside on third and goal?" I said
quickly. "Yeah, I had my head stuck up my ass." He remembered me, all right. It was all that anybody remembered
about my football if they remembered it at all. And his look
said that he remembered my prison stretch as well. That
didn't surprise me; I was a lot more famous for going to jail
than for anything I'd ever done playing football. I glanced
at the register. "You clearing me for takeoff?"

He hesitated, then said, "I'm not supposed to, if you're on
parole. Unless you're immediate family, that's different."

He was speaking too loudly, and I was getting some funny
glances from the people in line behind me. I leaned over the
counter and said in a low voice, "My time's up. Last year I
got a full release if you want to check it."

The deputy looked me over, then snorted. "Naw. No reason
to, we take everybody's word. Truth is, half the people coming down here are on parole. You want the eighth floor." He
wrote something on a pad, tore off the top sheet, and gave
it to me. "Give this to the guard. Go on, sit on one of those
chairs over there, you got ten minutes to wait. I got to tell
my brother-in-law you were down here, I'll get one up on
him."

I went over to where fifty or sixty people waited, picked
out a plastic chair, and sat in it. The fat black woman was
directly across the aisle and was now holding the kid in her
lap. He didn't look as though he belonged in anybody's lap.
A folded newspaper, a *Times Herald*, lay on an empty seat a
couple of places down from me. I picked the paper up and
spent the next ten minutes reading about Jack.

This was the first evening edition I'd seen in three or four days that didn't have Jack featured on the front page, but he still took up three columns beginning at the top of page two. Most of the story was about the bond hearing. There were quotes about Jack, from Fred Cassel and also from Norman Aycock. If the defense lawyer and prosecutor hadn't been quoted in the same article, I'd have never known they were both talking about the same guy.

There was a round clock on the wall at the end of the room, between twin elevator doors. At seven on the dot, the pudgy registration deputy came around the counter and told us that if we were visiting one of the lower six floors to take the car on the left, and that everybody else should pile onto the other car. Then he pressed a button on the wall and both elevator doors slid open. He operated the car on the left while a young Mexican deputy—a girl with shoulder-length hair who could have stood some dieting—drove the elevator that I was to ride. Each car held twenty people. I went up to the eighth floor in the second load.

Visitors in the Lew Sterrett Justice Center sit in a booth. There's a low counter to lean on, and beyond the counter is a thick plastic window. Prisoners come from the innards of the jail into a huge bullpen, look hopefully around, then take seats in front of the windows, and peer into the booths at the visitors. Prisoners and visitors converse over phones, and sitting in the confines of the booth makes the visitor feel as though he's switched roles with the prisoner. I set a ballpoint pen and a ruled pad up on the counter, lit my first Pall Mall of the evening, and inhaled as I watched Jack enter the bullpen. Even in a tan county-issue jumpsuit, and in spite of the extra pounds he's acquired over the years, Jack's slightly pigeon-toed athlete's walk stood out. He spotted me, grinned and waved, then came over to my window, and sat down. We picked up our respective phones.

"Hiya," Jack said. "Man, you've lost weight. How do you do it?"

"I jog most days," I said, "and I can't afford to eat much. I'll go two-twenty."

"Jesus Christ. You played at what, two-sixty?"

"Seventy, one year. Remember? Fined me a hundred a day until I knocked off ten pounds."

We laughed at that one, a short, strained laugh. I hadn't had a close look at Jack in a while. His jowls were beginning to sag and his thick black hair was going to salt-and-pepper. I suspected he'd gained about as much weight as I had lost, which would put him around two-fifty. Some blood vessels had ruptured beneath the skin around his nose. Booze. Jack couldn't be over forty, but Jesus. That would make Donna what, thirty? Thirty-one?

He said, "Donna come downtown to see you?"

He'd phrased the question that way on purpose. I decided to lie. "Yeah. We had a long talk."

"They're putting the jacket on me, Ricky-boy. It's a pure frame. I swear to God." Jack had played college ball at East Carolina. He'd lost most of the accent, but not all of it.

"How pure of a frame?" I said.

"Huh? How . . . ?"

"Jack. The feds frame everybody to one degree or another. That doesn't mean they're locking up a bunch of Simon Pures. So you'll know, I've got one rule. I don't work for anybody who bullshits me. If you've been running some dope, so what? So have ten thousand other guys. I don't give a fuck. But if you lie to me and I find out about it, I'll quit you cold." I gave him a smile that I hoped was reassuring. "So between a running back and a washed-up old tackle. What's the deal, you selling a little cocaine? Smuggling it, what?"

While Jack took a few seconds to decide whether or not to level with me, I glanced beyond him around the bullpen. Six or seven other inmates were talking to people who were in booths identical to mine. The inmates all wore jumpsuits like Jack's, with "COUNTY JAIL" stenciled between the shoulder blades in bold black letters. Finally Jack set his jaw and said, "Well, yeah. A few times, but only when business wasn't too good. Not this deal, though. Sure, yeah, I went for the deal, but the feds set me up from the word go. Fuck, I come to find out it was even their money financing the coke."

Their money. There wasn't anything new about the feds setting up drug deals, but I still clenched my jaws thinking about it. I looked around for an ashtray, found none, flicked a gray cylinder from the end of the Pall Mall, and watched it break up on the concrete floor. "I'd think you'd know better, Jack. On second thought, probably you wouldn't. Full-time dealers, guys that've been around, know what's going on and don't take the bait. Part-time guys are easy meat for them. So. Who'd they set you up with?"

"Skeezix, is all I know. Look, buddy, I didn't just run and jump into anything. Skeezix came with references. Some guys I know said he was solid as a rock. I arranged four different meeting with the guy and had him checked from A to Z." Jack's forearms rested on the counter, and he was cracking his knuckles by pressing the fingers of one hand against the receiver as he held it against his ear.

My little cubicle was getting hazy with smoke, so I dropped my cigarette on the floor and ground it under my heel. "So it turned out this Skeezix had money and a plane but no connect to make a buy," I said.

"How'd you know that?" Jack said. "You know Skeezix?"

"No, but Breaux will. Or he'll find out. Breaux's a friend, a guy I know from El Reno. Hey, I don't have to know the particular guy. It's always like that. Skeezix will turn out to be a junior-grade dealer they've busted. As long as he'll keep setting guys up, they'll leave him on the street. Keep right on dealing dope if he wants to, the feds don't give a shit. But the first time he doesn't come through for them it's bye-bye Skeezix, off to the joint. How much coke was it that Skeezix was going to buy?"

"Two hundred kilos is what he said. He was really flashing some money around. That's entrapment, isn't it? I mean, the guy came to me, not vice versa."

"Sure, it's entrapment, but that's not going to save you. Not too many people understand the entrapment laws. The feds are going to say you were in the business all along, that this Skeezix didn't get you to make any dope deal that you wouldn't have made anyway, with somebody else. The only way an entrapment defense will fly is if you were standing around doing nothing and the guy talks you into committing a crime that you wouldn't have committed anyway. It's the shits, Jack, but that's the way it works."

He closed his eyes and just sat there for a moment. Across the bullpen one prisoner, a black guy with an Afro, was shaking his fist through the window at a young, pretty, light-skinned black girl. Dear John visit.

Finally Jack said, "So what do we do, buddy?"

"The first step is to get you out on bond if we can. This Skeezix. He your only contact up until the feds arrested you?"

"That's it. Hell, I wasn't even there when the plane landed. Did Donna tell you? They walked right into Chateaubriand while we were having dinner. Cuffed me right at the table. Jesus, it was—" He halted, his shoulders heaving. I couldn't stand to watch Jack cry, so I studied my knuckles.

I said, "Well, then, Skeezix is the key. He's going to be the feds' witness at your bond hearing."

He rubbed his eyes with a thumb and forefinger. The eyes were bleary, as though he wasn't getting enough sleep. In his surroundings I doubted that he was. He said, "Look, buddy, I don't know how far Cassel's gone into this with you. Your money's there, I got that. In fact . . . look, Ricky, I'm going to tell you something Donna doesn't even know. There's a key. Bookcase in my den, there's a key taped inside the front cover of *Moby Dick*. I picked one nobody's likely to read. The key opens a mini-warehouse locker in Mid-Cities. In Hurst, on Bedford-Euless Road just south of the Airport Free-way. It's the only mini-warehouse out there, you can't miss it. The locker's rented under the name of Jack Landry. Sort of a name you and I would both recognize, huh? Anyway, worse comes to worse . . . well, there's enough money in there to pay you if anything happens. A helluva lot more than enough. There's—and to hell with what you might think about this—but there's two kilos of almost pure Bolivian in there, too. If anything happens, I'm looking to you to see that Donna gets what's left after you get yours, okay?"

I shrugged. It would be okay and Jack knew it.

"Anyway," Jack said, "I don't want you to take any of this the wrong way. But as for what Cassel's told you about you taking all the heat if anything goes wrong . . . well, it has to be that way. I can't afford any more trouble than I've already got, Ricky."

"A deal's a deal," I said. "Look, as long as we're spilling our guts to each other, you're talking to a guy that doesn't have much to lose. Jesus, I don't have a pot to piss in. I'm driving a Corvette that's two payments behind, and that Sweaty Mathis—you don't know him, he's a bail bondsman. Sweaty says he's going to tip off the finance company where I keep the 'Vette parked if I don't start locating some people for him. Hell, I'm lucky to locate myself most of the time. About the only thing I got going for me in a deal like this is that jail doesn't scare me like it does most people. Hell, I've been there. So whatever I do, you won't get any kickback from it. It stays right here with me."

Jack scratched his nose. He tugged at his ear. He smoothed his thick graying hair. Just as I was about to decide he was imitating a third-base coach, he grinned and said, "Well, sic 'em, then."

I pulled the envelope from my inside pocket, the one Donna had given me. I held it against my forehead and winked at him. "I already have," I said. "I'm just making sure you're not going to yank on the leash before I can sink my teeth in."

FOUR

Bodie Breaux once had hauled eighteen thousand pounds of marijuana north along the eastern shore of Mexico, hidden under the deck of a Honduran lobster boat. Somewhere north of the Yucatan Peninsula, Bodie ran afoul of the U.S. Coast Guard. They dispatched one cutter to keep pace with Bodie astern, sent a second, speedier vessel along to stare him down over his bow, and hovered a whirlybird over his mast for good measure. Thus backed by firepower, the captain of the Coast Guard mini-fleet politely requested permission via radio to board. Bodie thought it over, spat a stream of Beechnut tobacco juice over the side, and said into his mike, "That's your fuckin' ass, Captain. This ain't no American tub you're talkin' to."

During the two hours required for the Coast Guard to get permission from the Honduran government to board and search, Bodie pointed the lobster boat's nose toward the open sea. As more Coast Guard ships joined in the chase, Bodie found himself leading quite a parade. He damn near made it, too; when the helicopter's crew finally leveled machine guns at Bodie's people—a grinning black giant with a shaved head and a skinny Puerto Rican with a patch over one eye—while one of the cutters clamped onto the lobster boat, the distance to the point where the ocean floor dropped off to bottomless depths was less than half a mile. Halted, Bodie tried to sink his boat anyhow, right there in the shallows. A seaman first class wearing a bulletproof vest, his gaze darting furtively about, burst into the engine room and pointed a shotgun at Bodie. His voice cracking like an adolescent's, the young sailor said, "Hold it right there!" At the time Bodie had all valves open and gushing and was himself waist-deep in salt water. He grinned, raised his hand, and shot the swabbie the finger.

Two weeks later in a Miami grand jury room, Bodie stood at attention in front of a court reporter. The steno took time out from running his shorthand machine and had the prisoner raise his right hand. Then he asked whether Bodie solemnly swore to tell the truth, the whole truth, and nothing but the truth, so help Bodie God. The two U. S. marshals who'd escorted Breaux over from the Metropolitan Center stood at ease and waited for the prisoner to answer.

Bodie glanced first at the ceiling, then at his feet, shifted his weight, and finally told the grand jurors loudly, "Fuck no." The stunt cost Breaux eighteen months for contempt plus a five-year beef in the federal joint for trying to smuggle the dope. But it gained him a lot of respect in some circles, too.

I found Bodie lounging in a dark corner at Cafe Dallas. His hand was resting on a leggy redhead's thigh, and I told him that we had some work to do. He said, "That's your fuckin' ass, Bannion."

I sat down in a cushioned chair. A small round table between us was clear plastic with old *Dallas Morning News* clippings molded in. I looked down at a photo of Melvin Belli, glasses askew, gray hair wild, shaking his fist at the camera on the day of Ruby's conviction. Bodie's Jack Daniels, neat, was on the table in a rock glass, his water back in a tumbler beside it. The redhead's drink was a green, frothy something-or-other in a stemmed champagne glass. Heard on the club's muted sound system, the Bee Gees rocked through "Stayin' Alive."

"Look, Bodie, I hate to interrupt, okay?" I said. "But I don't have much time on this."

The redhead leaned close to Breaux and whispered something. Bodie's eyes widened. He had a square, jut-jawed face and a day's growth of dark beard. Funny thing about Breaux. If you see a guy and he's got a day's growth, and then you see him again the next day, by then he should either be clean-shaven or have two days' growth. Not Breaux. Each and every day, one day's growth of dark beard. When the redhead had finished whispering, Bodie said to me, "You want Gloria to call her roommate?"

The redhead was in tight blue slacks and showed a lot of hip curve, and the roommate would be quite a number or Breaux wouldn't have given the okay. I sighed and said, "No time. You know a guy they call Skeezix?" I paused and glanced at the redhead. Bodie nodded and winked; it would be all right to talk in front of her. I went on. "Real name's Herman Moore, but I doubt you'd know him by that."

Breaux slightly rotated his thick shoulders. He was wearing a red T-shirt with a cartoon of a giant crab on the front along with a red-billed cap advertising Inland Marine Co., Metarie, La. Thick black chest hair was visible over the shirt collar. He said, "I hope I didn't hear you right. Do I know a guy named who?"

"Skeezix."

"That's what I thought you said. Yeah, I know him, and so do the feds. Look, the only reason Skeezix ain't dead is because his spirit might rise up and stool somebody off. I'm serious. The fucking guy is dealing coke with one hand while the other hand is on the hotline to the U.S. attorney's office."

"That's the guy," I said. "He set up Jack Brendy."

A cocktail waitress appeared at my elbow wearing a farmer's daughter outfit, complete with floor-length pleated skirt. I ordered plain soda and lime. The drink I'd had earlier with Donna had made me a little dizzy, and I didn't want to get started again. The waitress showed a disappointed pout, then jiggled off toward the island bar in the center of the club. The bar stools were elbow to elbow, guys in suits and guys in jeans and women in everything from shorts and halters to shoulderless dinner dresses. Most were stag, in twos and threes, and the guys and the women shot glances at one another over the rims of their glasses. A few had gotten up the nerve to start conversations.

Breaux said, "That Brendy guy must be pretty dumb, whoever he is, fooling with that Skeezix."

The redhead spoke up. "*Bo*-die, he's been in the paper every day. He used to play for the *Cowboys*." She spoke in a high nasal twang, and I'd just as soon that she go back to whispering her messages through Breaux. The way a lot of Dallas folks put reverent emphasis on the name of their silly football team just knocked me over. As though whether the Cowboys won or lost was right up there in importance with the world economic crisis. I'd had a decade-long relationship with the town that I loved as a member of the football team that I hated, and I didn't want any more of it.

"Oh," Breaux said. "That guy. Brendy. I saw him in the Super Bowl down in New Awlins in what, seventy-eight? Against the Broncos. You'd already shot your wad in football by then, hadn't you, Bannion?"

I'd always assumed that tact was something they didn't teach in the cajun home. I nodded.

The redhead brightened, sat up straighter, and leaned closer to me. She had a cute button nose and a spray of freckles. She gave me a pretty porcelain smile. "You played for the *Cowboys*?"

I thought, Jesus Christ, I've got to get out of here. I forced my lips into a smile that probably looked more like a grimace, then turned once again to Breaux. "I got reasons I got to find this Skeezix before Thursday morning. You got any idea where to look?"

"I damn sure know where not to look," Bodie said. "That's anyplace where Muhammed Double-X might find him. A few months back Skeezix set up Muhammed's baby brother, or that's what they say. I always say I ain't afraid of anybody, but that don't include that double-scary cat. Muhammed Double-X, Jesus."

I had a fleeting mental image of Muhammed's kinky hair, sharp ebony features always hidden behind mirrored shades. He'd once cut off a man's hand for shorting six grams out of a kilo. I said, "So I don't look in South Dallas. Where do I look? It's nighttime, and whatever bad habits Skeezix has, he's probably into them. You know his bad habits? He just a dealer, or a user, too?"

"I don't know the guy that good. I've seen him around, and hell, it's my business to know about him. But, yeah, he'll be a user, you get to where you can spot 'em. Dancy little fat guy, always talking a mile a minute. Thinks he's a real cool dresser, but if you ask me he looks more like a circus clown. Neon sport coats, two-tone shoes, that kind of shit. Tell you something else, this Skeezix is a gambler. I know one guy—hell, Bannion, you know him, too. Ace the Book." I nodded. I'd had a passing acquaintance with Ace the Book back during my playing days, at a time when I wasn't supposed to know any gamblers. Breaux went on, "Ace says this Skeezix shoots craps with one hand while he's got the phone in the other, getting his bets down."

The waitress had brought my drink, and now I sipped it. It was tart and bubbly. "That should narrow it down, Bodie. We'll start with the gamblers. Chances are one of 'em has seen him."

"What you mean, 'we,' white man?" Breaux said. "I told you, I got something to do." He squeezed the redhead around the shoulders. She giggled and scootched closer to him.

I intertwined my fingers on the tabletop. The Bee Gees' song had ended and Michael Jackson's "Billie Jean" was now jumping over the sound system. I said, "I need you. Tell you what, two hours. Two hours max, and if we can't find the guy I'll take it from there."

"You ain't getting through to me," Breaux said.

I figured to have a twenty-five percent chance of finding Skeezix alone. With Bodie as a guide I was a lead-pipe cinch. He knew every nook and cranny and then some. I said, "It's important to me, Bodie. Just this once, huh? It'll be plenty worth your while."

I guess he caught something in my tone of voice. He studied me for an instant, then untangled himself from the redhead. Without looking at her, he said, "I guess I got some business, Gloria. Be around later, doll."

Ace the Book had an Adam's apple the size of an eight ball. He was tall and skinny with a hawk nose. His hair was graying at the temples and he had slim, delicate hands. At the moment he was popping hundred-dollar bills from a roll the size of a softball and stacking them in a neat pile in front of him. In a foghorn voice he said, "Shoot eight hundred. Take any or all of it." He picked up clear red dice, rattled them, and peered around through the hanging smoke at the circle of faces.

Breaux and I stood beside the sliding accordian gate at the head of a staircase that descended to a door set into an old brick building on Lower Greenville Avenue, a couple of blocks north of Ross. A few moments ago we'd told the doorman that Ace the Book would okay us and, eyeing us suspiciously, he'd let us in and followed us up the stairs. I read the sign above the entrance: "VETERANS OF FOREIGN WARS—MEMBERS ONLY." The only war of which Ace the Book was a veteran had taken place somewhere on Akard Street.

The doorman, a stocky, balding guy wearing a white shirt whose collar was grimy, said from the side of his mouth, "You better hope Ace knows you. He don't, you seen too much already." He had stained yellow teeth and was chewing a cigar butt. He wore baggy gray slacks. The bulge in his hip pocket was probably a sap, but might have been a gun.

We'd stopped by my place for me to change into Levis, pullover knit short-sleeve shirt, and white Nike sneakers—Breaux's idea. The people in the places where we were going didn't talk to men in coats and ties. I leaned against the folded gate and jammed my hands into my back pockets. My right fingertips brushed the handle of my Smith & Wesson .380, a cheaper imitation of a Walther PPK. "There's Ace over there," I said. "Ask him."

Breaux folded his arms and showed an insolent leer.

The doorman was built like a barrel with arms and had too much of a roll around his middle. "Ace is shooting dice, pal. You don't want to interrupt a man's shooting." He sounded as though we'd just asked to break into Ace's confessional booth.

There were eight or nine men hunched over the edges of a pool table. Ace stood at one end rattling the dominoes. A black, beefy-necked citizen peeled off four fifties and dropped them beside Ace's eight hundred. A sleepy-eyed young guy with diamond pinky rings on both hands covered the remaining six hundred, then laid two hundreds and a fifty off to one side. "Laying five to one, Acie," he said. "Two-fifty to fifty, no seven."

Ace hesitated. "You giving me a short price, Herkie. Make it six to one, you got a bet."

The young guy had a black handlebar mustache. He fingered his bankroll, shrugged, and added another fifty to the stack. Ace faded the bet, grinned, and rolled a natural seven, six-one. The young guy blinked and scratched his head.

As Ace grabbed the money and stacked it, I turned to Fireplug the doorman. "How about asking him now," I said. "Or is interrupting a man collecting the same as interrupting a man shooting?"

Fireplug mumbled to himself as he left me and Breaux standing there, continued to mumble as he crossed the room. A single shaded light hung over the table, and smoke and dust particles swirled in the beam like confetti in a fog. Fireplug skirted the table and sidled up to Ace. The cigar stump came out of Fireplug's mouth and he whispered something. Ace passed the dice to the next shooter and came over with Fireplug trailing a step behind.

"I know 'em, Jackie," Ace said, and Fireplug showed a glum scowl. "I ain't going to say they're okay," Ace said, "but I know 'em. Let 'em on in." He smiled slow and easy and extended his hand to me. As I shook it, Ace said, still to Fireplug, "This here cat cost me pretty good one year. How 'boutcha, Mr. Offside Man, you ever learn to wait for the snap?"

"I'm still waiting for it," I said. "Long time, Ace."

Ace clapped Breaux on the shoulder. "Hey, Bannion, you got Captain Crawdad along, huh? What you doing on dry land, Bodie, your boat sink or something?"

"Just came in to clean my pipes," Breaux said. "You need to send your doorman to school, Acie. He leads us upstairs to where we can see the action, then starts checking to see if we're okay. Jesus Christ, if we was working for the sheriff you'd all be in a paddy wagon by now."

Fireplug drew himself up as if to say something, but Ace the Book cut in. "Jackie? Jackie's my boy, he's doing okay.

Tell you what, Jackie, I got a bottle of Johnnie Walker in the kitchen under the sink. Bring it for my friends, huh?"

The kitchen was to the rear, behind a Coke machine and a standup cooler that probably contained Lone Star and Pearl Beer. The place must have been a real VFW before Ace had bought the license, and it would be a good idea to keep appearances up in case some legitimate veterans wandered in. Fireplug kept scowling as he waddled toward the kitchen. I hoped that the whiskey bottle's seal was intact; otherwise Breaux might get scotch and rat poison.

Ace edged between Bodie and me and slung an arm over each of our shoulders. I've never liked having men put their hands on me, even in good cheer, and not so many years back the gesture would have cost Ace a sore jaw. But it's something I've learned to live with. Ace said, "Between you and me, Jackie's married to my sister. What you going to do? If I don't put him to work I'm never going to hear the end of it. So what's it, you looking for action? Tell you what, the limit's a thousand, hundred on the proposition bets. But for a couple high rollers I can get the limit raised. I got some clout."

The kid with the handlebar mustache and the pinky rings had the dice ready to roll, but now froze with his hand beside his ear. He eyed Bodie and me as though we were slices of white meat chicken. The other players licked their lips and did the same.

I gently removed Ace's paw from my shoulder. "No dice, Ace, no pun intended. We need to talk. You got a quiet place?"

Ace cocked his head. "I guess I do." He took his other hand from Breaux's shoulder. Breaux enjoyed being pawed about as much as I did, and he brushed the sleeve of his T-shirt. Ace said, "I should have left Jackie by the door, I could have picked up the Johnnie Walker on the way. I got an office behind the kitchen. I'll tell you before we go, I ain't buying nothing."

"We're not selling," I said. "Lead the way, Ace, it might be worth something to you."

He nodded and led us through the kitchen. The linoleum floor was cracked and grimy; in one corner was a jumbled pile of empty boxes. We passed a rusty icebox and a stove that had black grease encrusted on its burners. Fireplug met us going in the opposite direction, and Ace took the scotch from him. Fireplug shot Breaux a glare that would stunt growth as he went by. Breaux grinned and nodded. The bottle swung at Ace's hip as we entered his office.

The office was more like a closet with a desk inside. The desk was old and scarred, with chipped brown paint; I read the initials "J.R." where someone had carved them into the wood. Ace had to inhale in order to squeeze between the desk and wall, then he sank down into a rickety swivel chair that squealed in protest. At one time this had been a pretty nice little room; there was a cherry-patterned wallpaper that was now faded and wrinkled and a light green carpet that had brown stains in places, and whose backing was showing through. On one wall was a calendar advertising Midas mufflers; the calendar was showing the month of June. I told Ace that he needed to tear off a couple of months in order to be current, but he snorted and pretended not to hear me. A Playmate of the Month from a couple of years back peered at us around her saucy behind from another wall. A cloth couch that was sagging in the middle was in front of Ace's desk. Breaux and I sat on it. Breaux sneezed as dust flew. There was a phone on the desk, sitting on top of a pile of football betting sheets from the previous fall. The phone was ringing.

"Don't pay it no mind," Ace said. "Bastards. They know I don't take action after seven, but some of 'em wake up in the middle of the night. Got a vision about some baseball game on the West Coast." He slammed open a bottom drawer and produced a stained coffee cup along with two glasses. One of the glasses was only dusty; in the bottom of the other was a sticky brown residue. Ace broke the seal and poured scotch into the cup. The sudden smell of the liquor mingled with the odor of stale cigars—probably Jackie's. Ace hadn't been a smoker the last time I'd seen him. He took a slug from the cup, his Adam's apple bobbing as he swallowed, then started to fill the glass with the sticky stuff in its bottom. He looked at me and said, "Say when."

"Nothing for me, Ace," I said quickly. "I'm working."

"Uh, me either." Bodie's nose was wrinkling. "I just had a couple down the road."

Ace's eyebrows lifted. He set down the bottle, screwed on the cap, and emptied the glass into the coffee cup. He took another swallow. "So you won't drink with me. It must be serious what you're wanting. Working at what, Ricky? You ain't joined no police force, have you?" His eyes narrowed. A slob, yes. A dummy, far from it.

"Just the opposite," I said. "I'm working for a guy against the cops. Federal cops. FBI, DEA, all the same difference."

"A man after my heart," Ace said.

"I'm looking for a guy," I said. "Herman Moore. Skeezix. I think he might bet the sports. Football, some baseball maybe."

Breaux shifted beside me and crossed his legs. His shin brushed the corner of the desk. "I brought him here, Acie, so I already told him Skeezix bets sports with you."

Ace swiveled in his chair and eyed the playmate on the wall. He had a small bald spot at his crown. He said, "This guy, Ricky, the one you're working for. It ain't Muhammed Double-X."

"No way," I said.

The phone had stopped ringing, but now began once more. Ace ignored it. His gaze still on the playmate, showing us the back of his head, Ace the Book said, "Look, Skeezix is double-hot and don't I know it. But I can't help you. The guy is on the mattresses, which is better than being dead, which is what he'll be if Muhammed runs across him. So I might not like Skeezix any more than anybody else does, but he's a good player. One of the best I ever saw. Five grand a week he blows on the sports, pays of like Caesar's Palace. I can't afford to have the guy dead. So I can't give up his location to nobody." He turned around and faced us. "It's business is all, I ain't going to bullshit you."

"You don't understand," I said. "I got to have the guy and quick. I got no choice. If I—"

Breaux place a restraining hand on my arm and shook his head. He said to Ace, "I dig that you're making too much off the guy to give him up for nothing. So how about a trade?"

"A what?"

"Trade. You tell us about Skeezix, I don't tell the boys out front about those six-ace flats in your pocket."

Ace had been about to take another slug of the scotch and God-knows-what, but now he froze. "Six-ace flats? The fuck you—"

"Or lead-loads, whatever," Bodie said. "You palmed 'em, Acie. They're in your right pants pocket."

Ace shifted his gaze from Breaux to me and back again. You could practically hear the wheels turning; he was figuring whether Skeezix's business was worth losing the boys' out front. Getting caught cheating wasn't that big of a deal— every man in the game was likely to have a pair of loads on him; the penalty for cheating in Ace the Book's circle was the gambler's equivalent of standing with one's nose in the corner—but it was Ace's game. The house man was supposed to watch for cheaters, not cheat himself. Ace wouldn't bother lying to us about the crooked dice—it wasn't as though his conscience was bothering him. I didn't really like to put this kind of pressure on, but Breaux was doing the right thing. I needed this Skeezix and I didn't have time to screw around.

Ace let go a long sigh and said, "Two things. Skeezix ain't to know I'm the man that told you. And bigger than that, Muhammed Double-X ain't to know that I know where Skeezix is at. Jesus Christ, I got enough trouble without a bunch of Muslim smokes in here beating the shit out of me."

"Yeah, they're not exactly a pack of Uncle Toms," Breaux said.

I leaned forward, rested my forearms on my thighs, and put my fingertips together. I looked down. A prominent vein ran the length of my right forearm, outlined against the muscle. "You got my word on it, Ace," I said. "All I want is to find Skeezix."

Ace drummed the desktop with his fingers. "You know Lewisville, Ricky? Up by the lake?"

"Pretty well. I don't get up that way much, but I know the general area."

"There's a house. The owner's Lorraine Daley—she's a titty-shaker, dances as Connie Swarm over at Baby Doll's. But Skeezix pays the bills on the joint, I think Connie Swarm gives him a little sniff once in a while. Anyhow, that's where Skeezix is at. Ain't stuck his head outside in a week. Take Hawley Road west off the freeway, it winds around behind the lake. The house is on the left, maybe a mile from the dam. It's got a green windmill in the yard, you can't miss it."

"Skeezix and Connie Swarm," I said. "Who else is up there?"

"There'll be more, they come and go. Besides the other titty-shakers there's poker players. Skeezix is the main sucker, he keeps the game going around the clock. Only when Skeezix stops to sleep, the other players just sit. Jesus, I never saw anybody has to have action as bad as that sonofabitch. There'll be a little muscle, but nothing the pair of you can't handle. Who you working for, Jack Brendy?"

I wasn't ready for the question, and I tried to hide my surprise as I said, "How'd you know? There's been nothing in the paper to connect Skeezix to Jack."

Ace snorted. "It's the feds, shit, the word's out all over town. I can't figure Skeezix. Anybody that thinks the feds are going to give them any protection just 'cause they're a snitch—shit, them FBI's gossip worse than old women. Once they're through with Skeezix on the Brendy deal they'll throw him to the dogs. Or the Muslims. You watch what I say."

Breaux and I exchanged glances. "I guess we got what we came for," I said.

Breaux got up from the couch. "Yeah, we better be going. You need to get back to your game, Acie. You got to watch to make sure the game is on the square. You wouldn't want nobody getting fucked in your joint now, would you?"

I sat in my chocolate brown Corvette with the engine running and watched Bodie Breaux come out of the Quik Stop and jog around the Citgo gas pumps toward me. The interior of the Quik Stop was lit up like broad daylight. Between the long shelves which held the usual convenience store junk—soap, shaving cream, canned meat, tuna and sardines; every brand of candy bar known to man, giant dollar-and-a-half bags of M&M's, plain and peanut—stood a big transparent plastic bin that was filled with murky greenish water. A stack of aluminum minnow buckets was alongside. The overhead lighted sign announced that the minnows were two sixty-nine and the buckets twelve dollars. When I'd been a kid in South Texas we had used earthworms as bait, worms that we had dug up on our own. I looked to my left, toward the narrow strip of asphalt pavement. Hawley Road had narrowed from a boulevard into a two-lane blacktop a mile or so after we'd left the interstate. Beyond the asphalt, past two hundred yards of mesquite trees and scrubby brush, Lake Bruce Alger shimmered and rippled under the full August moon. Breaux opened the passenger door, and the 'Vette shifted slightly under his weight as he slammed the door.

Between winded huffs and puffs, Breaux said, "Twelve and a half for gas. I got a Hershey." He showed the candy bar, then handed over my change—a five, a single, and a couple of quarters. As he lifted his cap and rubbed his smooth, bald head, I looked from the money in my hand to Breaux and back again. He said, " 'S matter?"

I put the car in gear and sprayed gravel as I wheeled back onto Hawley Road. "Nothing. Nothing's the matter. Only every time you take that hat off it's a shock that you're bald. You sleep in that hat?"

He bit off a chunk of Hershey. "You ain't ever going to find out how I sleep. Can't everybody have as much hair as you. At least what I got is still black. I think I'll start calling you the Silver Turd, Bannion, how 'bout that?"

He got a laugh from me. I began to gray in my twenties and I've gotten used to it. "You make the call?" I said.

"Yeah."

I waited for him to go on. When he didn't say more, I asked him, "Well? You set it up?"

"Yeah," he said. "How much I'm getting for this shit? I'm running around calling guys, setting things up, finding guys for you, pumping gas, you're driving around like Stud Stingray asking questions."

"Oh, you know me," I said. "I'll make it worth your while." I quickly switched on the radio and increased the volume. Clarence Fogarty was singing "Put Me in, Coach" over KVIL.

The house wasn't near as easy to find as Ace the Book had

said. It was set back a hundred feet from the road behind a thick six-foot hedge. The windmill was a small one and partially hidden by the house; the blades turned ever so slightly and reflected moonlight. I didn't notice the house as we passed, but caught a glimpse of the windmill in my sideview mirror, made a squealing U-turn, and parked fifty yards short of a long, winding gravel drive. In the driveway sat an Eldorado, a Ford Bronco, and a Dodge Caravan. I cut my headlights and Bodie and I climbed out, moved from the road onto the grass, and approached the house.

The house was white frame with dark shutters on the windows, and appeared well kept. Light streamed from the windows. The backyard extended to the lake shore. A boat—a pretty good-sized inboard job, probably a Cris-Craft—was moored to a dock with steps leading down into the yard.

Breaux was moving silently along on my right; the bill on his cap threw a shadow that hid his face. Visible in the distance, tiny flashes danced across the surface of the lake like fireflies. Crickets whirred nearby and, farther away, water lapped against soggy wood. I whispered, "How long have we got?"

"Well, it took us, what, a half hour from Ace the Book's? Muhammed's way to hell out in South Dallas, but he'll be stepping on it since I told him Skeezix was out here. I figure forty-five minutes, maybe more," Breaux said.

"We've got to get inside before the Muslims show, and that may take some talking, jumpy as Skeezix is going to be. You got any idea how we're going to get invited in?"

"Yeah," Breaux said.

We were now crunching gravel as we went up the drive. I stopped beside a low cedar bush, the odor of sap in my nostrils. "Through the garage? Around back, what do you think?"

"Well, I don't know about you," Breaux said, "but I'd just as soon not get my ass blowed off running around like a second-story man. The best way to get inside is to ring the doorbell." Shaking his head, Breaux ambled across the front yard to the porch, ascended the steps, and pressed the buzzer. I followed a couple of steps behind him, my gaze darting warily from side to side. As we waited, he murmured, "Through the garage the man wants to go. Jesus Christ."

So there we stood, me first on one foot and then the other and Bodie in a bored, hip-cocked stance. In a few minutes a yellow overhead light came on; a herd of fat june bugs attacked the light, wings whirring and bodies bumping against one another. The handle turned and the front door swung open a foot. My hand crept involuntarily toward my back pocket, where the Smith & Wesson rested.

A soft female voice said, "Bodie? *Bodie*? What you doin' out here, darlin'?" Then a pure knockout wearing snug jean shorts and a bare midriff halter came onto the porch and threw her arms around Breaux. Blond hair cascaded around her shoulders. She kissed him and she was anything but sisterly about it. I let my arms fall to my sides and counted to twenty before they came up for air.

"Don't mess with my hat, doll," Breaux said.

I had to admit, it wasn't a bad line.

The blonde stood on one foot, suspended the other a few inches off the concrete, and used her arm around Breaux's neck to balance herself. She peered at me. "Who's this dude, Bodie? And how'd you find me? Nobody's supposed to know about this place, it's my secret hideaway." She had wide blue, China-doll eyes and a cherubic, pouty chin. I thought she would have been a whole lot prettier with a couple of coats less of makeup, but to each his own.

"I asked around," Breaux said. "Don't matter how I found you." He jerked his head in my direction. "This here is Ricky. Don't get too close to him, he bites. Ricky, meet Connie Swarm. She dances. We . . . know each other."

She stood away from Breaux and curtsied cutely. "Pleased to meetcha."

This had all been happening so fast that I was having hell getting my thoughts organized. Connie Swarm's name had rung a little bell the first time I'd heard it, back at Ace the Book's, and now I snapped to and sorted out what I knew about her. Feature attraction at Baby Doll's, the Madonna of the shitkicker set. Her name had been linked to one gubernatorial candidate—a slightly cornpone type whose TV ad campaign featured pictures of all the death-row inmates he was going to execute if he was elected—and his opponents had blown the affair up big. Let's see, hadn't there been a shooting? Yeah. Her ex-husband, she'd shot him right in the balls (the papers had said, "in the groin"), and she'd been mixed up in a marijuana bust that had gotten a lot of ink as well. No Miss America candidate here, and with this chick's credentials it would have been surprising if Breaux *hadn't* known her. Of course, he could have told me. The s.o.b.

"Hi, Connie," I said.

Breaux showed me a shit-eating grin and a one-up wink, then said to Connie, "Ain't we invited in?"

Her gaze flickered hesitantly. "I don't know. There's this guy . . . Bodie, he's not my *man* or anything, but, well, he's here now. And some friends of his."

"No sweat about that," Breaux said. "He's got friends, you got 'em, too."

She frowned in thought. I'd just met Connie, but it was already apparent that her IQ was somewhere around the score of your average football game. Make that your average defensive battle. Finally she brightened, shrugged her slim shoulders, clutched Breaux's hand, and led him inside. Apparently she'd forgotten about me; probably two people at once were a bit much for her to keep up with. In a few seconds I got lonely on the porch and went in after them.

I was standing in spooky, greenish light from a single painted bulb hung from the ceiling of the living room. Bodie and Connie, hand in hand, were just disappearing through a doorway that led farther into the house. They left me alone with a long cabinet-model stereo that was playing a heavy metal tune by Twisted Sister, and a long tall brunette who was seated on a cloth divan. She wore a short, Dorothy Hamill hairdo along with bikini panties and a wispy half-bra. Her eyes were dark holes in her face. A Sherlock Holmes pipe hung loosely from one corner of her mouth. She was freebasing; I got a whiff of crack smoke, followed by a quick, heady rush.

The girl took the pipe from her mouth and pointed its stem at me. She said in a childlike monotone, "Want to get high with Crystal?" I shook my head and went on through the living room. As I passed through the doorway, Crystal gave a hollow, mirthless laugh.

I entered what had once been a formal dining room, a pretty nice one. There was a chandelier hanging dead center from the ceiling, putting out clear white light from teardrop bulbs. The wallpaper was a tasteful beige. A portable bar stood close to one wall in front of a glass breakfront cabinet. Connie and Bodie were at the bar. She was filling two stemmed glasses from a bottle of white wine.

A second guy was at the bar, mixing bourbon and water, and I'd seen him someplace before. He was tall and stoop-shouldered, about forty, with close-cropped brown hair and jug handle ears. I rattled my memory bank. Nothing. As I approached, the guy regarded me through sleepy-lidded eyes that showed the barest flicker of recognition. I was trying to place the guy and he was doing the same to me. As I leaned against the bar, he said from the side of his mouth, "This one with you, Connie?"

She encircled Breaux's bicep with her hands and looked at me. "Him? Yeah, yeah, he is. I invited him." Connie Swarm might have been an airhead, but she was a pretty good liar. Probably had a lot of practice.

The stranger nodded to me. He didn't seem to want an introduction; he picked up his drink and retreated toward the living room. Probably this citizen was more interested in getting high with Crystal than he was in meeting me. I mentally filed his image away; when I had more time, I was going to remember where I'd run across the guy. Connie and Bodie carried their drinks farther into the house with me trailing a step behind. The two of them and the one of me. I took one long step into the next room and froze in my tracks. I blinked.

I've seen a lot of poker games, and normally it takes some observation to figure out who the sucker is. He's the guy who gets the most sympathy from the other players when he loses a pot, and who gets the loudest laughs when he tells a joke that isn't very funny, but it takes a while for a new-comer to the game to get the drift. That's in *most* poker games. But in the game that was going on in the back room at Connie Swarm's house, the sucker stood out like a sore thumb. I probably would have known Skeezix even without the description that Breaux had given me, just with the information from Ace the Book that Skeezix was the pigeon in the poker game. The guy might as well have had a spotlight trained on him.

He was fat, all right. The folds of his neck puffed out over his collar like water-filled balloons, and his cheeks were round as Porky Pig's. He was dressed like Liberace off his diet, in a maroon silk blazer with velvet lapels. A full ten inches of snow-white cuff protruded from each sleeve, and he had thick, dark, wavy hair. There were rings on three of his stubby fingers—one diamond, one ruby, one emerald. He wore a maroon bow tie that matched his coat. The coat was unbuttoned and even with his chair pushed back, his belly spilled out over the edge of the table. On the table in front of him were three foot-high stacks of poker chips. They were professional, monogrammed chips, probably straight from Vegas. One stack was white, one blue, the other hundred-dollar blacks.

The round table was about five feet in diameter, covered in off-white burlap stretched taut over a cushion of foam rubber. Besides Skeezix there were five players in the game. Two were women, a Mexican pepper pot with giant boobs rolling out from a teeny-weeny string bikini top, and a black girl with blue mascara worn on lashes long as taut fishing lines. The black girl wore jean shorts and a halter, like Connie's outfit. The women sat on either side of Skeezix. The Mexican broad had a few chips in front of her, the black girl none. As I watched, Skeezix tossed some black chips into the pot, then peeked groggily at his hole cards. "Bet five hundred, Joe Bob. How you like them apples?" He sounded like Froggy the Gremlin.

The black girl sat on Skeezix's left, and had first action on his bet. She peeked at her hole cards—they were playing seven stud—then wiggled around so that she brushed against Skeezix, and stuck out her lower lip in a pout. "I got nothing to call you with, darlin'. Missy's cupboard is plumb bare, bay-be."

Skeezix rubbed his fat palms together. "Don't matter, hon, it's all coming home to papa anyway. Here." He handed her some black chips from his own stack. She batted her long lashes and called the bet. There was a white powdery residue on his upper lip, below his nostrils.

I'd been watching the Skeezix Show so closely that I hadn't taken a look at the other players. Now I did, and two of the three remaining poker players I recognized. Joe Bob Cleveland was directly across the table from Skeezix. Joe Bob was a rawboned, cigar-smoking, straight-off-the-range type who'd finished high in Binnion's World Championship a few years back. He wore a flowered western shirt and a black Stetson tilted back on his head, and smoke curled upward from a fat cigar resting in an ashtray by his elbow. Sitting beside Joe Bob was Hubie Peters, an ex-N.B.A. basketball player. In his playing days he'd been a real showboat, behind-the-back passes and alley oops and in-yo-face slam dunks. The league had booted Hubie for shaving points, and from what I'd heard he hadn't hit a lick since except for booking sports and playing poker. He was nearly seven feet tall, sprawled out in a chair with his knees bumping the table from underneath. His arms and legs were pretty thin, but his midsection had expanded at least as much as Jack Brendy's, maybe even more. Hubie was now built like Big Bird. He saw me and raised a hand. I nodded.

I didn't know the remaining player, but the guy had all the moves. He was young, probably middle twenties, sporting a neatly trimmed beard and wearing a blue knit Polo shirt. At the moment he was shuffling a stack of chips one-handed, *click-click-click*, with the practiced ease of a Vegas dealer. I'd say this for Skeezix, he wasn't picking on any softies. Jesus, Amarillo Slim himself might have been a slight underdog in this game.

Joe Bob Cleveland studied his hand, scratched behind his ear, dragged at his cigar, and blew a wispy line of smoke at the ceiling. "Well, I'm a fool for it," he said, "but I just got to see what you're so proud of, Skeezix man. Call. Here, I'm calling you." He gently nudged a cylinder of blue chips into the center of the table. Hubie Peters folded, airplaning his hand across the table to fall among the discard. The young guy, looking bored, did the same.

"What you got, Skeez?" Joe Bob said.

Skeezix peeked at his hole cards. Then he peered squint-eyed at his four face-up cards. Then he checked his hole cards again. "I got . . . I got . . . shit, I ain't got nothing." He giggled as though he'd just said the funniest thing in history. "I ain't shitting, I don't even have a pair."

"Well, I do," Joe Bob said, rolling his cards over. "A little bitty pair. Threes." He raked in the pot while Hubie Peters and the young bearded guy shot Jesus Christ glances at one another.

Skeezix's face screwed up into a sullen frown. The Mexican girl consoled him with a kiss on the cheek, palming a couple of blue chips from his stack as she did. His eyes rose and, for the first time, met mine. He stood up pretty fast for a dumb fat guy. His stomach bumped the edge of the table.

Skeezix said, "Connie, how many times I got to tell you about letting strangers in here?" He looked around frantically, and his gaze now came to rest on Breaux. "Jesus Christ, bring me a lobster," Skeezix said. "What's Bodie Breaux doing at this here poker game?"

Connie let go of Bodie's hand and stepped forward, her shoulders squared. "He came to see me and he brought along a friend. It's my place, I guess I can have friends over if I want to." She didn't sound any smarter than she had outside on the porch, and I decided that Skeezix and Connie Swarm were pretty close to a dead heat in the brain department. I've had occasion to know a few dope dealers. There are some smart ones, but they're definitely in the minority. Breaux was a rare exception.

Breaux said, "How you doing, Skeeze man? Small world."

Skeezix sat down like a kid who'd just been told to stop playing Nintendo and take out the garbage. "Yeah, okay," he said. "It's okay this time, Connie, but that don't change anything. This is your place so long as I say it's your place, so from now on no visitors unless I clear 'em first." He peered once again at me. "I know Breaux, but who's *this* dude?"

Just when I thought Connie was stumped—I doubted that she could remember my name; it had been five minutes since she'd met me—Breaux came to the rescue. "He's my buddy. Rick. Ricky, say hello to Skeezix. Big man on this street."

I grinned and tried to look impressed. The grin was easy,

but the impressed expression was a little harder. Skeezix regarded me through fat-lidded eyes, then, without so much as a hello gathered the cards in front of him on the table. The black girl and the Mexican chick leaned closer to him and appeared interested. Skeezix began a butterfingered shuffle. "Come on, let's play, I got to get even," he said.

The other players exchanged glances that told what they thought Skeezix's chances of getting even were. Hubie Peters threw me a wink and a slight head shake that told me not to let on that I knew him. That was fine with me, and my nod told Hubie so.

I moved over close to Breaux and whispered, "Since you're the in-crowd around here, I guess you'd better stay at the party. I'm going up front to have a look. Time's getting short." As I spoke, I checked out the room. Nobody was paying any attention to us; they were all too busy watching Skeezix make an ass of himself. Bodie nudged me and his chin moved up and down. I went back through the dining room and into the living room.

The stoop-shouldered guy I'd seen earlier and couldn't quite place was on the couch with Crystal, getting high. They were on their sides with their noses practically touching, and were passing the crack-filled pipe back and forth between them. The guy was alternating hits on the pipe with swigs from his bourbon and water. He was headed for never-never land at breakneck speed. I tried to make him again and couldn't; that was okay, it'd come to me. The two of them ignored me. He was stroking her bare thigh, but I doubted that either of them was getting any kind of charge from the contact. I went to the window and peeked outside between the drapes.

Nothing yet. The cedar bush by which I'd stood earlier was outlined in moonlight across the drive. Down the road a piece, reflected light from the lake danced across my Corvette's hood. The night was windless; the mesquite trees stood like stone carvings. I looked hastily around behind me, found a chair, and placed it beside the window. I sat down and looked outside again. The asphalt pavement on Hawley Road stretched in the distance into nothingness.

I didn't have long to wait. I'd barely lit up a Pall Mall and inhaled the first puff when headlights twinkled far away and came nearer. Whoever was coming was driving like a bat out of hell. As the headlights passed swiftly in front of the house, a sleek, long limo materialized behind them. It was probably a Caddy, though in the moonlight I couldn't tell. The limo's windows were one-way black. An antenna waved from the center of its trunk. The car moved away down the blacktop, made the same squealing U-turn I'd made earlier, and came back to stop behind my 'Vette. Its lights went out. The front doors opened as one.

Mr. T got out on the driver's side, at least the guy looked like him. Light reflected from his shiny black forehead. He was solid muscle stretched over a frame the size of a jeep, wearing a sleeveless dark T-shirt that struggled to hold itself together. A lone strip of hair ran down the center of his head; the back and sides were shaved into a Mohawk. He was drinking from a can—in the dimness I wasn't sure whether it was a soft drink or a beer—and I wondered whether he'd opened the drink with the conventional tab, or to save time had just poked his thumb though the top. He turned up the can, finished off the drink, crumpled the can and dropped it on the limo's floorboard and closed the door.

The black man who exited from the passenger door was a lighter, coffee-and-cream color. Taller and slimmer than Mr. T, he was wearing a checkered sport coat, and even looked human. A black patch covered one eye. He went around the limo's nose and talked to Mr. T for a moment, then the two of them walked up to the Corvette and gave it the once-over. Mr. T bent over, and for just an instant I expected him to lift the Corvette and look underneath, but he didn't. He moved back to the limo, opened the rear door, and stood aside. Muhammed Double-X got out and looked around.

I'd run across Muhammed Double-X several times over the years. The first time had been around fifteen years ago in New York, at an otherwise forgettable postgame party after we'd squeaked by the Giants at the Polo Grounds. We'd had a good-looking rookie cornerback that year, Willie Bowles out of Grambling, and it had been Willie who'd introduced Muhammed around as his "main man." Before that season had ended they'd found Willie dead in his apartment, enough heroin in his veins to put South Dallas in orbit. Another occasion I remembered seeing Muhammed had been in downtown Dallas, on Jackson Street. Muhammed had approached one of Sweaty's bond customers, a small-time coke dealer named Billy T, and had whispered something to him. Just whispered, nothing more. Billy T's eyes had grown round as saucers and he'd looked as though he might have a stroke on the spot. Billy T never showed up for trial; Sweaty had paid off his bond and was still looking for the guy.

Muhammed was wearing a tailored dark suit with skin-tight pants. Mirrored shades covered his eyes; he had sharp cheekbones and a pointed chin. He adjusted his Windsor knot with an ebony thumb and forefinger, said something to Mr. T, and motioned toward the house. T and the man with the eye patch fell into step side by side and led Muhammed Double-X across the yard.

I let go of the drapes and stood as they fell back into place. I didn't have to worry about disturbing the pair on the couch; now the guy was on his back and Crystal was lying on top of him. They were looking into each other's eyes and taking turns giggling. There was a small utility closet just inside the front door and I hid in it, knocking over a chrome vacuum cleaner extension as I did. I left the door open a crack and peeped through the slit.

Mr. T didn't bother to knock. He hit the front door like a battering ram; wood splintered and T came into the house accompanied by a rush of air and a loud crash. He never paused but headed straight over to the couch and put hands the size of hams around Crystal's waist. Then he lifted her as though she was foam plastic and showed the guy who'd been lying beneath her a King Kong grimace. It was probably a good thing that the guy had been smoking all that crack and drinking all that whiskey; he grinned at Mr. T as though he was watching a cartoon. The hood with the black patch over his eye now passed my line of vision; still holding Crystal aloft, T turned to his buddy and said, "Ain't him." Then he dropped Crystal back on top of the guy in a tangle of arms and legs, and lumbered purposefully toward the back of the house with Eyepatch close on his heels.

Muhammed Double-X now sauntered through the living room and followed. As he passed the couch, Muhammed said to Crystal, from the side of his mouth, "Be cool, sister."

I decided that I'd better follow as well, slid out of my closet, and made tracks through the living room. Crystal grinned vacantly at me as I went by. From the rear of the house came a loud bang followed by a gargling, squawking sound, as though someone were strangling a rooster. I quickened my pace, double-timed it through the dining room, and came to a screeching halt just inside the poker room. I was digging my hand into my back pocket and wrapping my fingers around the handle of the Smith & Wesson.

It was Skeezix who was doing the gargling. The Mr. T character had the fat guy by the throat and was holding him about a foot off of the floor. Jesus, Skeezix must have weighed close to three hundred pounds, but the big guy didn't even seem to be breathing hard. Everyone else—Breaux, Connie Swarm, the Mexican cutie and the black chick, Hubie Peters and the two other poker hustlers—was lined up against the wall with Patch-on-the-Eye holding a big .45 pistol pointed loosely in their direction. Patch was watching with mild amusement as Mr. T choked the daylights out of Skeezix. Muhammed Double-X had his back to me, about two yards away. His shoulders and waist formed a *V* underneath the coat of his dark suit.

I had to admit that I was sort of enjoying the strangling myself, but I reluctantly sprang into action. I took a long step forward, brought the Smith & Wesson up, and placed the barrel inside Muhammed's ear. "Hate to spoil your fun," I said. "Call the gorilla off."

Muhammed tensed. His right eye was visible from my side-angle view, behind the lens of his mirrored shades. The eye blinked once. "Who that?" Muhammed said. "You sound like Rick Bannion. Rick Bannion, that you?" Only his lips moved; the rest of him was still as stone.

"The last time I checked I was. Come on, high priest, call him off. Skeezix is getting sick."

"Man, you working for *this* honky snitch muthafuckah?" Muhammed said. "I ain't believing this. I thought you was Sweaty Mathis's man."

Come to think about it, I was having a tough time believing it myself. I pressed the S&W's barrel harder against his eardrum. "I don't have time to bullshit. The gorilla drops Skeezix and Skinny drops his gun."

Muhammed showed gritted teeth in a half snarl. "Put the fat ass down, Honeybear. Yo pistol, Snakey, put it away. We got us a turncoat sonofabitch here." He meant me.

Honeybear let go of Skeezix, who thudded clumsily to the floor. Honeybear looked as though his raw-meat ration had just been canceled. I still thought he resembled Mr. T. Snakey laid the .45 gingerly on the poker table and regarded me mildly though his one good eye. Skeezix flopped into his chair and clutched his throat, gasping for air. His face was the color of ripe plums.

"Get the piece, Bodie," I said.

Breaux sauntered over, picked up the .45, rested his hip on the poker table, and aimed the gun loosely in Honeybear's direction. Honeybear looked about as afraid of the gun as he was of Skeezix. He blinked dully. I briefly wondered whether bullets bounced off him.

I said to Muhammed, "Now we're going to inspect the shoreline. Come on, the three of you first." I took the S&W's barrel out of his ear and motioned toward the back door. It was located down a narrow hallway at the rear of the poker room.

Honeybear didn't move a muscle. He said to Muhammed, "What I do, boss man?" I mentally held my breath. If Muhammed gave the word, this monster was going to charge us, guns or no.

I put the barrel against Muhammed's right temple. "You give him the right orders, bro," I said. I showed Honeybear my version of steely gaze. He appeared bored to death.

Muhammed shrugged. "Do what the mothafuckah say, Bear. There be another time, you see." He didn't sound frightened, either. I began to wonder who had the drop on who.

Honeybear led the parade through the back door into the yard, his thick arms slightly akimbo and his palms to the rear. His shoulders rotated in a half swagger. Snakey went next. He paused in the doorway, adjusted the patch over his eye, glanced at my pistol, then at me. He said, "What you think this honky gonna do, Bear, shoot us down like dirty dogs? At least he don't tell us 'Reach for the sky,' or none of that Hopalong Cassidy shit." Snakey and Honeybear broke up, whooping and giggling. Muhammed Double-X followed them into the yard like he was strolling down Broadway. I went out after them, my gun at waist level, in full control of the situation. Breaux trailed a couple of paces behind me. He mumbled, "Jesus Christ, Bannion, I think you got 'em."

The Bermuda lawn slanted toward the lake. We'd made it about halfway down the incline, crickets whirring nearby and frogs croaking in the distance, when heavy running footfalls approached us from behind. I turned, tensing, and came within a whisker of shooting Skeezix. He'd come only about thirty yards, but he was huffing and puffing as though he'd run a couple of miles.

Skeezix showed me his version of a friendly smile, which didn't look particularly friendly. "Hey," he said, "I got to apologize for not trusting you, man. You're all right. Fucking niggers, sneaking up on people. We gonna deep-six the fuckers, what?"

Honeybear halted and swiveled his massive head around. Breaux motioned with the .45. Honeybear moved slowly on.

As we neared the dock, the lapping of the waves grew louder and the boat bobbed up and down. I'd been right, it was a Cris-Craft, a twenty-footer with a steering wheel behind a curved windshield. I shifted my gaze warily between Snakey, Muhammed, and Honeybear. Skeezix stayed at my elbow, chattering a mile a minute, but I ignored him. I didn't have time for him. Not just yet.

Skeezix was really getting into the act. "You fucking smokes think you're big-time, huh? Muhammed Double-X, hot shit. Hell, that ain't even your name. I know your name, you jungle bunny. Hey, you guys, you want to know the head nigger's real name?"

Muhammed paused and turned. "You don't use that name, you fat honky. Don't nobody use that name, you heah?" I couldn't see the expression in his eyes, but the sneer on his lips was enough.

Skeezix laughed, a high-pitched, pig-like squeal. "Don't *use it*? Man, you smokes with your phony names kill me. Pork-

pie. *Porkpie*, you hear me? Porkpie Stevens is the head nigger—I seen your FBI file. Porkpie Washington Stevens, just
like one of them smokes on *Amos & Andy*."

Up ahead, Honeybear grunted. "*Porkpie*? Boss, he's shittin',
ain't he?"

Muhammed said to Skeezix, "You one dead mothah-
fuckah, boy."

I said, "Cut the crap. You three, in the boat. Now. Move
it, over the side." I waved the Smith & Wesson. I was snick-
ering. I couldn't help it.

The hoods climbed aboard. Honeybear staggered a bit to
keep his balance in the gently rocking boat. Snakey was a
bit more graceful; he swung one leg, then the other over the
side and sat on a cushioned bench, watching me with one
unblinking eye. Muhammed Double-X clambered aboard,
then propped one foot up on the driver's chair, and leaned
on his thigh like Washington on the Delaware. Off to my
right a big fish—a bass or crappie—broke water, wriggled in
midair, and splashed back down into the depths. I smelled
wet moss.

"Hey, Bodie," I said. "Keep an eye on the crew for a
minute."

Breaux stepped forward. He'd come up with a flashlight
from somewhere, probably in the house, and he switched it
on. The beam stabbed the blackness and illuminated the
Afro Mafia aboard the Cris-Craft. Bodie pointed the .45 with
his right hand and held the flashlight in his left.

I turned to Skeezix. He raised his fat face to me and
grinned. "You going to pop the niggers right here," he said,
"or wait till you get 'em out in the middle? Man, a nigger
sinks good with a rock tied to his ass."

I pointed the S&W at Skeezix. "You want to go for a boat
ride?" I said.

His gaze shifted uncertainly. "Huh?"

"A boat ride." I raised my voice. "Hey, Muhammed, you
want to take Skeezix for a boat ride?"

From aboard the Cris-Craft: "Man, you kiddin'? Give us
the fat muthafuckah."

Skeezix's uncertain look went away, replaced by knowing
fear. He glanced in the direction of the house, tensing, about

to take a running step in that direction. I raised the Smith & Wesson and put the barrel against the slight cleft in Skeezix's chin.

He said, "Man . . . please . . ."

" 'S matter, Skeezix, you don't like boat rides? You have to get your sea legs. Come on, get in the boat."

His eyes widened and his puffy mouth twisted. He shot a fearful glance in the direction of the Cris-Craft. He whimpered. "They'll fuck me up bad."

I kept my gaze on Skeezix and said to Breaux, "What do you think, Bodie? You think we ought to let Muhammed have him?"

"Do one or the other," Breaux said. "Just quit fucking around. I'm tired watching these guys float. It's making me seasick."

Muhammed said, "You give us the fat shit, Bannion, we forget about you." He was practically drooling.

I softly chewed my lower lip. "Look, Skeezix, you want to stay alive? Make a deal?"

"Anything." Skeezix was breathing like a cardiac patient.

I pretended to be deep in thought, then said, "We're going to give you a break, Skeezix. You're going to leave here with me and Breaux. You're going out of town, like a trip, okay? Now I'm going to know where you are, every day, all the time. Always, don't you doubt it for a fucking minute. And if you don't stay exactly where I want you, Muhammed is going to find you. Okay? Now don't lie to me, Skeezix. You understand?"

"I said anything, man. Just get me the fuck outta here."

"Shove 'em off, Bodie," I said.

Bodie made Snakey hand him the two oars from the boat. He untied the rope, tossed it aboard, and used one oar to shove the Cris-Craft away from the dock. And they floated slowly away, watching us, the three black thugs like glum statues.

"So don't take no wooden nickels, Porkpie," Breaux said.

Driving the Corvette with Skeezix sitting on the console was like trying to steer with the world's largest bag of marshmallows bumping my elbow. Twice on Airport Freeway he knocked the shift lever into neutral, and the engine revved and raced while I fought to get the car back in gear. The exhaust pipe rattled against the Corvette's underbody with every bump in the road.

As we made the slow northbound curve off the freeway and headed for the twinkling red and green lights strung over DFW Airport's entry toll booths, Skeezix said, "Well, yeah, he's my baby brother and all. He'll put me up for a while, but Jesus Christ, showing up in town without any clothes—"

"You'll have to think something up to tell him, Skeeze," I said. "I don't know how long Muhammed and the boys floated around in the lake, but I'll bet not over a quarter of an hour. The first thing they're going to do is make a beeline for your pad, so we can't afford to go by there for you to pack. What're you worried about? You got all that federal stoolie money in your pocket, go buy yourself a new wardrobe. And Skeezix, show some taste this time, huh? No more purple sport coats. Minneapolis, huh? You better not be shitting me, Skeeze. I know a guy in Minneapolis and I'm going to have him check on you every day."

Skeezix bit the nail on his right index finger. He was acting more and more nervous, and I suspected that he needed a little cocaine in order to get his head on straight. They all think they do. He said, "You don't believe me, check on it. Moore and Stanton, CPA's, downtown Minneapolis. It's in the book."

On Skeezix's right, Breaux snorted. "Skeezix, your brother's a CPA? I bet he does a lot of bragging around about you."

I steered into the inbound lane, slowed, accepted the blue ticket that the machine spat at me, then pulled back into the whizzing traffic, following the taillights of a Chevy van. The jammed parking areas and lit-up terminals whooshed by on either side. We passed a luminescent green sign that told us the next exit led to American Airlines. I checked the digital clock on the dashboard: 11:42.

"You'll be just in time, Skeeze," I said. "Red-eye special."

I thought he was going to say something, but at that instant we bounced over a freeway expansion joint that was deeper than normal. Skeezix jiggled up and down and steadied himself with his fat palms against the dashboard. I made the winding up-and-down circle and screeched to a halt in front of the American terminal, probably making the ride a little rougher on Skeezix than necessary. I wasn't doing it on purpose. I didn't think.

"Bodie, escort our guest to the departure gate," I said. "He's got ten minutes." Then I put my lips close to Skeezix's ear and whispered, "Don't fuck with me, Skeeze. I'll be watching you. Every day." I winked. "No fooling." He nodded. He was blubbering. Probably sad over leaving his setup at Connie Swarm's. I couldn't say that I blamed him.

I watched Skeezix waddle into the brightly lit terminal with Breaux at his side, then put the 'Vette in gear and made the circle once more. The 'Vette seemed a whole lot peppier without Skeezix riding the console. I only had to make the circle once; the first time by the terminal, Breaux waited on the curb, hands on hips. I stopped and he climbed in. "Fucker barely made it," Breaux said. "Jesus, I'd hate to have to pay for the petrol it takes to fly that fat son of a bitch around."

The Cafe Dallas was jumping, bodies now writhing on the dance floor. As I pulled to the curb in front, I peered inside through the windows. I didn't see the redhead, but I'd have bet she was still inside. Breaux affected certain kinds of women like that.

He said, "You coming in?"

"I don't guess so, Bodie, I'm worn out. I think I'll go on to bed." I fished a roll of bills out of my pocket and peeled off five hundreds. "Here. You're high, bro, but you're worth it."

Breaux eyed the money, then me. "Bannion, you're a real fucking Daddy Warbucks, you know that?" he said.

I told Donna, "I think it's going to be all right."

"Are you sure? I don't want you to get in any trouble, Rick. What did you do?"

"Don't ask." I was standing outside a 7-Eleven store using a public pay phone. The 'Vette idled at the curb behind me, its hood vibrating more than it should have. Probably needed plugs. "Let's just say, I think they'll have to set bond. It'll be high, but I think you'll be able to post it."

There was a brief silence on the line, broken by the faint noise of static, like paper rustling. "Rick?" she said.

"Yes."

"Can I see you?"

I'm not sure whether I'd expected it or not. To give her the opportunity was probably the real reason I'd called. "Tonight?" I said.

"Jacqueline's spending the night with her friend. Tonight, yes. It . . . might be our only chance."

Long-ago images flashed through my mind. One was a scene at Jack and Donna's wedding reception, the warm, nearly feverish squeeze she'd given my hand as I'd passed through the reception line. "We might be sorry," I said.

"I'd be sorrier if we don't."

I sighed. "Me, too. I don't want to come to your house. I wouldn't feel comfortable."

"Where, then?"

"You're sure you want to?"

"I'm sure I have to," she said.

I gave her an address, returned to the 'Vette, and headed south on Greenville Avenue. Deep down I'm a real bastard. I've gotten used to the feeling.

FIVE

I lay on my side on cool satin sheets, propped my head on my elbow, and peered through the dimness at Donna's outline against the sliding patio door. She was standing with her feet slightly apart on the carpet, her back to me, her chin pointed downward and to her left. She was looking across Turtle Creek Boulevard toward the stately elms and sycamores that grew in Lee Park. There was a big bronze statue of General Robert E. himself over there, in full Rebel battle dress astride his horse. I'd stood where Donna now was countless times, and General Lee would be visible to her. There was a spotlight in the park, trained on the statue, and the general showed up pretty well at night. Underneath the horse's belly there'd be a few spent roaches on the ground.

She shifted her weight from one foot to the other; one round hip moved upward, the other down. There was a stark white strip across her buttocks that contrasted with her tan. "That doorman called you Dr. Peters."

"Peterman," I said.

"God. The eternal phallic symbol."

"I never thought of it that way," I said.

Her slender arm moved; the point of her cigarette glowed

hot, then dimmed. She snuffed it out in an ashtray on a small round table just inside the door. I'd put an oldie album on the stereo, Johnny Mathis. "Chances Are." Old lost times with old lost loves.

"Why the alias, Rick? You're not a spy or anything." Her rich mahogany hair hung below her shoulder blades. She tossed her head. Visible beyond her outline, the full August moon touched the tops of the trees.

"This isn't really my place," I said. "I clear out a couple of times a week so some bookmakers can take over the phone. If this place gets too hot they'll move on. *We'll* move on. Then I'll be living someplace else and there'll be a different name on the mailbox. What I get out of it is a free place to stay. What they get is a safe place to operate. It works out."

"I don't get it, Rick. I don't get any of it. My husband, a guy I've lived with all this time without knowing he was a cocaine smuggler. You, the way you're living. What's happened to all of us?"

"I can only answer for me," I said. "And my story's pretty simple. I live whichever way it takes to get by. Oh, sure, I could work on an assembly line, but prison didn't leave me a lot of choices. As for Jack, well, nobody's proved anything about him."

She came over to sit on the bed, and I scooted over to give her room. She leaned her back against my bare midsection and crossed her legs. One small foot began to swing. Johnny Mathis was now into "Small World."

There was a stuffed zebra head on the wall over the bed. She looked at it. "At least your friends go first-class. God, the first time I looked up and saw that . . . *animal*, it scared me to death. Nothing against you, Romeo, but it was the zebra that made me yell the first time. Turtle Creek North is a pretty fancy address for a temporary pad."

"You should have seen the last one," I said. "Out in Southeast Dallas. If I still lived there I would have had to put tight jeans and a crash helmet on you and smuggle you over there on the back of my Harley."

She laughed, a silvery tinkle like crystal dinner bells. Her voice was slightly higher-pitched than I'd remembered. "Jesus Christ, Rick . . . yes, it's funny. But at the same time it's a little sad to see you living like this, with no future. You don't have much of one, do you?"

"No. Whatever future I might've had, well, the feds took it away."

"I couldn't believe it when you went to prison," she said. "And having to read about you in the papers, well . . . I'm not sure that wasn't more of a shock than finding out about Jack."

I rolled onto my back and clasped my hands behind my head. She draped an arm across my chest. I smelled faint lilac in her hair. "I guess it's a shock if you don't understand what's going on," I said. "But turning to dealing drugs isn't peculiar to Jack and me, it's happened to a lot of worn-out jocks. The one bonehead offside play against the Forty-Niners, that wasn't the real reason that Dallas got rid of me. That's all baloney. They let me go because I was short on talent. The Rams found that out and quick."

I'd fixed her Drambuie in a tiny stemmed glass earlier, and her drink sat half full on the nightstand. She had a dainty sip. "That's not what Jack said. Or the other guys on the team, either. They—"

"Donna, it's great of them, but those other guys aren't coaches. I've never seen a ball player yet who knew beans about talent. They've got talent, but they can't recognize it. So let's let me go ahead and feel sorry for myself, it's kind of fun. The long and short of it is that when the Rams finally had enough of me and let me go, there I was. In L.A. with about two cents to my name and a phys ed degree to fall back on. Man on the move, huh?"

"Soh-oh," I said. "Well, I don't guess I went to a party the whole time I played football where there weren't some drugs around. Uppers, downers, cocaine, grass, you name it."

"I went to some of those," Donna said. "Remember?"

"Yeah. I don't remember you taking any dope, though."

"My point exactly," she said.

"And your point's well taken. So I wasn't so smart and hindsight's twenty-twenty, what can I do about it now? I had a habit of living high that was harder to break than a dope habit, what can I say? Only I wasn't making any money anymore. So I knew a guy in L.A. I'd met at some of those parties and he knew a guy back here in Dallas and the two of them were in need of somebody desperate for money and too dumb to know better. Which was me. I was going to get twenty thousand dollars just for flying to Dallas, picking up a package, flying it back to the coast, and driving it down to Newport Beach. Easy money, huh? Only when the guy in Dallas handed me that package at the Marriott, boom. Lights came on and guys in dark suits came in. This Dallas guy had been working with the feds all along."

"God, didn't you know that was the way it works? All you have to do is read the paper."

"Hindsight, Donna. Hindsight. You'd have to have been there. And understand this, I'm not bitter about what happened to me up to that point. I'd made my own bed and I was ready to lie in it. But then along came Mr. Norman Aycock."

Her chin lifted. "The same one that's prosecuting Jack?"

"The same old guy. Small world, huh? Aycock's been around here since the Alamo. He wanted me to testify against the guy in L.A., the one who sent me, and I wouldn't do it. I guess somebody somewhere taught me that you're supposed to take your own medicine. Since I wouldn't cooperate, Aycock decided to frame me. Hell, Donna, what I did was worth two years in the joint, tops, but by the time Aycock got through running in all these phony witnesses to testify about things that never even happened, I wound up with a ten-year sentence. Of which I served half. Which I'm not really thrilled about." I tried some of the Drambuie myself. It was warm and sticky and burned going down.

"Is that what's going to happen to Jack? God, you're scaring me." She hunched her shoulders and hugged herself. The movement squeezed her breasts together, and their tips quivered like pink lambs' noses.

"It ought to scare anybody, babe. The old gnome has got the power of God, and he's crooked enough to do just about anything. That's why Cassel wanted me. So some of the things I'm doing aren't exactly cricket themselves, but on this deal my conscience isn't going to bother me. Call it rationalization if you want to."

Donna got up, rose on her tiptoes, and stretched. Then

she knelt beside me and massaged my chest and shoulders. Her hands were cool and firm. Her forearm muscles rippled with the movement of her fingers. "Rick," she said.

"Yes. *Ouch*. Careful, Donna, that's tender."

She traced the scar on my shoulder with her fingernail. "That's still sore after all this time? You had that operation right after Jack and I married, didn't you?"

Four months to the day after the wedding, to be exact. "I'm not sure," I said. "Sometime around then. It still hurts if you touch it a certain way, I guess it always will. Another thing to thank football for."

"Poor baby." Her tone was gentle and teasing. Then, more seriously, she said, "Do you think about me?"

I wasn't sure how to handle that one, but I decided to tell her. "Sure I do. But things have worked out. You wanted things I couldn't give you. That I still can't. Like homes and permanency and fidelity and whatnot. Things you're entitled to."

"I'm not sure I've got them now," Donna said. She lowered her gaze to her lap and rested her hands on her round thighs. "I do love him in a lot of ways. And Jacqueline's my life. One problem we've had, well, Jack has real problems with you and me and what was. If he knew about tonight . . ."

"It might put him under," I said. "I told you we might be sorry. I just don't know what's right. What we want? What Jack wants? I'm pretty sure he's going to be home in a couple of days, out on bond. You going to have trouble facing him?"

She turned her back to me and lay on her side. "I suppose I'll have to deal with that when the time comes." She groped for my hand, found it, pulled my arm around her. "For now just hold me," she said.

S I X

Norman Aycock probably hadn't looked so glum since the Supreme Court threw out the death penalty, way back in '69. He turned his craggy face around and peered birdlike toward the rear of the courtroom. Nothing there. He piddled around at the prosecution table, picking up typewritten pages one at a time in long, skinny fingers and pretending to read them over. He poured himself a glass of water from a chrome-plated carafe. In the hushed courtroom the sound was like a waterfall.

From his seat at the bench, Judge Sid Fitzwater said impatiently, "The court has a lot of business, Mr. Aycock. Can't we get on with this?" Fitzwater was a recent appointee by the Reagan administration, the youngest federal judge in the history of the Northern District of Texas. His flowing black robe was a couple of sizes too big for him. He looked like a high school kid playing dress-up judge.

Fred Cassel stood at the defense table, wearing a navy Brooks Brothers (I briefly wondered how many identical suits Fred owned), and today a maroon silk hanky in his breast pocket. He took his glasses off and tapped an earpiece against his front teeth. "I agree with the court, Your Honor. My client's been in jail for a week, and it's high time he learned something about his bond." He threw an encouraging sideways glance in Jack's direction. Jack was seated at the defense table wearing a dark brown suit. The two U.S. marshals who'd escorted him over from Lew Sterrett Justice Center were lounging against the rail. There was a slight stoop to Jack's posture that I'd never seen before.

Aycock lifted his bony frame and stood as well. His suit was black, the sleeves about a half inch too short. His hair was gray-going-to-snow-white, cut short in the fifties style and parted on the left. Aycocks's idea of liberal was a woman whose skirt showed her knees. He said, after clearing his throat, "Please bear with us a moment, Your Honor. This case is of the utmost importance to the government, and I assure you that we're not taking up the court's time intentionally." He was doing his best to speak respectfully, but I caught a tone in his voice that said the old prosecutor thought that the young judge was an upstart twerp. I wondered whether Fitzwater had caught it as well.

Fitzwater tapped on the bench with the eraser end of a pencil. "I'm giving you two minutes, Mr. Aycock. Then we're proceeding with the bond hearing, ready or not." A giant Stars and Stripes hung from a gilt pole on his left.

The door behind me swished open. I turned. There was a muted rustle as fifty or sixty spectators—three reporters I'd counted, four or five lawyers with other cases on the docket, the rest the usual gawkers and hangers-on—turned as well. I was seated five rows behind the rail, practically in the center of the spectators section. I had to crane my neck a bit to see what was going on at the rear of the courtroom.

A Mutt and Jeff duo came in, one tall and wearing a charcoal suit, the other short and squat and wearing a plaid sports coat. I'd never seen either one of them, but they'd both be federal agents. When you've been through the system as I have, you get to know the look. Mutt looked perplexed while Jeff signaled Aycock, then extended his hands palms up and shrugged. We got no witness today, boss. My lips were spreading in a grin as I turned back toward the bench. I froze. Aycock had spotted me.

The look that the old prosecutor was shooting in my direction wasn't exactly a glare. It was more the look of a man

who'd picked up a rock in the creekbed and found a mocca-
sin writhing underneath. Or who'd just walked into his bedroom unannounced and found the plumber banging his wife.
He turned back to the bench with a snap that must have
popped a couple of vertebrae in his neck. Now it was Cassel
who was staring at me. He was a little green around the
gills. I grinned, tossed old Fred a wink, folded my arms, and
slid downward in the cushioned pew.

Aycock said, "Your Honor, may counsel approach the
bench?" His voice was raspy and sounded old.

As Aycock and Cassel converged on Fitzwater, I watched
Donna. She was sitting in the front row, in front of me and
to my left. She'd worn conservative gray, a modest business
dress that buttoned up to her throat. Her luxuriant hair was
confined in a bun and she wore a small gray hat. Her neck-
line was elegant and slender, and there was a royal tilt to
her chin. Jack turned around and smiled hopefully at her.
She raised a manicured hand and gave him the thumbs-up
sign.

There was quite a show going on before the judge. Aycock
was talking a mile a minute, gesturing frantically with his
hands. Cassel had one ear bent in the prosecutor's direction
as he listened. Good old Fred's mouth was agape in disbelief,
and he now turned and stared in my direction as though
he'd never seen me before in his life. At the same time Judge
Fitzwater leaned forward and regarded me through narrowed eyes. Finally Aycock made it a threesome, interrupting his discourse long enough to fix me with a beady-
eyed stare. I put on my blandest, who-me expression and
looked at the ceiling.

The judge shrugged his shoulders and said something to
the lawyers. Both Cassel and Aycock returned to their respective places. The judge popped his gavel. In the foreground,
the slim female court reporter sat up straight, her fingers
poised over the keys on her shorthand machine.

Fitzwater droned, "The court calls Case No. 87-CR-371-J,
United States of America versus Jack Stuart Brendy. Are the
government and the defendant present in the courtroom?"

Cassel and Aycock stood as one. Jack rose slowly to his

feet at Cassel's side. Both sides said that they were there. Fitzwater went on.

"The matter at hand is a bond hearing, ladies and gentlemen. Before we begin, are there any announcements?"

"The government has something to say, Your Honor," said Aycock, squaring his shoulders. The rasp was gone from his voice and he spoke in a rich, youthful baritone. Norman Aycock might be an asshole, but he was some kind of orator when the spotlight came on.

"Proceed," said the judge. He sat back and folded his hands.

"We'd planned to present probable cause evidence, much more than probable, that the defendant here, Jack Brendy, did conspire to transport two hundred kilograms of a controlled substance—to wit, cocaine—into this country from Colombia. But it seems we can't. It seems our witness has disappeared. Disappeared under circumstances, I wish to go on record as saying, that lead me to suspect foul play." He sounded like the guy on "Inner Sanctum." He turned to stare once again at me.

There were whispers and rustles in the courtroom. People stared. An elderly woman in a blue dress, her white hair tinted electric blue to match, regarded me from an aisle seat like, Oh, you dirty dog. I cleared my throat and kept my gaze straight ahead.

Now Fred Cassel chimed in. "I want to go on record also, Your Honor. I want to go on record as saying that if something has happened to their witness—and I'm not agreeing that anything has happened, Your Honor; there isn't any evidence that anything has—but I want to go on record as saying that I know nothing about it. The law offices of Fred S. Cassel wouldn't get involved in anything that even hinted of being so . . . so wrong." Now it was Cassel's turn to stare at me. Old standup Fred.

"Well, that's a matter for the U.S. prosecutor and the FBI," Fitzwater said. "And I'm sure, Mr. Aycock, that you'll see things are fully looked into." Now the judge looked at me. I'm sure that he wasn't, but I got the feeling that Fitzwater was about to laugh. Then he said sternly, "But that doesn't solve our current dilemma. We must proceed with the hearing, witness or no witness. The statute says plainly that the defendant is entitled to a bond hearing within seven days of his arrest."

Aycock cleared his throat. "Your Honor, since we're currently without any ammunition, the government withdraws its request to hold the defendant without bond."

"I should think you'd have to," Fitzwater said. "Request granted."

Now Aycock bowed his neck and stuck his chin out like an old bull pawing the ground. "But we're going to ask the court to set substantial bond. The defendant is charged with drug smuggling, one of our highest crimes. Higher than high. He has assets. His assets are going to be the subject of a seizure order that I'm going to ask the court to consider in the near future. But for now, anyway, he has assets. He's known to be connected; he can step aboard an airplane and be halfway around the world in hours. And foremost, we feel he's a risk to commit further crimes while he's out on bond. These—these *drug dealers* have a tendency."

"Objection." Fred Cassel's voice was a mild tenor and didn't carry very well. On the heels of Aycock's rich baritone, Cassel sounded like a scratchy old Dennis Day album.

"Sustained," Fitzwater said. "Mr. Aycock, you haven't presented any evidence that the defendant has done anything in the past, much less that he's going to do anything in the future."

Cassel strutted in place. The reporters scribbled notes. To the unwashed masses it looked like a timely move for the defense, but I'd been around the courthouse enough to know better. With no government witnesses to point the finger at Jack, Fitzwater *had* to sustain the objection. His hands were tied.

Aycock plunged on. "Nevertheless, Your Honor, we are asking for a substantial bond to guarantee the defendant's presence. Two million dollars, Your Honor. Two million minimum." He stepped back and folded his arms.

Fitzwater arched an eyebrow. Then he said to Cassel, "Does the defense have anything to say?" This part was for show. Fitzwater already knew how much Jack's bond was going to be, but he was going to give Cassel a chance to blow and go anyway. Make it look as though Cassel was earning his fee. It was like a goddamn fraternity.

Cassel took the judge up on it. He tweaked, "Yes, we do, Your Honor. We ask the court to bear in mind that Mr. Brendy is well established here, a homeowner with wife and child." He gave Donna an over-the-shoulder glance that reminded me of an Oral Roberts sermon I'd once seen on TV while waiting for a Giant-Bear kickoff. "Also," Cassel said, "and this is in the past, but Mr. Brendy is not an unknown. He was an outstanding player with the Dallas Cowboy football team. He'd have a hard time going incognito."

"And I'm sure his old teammates would back him up," Fitzwater said. He threw a smirk in my direction.

"To the hilt, Your Honor," Cassel said. I cringed inside. Cassel said, "And under the circumstances the defense asks that bond be waived and the defendant be place on personal recognizance. Thank you."

Fitzwater regarded Cassel for a moment, and I got the feeling that the judge thought old Fred sounded just as dumb as I thought he did. Finally Fitzwater said, "Well, I hear two million and I hear personal recognizance. That's quite a spread, gentlemen. Mr. Brendy"—now he spoke directly to Jack, ignoring everyone else—"Mr. Brendy, I've no choice but to set bond for you in this matter. I'm also telling you here and now, sir, that if the government can prove its allegation regarding what's happened to their witness, things will not go easy on you. Bond is set at five hundred thousand dollars."

Fitzwater's gavel banged and echoed. The courtroom buzzed and tittered. Jack's shoulders sagged even more.

Donna half rose and turned to face me. Her look was close to panic and there was a mist in her eyes. She mouthed silently, "We can't."

It wasn't a big surprise that Jack couldn't post bond. He had some assets, yeah, but the reason he'd gotten into the drug deal in the first place was that he'd been in a bind. Hell, Aycock probably knew exactly how much bond to post; five would get you ten that he'd briefed the judge on what to do if they couldn't deny bond altogether. I winked at

Donna, at the same time mouthing back to her, "You can."
Then I turned around and looked for Sweaty Mathis.

Sweaty was making tracks. I spied his round form just as
he hustled out of the courtroom into the hallway. I charged
after him, almost knocking over an old gent with a cane in
the aisle. Steadying the old fellow and mumbling, "Excuse
me," I caught Sweaty halfway to the elevators.

"Where you going, Sweat?" I said.

Sweaty was living up to his name. Rivers of perspiration
ran down his forehead and made little tributaries around his
eyebrows. He was round-faced with pudgy cheeks, about six
inches shorter than I was. He was wearing a dark green suit
that was too big for him, and that needed pressing.

"Jesus Christ," he said. "Half a mil. Half a fucking mil.
What I'm going to do if the guy runs off?"

"Sweaty. Did I ask you what I was going to do if I got
caught when I was helping take a little income tax heat off
you? If he runs you're going to hire a bunch of lawyers to
keep you from having to pay off, that's what you're going to
do. You're going the wrong way, Sweaty. The bond posting
desk is in the other direction. Jack won't run, take it from
me."

Sweaty sweated even more. He closed his eyes, and I figured he was seeing images of dollar bills, wings attached,
flying away. Then he shook his head and started reluctantly
toward the marshals' office down the hall, muttering, "Jesus
Christ. Half a fucking mil."

"No sweat, Sweaty," I said.

Norman Aycock paid me a visit just as Sweaty was posting
bond. He said, "I'm going to tie you into this. Mark my
words."

"That won't be hard, Mr. Aycock," I said. "Jack Brendy's
been my friend for a lot of years. I wouldn't be much of a
pal if I didn't at least show up for his bond hearing. You
know, give moral support." Visible over Aycock's shoulder,
Sweaty was checking the bond form over, item by item. If
there was a loophole, Sweaty would find it.

"Buddies through thick and thin, eh?" Aycock looked like
Moses on the mountain as he glared at me. "Oh, Bannion,

are you ever going to be a hit at Leavenworth. They just love funny guys up there."

"Well, they might," I said. "That's why Jack shouldn't go there. He's not much of a comedian."

I didn't see Jack and Donna again until I'd reached the Federal Building's lobby. There was a pretty good crowd standing around them, five or six reporters, a harried-looking guy who was aiming a hand-held video camera, and the frosted-haired, curried and manicured dish who served as anchor for Channel 8's evening news. The newslady and Jack faced the camera. She held a cordless mike between them, asked Jack questions, then showed Pepsodent whites to the cameraman while Jack did his best to give the answers. Donna stood by Jack and his arm was around her shoulders. I glanced at the newslady dish, then back at Donna. Donna was better looking, hands down.

Sweaty followed me through the revolving door onto the sidewalk; sudden August heat battered us like a furnace. Sweaty really showed the temperature, the guy was a human thermometer. Now he looked like a guy taking a steam bath with his clothes on.

He spread his chubby hands, palms down, like an umpire's "safe" signal. "That's it, Bannion. That is everloving it. You got any idea how much I'd charge somebody else for a bond that size? Way I figure, you owe me about six hundred skips free of charge." To my left on Commerce Street, horns honked and buses chugged. Sunlight glinted from the mirrored walls of the Interfirst Tower, two blocks away. There was a big Park 'n' Lock lot across the street. I watched with sudden interest as a four-door Mercedes toured slowly to the lot's exit, then paused as if waiting for someone. There were four men in the car, two in front and two in back.

Jack and Donna were coming out of the Federal Building with Fred Cassel strutting between them. Jack looked better, as though a load had been lifted. Cassel halted in his tracks, said something to Jack, then went back inside the building as if he'd forgotten something. Donna rose on tiptoes and gave Jack a wifely peck on the cheek; as she did, Jack caught my eye and waved. Try as I might, I couldn't shake a pang of jealousy. I returned my attention to the parking lot across the street.

I'm not sure where the warning bell comes from, it just comes. Maybe it's the result of too many nights in prison, sleeping with one eye open, but the warning bell is right a helluva lot more times than it's wrong. The Mercedes moseyed out into traffic, then cut across three lanes, and angled to the curb right beside Sweaty and me.

Sweaty was saying, "And if I have to pay off, you'll owe me six *million* skips, you hear? I can't take it, Bannion, I lose too much sleep. Half a million—"

"Get a move on, Sweaty," I said. "Haul ass out of here." Even as I spoke, I was taking a long, running stride toward Jack and Donna.

The Mercedes's rear curbside door opened. I had a first impression, a crazy one, that the guy who got out didn't have a face. But it was a mask, a makeshift job made from a bedsheet or pillowcase with eyeholes cut in the fabric. He wore a tan overcoat and a dark hat pulled low. Cradled in his right arm was a very real, very ugly Uzi submachine gun.

I reached Donna's side, folded her into my arms, and hit the cement rolling. My right shoulder, the one with the football scar, landed first and pain sliced into my collarbone. Donna gasped and her fast breath blew sweet and warm on my cheek. I rolled onto my back with her weight on top of me, firm flesh over vibrant muscle. I rolled again and shielded her. "Move it, Jack," I yelled. "It's the Mercedes." I buried my face in Donna's shoulder.

The Uzi chattered and spat fire. Someone screamed behind me; it could have been a woman or a very terrified man. Donna whimpered. Bullets whined close overhead in rapid succession. A car door slammed and tires squealed. I looked up. The Mercedes careened into the middle lane on Commerce, sideswiped a Dodge pickup, made a squealing right turn, and disappeared.

Jack lay spread-eagled on the sidewalk. One brown pants leg had ridden up to expose his calf and a long black sock. My gaze swept his body and my stomach churned. The top half of his head was missing.

I cupped my hand behind Donna's neck and held her face against my shoulder. "Don't look, babe," I said.

Her body was heaving with her sobs. Right then I felt like letting go myself. It happens that way sometimes.

S E V E N

They buried Jack on a Saturday that began with the sky overcast and with sooty thunderheads lumbering across the horizon. The chapel at Park Cities Baptist Church was standing room only; Roger Staubach gave the eulogy to the solemn accompaniment of rain sweeping across the roof. By the time I'd followed a string of fifty or sixty cars—mostly Caddy's, Lincolns, and Mercedes: Jack had run with a pretty blue-blooded crowd—to Hillcrest Memorial, stood off to one side and watched Donna's filmy black veil move gently in the breeze at the short graveside service, the rain had gone and the clouds had disappeared. The grass was suddenly a brilliant sun-washed green and the flowers at Hillcrest sparkling shades of red and yellow and blue. Somehow the day didn't seem any brighter because of the sunshine.

I stood between Bobby Mitchell and Larry Morgan as a line of men with raincoats draped over their arms went by. The men escorted ladies dangling parasols by straps out into the parking lot to head for home. One sandy-haired man of forty was walking arm in arm with a girl of twenty, whispering just inches from her ear. As they passed, she winked at him and giggled. A natural amphitheater stretched out below us, formed by rows of clipped hedges and rows of white and pink marble tombstones. Donna was far down there, standing with her arm around Jacqueline's shoulders. They were beside the oblong pit into which some men had lowered Jack's coffin a half hour earlier. Their heads were bowed.

"Sumbitch was a runner," Bobby Mitchell said. "If you didn't get your ass in gear when you was leading him, he'd run right up your backbone. Dude could hum it." His skin was chocolate brown in color. He was wearing a powder blue sport coat, and his arms were folded across his chest. He owned a seafood restaurant near Six Flags Mall and he'd gotten way too fat.

"Heady ballplayer, too," Larry Morgan said. "Could think on his feet. I still remember one run he made in New Orleans. Wadn't but five yards, but Jesus. Wadn't another back on the field could have made an inch the way they were stacked up in there. Could pick his holes." Larry was in real estate sales and wore dark brown snakeskin cowboy boots with a dark brown pinstriped suit. He rose on the balls of his feet, then sank back onto his heels. He weighed about the same as when he'd played free safety.

"What movies did he like?" I said. "What kind of books did he read?"

Larry cocked his head slightly to one side. "Huh?"

"What was his favorite food?" I said.

Bobby Mitchell chewed his full ebony lower lip. "Seem like he ate a lotta T-bone. Yeah, pregame meal he used to put away two of 'em."

They'd never get it, either of them. Never in a million years. "Hey, guys," I said, "great seeing you. Let's all hope it's for a happier occasion next time." I walked away, went up on the crest of the hill, and stopped at the entrance to the parking lot for one last, faraway look at Donna.

"I'm going out of town for a while," she'd told me the day before on the phone. "I think I'll take Jacqueline to Disney World. She's never been and the trip will take her mind off of . . . oh, Rick."

"You should, Donna. Keep moving, keep doing things."

There'd been a pause during which she'd uttered a tiny sob. Then she'd softly cleared her throat and said evenly, "Rick?"

"Yes?"

"Will you be there for me?"

I'd hesitated. It hadn't seemed like the right time. "You know I will," I'd said.

I'd almost sent her money back that morning. Squaring accounts, I'd thought. As if any amount of money would even things with Jack after what Donna and I had done. But after thinking about it, I'd decided that the gesture would be far too corny. Besides, what was left of the five thousand dollars was all that stood between me and a curbside seat by the Salvation Army headquarters. I went into the asphalt parking lot of Hillcrest Memorial, and it took me a few minutes to locate the 'Vette. Guess I had other things on my mind.

The three guys who were lounging around my Corvette definitely weren't sportscar fans. They were strictly four-door Impala candidates—AM-FM radio, power and air, and you could forget all of the other extras. The two who had hair wore fifties flattops, and the bald guy's fringe was a half inch long. All were in shirtsleeves, slacks, and ties.

The bald guy was leaning his rump against the 'Vette's driver's side door. His hands were in his pockets. I said to him, "Show me a warrant or fuck off. My friend just died."

He gave me one of those wide, plastic smiles that said he was used to having people insult him. He had thin lips and a long nose underneath watery green, I'm-suspicious eyes. "I can show you the shield, Mr. Bannion, but I probably can't get a warrant before Monday. I can hold you for questioning until then if that's the way you want to do it."

He fished in his back pocket, snapped open a Naugahyde wallet, and held it in front of my face. Thompson. FBI. *Dumm de dum-dum.* He waited for me to start shivering. I didn't.

"This is Agent Whittington"—one flattop nodded—"and Detective Atchley, Dallas County. He's helping us with—with this thing we've got going." The county guy, the real cop, looked slightly embarrassed about the company he was keeping. I didn't blame him.

I gave Detective Atchley a friendly wink. "A cooperative task force, hey?" I said. "You provide the cooperation and

do all the tasks, they provide the force. What a team."
Atchley's lips twitched as though he wanted to laugh. The
federal cops didn't think I was funny.

"The Dallas police department has been kind enough to
provide us with a meeting room, Mr. Bannion," Thompson
said. "It's at the Whiterock Precinct, just a ways up the road
from here. You can ride with me and Detective Atchley if
you would. Agent Whittington can follow along in your car,
if you'd just give him the keys."

Agent Whittington's flattop was blond. He wore a yellow
tie and brown pleated slacks. A new recruit, not over a year
or two out of college. I thought he looked like Troy Donahue,
back when old Troy played on "Surfside Six." He stepped
forward and held his hand out, palm up.

"Agent Whittington doesn't look old enough to have a driver's license," I said.

Thompson took a short stride in my direction, bent his
elbows, and put his hands on his waist. "We're not here to
give you a hard time, Bannion. Now you don't give us one,
either. The keys, Bud. Now."

My upper body tensed the same way it used to during
barked signals just before the snap. I said, "I know where
Whiterock Precinct is, Bud. I'll meet you there. But nobody
rides with me and nobody lays a finger on my car. I can't
be seen riding with you guys. Hell, I've got a reputation to
maintain."

Thompson studied me, and whatever he saw made him
back off. He stepped aside. "Have it your way. Come on,
men, we'll follow him. And Bannion. Don't get lost on the
way, huh?"

The three guys became five in the meeting room at
Whiterock Precinct. One addition was Norman Aycock, glaring at me with a nearly maniacal gleam in his eye. He made
me feel like Bob Cratchitt must have felt just before he asked
old Scrooge for a raise. The other newcomer was a milder-
mannered guy, late thirties, with thinning brown hair and a
clipped mustache. He had a round, pleasant face and he'd
spent quite a bit of time out in the sun. There was a yellow
legal pad before him on the table, and he was taking notes

with a gold ballpoint. He was wearing a dark green Mac-Gregor golf shirt with "LAKEWOOD CC" stitched in gold thread on the sleeve. Middle-class club, probably just within the price range of a county prosecutor. If the guy cut a few corners.

We were seated at a small, round conference table. There was one tall window in the room; outside, carpets of Bermuda stretched among sycamores, weeping willows, and elms. One adjacent white stucco wall of the building was visible, and some stone steps leading down from the building to a sidewalk. Whiterock Lake wasn't in sight from where we were; it was behind us, across from the front of the station.

"You can save us all a lot of trouble, Bannion," Aycock said.

"Why would I want to do that?" I said. Agent Thompson was on my left, Detective Atchley on my right. Agent Whittington, the Troy Donahue type, was directly across from me between Aycock and the guy whose name I didn't know.

Aycock pretended he hadn't heard me and continued to bore holes into my chest with his gaze. He said, "I know you get a kick out of being a thorn in our side. Or thinking you are. But you're not even worrisome enough to be classified a thorn. You're more like a gnat or mosquito. You're not ever—"

"Let's can it, Norman." The mild-mannered guy in the golf shirt lifted a hand. "Look, this is Saturday and we've all got better things to do. So please carry on your personal campaign against Mr. Bannion on somebody else's time." Then to me he said, "These men are rude, Mr. Bannion, they haven't introduced us. I'm Tom Pierson, D.A.'s office, and I don't have any bones to pick with you. Not personally, anyway." He glanced at Aycock, then back at me.

Now Aycock turned one of his wild-eyed stares on Pierson, and I wondered if the old federal prosecutor was going to have a stroke. Aycock shut his eyes tightly and shook his head. He took a deep breath and let it out slowly before saying, "The case against Jack Brendy is history, but this investigation is still quite active. Brendy was involved with quite an extensive ring of smugglers, Bannion. Of course"—he smirked—"I'm not telling you anything you don't already know, am I? We intend to snare the others with or without your help. But if you'll help us you can make it easier on us *and* you."

I scratched my cheek, doing a slow burn and trying to control myself. I hadn't forgotten what Aycock had the power to do. I never would. "That's not right, Mr. Aycock," I said. "You know it isn't. Jack might have been mixed up in a dope deal or two, but a *ring*? No way. That Skeezix, the man Jack was dealing with, he was your setup all along."

"I'm not going to discuss our case against Brendy," Aycock said. "It's closed. But there is a ring and your friend Jack Brendy was up to his ears in it. I want you to help us bag the others."

I was still hot under the collar, but now was getting puzzled as well. What others? And why in everloving hell did Aycock think for a minute that I was going to help him, ring or no ring? Thompson was leaning forward, one corner of his mouth upturned. Atchley, the county cop, was keeping a poker face. I decided to let Aycock have it regardless of what power the old goat had.

"Well now, Mr. Aycock," I said, "I can't see as how I blame you for not wanting to talk about your case against Jack. Especially since it was a phony setup from the word go. I'll tell you something. Skeezix—Mr. Herman Moore, you know—he's not going to be much good to you as a snitch any longer. Everybody in town's got his number, and five'll get you ten he winds up crippled or dead. Of course, you don't give a shit what happens to Skeezix, do you? Just another stoolie, hell, they're a dime a dozen. Now I don't know anything about any dope ring. But if I did—well, you're talking like a truck ran over you, thinking I'm going to help you any."

Aycock's brows knitted. "Bannion, I guarantee you I won't like it any better than you do, working with a man of your stripe."

"Stripe? Well, what stripe are you, you—"

"Shut up and hear me out," Aycock said. "The group we're talking about—and we've got a couple of names—they're simply too sophisticated for our usual tactics. They have their own planes and their own money, so we can't trap them that way. Phone taps are a joke—hell, for all I know they might be recording *me*. So we need somebody they're going to trust, somebody that's right down there on their own level. Which brings us to you."

Now I'd really heard enough. *Their level*, huh? I stood. "You gentlemen can collectively go and fuck yourselves," I said, and turned to leave.

Pierson, the county prosecutor, said, "I don't think you're going to like the alternative, Mr. Bannion." His voice was calm and steady. Where Aycock came across like a ranting loony, this guy was cold steel. I sat back down. I didn't say anything.

Pierson tugged at his shirtsleeves, then folded his hands on the table. His right hand was a few shades browner than his left: lots of golf. "The feds are investigating drugs, Mr. Bannion. I don't stick my nose in their business. But a man's been gunned down on the streets of downtown Dallas, and that is my business. Plus the dead man's lawyer is threatening to sue us for not protecting his client, even though the client had been a federal prisoner. He says the shooting happened on county property. Now, I don't know how well you know Fred Cassel, but I suspect he's blowing a lot of smoke. But he talks a lot to the papers, you know what I mean?"

I did know. I nodded. He went on. "So we've got to come up with the perpetrator. My first thought is somebody involved in drugs, somebody that was afraid of the cats Brendy could let out of the bag. It's a strong possibility."

"Sounds reasonable," I said. "So why don't you blow and go? Hell, you've got ten million cops running around."

"I said a *possibility*, Mr. Bannion. But there's another option, maybe even better than a druggie." He watched his folded hands for a moment, then looked directly at me. "You and Mrs. Brendy are quite a bit closer than friends, aren't you?"

There it was. My stomach dropped a foot and my insides were suddenly cold. "I've known Jack and Donna for a lot of years," I said. My voice cracked slightly. I couldn't help it.

Pierson didn't change expressions, leaned over and flipped through his legal pad. Inserted between two pages was a dot-matrix computer printout with lines in alternating shades of green. The paper rustled between Pierson's fingers. He read aloud from the printout.

" 'Donna Sue Morley, born nine-two-fifty-six. Birthplace, Corpus Christi, Texas.' That's your hometown, too, isn't it? In fact, you and Mrs. Brendy attended the same high school."

I shrugged. "Small world. Corpus Christi Ray's one of the biggest schools in the state, or it was back then. Look, Donna's a lot younger than I am. We never went to school at the same time."

Pierson slid the printout back inside the legal pad. "Eight years younger. But she had older brothers. One in fact who was in your graduating class."

They'd really been checking up. The first time I'd gotten laid, Buddy Morley and I had driven to Matamoros and spent the night in a joint called the Rhumba Casino. Our folks had thought we were in San Antonio playing a baseball tourney. Funny, I hadn't thought to ask Donna about Buddy and what he was doing now, we'd had too many other things going on. I said to Pierson, "She might've. Yeah, seems like I remember some Morleys." Across the table, Aycock was showing a crooked grin.

"Let's don't waste time," Pierson said. "Like I said, it's Saturday. You were playing pro football when Donna got out of high school and moved to Dallas. You got her a job at Wilson Drilling; Wilson was a buddy of the team owners. You and Donna got to be an item during the same time you were sharing an apartment with Jack Brendy. Your apartment was at the Corners, on Southwestern Boulevard. How'm I doing?"

They had too much of it. I let a long rush of air escape from my lungs. "Actually, it's on Shady Brook Lane, a half block from Southwestern. The leasing office is on Southwestern, I guess. You're doing okay."

Pierson laughed without humor. "Nothing to be ashamed of, Bannion. You make guys like me jealous. Hell, I've been married all my life, never got much of a chance to swing."

"So okay," I said. "So I had a thing with Donna. Then we didn't have one. Then she married Jack. So what?"

Light reflected from Pierson's gold ballpoint pen as he played with it, exposing the point, retracting it. "Mr. Bannion doesn't want to own up, fellas. Go ahead, Toby, show him."

Detective Atchley looked more like a Toby than the others, so I looked at him expectantly. But it was Thompson, my FBI buddy, who reached under the table and produced a Ziplock plastic bag. He took out some color photos, thumbed through them, tossed two pictures in front of me. I didn't want to look, but picked them up anyway.

The first picture didn't really surprise me. It was a shot of me by Jack's swimming pool, talking to Donna, taken from a slightly overhead angle, probably from atop the wall that surrounded the pool area. Jack had been a government target, and I guess it would have been surprising if the feds hadn't had a picture taker lurking in the bushes. My gaze lingered for a second on the image of Donna. She could have made a living as a swimsuit model. I shrugged, flipped the photo back to Thompson, and picked up the next one. I froze.

Considering the time of night and the circumstances, this guy had been a hell of a photographer. In the background behind Donna and me was the east side of Turtle Creek North, some tall elms, ivy crawling up a brick wall. We were standing beside her Mark VI with the door open. Her face was upturned to mine. The shadows on my face made my silly grin look more like a snarl; just seconds after this picture had been taken she'd kissed me. Then she'd driven away. I laid the picture on the table and gently closed my eyes.

Thompson tapped a finger on the stack of remaining photos. "There's more. I'd have to get the censorhsip committee to rate them before I could show them to you." He showed me the standard, I-work-for-the-government smirk.

I said evenly to Thompson, "Fuck you."

"That's probably an appropriate comment," Pierson said, "but we're doing our best to keep personalities out of this. We're simply working hand in hand, our county people and the feds. The federal matter is the drug business, and we're interested in the shooting. One case goes along with the other. Probably when the feds get their hands on the drug folks we'll have the shooter as well. But not for certain." He blinked. "I think you're getting my drift."

"Yeah, I'm getting the drift," I said. "Either I can help the feds or you're going to railroad me for Jack's killing. Since you know goddamn well that I didn't have anything to do with it, that's exactly what you're saying."

Pierson took out a cigarette, a Vantage, and fumbled in his pockets. The young FBI agent, Whittington, produced a butane mini-flamethrower and lit Pierson's smoke, then got an ashtray from a bookcase, and set it on the table. Good job for the kid. Pierson said, "Do we? Do we know it goddamn well? You're sleeping with guy's wife, he gets popped. You would have known it would look like a drug killing, plus you're connected. You know people that would do the job, and some of them might even owe you favors. Oh, yeah, and Bannion. Not just you alone. It takes two to tango."

I didn't get it for a couple of seconds, then I did. I sat up straighter. "Yeah, you bastards would charge Donna, wouldn't you?"

On my left, Thompson said, "Well, he damn sure couldn't charge Liz Taylor."

Aycock cackled like Walter Brennan. "You should watch out who you're sticking the pork to," he said.

"I think I'll sleep in the sewer tonight," I said. "The smell is better."

"Cute, Bannion," Aycock said. "But cute won't get it. Not this time."

I got up, went to the door, then faced the room. "I'm not saying one way or the other. Give me some time."

"Sure," Pierson said. "I couldn't get a grand jury together before Tuesday anyhow. Call us before then, Mr. Bannion. If you would."

Donna's face softened as she said to me, "I'll be so worried." She was holding Jacqueline's hand. The child was wearing a spotless white lace dress, her face was scrubbed, and she had on black patent leather shoes with tiny buckles across the insteps. Behind mother and daughter, a long line of men in suits and women in business dresses paraded by a uniformed Delta flight attendant, showing her their boarding passes. Visible through the big plate glass window, a 747's hull blocked the view of the runways beyond.

I said, "I can't tell you not to worry. I'm not even sure this is the right thing to do. I just have this gut feeling that you should be a long way from here. The Ramada Inn, just outside the gate to Disney World. Prepare yourself, Florida's one hot sucker this time of year."

Jacqueline did a little hop-skip and said, "I'm going to see Mickey Mouse."

I knelt before her. "Sure you are. And Donald and Goofy and whatever other guys are around." I kissed the tip of her nose.

"You still won't tell me what's wrong?" Donna said.

I stood. "Not now, babe. You just make sure that nobody, and I mean nobody, knows exactly where you are except me."

I was conscious of Jacqueline's gaze on me as I gave Donna a brotherly kiss on the cheek and turned to walk away. Over my shoulder I said, "Bring me one of those golf shirts with Mickey on the pocket. Extra large."

On my way home I decided to begin with Muhammed Double-X. It seemed as good a place to start as any.

EIGHT

If it's rats you want, you go to the sewer. Muhammed Double-X's personal sewer began somewhere around the intersection of Martin Luther King Boulevard and South Central Expressway. Its network of streets and alleyways sprawled from there to the southeast; its southeast boundary was near the intersection of Oakland Avenue and Hatcher Street. On a lucky night a guy could walk all the way from South Central and Martin Luther King to Oakland and Hatcher with his wallet intact, and without someone sticking a knife between his ribs. The odds were against it, though.

It was after dark, about nine-thirty, when I steered the 'Vette through South Central's exit ramp, made a left on Martin Luther King, and tooled on over to Oakland. I passed a theater that was showing *Hot Thrusts*. An old black man with a snow-white fringe of hair glanced furtively around as he stepped up to the ticket booth. Martin Luther King's a wide boulevard, and that's not its original name. Decades ago it was Forest Avenue, and the stately, pillared houses on both sides had been the homes of Dallas's upper crust: the Neimans, the Marcuses, the Stanley B. Woodalls. Those people don't live there anymore.

I waited at the light at the Oakland intersection, the 'Vette's padded steering wheel vibrating under my fingertips and Gladys Knight on the stereo moaning heavily through "Midnight Train to Georgia." At a sudden rapping on the passenger-side window, I tensed, my hand moving automatically toward the Smith & Wesson on the floorboard. A young black girl, not over twenty-five, milk chocolate skin, wearing a skin-tight mini and knee-length boots, peered at me from outside the window. She wore a long blond wig and heavy lip rouge. She winked at me and wrinkled her nose, then pointed a glistening silver fingernail at the door lock. Open up, sugar. I shook my head. She stuck out her tongue, then retreated to the curb with her bottom jiggling. A black dude in a T-shirt and jeans said something to her. She pointed at the 'Vette with one hand and gave me the thumbs-down sign with the other.

I made a right on Oakland and steered carefully through bumper-to-bumper, stop-and-go traffic, fifteen blocks south to the Green Parrot Lounge. The locals were back to back and belly to belly on the street corners and in between. I made the block and drove past the Parrot a couple of times before I located a parking slot nose-on to the front door.

I hadn't been to the Parrot in fifteen years or more, and I couldn't see that its exterior had changed any. Same neon green and yellow parrot's outline over the door, more neon, some of it not working, forming script letters that read, "G een Par o." In the old days we had come to the Parrot to hear good rhythm and blues and listen to Louis Armstrong clones blow red-hot jazz.That was in a different world, when gay meant happy and a joint was the place where you were hanging around. I cut the engine, got out, and took a couple of steps down the sidewalk. There was a kid of about eighteen lounging against the wall with a toothpick dangling from one corner of his mouth. He wore dirty jeans and a blue stocking cap, and his gaze darted from me to the 'Vette's Fiberglas nose. I doubled back and locked the car, then went inside the Parrot.

Inside, rows of long tables surrounded a scarred hardwood dance floor that was maybe ten by twenty. Marvin Gaye was blasting "I Heard It Through the Grapevine" on the juke— an ancient Wurlitzer with a clear plastic cover through which you could watch the forty-fives spin. Cigarette smoke mixed with the odor of grease-cooked meat. The place was about half full; it was early yet. There was one couple on the dance floor, a young guy in a sleeveless leather vest with a red bandanna tied around his head and a gold ring through one pierced ear, and a light-skinned, mulatto chick in tight designer jeans and a white body shirt. They were getting after it. I wound my way between the tables, past the edge of the dance floor, and leaned my elbows on the bar.

A pudgy, ebony-skinned guy yelled over the music, "Whatcha want?" He was carrying an empty glass mug, wiping it off with a dirty towel. He glanced carefully behind me, then looked relieved. One honky generally meant a man after pussy; two honkies usually meant the law.

I said, nearly straining my vocal cords, "Bud. In a bottle if you got it. If it's in a can, gimme a glass. A clean one." I glanced at the grimy towel. Now he was wiping down the bar with it. "If you got a clean one," I said. "Jesus Christ, how do you hear in this joint?"

"You don't. You want to hear, you go to a movie. Or find a motel room. Shit, who wants to hear?" He slid open a rolltop cooler and fished out a longneck. Its brown glass was frosting over. As he popped it open, he said, "You in luck, we got bottles. If it was me I'd drink straight from the can 'fore I'd use one of them glasses. Filthy mothafuckahs. Listen, you looking for action, you got to change you style."

I took a swig of the beer. Pretty good, though not as cold as it looked. The Marvin Gaye song ended and the arm on the Wurlitzer searched mechanically for another platter. I took advantage of the break in the noise to say in a normal tone, "What's wrong with my style?"

"Man, you kidding? You look too hip. You got nice knit shirt and tailored jeans, ain't no fat around you middle. Ho, she gonna think you too nice-lookin' to pay for no pussy. She think you the Man. Pimp, too, he think the same." He had to raise his voice as Tina Turner howled suddenly over the juke.

"Yeah? Well, maybe I want a colored broad and I don't know any to ask for a date, you know, take her to dinner."

"Change you luck? Shit, ho don't fall for that, either. She *convinced* you the Man, you start that shit."

I bent closer to him and motioned. He leaned and turned an ear toward me. I said, "Well, really I—hey, what's your name?"

"Elmo."

"No kidding. Hey, I had a cousin named Elmo. Grew up with him."

"Yeah?" He cocked his head. Artificial light reflected from his shiny cheeks. "Well, I don't got no cousins name Honky. The fuck you lookin' for?"

I decided that Elmo wasn't going to be my pal. I fished in my pocket and dug out two ten-dollar bills, then held them just above bartop level between my index and middle fingers. I said, "Three, four nights ago a friend of mine called a guy in here. I think the guy's a regular, I'm not sure. I need to talk to the guy."

Elmo took a long, slow look at the money, then did a Stepin Fetchit eye roll. He reached underneath the bar, found a toothpick, and chewed on it. Then he motioned to me. I bent closer and smelled the garlic on his breath as he said, "You one I can't figure. You ain't no law or you be flashin' hunnerds, talkin' about buyin' a load of twenty-five-dollar papers, shit like that. You ain't lookin' fo' no ho's. You ain't no homosectual, but now you lookin' for a guy. What guy?"

"Muhammed. Muhammed Double-X." I tried to put on a cagey, in-the-know expression. The couple on the dance floor must have been pretty close behind me; the floor vibrated with the slap of shoe leather. Elmo's glance flicked over my shoulder, then back to me.

"You ain't no homosectual and you ain't no law," he said. "You jus' crazy. Find you a ho, man. Worse she gonna do is roll yo ass."

"Muhammed," I said.

Elmo shrugged and plucked the two tens from between my fingers. "I goin' to collect while you still kickin'. Don't no Muhammed hang in here. I can call somebody, they come down here an' take you to Muhammed. I tell you, though.

Muhammed don't like no honky bullshit. You better have you some business, man."

"I got business," I said.

"You sit in that booth at the front." Elmo pointed. "Up there, right where somebody see you when they walk in. Try to look at home, baby. It won't be long."

There was a pay phone at the end of the bar. Elmo opened the cash drawer and found a quarter, then motioned to me again. As he waddled toward the phone, I wound my way through the throbbing sea of noise and sat in the front booth.

Things were really picking up inside the Parrot. They were drifting in in twos and threes, some of them already high and most of them getting that way if they weren't already. One girl, a tall, lanky chick in a tight pink dress, glanced in my direction and curled her lip. A second couple, this one a jiggling fat woman and a tall, skinny mustachioed dude, joined the first couple on the dance floor and began to shuck and jive. Elmo came over and whispered, "Man on his way, be here in a minute." I nodded, handed him my half-empty beer, and ordered a Coke. Elmo brought it. I sipped it through a straw and watched three guys at a corner table watch me. Just as their glances changed from mildly curious to openly hostile, Snakey came into the Green Parrot and sat down across from me.

All of a sudden. It was as though he'd materialized. He said, "You maybe not doing the smartest thing, cowboy." He adjusted the patch over his eye. Tonight he wore a white shirt with bright red flowers printed on it. The shirt was satin, with tight cuffs and puffed sleeves.

"Maybe," I said, sipping. "Hey, by the way, nice shirt, man . . . Hey, you want a drink?"

Snakey said that he didn't. Elmo had waddled around the bar and come halfway to the booth. I waved him away.

"So maybe I'm not too smart," I said. "What's a better idea? Stay on my own side of town, wake up some night with you and Honeybear playing tag in my bedroom? With me as 'it'?"

He folded his hands on the table. Still the same look: no anger, no curiosity, just a mild amusement. I doubted you could shake this guy up if you punched him in the stomach. "Don't guess it make any difference at that," he said. "You might have a better chance on yo turf. But yo turf, our turf, you dead anyhow. I say this, you got better chance now than when you left us floatin'. We know some stuff now we didn' know." He looked toward the dance floor. The fat woman was really into it, belly jiggling. Snakey said, "I tell you, offside man, you don't make no sense. You workin' fo Brendy, you should have give us the fat man. Poof, Skeezix gone, no mo fedral witness for Brendy to fuck with. Plus you got no problem with us. Shit, you don't make sense. Now Brendy, poof, he gone. Now you don't work fo nobody an' you got us thinkin' 'bout killin' you."

I couldn't argue with his logic. Principles? I was pretty sure that Snakey wouldn't know what they were. I might have been better off if I didn't have any principles. But I just didn't like getting people killed, even slime like Skeezix. It went against my grain. I said, "Am I going to see Muhammed, or are you and I going to draw on each other right here?"

"Oh, you goin' to see him," Snakey said. " 'Co'se, I ain't sayin' what's goin' to happen when you do. Muhammed might talk. He might jus' off you, too. I hope he don't. If he off you, I got to find a place to dump you."

I finished my Coke, took a final mouthful of crunchy ice, and set the glass on the table. "Well, lead the way. We going to ride or walk?"

Snakey didn't answer me. He got up and went to the door, jerked his head in a follow-me gesture, and left as quickly as he'd come in. I followed him as "Love Potion Number Nine" throbbed from the jukebox; the door closed behind me and muffled the sound of the music. Snakey was a half block ahead of me, strolling casually among the dudes and chicks of Oakland Avenue after sundown. I thought fleetingly about going over to the 'Vette and getting the Smith & Wesson, then forgot the idea. Snakey would never let me within a country mile of Muhammed if I was carrying a piece, and letting him find one on me was just asking for trouble.

A white Eldorado waited at the end of the block, and Snakey glanced at me over his shoulder just before he climbed into the driver's seat. I quickened my pace, drew alongside, and climbed in. He was waiting for me with a big red scarf in his hands. "Look out the window," he said. "I going to blindfold you. Iran hostage kind of shit."

I watched the neon sign over the Green Parrot until the scarf blotted out all sight. He tied the knot firmly at the base of my skull; the fabric dug sharply into the bridge of my nose. I moved my eyes upward, then down; I couldn't see anything except for faint brightness at the top of the blindfold. "I'm not tying yo hands, Bannion," Snakey said. "But if you touch the rag I'm going to shoot you." He sounded as though it didn't matter to him whether I tried anything or not. The Eldo lurched as he dropped the shift lever into drive.

The ride was about ten minutes, though I didn't have any idea how far we traveled. I was pretty sure that Snakey doubled back at least once in order to throw me off; for all I knew, Muhammed's place was within a hundred yards of the Green Parrot's front door. Not that it mattered; Muhammed Double-X's address was something I was better off not knowing.

My weight surged forward and then back against the seat as Snakey applied the brakes. He shut off the engine. His breathing was calm beside me. His door opened, then closed with a solid *thunk*. In less than a minute my own door swung outward; a strong hand on my elbow helped me climb out of the Eldo and stand up.

We moved a short distance on concrete, then took twenty counted steps on sparse grass over grainy dirt. My foot collided with a stone step; I stumbled and nearly fell. Snakey aided me up four stairs, one at a time, then my feet thudded on wooden planks. Smoke from someone's cheap cigar stung my nostrils; someone nearby on my left said, "Ain' nobody up there with him. You go on up, bro." A screen door creaked in front of me, and a heavier wooden door swung away. Snakey guided me over a threshold; the wooden door thudded behind me. Snakey fumbled at the nape of my neck, undid the knot, and my blindfold fell away.

I said, "Some digs."

"What you 'spect?" Snakey said. "A dirt floor and a pile o' chitlins? You ain't calling on no people from 'Roots.' "

We were in the entrance hallway of an old home that had been restored. There was a thick beige carpet on the floor. Yawning double doors on my right opened into a mammoth living room with a fireplace that would accommodate a peprally bonfire. In the living room was a long, overstuffed divan on which a white girl sat. She was a compact brunette wearing a tennis dress, watching television with one leg drawn up underneath her and one foot swinging to and fro. The TV set was a console with a forty-inch screen; a mellow piano played the theme from "Hill Street Blues" as squad cars peeled out of the station parking garage and splashed through mud puddles. The girl on the divan was chewing gum, her jaw working slowly.

Directly in front of me in the entry hall was the foot of a carpeted staircase with a polished mahogany bannister. Snakey told me to go upstairs, which I did with him following. On the way up, I passed an oil painting of Martin Luther King, Jr., his eyes wide, his clenched fist raised in a salute. Another hallway ran perpendicular to the head of the staircase; the wallpaper was pink with a rosebush pattern. Snakey motioned toward a closed door at the end of the hall. "Wait in there," he said. "If Muhammed don't off you, I see you later." He went downstairs and left me alone. I swallowed a lump in my throat and went through the door.

I entered a converted bedroom with a portable bar against one wall and a green felt poker table directly in the center of the floor. Honeybear was leaning on the bar. He was wearing a black mesh muscle shirt, and he looked like an ad for Joe Weidner's Gym. One hand was in his pocket and his ankles were crossed.

I said, "Hi."

Honeybear grinned, straightened, and punched me in the stomach.

I'd taken a lick or two in my time—one in particular that crossed my mind was a submarining, assassin blow from a Pittsburgh linebacker named Jack Lambert as I'd pulled to lead the blocking on a wide sweep—but nothing like this. Or maybe time had dulled my memory.

Honeybear didn't seem to put much effort into it, either. One second he was standing there, relaxed and grinning; in the next instant he hammered his clenched fist into my midsection. The punch couldn't have traveled over eight inches, but it felt as though it had come from the end zone. All of the air whooshed out of my lungs; stunning pain shot upward into my shoulders and down into my ankles. I sat down hard, and more pain jolted through me as my rump collided with cushioned hardwood. I doubled over and clutched my belly. Hell, I wasn't just hoping that Honeybear wouldn't hit me again. I was praying that he wouldn't.

Through a red-tinted haze I watched him rub his knuckles. "Man," Honeybear said, "you need to do some working out. Work on yo ab muscles. Shit, you like a bowl o' jelly." He reached down, bunched the front of my shirt in his fist, and hoisted me to my feet. One-handed, as though he was lifting a bag of feathers. He held me that way and patted me down with his free hand. Then he let go and took a step backward. I resisted the urge to sink back to the floor. He said, "Shit, you ain't got no piece. I was gonna break yo arm if you'd had one."

I could barely drag enough air into my lungs to speak. "Sorry to mess your plans up," I said.

Honeybear's dull eyes narrowed. "You ain't being funny, are you?"

"No. I'm being sick," I said. And I was. With most guys I'd have been looking for a chance to bore in and whale the daylights out of them. Not with this guy. I'd had more than enough of Honeybear. Hell, I was wondering what it would take to hire him away from Muhammed. If you can't beat 'em, join 'em.

"Well, you clean," he said. "You ain't funny, but you clean. Boss man, he in there." He jerked his thumb toward another closed door, this one at the rear of the room behind the poker table.

I wasn't too crazy about seeing Muhammed at this point, but I'd gone this far. I said to Honeybear, "I'm with you."

He led the way around the table, opened the door, and stood aside. I went past Honeybear with my knees clanking like the Tin Woodman's on his way to see the Great Oz. I wondered briefly if I should ask Muhammed for a heart. Maybe Muhammed would think I was funny.

Muhammed's office surprised me. No skull and crossbones, no shrunken heads. Just a black-and-white aerial photo of downtown Dallas on one wall, a painting of two white-maned black horses charging across a meadow on the other. Muhammed's desk wasn't much bigger than the Green Parrot's dance floor, but the wood was in a whole lot better condition. You could have used the surface of the desk as a mirror. Muhammed was reared back in a stuffed leather swivel chair with his feet resting on one corner of the desk, his ankles crossed. His black shoes were spit-shined. He wore a charcoal suit, white shirt, blue tie, and his trademark mirrored shades. There was a two-shot derringer lying on the desk just inches from his elbow. He was smoking a cigarette through a long plastic holder that was encircled by two gold rings. He set the cigarette in a round glass ashtray and touched his fingertips together.

"How you like my honky downstairs maid, mothafuckah?" Muhammed said.

"Is that what she is?" I said. "I thought she was Martina Navritalova."

"Martina Navritalova? Shit, I don't need no ballet dancers." Muhammed said. He motioned to Honeybear. Behind me, the door closed with a soft thud. Muhammed scratched his cheek with the nail of his little finger. "So, Bannion. You got fifteen seconds to tell me a good reason not to kill you. You got me curious is the only reason you got the fifteen seconds. You make me mad the other night. But now you down here in my town hunting for me. So what you want, boy?" He picked up the derringer, pointed it at me, and sighted down the barrel. Wearing the mirrored shades, he looked like Ray Charles.

I was rubbing my midsection. I was going to have a nice blue and green and purple bruise there in the morning, if I lived that long. The sight of Muhammed squinting at me down the barrel of the Derringer raised goosebumps along my spine the size of robins' eggs. "Hey," I said. "Let me sit down and catch my breath for a second."

"Sho," Muhammed said. "If it take you five seconds to

catch yo breath, that mean you got ten seconds left. My baby brother, he sweating in a cell down at Bastrop right now 'cause of that fat stoolie you palling around with. So like I say, boy, what you want?" He aired back the hammer. He wasn't kidding.

I sat in an overstuffed chair across from him. "I have to find some guys," I said. "The law's putting heat on me."

"So that ain't nothing. The law's been putting heat on me fo years. What guys an' what you want 'em for?"

"Jack Brendy. The guys that offed him."

"Bannion, you really gone crazy, man. What I give a fuck about who offed Jack Brendy?"

I draped a leg over the arm of my chair, being careful not to put too much strain on my stomach muscles. They were really beginning to throb. "Muhammed, believe me, if I don't come up with the guys that offed Brendy in the next few days, you're going to see heat like you've never seen. Federal heat. State heat. You got a man shot down on the streets right in front of TV. The law is serious about it. If somebody doesn't go down on the Brendy hit, and fast, heads are going to roll. My head. Your head."

He laid the derringer down and looked thoughtful. He picked up the holder, puffed on the cigarette, watched the smoke drift upward toward the ceiling. Finally he said, "Yeah, stupid mothafuckahs. You don't make no hit in broad daylight. Dumb. Dumb."

"Not only dumb for them, dumb for everybody else." I decided to try flattery. "So that's why I'm coming to you, you're number one. If anybody knows who did Brendy, you will. Maybe not who had it done, but at least who pulled the trigger. I was right there, saw the hit with my own eyes. Hell, the guy with the Uzi had on some kind of flour sack mask. I wasn't looking at the other guys in the car, so I don't know if they were white dudes or black dudes."

Muhammed began to wave the cigarette around, making trailing circles of smoke in the air. He seemed to have forgotten the derringer. I hoped it stayed that way. "That Mercedes them dudes had," he said. "They stole it off a cat I know, out on Illinois Avenue. I'll tell you one thing, it wasn't no black dudes did it. Black dudes, they dumb as shit about offing anybody, but they got more sense than to do it in broad daylight. I'd never hire no black dudes for no hit, they too much jive-asses. They'd have been black dudes somebody would have hollered, 'Death to white mothafuckahs,' given some black power salute, some shit like that. Them dudes that done it, they probly . . . lemme see." He raised his voice. "Bear. Yo, Honeybear. In heah, boy."

The door behind me opened. There was the sound of heavy breathing and wind blew against the back of my neck. Honeybear displaced a lot of air. He said, "Yeah, boss."

"Bear, what that cat's name been hanging on the north side? Been putting the word out he available. Crazy white mothafuckah, just up from Texas Penitentiary."

"Aw, you mean that Catfish dude," Honeybear said.

"Yeah. That the suckah. He still been hanging up around Harry Hines Boulevard?"

I sat up straighter. "Up where all the titty joints are?"

"Naw," Muhammed said. "Further north than that. This dude's a cowboy, hangs out where they play Willie Nelson shit. Longhorn Ballroom shitkicker. He's probably you boy, Bannion. Ain't too many guys around talking about doing hits. Catfish been soliciting."

"Seems to fit," I said. "Evidently he found somebody that was buying what he was selling. You got more of a name than just Catfish?"

"Shit, I don't know nobody's name," Muhammed said. "I don't even know Honeybear's name." I thought fleetingly about Muhammed's name, Porkpie, as he went on. "I think I give you a break, Bannion. I ain't going to kill you, how about that?"

"Sounds good to me," I said.

"Catfish probly going to kill you if you find him, but if he don't, then it's good for me if he's out of the way. If he kills you, I don't have to fuck with you. If you kill him, I don't got no heat from no law over Jack Brendy being dead. That I like."

"You ought to like it," I said. "Either way you win. I need something more definite to find this guy. I can't just walk up and down Harry Hines Boulevard yelling, 'Anybody seen this Catfish?' "

Honeybear loomed over Muhammed's desk; even Muhammed looked just the slightest bit jumpy when Honeybear came close. Honeybear said, "You could go talk to Catfish lady."

"Who's that?" I said.

Muhammed pushed his shades up on his nose with his middle finger. "Dude like Catfish don't keep no lady for long. The one he's seeing now name Candy. She waits tables at Bullrider Danceland—it's a hillbilly joint a mile off Harry Hines, out on Northeast Highway."

"I know the place," I said. "I've been by it."

"Well, that where you find Candy, till two. Catfish might even be hanging around there waiting for her. You kill two birds with one stone, if one of the birds don't kill you first. I wouldn't be asking this Catfish about no hits he did unless you got a gun on him. He's one crazy white mothafuckah."

"Well, I'd better get going," I said. "Can't tell you how much I appreciate the help."

"Hey, no problem," Muhammed said. "Just go downstairs and get Snakey, he take you back."

I got up and walked toward the door. As I reached for the knob, Muhammed said, "Ho, Bannion."

I turned.

"You still owe me that Skeezix," Muhammed said. "I ain't forgetting that. No matter what happens with Catfish, you and me going to talk about you giving up that fat mothafuckah."

The honky downstairs maid rode along with Snakey to take me back to the Green Parrot. She sat between us in the front seat as I leaned on the armrest and forced myself to keep my hands away from my blindfold. The girl changed the station on the radio five or six times before settling on "Material Girl" by Madonna. She leaned back and smacked her gum in rhythm to the music. She smelled like Juicy Fruit.

Finally, Snakey pulled the car over, stopped, and said, "Here, man, you can take yo blindfold off yoself."

I did, fumbling with the knot for a few seconds before finally getting the hang of it. When the blindfold came off,

I blinked my eyes a couple of times. We were idling at the curb across the street from the Green Parrot. The night had come alive and black dudes and hip-swinging, finger-popping dark-skinned women were now filing into the nightclub in a steady stream. I said to Snakey, "Thanks for not killing me."

I waited for him to deliver the punch line. He simply raised and dropped his shoulders, tugged on his eyepatch, and said in a bored tone, "Yo welcome, man." The guy *had* to have a sense of humor of some kind; maybe it was just that I was a flop as a straight man. I got out of the Eldo and they drove away. As they rounded the corner the girl slid over close to Snakey and draped her arm around his shoulders. I went across the street to get my car.

Someone had plastered the upper right portion of the 'Vette's windshield with an egg. Pieces of shell had stuck to the glass and gooey yolk had dripped and oozed down into the windshield wiper compartment. I gingerly touched the sticky stuff. Some of it was already dry. I started to get mad, then cooled off; I supposed I was lucky that this was all that had been done. The kid I'd seen earlier was still lounging against the wall in front of the Parrot as I drove away. His hands were in his pockets and he was chewing on a toothpick.

I stopped for gas in a Gulf self-service on the corner of Martin Luther King and South Central, and used the water hose along with an ice scraper to clean the egg off of the car as best I could. Some of the spots had hardened to the point that I had to leave them alone for now. The attendant, a round black guy with a bulbous nose, gave me a curious sideways glance as I paid for the gas. I got four quarters from him in change for a dollar and went to the pay phone at one corner of the gas island. I'd spent three of the quarters before I located Breaux at Humperdinck, Hornblower, and Witts, a bar on Greenville Avenue.

Bodie said over the phone, "I don't want to go to no hillbilly joint. I don't know about you, Bannion. I should have steered clear of you the first time I met you in the hole at El Reno."

I told him what Muhammed and Honeybear had told me about the guy called Catfish. He didn't say anything for a moment, and I listened to the rumble and click coming from the pool tables in the background. Finally Breaux said, "I ain't sure if I know any Catfish. I might."

"Even if you don't, I need your help," I said. "Tell you the truth, I got all I wanted of playing lone wolf out at Muhammed's place."

"You must have done okay if you're still alive," he said.

"How 'bout it, Bodie? Meet me at Bullrider Danceland."

"Jesus Christ, what a name for a joint," he said. "Okay, I'll be there, but it's gonna be a while. You behave yourself, Bannion. Shitkicker cowboys ain't any more in love with guys that come nosing around than Muhammed Double-X is."

NINE

Bullrider Danceland was country long before country was cool, and still was country ten years after country wasn't cool anymore. During the hillbilly craze of the seventies, urban cowboys looking for the real thing had come to the Bullrider, and often had been carried out with their brand-new, quilted-on-the-shoulder western shirts ripped to shreds. Willie Nelson had played the Bullrider in the years before he himself was "in," and during Nelson concerts the Bullrider had had the good sense to replace the longneck bottles with paper cups, and to hide the glass ashtrays and put molded tinfoil on the table.

The place is a corrugated steel building the size and shape of a double airplane hangar, a long stone's throw from Harry Hines Boulevard on a two-lane stretch of Northwest Highway that slices through Trinity River bottom land. Marshy swamp surrounds the Bullrider and its gravel parking lot; a row of gnarled and twisted horror-movie trees hides the nightclub from view of highway passerbys. If you weren't looking for the Bullrider, you'd never know it was there, and the people who frequent the joint like it that way.

I steered the 'Vette off the highway across an elevated gravel road built six feet above the Trinity's flood level. Tiny pieces of rock banged and pinged against the 'Vette's underbody; the probing headlight beams showed foot-high weeds on both sides of the road. A skunk moseyed across the road directly in my path. As I threw on the brakes, old Skunky purposefully turned his rump to me, raised his tail, and peered at me over his shoulder. I cringed and waited. Apparently deciding I wasn't worth the effort, the skunk lowered his tail and waddled off into the underbrush. I continued on into the Bullrider's parking lot, stopped between a GMC three-quarter-ton pickup with a gun rack and a Ford Bronco with a thick layer of dried mud on its wheels. I got out, patted the 'Vette's roof, and mentally crossed my fingers in the hope that the car would be in one piece when I returned. Then I crossed the lot and entered the dance hall.

The Bullrider was collecting a cover charge; directly in front of me was a low counter. Behind the counter sat a Dolly Parton blonde with a sprayed beehive hairdo, wearing a plaid shirt opened to the third button. As I handed her ten dollars, she gave my knit Polo shirt and brand-new tailored jeans a disapproving once-over, then counted out six bucks in change. I sidestepped a bearded cowboy at the entryway and moved on.

On a stage around a hundred yards in front of me, a country and western band was playing "Lost in the Fifties Tonight," a Ronnie Millsap tune. The band consisted of a drummer, two bass guitarists—a tall, skinny drink of water in boots and Stetson who finger-strummed his guitar at hip level, and a short, fat, bald guy who carried his instrument up under his armpit and used a plastic pick to twang the strings—a lead guitar played by a youngster with shoulder-length hair billowing from underneath the brim of his hat, and a full-hipped, big-breasted girl in tight jeans and a bare-midriff halter who held a cymbal in each hand and wiggled her fanny in time to the music. The singer was a square-shouldered gent who stood in an Elvis Presley, hip-cocked stance and kept his lips pressed to the hand-held microphone. The big dance floor was elbow to elbow, men in Stetsons and women in boots and jeans or flowered square dance dresses. The tune was a slow one and the crowd was doing some belly-rubbing; couples held each other close and did box steps together. On the far side of the dance floor, one cowboy tried to cut in. The cowboy who was already dancing didn't like that; he shook his head. The cutter-in yanked on the dancer's elbow, and the two men squared off with fists balled. A bouncer, a huge guy carrying a flashlight, stepped in between the pair and said something. The cutter-in eyed the bouncer, thought it over, and melted into the crowd.

The bar was fifty yards to my left, past rows of long tables and a cluster of smaller tables for more intimate seating. Leggy waitresses in jeans carried round metal trays, taking orders and hustling back to the bar to get the orders filled. The nearest waitress to me was a lanky brunette who at the moment was standing behind one of the long tables while a cowboy leaned back in his folding chair and talked to her over his shoulder. I went over to her and said in her ear, "I'm looking for a girl named Candy, supposed to work here."

She cut long-lashed eyes at me and shifted her tray from one arm to the other. "Who's looking for her?" she said.

I showed her my version of a disarming grin. "Rick. Tell her Rick wants to see her. I'm a friend of a friend."

The cowboy with whom she'd been talking eyed me, then said to her, "You know this guy?" He'd been drinking a lot; sober he could probably handle himself pretty well.

She leaned over and said to him, "Just a minute, Billy." Then, to me: "Well, you've got Candy, sweetie. Me. What friend are you a friend of?" Her dark hair was cut short in a Dorothy Hamill style. She was wearing flats; her nose was on a level with the cleft in my chin, which would make her around five foot nine.

"Well, it's . . ." I began, then said, "listen, is there a place we can talk? Won't take but just a minute."

Now Billy rose unsteadily to his feet, moved between Candy and me, and put his nose about six inches from mine. "The lady's busy, bud. Whyntcha take your tenderfoot ass away from here?" He eyed my clothes. He was a youngster, early twenties, with a broad chest and burly arms, about my height. He'd shaved clean as a whistle, and the strong scent of Old Spice Lime mixed with the smell of beer on his breath. Farmboy gone afunnin' on Saturday night. He was a strong kid, but I thought I could probably take him even when he was stone sober. In his current condition it would be a lead-pipe cinch. There were three more cowboys seated at the table, and they were glaring at me. I showed the kid my we're-old-buddies grin. "No trouble," I said. "I'm just wanting to talk to her for a minute."

Candy stepped around the youngster and faced him. "You behave, Billy. You wait, I'll be right back." Then to me, she said, "Come on with me. I got tables to wait on, you'll have to hurry." Billy flopped back into his chair. She led me to a table for two near the bar. Candy walked with a come-on, hip-swinging gait, and, following her, I decided that Billy would probably sit and wait until hell froze over. She sat down and put her tray on the table. I took a seat across from her.

The band launched into "I Don't Think Hank Done It This Way," a Waylon Jennings number backed by throbbing, loud guitars. I leaned over the table and practically shouted to Candy, "I'm wanting to talk to Catfish."

Her full lips twisted violently. "I thought you said you were a friend of a friend. Get lost, asshole." She got up and took a long step away from the table.

I got up and took her by the arm, none too gently. She'd thrown me a curve, and my mind was racing. Whatever it took, I had to find this guy. I said, "I was lying. He's not really a friend, and he's not going to like what happens when I find him."

She looked down at my hand on her arm, then back up at me. I let go of her. She said, "You a cop?"

"No."

"Too bad. I was hoping you were going to bust him. I got bruises from that bastard, mister." She sat back down at the table.

I joined her once again and said, "So I made the wrong approach to you. The word I had he was your boyfriend."

"Was. For about two weeks. I got plenty of getting the shit

beat out of me when I was with my old man. I don't need the same treatment from Mr. Donald Lund. That's his name, Catfish. If he bothers me again I'm going to a lawyer I know and have him slapped with a restraining order."

This was working out better than I'd expected. As long as she was riled up, she'd talk to me without thinking over her answers. I said, "Yeah, well, you're not alone. He broke my sister's arm the other night, and me and Mr. Catfish got a score to settle." I was pretty sure I was reading her right. In Candy's circle of friends, scores were settled every day.

She didn't bat an eye. "I'll tell you something, mister. I'm all for you, but you'd better take a baseball bat. Or a gun. This is one bad sumbitch you're talking about."

"I can be one, too, when somebody messes with my sister. You know where to find him?"

"You'd better be," she said. "If he ain't moved, he lives at four-twenty Wycliff Place. Off Lemmon Avenue. I don't know the apartment number, but it's right in the breezeway by the pool. Last apartment on the left. Listen, I got work to do." She glanced toward the bar. The bartender, a burly, bearded guy, was watching us through slitted eyes.

"Okay, I told you I only wanted a minute. And thanks." I stood.

"You might not thank me after you see him. But like I said, I'm pulling for you. You don't tell that s.o.b. who tole you where he lives, you hear?" Her big eyes became rounder, and slightly fearful. No, more than slightly; she was terrified of the guy.

"No way. No way would I." I patted her arm and walked toward the exit. At the doorway I turned and looked over my shoulder. Candy was back on duty, going from table to table, taking orders. She stopped and threw me a good-bye wave. I went on through the lobby and out to the parking lot. The Dolly Parton clone showed me a bored yawn as I went by.

Outside, the moon was behind a cloud bank, and the cars in the parking lot were faint bulky outlines. It was hot, the still heat of an August night in Texas, the steamy humidity rising from the marshland surrounding the nightclub. I stood on the short wooden porch for a moment, my gaze traveling beyond the parking lot to the narrow road leading to the highway. I was wondering about Breaux. Damn, he should have been here by now. I took two steps down and felt warm asphalt through my shoes as I walked between an Isuzu Trooper II and a Chevrolet pickup, headed for the 'Vette.

On my left a slurred male voice said, "Sum-*bitch*." At the same instant something stout and wooden slammed into the side of my head.

I was lucky enough to see it coming, a dark shape moving among darker shapes in the corner of my eye, and instinct moved my head to one side. The little head jerk didn't save me altogether, but instead of landing on the button, the blow glanced off my ear, painfully scraping my cheek. And instead of going down for the count, I went only to my knees.

The moon was suddenly out from behind the clouds, bathing the parking lot in muted light. The light illuminated the young cowboy Billy, the one Candy had been talking to when I'd interrupted. He staggered slightly, hefted the thick tree branch over his head, and brought it crashing down a second time. The booze played hell with his timing; I got my feet under me and sprang to one side and the branch thudded harmlessly on asphalt. It slipped from Billy's grasp, bounced once, rolled over twice, and was still.

My backside was flattened against the front fender of the Isuzu. I extended a hand, palm out. "What do you think you're doing, son? You got no problem with me."

Billy clenched his hands into fists, his breathing ragged, and took a step in my direction.

A second, deeper voice, also slurred, said, "What he's doin' is, he's gonna whip yore ass. Teach you to come 'round here fuckin' with these women."

From behind the Chevy pickup stepped reinforcements, the three other cowboys who'd shared Billy's table. Two were short and burly; the third was a couple of inches taller than I was and built like a whipsaw. All three were drunk, weaving in place. I was pretty sure I could handle Billy, but four on one was a different story. I wondered if I could outrun them, jump into the 'Vette, and speed away. I doubted it.

I said, "I had business with the girl is all. Hell, I wasn't butting into anything."

The tallest of the three snickered. "We got business, too, bud. Our business is goin' to be beatin' the shit outta you, how 'bout that?" The four men formed a semicircle around me. Visible beyond them, headlights came down the narrow road and into the parking lot.

One of the chunky cowboys grabbed the front of my shirt and yanked. I tried to swing at him, but somebody grabbed hold of my arm. An arm encircled my throat; my own hand came sharply up behind me in a hammerlock. Billy squared drunkenly off before me and spat in his palms. One of the cowboys said, "Knock his fuckin' teeth loose, Billy."

The headlights came down the row, bumping up and down. Breaux's Jeep convertible, top down, appeared behind the lights and came to a screeching halt just feet from us. Bodie was behind the wheel. He raised his hand, and in it was the .45 he'd taken from Muhammed's man Snakey out at Connie Swarm's. Orange flame spurted upward as a roar split the night like artillery.

The three in front of me froze like a stop-action photo. The arm around my throat loosened its hold. I took a step to one side and rubbed my windpipe. Breaux was up on his running board with the .45 leveled at the cowpokes.

"Stand away from him," Breaux said. "Get in, Bannion. Jesus Christ, I thought you was only going to talk to somebody."

I left my buddies and climbed aboard the Jeep. Breaux was wearing a grimy T-shirt and his yellow hat was soiled. To me he was pretty as a picture. "Where you been?" I said.

Breaux kept the pistol trained on the cowboys as he slowly lowered himself behind the wheel. He dropped the .45 between us, threw the Jeep into gear, and we bounced away. "I told you I'd be awhile," he said. "I told you not to get into any shit, too. Guess you don't listen to nothing, Bannion."

*   *   *

Breaux ran over the curb while parking the Jeep. The hood bounced up, then down. So did I, holding grimly onto the dashboard. Under the circumstances I'd had no choice but to leave the 'Vette parked at Bullrider Danceland and ride with Breaux. But after a heart-stopping thirty-minute trip with Breaux cussing under his breath, grinding gears and weaving in and out of traffic, I wasn't sure but what I'd have been better off to take the 'Vette and chance the cow-pokes catching up to me while I was getting the engine started.

Bodie turned the ignition off, and as the Jeep dieseled through a couple of vibrations before quieting, he said, "Jesus fucking Christ. Four-twenty Wycliff Place, here it is. You're going through a helluva lot, not to mention dragging me through it with you. The fuck is going on?"

The two-story, red brick apartment was sat far back from the street. There was a sidewalk leading to the building with a row of gaslights along the walk. Tiny flames wavered within the globes and formed small, moving shadows on the lawn. Beyond an ornate iron gate, blue-green lights wavered beneath the surface of the water in the pool. A diving board rattled and a body split the water with a small splash. Elm trees paraded down both sides of the street in neat rows, visible over the nose of the Jeep.

I yanked the handle upward and moved the door partway open with my shoulder. "Later, Bodie, okay? I'll tell you everything later. For now just trust me."

"I guess I trust you about as far as anybody else I know that the feds have got the heat on. Which ain't too far."

I'd already placed a foot on the curb and risen partway out of my seat. I flopped back down and faced Breaux. "The word's out already, huh?" I said.

Bodie shrugged and slung his wrist over the top of the steering wheel, teenager style. "Yeah, it's out some, to a few people. Plus I saw the broad on TV."

"What broad?"

"You trying to shit me?" Breaux said. "The same broad which was wearing a bikini and wrapped around your body, though I can't figure out why a broad looks like that would be wrapped around *your* body. Picture in our tank, up at El Reno. Remember? Who it turns out is Jack Brendy's old lady. Who it turns out is now dead. So like I say, the fuck is going on?"

I'd forgotten about the picture. Breaux had drooled over the photo of Donna and me at Las Colinas Country Club's pool so much that I'd finally put it away. Later the picture had turned up missing after the hacks had shaken down our cell. Probably good for me. It had helped take her off my mind, not seeing her picture every day.

I said simply, "Yeah. It's the same girl."

"So that part's none of my business," Braux said. "But what's going on with the feds is plenty my business."

I hesitated before deciding to tell him. Guys I'd met in jail and since jail didn't know much about my life before. About my football career, of course—things like that make one sort of a celebrity in the joint—but about my private life, nothing. I'd always tried to keep it that way. I said to Breaux, "Donna Brendy and I came close to getting married once upon a time. I grew up with her brother. Corpus Christi, you ever been there?"

Breaux tilted his hat back with a forefinger. "I was a seaman twenty years. Sure, palm trees and some pretty good seafood joints. I worked in Corpus, on the seawall after the hurricane in what, sixty-eight?"

"Sixty-nine," I said. "Hurricane Camille, only I was grown and gone to Dallas before then. Donna was still in high school. In fact, she had an uncle that died in Camille. She was Donna Morley then. Buddy's her brother, the guy I grew up with. The last time I talked to him was just before Donna moved to Dallas. He asked me to find her a job. Back then Jack Brendy and I were sharing an apartment. Jack went about as bonkers over Donna as you did over her picture up in El Reno."

There was a bright streetlamp across the way and, from my angle, Breaux's profile was outlined in the glow like the head on a coin. "I don't blame him," he said. "You still ain't telling me what I want to know, about the feds."

"I'm coming to it," I said. "Look, I had a lot of women in those days. I guess I looked at Donna as just another notch on my gun, or whatever you call it. I felt kind of guilty, her being my old buddy's little sister, but . . . Bodie, you never met a real horse's ass until you met me back in those days. I let her go on thinking we were going to get married when all the time I knew damn well I wasn't going through with it. The whole time I went out with Donna, Jack acted like he was her little puppy dog. It wasn't thirty days after I split up with her that he walks in one day and announces that they're getting married. Wanted to know if I had anything to say about it. At first I thought he was joking around.

"And then, it was the goddamnedest thing," I said. "All it took was for Donna to marry Jack and *whammo*: all of a sudden I couldn't get her out of my mind. Jesus, it was like dope. I used to wake up in a cold sweat just thinking about her. You ever had a woman affect you that way?"

Breaux's lip curled in the darkness in a kind of leer. "Not lately. I look like Dear Abby or somebody?"

"No, but right now you're the next best thing. Look, you're asking about the feds, I'm trying to explain what's going on," I said.

"So explain." He gestured toward the apartment house. "But this dude you're looking for is liable to move or die of old age before you get through. Jesus Christ."

"I'm hurrying. One night after football practice Jack had a press conference. He was a big star and all, he had 'em all the time. Donna was hanging around and she said—and I swear at the time I didn't know she wasn't telling Jack about this—she said since he was going to be busy, why didn't the two of us eat supper together? One thing led to another, you know. I saw her quite a bit after that, when he wasn't around. I'm not proud of it, but I'm not exactly ashamed, either."

"Brendy know you were fucking her?" Breaux said.

"I think he did. He never caught us at it or anything, but I'm pretty sure he knew. You can tell when two people are . . . Anyway, I got traded soon after that, and I never saw Donna or Jack again until, well, the other day. When he got arrested was when Donna got ahold of me. His lawyer hired me to get rid of Skeezix, and that's when I came looking for you." I took a deep breath and let it out slowly. "I was with her one more time, that night after I let you off at Cafe Dallas. I shouldn't have done it and neither should she. The FBI had a man on her tail, snapping pictures. So now Jack is dead, they've got me with his wife, and you know how the bastards work. They want me to finger Jack's drug connection, or they're going to have the state boys charge me and Donna both with killing Jack. Murder for hire, that's the death penalty. Jesus, I don't even know who Jack's drug connect is, but they don't give a shit. They want me to finger somebody, anybody. So I've got one chance. If I can get the folks that murdered Jack, the federal folks won't have anything to pressure me with. So far I've been to Muhammed Double-X and he's put me onto this Catfish guy that lives in this apartment. His girlfriend, or at least she was, she's not too in love with Catfish anymore. She works at the Bullrider Danceland, and that's what I was doing out there. She told me where the guy lives, or at least where he did. For all I know he's moved."

Breaux scratched the stubble on his jaw. "Didn't you think it was funny, them wanting you to get rid of Skeezix?"

"How's that?"

"Just funny. Face it, you ain't no torpedo. You chase bond skips, collect for bookmakers, shit like that. The fuck you know about running fedral witnesses off?"

"I just don't think they knew anybody else."

"Shit. You don't—" Breaux halted in mid-sentence. He opened his door and started to climb out of the Jeep. "So come on, let's go see the guy, if he's here. This ain't none of my business anyhow. I don't even know what I'm doing over here."

The door to the apartment was painted bright yellow, as though Catfish was saying, Here I am, come and get me. I was conscious of Breaux's soft breathing beside me as I rang the doorbell. Then I leaned against the jamb, watched a girl with sopping long dark hair, wearing a black one-piece swimsuit, clamber out of the pool and leave a trail of wet footprints along the bank as she went over to a beach table. She grabbed a towel and massaged her hair as she slipped into fuzzy pink sandals. Then she put on a yellow terrycloth robe, slung the towel over her shoulder, and walked away. I still hadn't heard any movement inside the apartment. I rang the bell again. We waited a few minutes more.

Finally Breaux said, "Well, maybe he's in the shitter." He reached past me, turned the knob. There was a soft click and the door swung inward, whispering over carpet. A gaslight was directly across the walk behind us, and it threw a flickering rectangle of light on green shag. Beyond the rectangle was only blackness. I pictured Catfish in there, crouched in the dark behind a table or chair with an Uzi trained on the doorway; if this boy *had* killed Jack, he was going to be jumpy as hell. I groped instinctively for my back pocket, then pictured the Smith & Wesson still resting on the 'Vette's floorboard at Bullrider Danceland, and relaxed. I nudged Breaux, placed a silencing finger to my lips, and pointed at the butt of the .45 jammed inside his waistband. He held the gun in both hands, barrel up commando style, as I said loudly, "Anybody home?" There was no answer, only the gentle lapping of the water in the pool. Breaux and I went into the apartment.

There was a dim glow ten feet to my left; I turned toward it. A lighted fish tank sat on a table, bubbles rising to the top in rapid succession and green imitation ferns waving gently. Yellow, inch-long piranahs darted among the ferns, whipped down to the bottom to wriggle and twist on white gravel. The light from the tank illuminated a four-seater cloth divan and two cloth stuffed chairs. There was a tall, shaded floor lamp beside the couch. Breaux went over and switched it on. I closed the outside door.

Catfish wasn't into decorating: the couch and chairs, along with the cheap dinette set in the alcove off the living room, were standard rental furniture. Aside from the fish tank there were no other knickknacks in the room. A portable fifteen-inch TV sat on a folding card table just inside the doorway. There was one picture on the wall, and it wasn't framed. Taped to the treated sheetrock was a photo of Old Sparky, the electric chair they'd used down in Huntsville before lethal injection was voted in, and I pictured Catfish sitting here with Old Sparky's picture and feeling right at home. There was a short hallway leading off the living room with a closed door at the opposite end. We walked side by side down the hall, Breaux still holding the .45, and went into the bedroom. I fumbled with the light switch and turned it on.

Now, this was quite a setup. There was a fairly normal king-size bed covered with a fairly normal green quilted spread. There was a chair beside the bed. On the chair were stone-washed jeans, freshly laundered and pressed, and an equally fresh blue western shirt. Polished brown western boots sat on the floor. The clothes were laid carefully across the seat and chair back as though someone had been planning to go out. The bed and chair were normal-looking, okay, but the apparatus sitting beside them was anything but.

I guessed that the thing was a torture rack. It was about three feet high and seven feet long, its top a padded cloth surface with foot stirrups at one end and a headrest at the other. Chains with locking bracelets attached were affixed to all four corners, and the top of the whatchamacallit was divided into two sections. There was a gear-toothed wheel underneath the center with a crank attached. By turning the crank one could make the top grow longer. Two brown leather quirts hung from a plaque on the wall behind the thing. Jesus, no wonder Candy had had enough.

Bodie gave a low, breathy whistle as he bent to turn the crank a couple of notches. There was a sharp *click-click* and the top lengthened three or four inches. I went over and leaned against a squat dresser of dark wood while Breaux crouched and looked the rack over from all angles. As I watched him I was dimly conscious of the *splash-hiss* of running water. I turned my attention away from Breaux and looked around.

I'd been concentrating so hard on the torture rack that the noise of the shower simply hadn't penetrated. On the other side of the bed, the bathroom door was partway open. Beyond the doorway were tiny green square tiles, both on the floor and on the walls. Hazy steam was coating the tiles with droplets of water. I touched Bodie's shoulder and jerked my head toward the bathroom. He rose. I led him around the foot of the bed and into the bathroom, then stopped in my tracks. Breaux grunted softly as he collided with me.

The guy Catfish—at least I assumed it was Catfish, and a closer inspection of the receding chin and drooping mustache convinced me that he looked sort of like a catfish—had been a weightlifter. His arms were big and muscular and his pectorals taut and hard. At least the right pectoral was; there was a gaping bullet wound through the left, over the heart. It was one of several bullet holes in Catfish. I didn't bother to count them.

The shower door was scattered about in jagged pieces of frosted glass. Catfish was on his back; his feet and shins were inside the stall. I guessed that the slugs had blasted away the top half of the door, and in tumbling outward Catfish had done the rest of the damage. His black eyes were wide and staring at the ceiling, his wet black hair drying and frizzing. It occurred to me that the force of the bullets should have thrown the body against the back shower wall; Catfish would have had to force himself, shot full of holes, out the door for one last, death-rattle lunge at the shooter. Mr. Catfish had been a plenty tough customer, and whoever had offed him had known that. That accounted for the extra bullet holes.

I stepped over Catfish and looked inside the shower stall. Several tiles were cracked; shards of green porcelain lay on the floor mixed with the broken glass. A misshapen gray lead pellet rested on the grating over the drain. Currents of dark red mixed with steamy water and swirled downward. Some of the blood was thickening and sticking to the walls.

Breaux said, "Guess he musta twisted that crank out there too hard on somebody. Pissed 'em off, huh?"

The steam was dampening my shirt, and I wiped my hand across my chest. "You ever seen this guy, Bodie?"

"Naw. Not nekked, anyhow. Let's split."

I hesitated. I wasn't too crazy about hanging around a dead man's apartment, particularly this dead man's. I thought about Pierson, the county D.A., and what he'd said about getting a grand jury together. "I want to look around a couple of minutes. Just a couple, okay?" I said.

Breaux wiped the bill of his cap, where moisture was beginning to collect. "Well, this cat here ain't going to stop you. Get a move on. Jails I don't like."

We went back into the bedroom with Breaux carrying the .45 loosely by his hip. I skirted the king-size, dodged around the torture rack, and returned to the dresser. There was a handkerchief in my back pocket. I wrapped it around the handle of the top dresser drawer and pulled. The drawer creaked slightly as it opened. I peered down inside.

Atop a stack of folded silk handkerchiefs—they were bright reds, greens, and purples, and I briefly wondered whether Catfish had known Fred Cassel—was a pair of steel handcuffs. There were flecks of rust on the bracelets. To the left of the hankies was something round and about a foot long, rolled up in linen. I picked it up and unwrapped it. I was holding a hard rubber imitation penis. It was quite a molding job; the thing looked real. I dropped it like a hot poker. The penis fell to the floor, bounced once, and rolled over. There were very real-looking black hairs sprouting from its upper end. Breaux's breathing quickened beside me and I resisted the impulse to giggle.

Breaux said, "Jesus Christ."

"That's what I say," I said. I looked back into the drawer.

A stack of five-by-eight color photos had been hidden behind the rolled-up dildo. The stack looked to be an inch-and-a-half high, maybe two dozen pictures. Slowly, carefully, using my own handkerchief to prevent any prints, I lifted the photos and laid them on top of the dresser. I bent my head to look. Breaux did the same, and his shoulder rubbed mine.

The top photo featured Candy, stark naked. She was on all fours on the torture rack. Her wrists were cuffed to the lower end. Catfish was in the picture, too, and I thought he looked a whole lot better as a corpse than when he'd been alive and walking around. In the photo he had a mean-looking grin on his face. He was behind Candy on his knees, and was naked also. There was a look of fear mixed with pain on Candy as Catfish plunged the dildo—I glanced at the thing on the floor and swallowed bile—deep into her from the rear.

"Jesus H. Christ," Breaux said.

"You sound like a broken record," I said. Still using the handkerchief, I nudged the top photo aside and looked at the next one.

My first impression was that the second picture was more to my taste. A tawny blonde was on the king-size bed in this one: supple, muscular legs, a flat belly, jutting, pink-tipped breasts. She was kneeling beside a prone naked man, and she was smiling wanton lust into the camera. Her lips were parted and she was holding the man's erect member between her palms. I looked at the girl for a second or two before it dawned on me that I'd seen her before. On a lit porch in nighttime with waves lapping against the shore in the background. Connie Swarm.

"It's your friend, Bodie," I said.

"Yeah. Old Connie-girl. Can ya imagine?"

"Sure is. She's—"

Whatever I'd been about to say stuck in my throat like a fish bone. I'd barely glanced at the man in the picture, Connie being the main attraction, but realization flooded over me as I looked at the man closer. Head back, eyes closed, a look on his face as though he was about to enter the gates of heaven. Which he finally had, just a few days ago. The guy was Jack Brendy.

"Jesus Christ," I said.

"That's *my* line," Breaux said.

I kept staring at the picture and felt a whole lot less guilty about what had gone on between Donna and me. I even managed to get mad at Jack—I was rationalizing, of course—as I nudged the photo off the stack and looked at the next one.

Jack and Connie again, coupled this time, Connie on top watching the camera, her pink tongue caressing her lower lip. Stage presence, probably the same expression she wore when her act at Baby Doll's reached a frenzied pitch. In this picture, Jack's eyes were open, his gaze directed at the ceiling, his lips parted in the early throes of climax. There was something about the way Jack looked that caused my eyebrows to knit. I reached for the other picture of him with Connie, laid the photos side by side, and compared.

I was pretty sure that I was right. Connie was playing for the camera, but Jack didn't even know that anybody was taking his picture. If Jack hadn't been Jack, had been a regular porno actor, then I probably would have felt differently. But no way could Jack Brendy strip down in front of a camera and play this scene so naturally. I left Breaux gaping at the pictures and made a circle around the room, checking out every foot of the walls and doors.

I found what I was looking for in a walk-in closet on the far side of the bedroom, directly opposite the bath where Catfish lay. The double closet doors were painted dark brown, the identical color to the walls inside the closet, perfect camouflage for the slit in one of the doors. The slit was about six inches wide by four inches high. I used my hanky to shut the doors behind me and squinted out through the opening. The back of one of Breaux's thick, blue-jeaned legs was visible—he was still ogling the pictures as though hypnotized—and beyond that the bed, at an identical angle to the scene in the photos.

So Jack had thought he was scoring for real. Blackmail? Seemed likely. But for money or what? Whoever was behind this—I somehow couldn't picture Catfish as the brains of the operation—would have to have known that Jack was into smuggling drugs. Hell, they wouldn't need a picture of him as he was banging Connie Swam to extort money. Didn't make sense. And what was Connie getting out of it? Her track record didn't seem to go with this scene, at least from what I knew about her. Connie had too many sugar daddies for her to have to sink to this kind of action for money. I decided to pick Bodie's brain, at least the portion of it where information about Connie Swam was stored.

I left the closet and started across the room. "Bodie, I need to know—"

A uniformed Dallas cop sprang into the bedroom and said, "Don't even breathe, assholes." He held his service .38 revolver in both hands, the barrel aligned with the bridge of his nose and aimed at a point somewhere between me and Breaux. The cop was a young guy, still with some baby fat puffing his cheeks. The bill of his cap was practically touching his nose. I stopped dead in my tracks and Breaux half turned in the cop's direction.

The cop moved warily, his gaze on us, moved around beside the bathroom door. He turned his head away long enough to peer inside, then said to us, "On the floor, facedown. Now. You, sea salt. Lay the pistol down easy."

I lay facedown on the carpet, the shag tickling my cheek. Breaux gingerly laid the .45 on the floor, then spread-eagled out beside me.

"Sea salt, my ass," Breaux mumbled.

T E N

The routine hadn't changed any. I followed the city jail guard down a steel-walled corridor between rows of cells with little rectangular windows in the doors and wondered where they were keeping Breaux. More than likely he was playing an identical scene, following another guard down another corridor in the jail to talk to a detective who had the same questions for him. I wasn't likely to see Bodie again until they felt they had all the information they were going to get. Keep the suspects separated, don't give them a chance to compare stories. I had to admit that the method usually worked, but I doubted if they were prepared for a couple of suspects like me and Bodie Breaux. We'd been through it before.

Unlike the modern Lew Sterrett Justice Center, the county lockup, the city jail was steel doors and tiny, dark cells, with bigger tanks for gangs of drunks who were sleeping it off. A good old-fashioned kind of jail. My guard was an older man with fat pouches jiggling underneath his shirt and sticking out over the back of his gray uniform trousers. I kept my gaze riveted on the small of his back as I followed him along. My feet were in soft jailhouse slippers, and the concrete floor hurt the soles like the dickens. The one-piece blue jumpsuit

I was wearing was too small and constricted the movement of my shoulders.

On my left, a sluggish, hoarse voice from within a cell said, "This dude goin' to see the Man, bruddas. He going to do some jive-talkin'."

Without thinking about it, I turned and said from the side of my mouth, "You talk like you been to see the Man yourself, you know right where I'm going. How many poor bastards you dropped a dime on?" Funny how quickly you get back into the swing.

A coal black face with thick lips and white, piano-key teeth appeared in the window. The face said, "Fuck you ass, honky. You come see me we have a talk, huh?" I did a snappy eyes-front and kept walking.

The guard halted and threw a lever. A panel in the wall clanged and slid on creaky steel rollers. The guard motioned like a traffic cop, and I went through the hole in the wall. The panel banged and echoed as it closed behind me.

The feds call them interview rooms. The cities and counties have other names for them. Bare white walls, yellow and gray from lack of cleaning and stale cigarette smoke. A long conference table with bare wood showing through the paint in places, two straight, hard chairs on either side of the table. One entryway from the innards of the jail, an exit leading to the cops' offices, a small window in the exit door in case the interviewer has to call for help. In the old days this was the room where the rubber hoses came out. I hadn't seen any rubber hoses in my career as a prisoner, but I'd seen some of these interviews get pretty rough. I hoped fleetingly that this wasn't going to be one of them.

The city detective seated on one side of the table was as typecast as the room itself. Sharp features, a long, skinny nose over a pencil mustache. Thinning short brown hair parted on the left. A white long-sleeved shirt, cuffs a couple of inches above bony wrists, a narrow black tie, no coat. He was thumbing through the stack of porno shots I'd found in Catfish's apartment. He really took his time with the photos featuring Connie Swarm, holding each one close to his nose and really going over the details. Solid police investigative procedure. I pulled out the chair opposite him and sat down.

He didn't look up. "Mr. Bannion."

I said, "Hiya."

"I'm Detective Willis. You ever been in trouble before?" His narrow eyebrows arched, and I wondered which of Connie's poses was now capturing his attention. The tone of his voice said that he already knew the answer to his question.

"Some," I said.

"Some. As in little some or big some?"

"Look, you've already run me up on the computer. So you tell me."

Willie laid the pictures down and looked at me. The act seemed to take some effort. His eyes were slate gray and twinkled with about the same merriment as drilling mud. "I didn't need the computer on you, Mr. Bannion. I'm an old football fan from way back. It's just that this kind of murder doesn't jive with dope smuggling, so I was wondering if you'd ever been in any trouble other than the drug charges that you did the federal time for. The computer doesn't show any other trouble."

Great. Another fan. As I tugged on the sleeve of my jumpsuit, I wondered if I should offer the guy an autograph. I didn't say anything.

Willis showed me a tiny smirk as he opened a drawer. He came up with a compact Sony recorder and depressed a button. Seen through clear plastic, the reels began to turn slowly. Willis said to me, "Somebody's already read your rights, haven't they?"

I shrugged. "I don't remember. They might've." The fact was that I'd already heard my rights, such as they were, two times: once from the cop at Catfish's apartment and another time from a stuttering night magistrate at police headquarters. But I might as well hear them from Willis, too. Inspirational work, the Constitution.

He told me I had the right to remain silent and that I could hire a lawyer and all of the other good stuff. When I told him I didn't want an attorney—eight years earlier I'd demanded one, then learned in the long run that it didn't make any difference whether you had a lawyer or not—he said, "Why'd you shoot the guy, Mr. Bannion?"

I scratched my chin. "I beg your pardon?" The recorder was making a soft whirring noise.

"Come on, Mr. Bannion, your partner's already told us you shot Lund. Why, is all I'm trying to find out. You help us, we'll help you." I supposed that he was trying to look reassuring. I didn't feel reassured.

"I'm going to save you some time," I said. "If you haven't already, then run Breaux up on your computer. He didn't do all that federal time because he told anybody anything. I didn't, either. So if you're figuring to make me think he told you I shot the guy, or make him think that I told you he did, then you're farting in the wind."

Willis carefully lifted both ends of his tie, held them away from his shirt, and looked at them. There were a few greasy spots, like gravy stains. "We're shorthanded in homicide," he said. "I can't even go home long enough to change this dungy tie. So let's both be reasonable. We've checked out the victim, too, and I don't think anybody's going to miss Mr. Lund very much. I doubt that the D.A. is going to go for your throat, not for killing that asshole. So talk to me."

"Tell all and it'll go easy on me? That bullshit's not going to work, either. Not on me. Not on Breaux."

There was a twitch of irritation at the corner of his mouth, and he tried to hide it by picking up the photos and thumbing through them again. I briefly wondered how he liked the one of Catfish and Candy.

"Look," I said, "there's only one guy I'm giving any information to. Get him in here and save us all a lot of trouble." I almost laughed out loud as I realized that what I'd just said was the cop's line in reverse.

Willis put the photos down. "I'm all ears."

"You know a Detective Atchley, down at the county?"

He picked up the pictures again and gave Connie some more of his undivided attention. "Yeah, but he doesn't work with us. He's county, we're city. Different jurisdictions."

I reached over and covered both of his hands with one of mine. He stiffened and blinked, shot a glance toward the exit, where reinforcements were if he needed them. I said, "Look, Willis, I don't give a fuck what department gets the credit for this. I didn't kill Lund. Breaux didn't kill Lund.

You ever want to find out who did, you get Atchley down here."

I tried to read something in Willis's expression. I couldn't. The way I was handling myself was apt to cost me a beating before this was over, but I had to see Atchley. If I'd been reading the county cop right, he didn't like the feds much more than I did. It was the only chance that I had.

Willis relaxed and firmly moved my hand away. "So okay," he said, "I'll call Atchley. What the hell, I got other things to do."

I leaned back and folded my arms. "That's more like it," I said.

Detective Atchley told me that I could call him Roy. That was okay with me. He looked more like a Roy than he did a Detective Atchley. Good ole boy, short sandy hair, full cheeks, a big, probing nose like a St. Bernard's. Not quite the cop look, until you noticed that his pale blue eyes didn't twinkle when the corners of his mouth turned up in a smile.

"You're really putting me in the middle," he said. "The city folks"—he jerked his head toward Detective Willis, he of the greasy stains on his tie—"have you dead to rights on a murder scene. The feds say you're the prime suspect in the disappearance of a witness. You're wanting me to interfere not with just one but two jurisdictions."

Atchley hadn't mentioned my meeting with him and the feds at Whiterock Precinct. If he didn't want to bring it up, I didn't see any reason why I should. I said, "You're the investigator on Jack Brendy's killing, Roy, at least so I understand. That's why I need to talk to you in private."

Atchley's imperceptible nod told me I'd said the right thing. He turned to Willis. "Steve, if he's got anything on the Brendy murder, I need it. How 'bout if you leave us alone?"

Willis quit studying his tie and looked dubious. "I don't know, Roy, the apartment murder is our baby. At least it is so far."

"Come on, Steve, you know me," Atchley said. "Anything the guy tells me that affects your case, you're going to get it right off. This is Roy Atchley, not some FBI you're talking to." I studied Atchley's expression and decided that he might make a pretty good political candidate.

Willis didn't look happy about it, but he stood and shrugged his shoulders. "I'm taking you at your word," he said to Atchley, then gave me a look that said he'd be seeing me later. He went to the exit and knocked. A peephole opened and an eye stared at him. A key turned in the lock. Willis left.

Atchley turned to me and said, "Bannion, you're one dumb son of a bitch."

I ignored the compliment. "Donald Lund, street name Catfish. The dead guy. I'm pretty sure he was the shooter that killed Jack, or at least that he was one of the guys in the car."

Atchley leaned back and propped a knee against the edge of the table. "He's got the record for it. That doesn't make you any less of a dumb son of a bitch for killing him."

"Roy, why would I kill the guy? He was my way out of the trap." It dawned on me that Atchley had known about Catfish, probably even before the meeting at Whiterock Precinct. And if he'd known about Catfish, Pierson and the feds had known about him, too. The bastards.

Atchley took a piece of Doublemint gum from his breast pocket and unwrapped it. "He might be. Or if you're the one that hired him, he might be your way *in*. To Hunstville. I don't see anything tells me you're not the guy that offed him." He stuck one end of the gum in his mouth, folded the stick over with his tongue, and began to chew.

I hesitated. If I was wrong, I could be cooking my goose. Finally I said, "Look, Roy, get me out of here. Breaux, too. I swear to God, forty-eight hours and I think I can find out who hired Catfish. You can't. It'll help you get the federals off your back."

The gum made a popping sound. He scratched his big nose. "This Breaux. Dope smuggler, isn't he?"

"He used to be." I hadn't actually seen Breaux making any marijuana deals lately, so I wasn't lying. Maybe fibbing a little.

Atchley stood and vigorously rubbed his upper arm. "Well, you're a dumb son of a bitch. But I'm dumber. Bannion, if

I go out on a limb and you saw it off, I'm promising you that you'll be better off if the feds get you before I do." His face softened. "But if you can help me, you won't be sorry. Jesus Christ, I've got to get rid of those fucking FBI's. I got indigestion so bad I can't sleep at night."

I thought that the Dallas city cops should furnish me transportation back to the Bullrider Danceland so I could pick up the 'Vette, and I said so. The desk sergeant, a chubby, bald guy with a snow white fringe, cupped a palm behind his ear and said, "I can't hear you, pal." Another funnyman. I picked up my brown personal property envelope, tore it open, and inventoried the contents—a wallet containing only my driver's license, a cheap Timex watch that I'd dressed up with a gold webbed band from Sterling's Wholesale, just under three thousand in cash that I had left over from the five that Donna had given me—as I went out the side exit from Dallas Government Center onto Ervay Street. The Timex was showing a couple of minutes after three in the morning. The air was still and hot, and the downtown buildings—Renaissance Tower, seventy-story Momentum Place with its roof in the shape of a parabola, along with ten or twelve other mirrored skyscrapers and assorted shorter tall buildings—had their silhouettes outlined in deep, hazy purple like sculptured Rocky Mountains. I was tired to the bone. My footsteps shuffled and dragged on the concrete.

Breaux was leaning against a parking meter, his feet crossed at the ankles. His head was down, only his chin visible under the bill of his yellow cap.

"They haul you downtown and then dump you out on the street," I said. "What about your car?"

"They towed the Jeep in. I got to go to the auto pound to get it. Coupla blocks." He kept looking down at his crossed ankles, and there was something in his tone that I didn't like.

"Well, at least we've got wheels," I said.

Bodie uncrossed his ankles and stood away from the meter. A lone pickup truck, a rusty old Ford with a tail lamp burnt out, went by on Ervay going north. Bodie thrust his

hands deep into his pockets. "Naw. *I* got wheels. You ain't."
His gaze was on the pavement.

I stared at him for a moment. Breaux wasn't a moody guy.
Finally I said, "What the hell is wrong?"

He had a strange, wary expression that I'd seen on Breaux
before, but couldn't recall where. He said, "Ain't much
wrong. You been fucking Brendy's old lady. Brendy gets his
picture took fucking Connie Swarm. They haul us to jail like
we was the Manson family or something, then poof, we're
back on the street. It don't look good is all."

Now it dawned on me where I'd seen the look. It had been
at El Reno, once when the hack had been grilling Bodie
about where a half pound of Colombian gold had come
from. I squared my shoulders. "Just what the hell is that
supposed to mean?"

"I got to spell it out?" he said. "Five, no, six times in my
life I been to jail. Three of the times I never come out again
till I'd done some time in the joint. The other times it took
a pile of lawyers and a vote of Congress to get bond set for
me. And them was all marijuana beefs, pissant charges. Now
this time I'm busted standing there with a dead guy and
holding a gun belongs to a nigger's got a rap sheet long as
the dictionary. And now, bim-bam, thank you, ma'am, I'm
standing here breathing the free, no lawyers, no bond, no
nothing. I ain't seen nobody get out of jail that easy without
somebody doing some snitching to the cops, FBI, some of
them fuckheads. And I ain't done no snitching, so that leaves
just one guy that did. You."

Now I was doing a slow burn. "Hold on. I haven't—"

"Well, maybe you have and maybe you ain't," Breaux said.
"But I ain't chancing being seen around with you right now.
I got a reputation. See you, Ricky, keep in touch."

He turned on his heel and walked away. I started to go
after him, then changed my mind. There wasn't any point
in arguing, and I really couldn't blame him. There was a
crazy code among guys like Breaux, and I didn't have time
to try to prove him wrong. I had three days before D.A.
Pierson put his grand jury together, and I had a lot to do. I
walked north on Ervay Street into the heart of downtown.

I waited about ten minutes on the corner of Ervay and

Commerce. Just when I'd decided that the two guys—a short one in work clothes and a tall dude with a bandanna tied around his head—who were lounging against a building front across the street were going to roll me, a Yellow Cab came by. I flagged it down and rode out to the Bullrider Danceland, dozing some along the way. At the Bullrider I checked the 'Vette over, and couldn't see that anyone had bothered it. Then I got in, started the engine, and went home to get some rest. I was probably going to need it.

"Hello?" Her voice was crackly and sleepy and sexy and made me want to crawl right through the telephone.

"Hi. How was your trip?"

There was a rustling noise over the line, and I pictured smooth brown legs moving under satin bedcovers. I turned my head and glanced at my patio door, remembering her outline as she'd stood with moonlight framing her slim bare shoulders and cascading dark hair. She said, "God, what time is it?"

"A few minutes until four. Guess in Florida it's almost five. Did I wake Jacqueline up?"

"No. She's dead to the world. Visions of sugar plums. You should see it, Rick, everything's so green here. Tall, shady trees like a forest, almost like the Everglades. It's hot as Hades but there's so much to see. On top of all the Disney stuff there's a Circus World and a Sea World. I swear we could stay a month and not see it all."

I shifted the princess phone's receiver from one ear to the other. I'd as soon have bitten through my lip as bring her down, but I was going to have to. "I've got to ask you some questions, Donna. About Jack."

"Oh." The fun was suddenly gone from her voice. "Well, I probably won't know the answers, but I'll try."

"I'm going to name a few names. I want you to put your thinking cap on and try to remember if you've met any of these people, or if Jack ever talked about them. I know it's late—or early, if you want to call it that—but try really hard. It could be important."

I listened to long-distance static as I fumbled on the

nightstand and lit a Pall Mall. Finally she said, "Don't you think you owe me an explanation for all of this?"

She had me there. Sure, I owed her one, but I thought more of her than to give it to her. I decided that a half-truth was better than a whole lie. "I'm no detective, Donna, but I've got to try to find out who killed Jack. The police have me on their suspect list. As number one."

"Why, that's absurd."

"Sure it is. It's my record, I guess. They've got to pin it on somebody." I thought about the photo that the grinning FBI agent had shoved under my nose, the one of Donna and me outside Turtle Creek North. And Pierson's threat that he would indict her as well. I said, "You ready for the names?"

"Ready as I'll ever be."

"Muhammed Double-X."

"Muhammed who?"

"Never mind. Donald Lund. Or Catfish maybe, that's the guy's nickname."

"Never heard of him."

"Now about Norman Aycock?" I was grasping at straws.

She sighed. "You must be kidding. He's Jack's prosecutor. Or was."

"Never mind him." I felt really dumb. "Connie Swarm."

She suddenly laughed. "Sounds like a beehive. God."

I was ready to admit to myself that I'd just used the names as an excuse to talk to her, when I remembered the name that Ace the Book had first called Connie by. Her real name. "Lorraine Daley," I said.

There was sudden tension in her voice. "Who?"

"Lorraine Daley."

"Well, yes. Not in person, but the name. I signed some papers for Jack. Something about a house he was financing, using some of our stock to collateralize a loan. He said the deal would bring more interest than CD's were paying, and that it was just as safe. Lorraine Daley was the name on the loan, I'm sure of it."

I thought, Jesus Christ. I said, "Where was the house located?"

"I'm not sure. Jack handled everything. Wait, I remember

now, it was on Lake Bruce Alger. He said that if she defaulted on the loan we could keep our boat up there."

Thoughts were swimming in my head like the piranhas in Catfish's apartment. I said, "I need to look through your house, Donna. Can I get in?"

"Sure. There's a key under the mat, by the back door. You'd better climb over the gate, you'll trip the alarm if you try to open it. Take a ladder with you. I've given the maid the week off, so nobody's there."

"I'll go this morning, as soon as I get some sleep," I said. "Listen, be in your room about noon, I may need to call you. Sleep tight, we both need some rest."

"Rick?" The sexy crackle was back.

"Yes?"

"I'm dying to see you. Is that wrong?"

I closed my eyes. "I hope it isn't, 'cause I want to see you, too, puddin'. You get some sleep." I hung up. Fast. Even as tired as I was, I didn't doze off for a while. I was picturing her wealth of dark hair, framing her face on the pillow as we made love.

ELEVEN

I couldn't remember having had the dream in a long time, not since the endless nights in the cell at El Reno. Those nights had been part sleep and part semiconsciousness, interspersed with long stretches of lying awake staring at the bunk springs overhead, and of listening to Breaux's gentle snoring and the monotonous *tick-tick* of the windup Baby Ben alarm clock, sold for an inflated price in the prison commissary.

In the dream I always caught myself. Up to the point where I caught myself, the dream was a replay of what had happened for real: Craig Morton's sweat-streaked, handsome face framed by a silver helmet with a blue star on its crown; Morton's face attentive as he listened to the play call from the sideline shuttle—a wide receiver that particular year, for Landry had a habit of changing the shuttle man from season to season. Morton in the huddle, screaming to be heard, sixty-five thousand leatherlungs creating an impossible whorl of sound. The play, Power Thirty-four. Jack's number, my hole. Jack winking at me, hissing, "Blow 'em out, bigun," slapping my rump. The spongy feel of the Astroturf underfoot as I jogged up front; the yawning hole in the Texas Stadium roof through which, in those days, it was said that

God could watch America's Team. The mob on its feet in front of the end zone scoreboard, waving thousands of arms, splitting the air with rabid screams. The scoreboard lights showing forty-two seconds, Forty-Niners twenty-one, us seventeen. The come-ahead sneer from the red-jerseyed defensive tackle—Charlie Krueger was his name, a Texas Aggie transplanted to Frisco. On my left the nose of the ball a foot from the goal line, Dave Manders encircling inflated leather with big, brawny hands, readying for the snap. Then the sudden sinking in the pit of my stomach as I jumped too soon, legs driving, unable to stop; the grunt of surprise from Krueger's lungs.

But in the dream I caught myself. A simple move it was, balancing my weight with one hand on the Astroturf, shoving off, scuttling beetle fashion back into position, lowering into my three-point stance for the required one-count. At the dream snap I blasted into Krueger, rammed him backward, arms flailing helplessly, beyond the goal line, and Jack took the handoff from Morton and waltzed in through a hole big enough for a forty-foot rig. Then in the dream I was hugging Jack, we were jumping up and down, he was slapping my helmet, joyous slaps like plastic tom-toms ringing in my ears.

I woke up. Suddenly. My eyes were at once wide open, and for seconds I listened for the clunk of the hack's boots in the hallway, the sound that had awakened me for three years at El Reno at five in the morning. But this wasn't El Reno. I rolled onto my side. Sun rays slanting over the carpet, the sliding glass door, beyond that the balcony, beyond the balcony the gently waving treetops in Lee Park. I shifted onto my back. My buddy the zebra, still up there on the wall. I stretched my stiff, aching muscles and sat up, then squinted at the illuminated clock radio on the nightstand: ten-thirty. I yawned and scratched my head. A familiar sinking sensation hit me.

The first time I'd felt it had been eight years ago when the indictment had come down; the sickening, gut-wrenching knowledge that what was happening was real, that it was happening to me and not some unknown someone in the newspaper. And here it was again, like a late-night rerun of a depressing movie. Jesus Christ, I was a target once more. I shook off the feeling as best I could and trudged in to take a shower. The steamy jets of water improved my disposition some, but not much. I shut off the nozzles, climbed out onto a green bath mat, rubbed my sopping hair with a towel. I finished drying off and stood naked in front of the lavatory.

I wiped a clear circle in the mist and looked in the mirror. Except for the dark circles under my eyes I didn't look too bad—square jaw, thin nose, a chin that I kept firm with a lot of facial exercise. There was a scab on my cheek where I'd scratched it during the night with a fingernail; such a scab generally appeared after I'd had the dream. The small wound itched slightly. I had a full head of thick and curly silver-gray hair; once when I'd been with the Cowboys an agent had tried to negotiate a TV commercial deal for me with Grecian Formula. If Joe DiMaggio could do it, why not me? When I'd gone to the Rams the deal had died on the vine.

I spread and stiffened my legs, put my hands on my waist, and rotated my upper body from side to side. A slimming exercise. Two hundred reps a day, plus bench presses, curls, dumbbell shrugs, and a lot of jogging, had trimmed off fifty pounds during my stay at El Reno without robbing me of any strength. Overall I'd done a pretty good job on my body. Hell, it was about all I had left. I finished the exercise and shaved, my hand so steady that I cut myself only once. I plastered toilet paper on the cut and went back into the bedroom. After the hot shower, the air-conditioning gave me a sudden chill. I sneezed.

I put on the same pair of jeans I'd worn the night before, along with clean white cotton socks, my Nike sneakers, and a red Lily Daché golf shirt with "GREAT SOUTHWEST G.C." stitched on the sleeve in white thread. Great Southwest was a step below D.A. Pierson's middle-class Lakewood Country Club. It was a haven for gamblers: bookies, poker players, gin hustlers, you name it. I was a couple of months behind in my dues, and as I rode the elevator to the ground floor I made a mental note to use part of the money I had left to catch up. To hell with food and car payments, I couldn't afford to come up on the club's delinquent list. Too embarrassing. I had a reputation to maintain. I went to the covered parking area and cranked up the 'Vette. I had some house-breaking to do.

The man at Rent-It-All, a skinny, sunburned guy wearing a white dress shirt with the sleeves rolled up to his elbows, had a ladder. It was a nifty eight-foot aluminum job. When he wondered aloud how I was going to carry an eight-foot ladder in a Corvette, he had me, so I wound up renting an old yellow Ford pickup as well. The guy even waived the deposit for the truck, as long as I left him the keys to the 'Vette, probably hoping that I wouldn't come back. I tossed the ladder in the bed and rattled off in the pickup, out the Dallas North Tollway to Donna's place.

Bent Tree wasn't really a neighborhood, at least not the kind of neighborhood I'd known growing up, with dogs trotting about and crapping on yards, and kids playing football with driveways as goal lines. Bent Tree was more like a Camelot: automatically watered lawns, clipped and manicured, spreading about high-roofed houses that were more like ski lodges; exposed aggregate drives, trashless streets, mind-boggling views of the rolling, tree-lined fairways of the kind of country club where everyone fixes their divots and no one yells, "Fuck!" after missing a short one.

Donna's house—Jack's house, too, but a woman like Donna seemed to me more to belong here than a guy like Jack—was a pale brown brick Gothic, homier-looking than most of the new-money shrines on the block. I parked in front, then carried the ladder up the drive and around to the side of the house. It was nearing twelve and the heat was stifling. I edged the ladder past a honeysuckle bush and leaned over to smell the flowers. A bee whined angrily by my ear. The temperature dropped sharply as I entered the shade at the side of the house. The ladder didn't weigh much, but the sweat was pouring down my face and sticking my shirt to my back.

The high stone fence surrounding the back portion of the property was designed like an ancient castle wall, miniature guard towers and all. I propped the ladder up, climbed up to vault one-handed over the top of the wall, and dropped into Jacqueline Brendy's playground. The tent on top of the swing set was drooping; one flap was torn and one wooden support was broken. I pictured Jacqueline and her merry band of little girls, and wondered that the poor old tent was still standing at all.

I hesitated before the waist-high cyclone fence that separated the playground from the backyard and pool area. I picked a leaf from the nearby hedge and chewed on it thoughtfully. Donna had warned me about triggering the alarm by opening the gate in the main wall, but she hadn't said anything about this little wire fence. I decided I'd better not take any chances, swung one leg up on top of the gate, and vaulted over. My pants leg caught on something; there was a soft, ripping sound. I stood inside the yard and examined the damage. A patch of hairy leg showed through a small triangular tear in my jeans. I murmured, "Shit."

The hot wind had picked up, now rustling the trees and hedges and sending small ripples over the surface of the pool. The water in the teardrop-shaped pool seemed bluer than when I'd sat there with Donna. The furniture was still in place, the cedar chaise longue on which Donna had reclined in the same slightly angled position that I remembered.

The trip across the front yard with the ladder and the climb over the two fences had kept my adrenaline pumping. But now, standing relaxed beside the pool, I was just a tad spooked. My rented ladder stood against the outside wall in plain view of anyone who happened by. "But, Officer," I'd say, "Mrs. Brendy told me to go right on in." "Sure, Mac," he'd say, "and I suppose she told you to climb over the fence so you wouldn't mess up the front porch any. Well, while we're at it, why don't I just run you up on the computer and see if you got a record or something." I suspected that if I were to get hauled downtown again, Detective Atchley would lock the door to the interview room, close the porthole, and take great pleasure in helping the city cop beat the everloving crap out of me. I took a deep breath, crossed the yard, climbed the two steps onto the redwood deck, stood in the shade beside the stained glass windows, and looked around. I didn't see anyone.

There was a straw woven welcome mat by the door; I lifted one corner. A gold brass Yale key lay shining in the sun, just as Donna had said. I grinned, picturing Donna hiding the key and thinking that she was being pretty slick. Under the mat is the first place that the bad guys look for keys; the second place is on the overhead ledge. I was still grinning as I picked up the key and went over to unlock the door. My grin faded. I wasn't going to need the key after all; someone had already been here.

The line that separated shade from sunlight was splitting the doorknob just about in half, and if it hadn't been for the sun rays I probably wouldn't have noticed the round hole in the pane, just to the left of the knob. I bent for a closer look. It was the work of a pro: a glass cutter used to make the hole, then the section of glass lifted carefully and silently away, probably with suction cups. I dug in my back pocket. As usual, I'd left the Smith & Wesson in the 'Vette, and I briefly wondered why I'd bought the damned gun in the first place. I tried the knob. It turned easily and the hinges creaked slightly as the door opened. I walked quietly in with a thousand tiny pinpricks parading up and down my spine.

I stood in the entryway and blinked a couple of times. I couldn't hear a sound, only the distant ticking of a clock. My gaze lingered for a moment on the Dimitri Vail painting over the mantel, and just looking at Donna's image in riding breeches astride the palomino started a rumbling in my breastbone. Jack's image seemed to be staring at me with a hands-off-my-girl look in its eyes. I thought, Yeah, buddy? Well, how 'bout you and Connie Swarm, huh? I made the journey through the den, past the long, low couch and baby grand piano, and leaned on mine and Jack's old pride and joy, the hand-carved bar. There was a faint odor of lemon Pledge, and I made a mental note to tell Donna that from now on the maid should use only real polish on the dark wood. Lemon oil would eventually ruin the bar's finish—at least that's what the Mexican guy we'd bought it from had said. I drummed my fingers on the surface, briefly thinking about fixing myself a drink, then changing my mind. The odds were that the burglary had been a random, nighttime affair, but if someone was still here in the house I'd best not be stumbling around having a toddy. A sudden flashback came to me, a recollection about an old habit of Jack's, so I went behind the bar and clicked open its lower cabinet.

The old habit had never changed. Jack had been squeamish about guns to the point of being silly about it. He'd refused to have a rifle or pistol anywhere on the premises where he lived, and even had once thrown away a pretty nifty derringer of mine when he'd found it tucked inside a kitchen cabinet. We'd almost come to blows over that one. But Jack had always kept a weapon of sorts, usually somewhere around the bar. I found the weapon on the second shelf, behind two unopened quarts of Jack Daniels Black Label and a jug of W.L. Wellers blended whiskey. It was a leg from a piano bench or small table, still with a threaded metal stud protruding from the fat end. I hefted it; the thing made a pretty good club. I carried it with me over to the hand-carved bookcases that ran the length of one wall. Surely, though, whoever had been here before me was long gone. Or if they were still in the house they'd turn out to be a seventy-pound midget without a gun. I stood on tiptoes and looked over the titles in the bookcase.

Jesus, what book was it that I was looking for? When I'd visited him at the jail, Jack had told me that the key to the mini-warehouse was taped inside the cover of a book that nobody would ever read. Well, as far as I was concerned, nobody would ever read any of these books. I went down the line: *Great Expectations . . . The Foxes of Harrow . . . Leaves of Grass*. Jesus Christ, Jack, who were you trying to kid? You never read any of this stuff in your life. *Oliver Twist . . . Hawaii . . . Texas . . . Moby Dick*, the great white whale. Or was it a shark? The book had a navy cover with gilt lettering that had faded in spots, and it looked really musty and old. I reached for it, then froze as, somewhere in the house, a board creaked.

It could have been nothing more than the house settling, maybe the wind causing the framing to shift. I wasn't sure. I stood away from the bookcase and listened. Nothing. I thought, To hell with it, stretched out, and took *Moby Dick* down from the shelf. The volume beside it, *The Great Gatsby*, tilted sideways and toppled against the remaining books with a soft thud.

I found the key taped inside the front cover, a small, flat little silver key like the ones that the post office issued. There was a number inscribed on the round end—14B. The key joined the door key I'd found under the mat in my right pants pocket. I softly laid the book on a nearby table and walked to the front of the house, holding the club in a death grip.

The foot of the stairs was about three yards inside the front door, which was heavy, carved oak and held an octagonal leaded glass window at eye level. Just beside the door stood a full-length grandfather clock, probably a real antique, with a gold pendulum the diameter of a basketball swinging back and forth, back and forth, ticking and tocking. The clock showed five minutes after twelve with beveled golden hands. I ascended the stairs. They were carpeted in rich blue, and as I went up, my feet sank noiselessly into three-quarter-inch foam padding. The bannister was dark polished wood supported by curved wrought iron. I touched the bannister every couple of steps or so.

Several pictures hung along the way in plain gold frames. Some were of Jacqueline, some of Donna, others of Jack, a few of the three of them together. One of Donna's poses caused me to catch my breath: her long, supple legs, bare and tan, in a pair of tight white shorts as she stood on tiptoes and grinned a little devilish cheesecake into the camera. She was on the deck of a yacht with swelling blue waves in the background, and one arm was raised over her head. Her fingertips were touching the snout of a huge fish—a blue marlin; Jesus, I knew guys back in Corpus who would've died to have caught that beauty—which was suspended tail downward over the deck.

Farther on down the line was a photo of Donna's dad, and beside it a shot of her brother, Buddy. They were old pictures, dating sometime around when I'd been in high school, and both Mr. Morley and Buddy looked exactly as I remembered them. Buddy in particular, deeply tanned, a wide grin on his square, honest face, in jeans along with white socks and black penny loafers, leaning on the roof of his '62 Thunderbird. I remembered the car as well—did I ever. It had transported me and Buddy on many a wild weekend across the border, when our folks had thought we were in for some weekend fishing. Mr. Morley had passed away in '71—I was pretty sure of the year—and as far as I knew Mrs. Morley still lived in the same house where Buddy and Donna had grown up. Next to Buddy's picture was a cuddly photo of Jacqueline Brendy, age about three, wearing a flowered party dress and giving a cute pixie smile over her shoulder. I went up two more steps, glanced at the picture just below the second-story landing, then did a double take, and stared hard at the photo. My mouth was hanging open like a fly trap.

It was Donna and Jack, arms about each other's waists, on the deck of the same boat where Donna had posed with the unlucky marlin. She was wearing the same pair of hugging white shorts, and one of the marlin's huge tail fins was visible on the far right edge of the picture. But it wasn't Jack and Donna I was gaping at. It was the guy in the picture with them: a tall, stoop-shouldered guy with jug handle ears and a big winning grin, and who was wearing a dark blue blazer with white deck pants. I'd seen this guy not too long ago, but when I'd seen him he'd been in a slightly different condition than in this picture. It was the same citizen who'd been on the couch at Connie Swarm's, getting high with Crystal. The one who'd recognized me, but whom I hadn't been able to place.

I snapped my jaw back into its socket, went on upstairs and found the master bedroom, stood just inside the door, and shook the cobwebs out of my brain. Who *was* that fucking guy? I still didn't know.

I crept inside both closets, one at a time, and sneaked up on no one. Ditto with the bathroom; I stood for several seconds with the shower curtain yanked aside, threatening thin air with my club. Then I went back into the bedroom and sat on the edge of the bed. It was a four-poster king-size with a canopy and a blue quilted spread, and the thought of Jack and Donna in the bed making love sent a quiver jumping across my scalp. I picked up the white princess phone, fished a folded slip of paper from my pocket, read the number, and called Ramada Inn Disney World, in Orlando.

An operator confirmed that I had the Ramada Inn and

told me to have a nice day, sounding as though she was talking through her nose. I gave her Donna's room number, and as I listened to a series of monotonous three-second buzzes, I had a fleeting moment of panic. I'd told her twelve o'clock—hell, in Florida it was a few minutes after one. What if she wasn't there? There was a sharp click on the line and Donna's soft, lovely voice said hello.

"I was afraid I'd missed you," I said.

"Rick. You nearly did. Jacqueline's ding-donging about going to the Haunted House and Twenty Thousand Leagues Under the Sea to the point that I can't hold her off much longer."

"Guess what, Donna. I'm sitting on your bed."

"I wish."

A small lump stuck in my throat. I cleared it away. "Your house in Dallas, goofy. I'm . . . looking around." I'd almost told her about the hole in the downstairs window, but decided she had enough to worry about.

"I don't think I'd like to be in that house right now," she said, her voice suddenly tiny and frightened. "Maybe later, but not now. Have you found anything?"

I touched the key through the fabric of my pants. "Not much. I've got more questions, though."

She laughed, the teasing lilt suddenly returning to her voice. "I'll answer on one condition, that you'll fly down here in a day or two. I'm keeping up a pretty good front, if I do say so myself, but I need some moral support. Some physical support, too." She breathed softly, then said, "Shameless, huh?"

Little Donna Sue, the subject of most of my dreams during the years at El Reno, now the target of a possible murder indictment that was mostly my fault. I said, "Sure, I'll come. The questions. They're pretty important to me."

"Well, ask them."

"I need to look at a copy of the papers you signed for Jack. The ones that have to do with Lorraine Daley's house."

"Oh, they won't be around there. Jack never kept anything like that at home. Fred Cassel will have a copy."

Good old stand-up Fred. The piano stool leg lay beside me on the covers like a small brown stump. I said, "I'll pay Mr.

134   A. W. Gray

Cassel a visit. Another thing, Donna, something I'm buffaloed about. There's a picture hanging by your staircase, of
you and Jack on a big boat beside a big fish. Who's the
guy in the picture with you, the one dressed up like *H.M.S.
Pinafore?*"

She laughed again. "Why, don't you know?"

"Should I?"

"Well, I don't guess he's that famous. Lou James, Louis P.
James. He was the state senator from our district, ran for
governor. Jack did a lot of chasing around after those kind
of people. That trip on the boat, that was the only time I ever
met the man, but Jack insisted on displaying the picture."

I guess the guy's identity should have surprised me more
than it did, but it figured. I even remembered where I'd seen
him before Connie Swarm's. At a couple of rah-rah, in-
crowd-only parties back when I was playing ball, another
time at a fund-raiser given by Clint Murchison, the Cowboys'
owner at the time. The press had had a field day with an
affair between Connie Swarm and a gubernatorial candidate.
Same guy, Louis P. James.

Donna's voice cut through the fog bank. "Is something
wrong?"

I'd been clutching the phone and staring off into space.
"Nothing," I said. "Just thinking." The grandfather clock at
the foot of the stairs was chiming twelve-thirty. For some
reason it sounded odd.

"I thought you were using the phone in my bedroom,"
Donna said.

"I am."

"You can't be. I can't hear the grandfather clock from my
bedroom. Doesn't it have the sweetest chime?"

Yeah, it did, just the cutest little chime I'd ever heard.
Only the tinny noise of the clock striking hadn't come to me
in the conventional way, with the sound waves traveling up
the stairs into the bedroom. The single bong had come to
my ears electronically, transmitted through the telephone.
As realization flooded over me, my gaze rested on a bureau,
a tall French Provincial piece against the far wall. The top
drawer was partway open and some papers—what looked to
be some handwritten sheets and a white business envelope

with some typewriting on it—were sticking in disarray from the drawer as though somebody'd been going through them.

I reached down and gripped the piano stool leg. "Think carefully, Donna. Picture me in your bedroom. Now, where are the other phone extensions? The downstairs ones first." I shifted my gaze to the open bedroom door; beyond the door in the hallway was a wood rolling server on rich shag carpet.

"Well," Donna said, "there's one on a little table at the foot of the stairs, on your left as you go down. Another in the den by the sofa. One on the kitchen that hangs—"

She stopped in mid-sentence as a sharp click sounded over the line. Donna then said, "Rick? Are you still there?" Suddenly her voice was clear as a bell and the static I'd been hearing had disappeared. She said again, "Rick?"

"Yeah, I'm here," I said. "Look, I'll have to get back to you." I dropped the receiver onto the hook as Donna's voice, tiny, frightened and far away, started to say more. I carried my club out into the hallway with beads of sweat popping out on my brow. On the rolling server was a vase holding long-stemmed roses. The flowers were beginning to droop and wilt.

There was no one on the stairs; from where I stood on the second-story landing the bottom half of the front door was visible. I brandished the piano stool leg over my head, took a deep breath, and charged downward. Between short, raspy breaths I yelled, "You son of a bitch, I'm coming." I was either going to scare the hell out of somebody or send them into giggling hysterics.

I thundered around the bannister, my feet thudding on hallway tiles, and raced into the den. I stopped in my tracks. There was no one in the den, only stone silence and the painting of Donna and Jack and the palomino. I pictured someone crouched behind the bar, took hesitant steps, club ready, had a look. Nothing. The Dallas Cowboy team picture was slightly tilted in its frame. I straightened it. As I did, a draft hit my cheek; I turned toward the back of the house. The door leading to the redwood deck stood open; the flowered drapes rippled and billowed in the wind. I went outside.

Not a sign of anyone on the deck; choppy, wind-generated

waves rolled across the surface of the pool. As I started to go down the steps, white light flashed in the periphery of my vision accompanied by a small explosion, like a Chinese firecracker. Something whanged close to my feet, knocked a good-sized splinter from the redwood. I went down in the yard, rolling, the jarring fall sending pain shooting through my knee. Another explosion and something whined a foot over my head.

I held my breath for an hour's worth of seconds as my heart tried its damnedest to tear through my rib cage. There were no more shots, no further sound other than the wind rustling the trees and hedges. Finally I rose, went over to the wire fence and looked into Jacqueline Brendy's playground. I was still carrying my club.

The gate in the high brick wall, iron painted white and molded into the shape of a grapevine, stood open. On top of the wall a yellow light flashed on and off, on and off, and I looked stupidly at the light for a few seconds before it dawned on me what had happened. Whoever had gone through the gate had triggered the alarm. Goody, the law was on its way.

I went back through the house and exited by the front door. My rented pickup stood where I had left it, and I got in and drove away. A half block down the street, a black and white Dallas police cruiser passed me going in the opposite direction. Its lights were flashing and its siren was hooting. Only then did I remember the ladder, still propped against the wall at the back of Donna's house. The metal tag from Rent-It-All was attached to one of the ladder's lower rungs.

It was obvious from the look on his face that the skinny guy from Rent-It-All had had a bad day, and he saw the missing ladder as a chance to give somebody a ration of shit. There wasn't much for me to do but listen to him.

He said, "Buddy, you got any idea how long I could stay in business if everybody treated my stuff like that? About that"—he raised a hand to ear level and snapped his fingers—"long. Hells bells." He folded pipe-stem arms and leaned against his side of the counter. He was chewing a toothpick and a yellow pencil was stuck behind his ear. The old black Burroughs cash register was showing a No Sale flag in its window.

"Look," I said, "I told you twice I was sorry and I'd pay for the ladder. What's it worth?" I fished in my pocket and brought out my bankroll.

He eyed the bills. A hundred was exposed. "How much it cost ain't really the point," he said. "It's the loss in income. Aluminum ladders is hard to come by as young pussy, case you ain't never tried to buy one. How much rentals it's going to cost me before I can replace the damn thing, that's the question." On a low shelf behind him sat three TV sets—two RCAs, and even an old Philco—which looked as though they'd been around when "The Milton Berle Show" was leading the ratings.

"Look," I said. "A couple of hundred should take care of it, shouldn't it?" I laid two bills face-up on the counter and shoved them in his direction.

He removed the toothpick, examined its end, then used it to spear a pulpy lump of something-or-other from between his teeth. He looked the lump over, then swallowed it. A real Emily Post fan. He said, "Make it three hundred."

"*Three*? Bullshit."

"Three," he said. "Or the Corvette stays parked right where it is."

I didn't have any idea how long it would be before the cops read the tag on the ladder and called this guy, but it could happen any second. The guy had me by the short hairs. I dropped another bill on the counter. "How's that?" I said.

"More like it," he said, dinging open the register, fishing my keys out—they were on a chain along with a big orange plastic numeral 1—and dropping them over in front of me. He took the pencil from behind his ear and held it poised over a pad. "I'll give you a receipt, everything legit."

The phone rang, a too loud, jangly sound. He gave me a wait-a-minute wave and picked up the receiver. "Yeah, Rent-It-All. Bob speakin'." Then arched a thin eyebrow in my direction as he listened. "Yeah, it's my ladder. What about it?" he said.

I scooped up my keys and walked toward the exit, trying hard not to break into a mad dash.

He covered the mouthpiece with his palm. "Hey, bud, wait a minute."

I broke into a jog, left the building, ran across the asphalt to the 'Vette. I cranked the engine and spun rubber, fishtailing, barely avoiding a crack-up with a Dodge van as I wheeled onto Cedar Springs Road. Visible in my sideview mirror, the Rent-It-All guy came out on the curb, shook his fist, yelled something I couldn't hear, and finally shot me the finger. He was standing there with his middle digit upraised as he disappeared from view.

As I passed the entrance to DFW Airport and continued west in Highway 183, a Delta 747 whined overhead and rode the breeze in a lumbering descent. I didn't have the slightest idea what the speed limit was. There didn't seem to be any signs; half the cars were going forty, the other half seventy. I couldn't afford a ticket; if a cop were to stop me I'd probably be breathing my last gulp of free air for a while. Likely there were already warrants on me for the break-in at Donna's house. I took a white-knuckled grip on the steering wheel, kept the needle firmly on sixty, and listened to a country singer look for love in all the wrong places on the wraparound. The sun was setting, a blinding ball of fire directly in my path on the western horizon; I lowered the visor, hunched over the wheel, and squinted down the road.

Euless Main Street flashed by; Central Drive, with its single tall bank building on the right; golden McDonald's arches and a green, blue, and white Wendy's Hamburgers sign on the Brown Trail access road. I passed underneath a green luminescent sign reading, "Bedford-Euless Rd—1 mi." I slowed gradually and eased over, took the Bedford-Euless exit, and came to a halt behind snarled traffic waiting for the light. When a Buick Park Avenue stopped behind me and honked, I jumped and banged my head on the ceiling. I was that jittery. The light changed and the traffic moved on. I followed, turned left in front of a Bennigan's Tavern, and crossed underneath the freeway, drove past Northeast Mall and its jammed parking lot, its big signs over the J.C. Penneys and the Sears, its marquee stating that the U.A. Cine was showing Steven Spielberg's *Empire of the Sun*, Danny DeVito in *Throw Momma from the Train*, and *Broadcast News*, starring William Hurt, Albert Brooks, and Holly Hunter. The mini-warehouse was a block down on my left. It was called U-Storit, and as I turned in and parked, I wondered briefly if these people knew the guy from Rent-It-All. I went inside, digging in my pocket for the key and tensing myself to break and run at the first sign of trouble.

For once, nobody gave me a hard time. The attendant was a young girl with stringy dishwater blond hair and braces on her teeth, and she was a whole lot more interested in the *National Enquirer* that she was reading than she was in me. I signed the register "Jack Landry," smirking at the alias in spite of myself, and showed her my key. She said, "Thank you," in a listless monotone, and went on reading about the trouble between Bonnie Prince Charlie and Princess Di. I found Jack's vault, 14B, in the second row of lockers. The vault had a thick blue steel door and a big padlock. As I inserted the key, I expected that it wouldn't work, sure as I was that there would be a foul-up *somewhere*, but the key turned easily and the lock popped open. Inside the locker was a brown Samsonite carrying case, and I opened it also.

I don't suppose that it was more than a couple of minutes that I stared at the bundles of hundred-dollar bills and the two cellophane bags of white powder, but it seemed much longer. The countless pictures of Benjamin Franklin seemed to leap from the bills, grin, and recite verses from *Poor Richard's Almanac*. Seen through filmy cellophane, the cocaine was the color of tapioca pudding. I picked up one of the bags and hefted it; it was as heavy as double ankle weights. I snapped the case shut and took it with me. The girl continued to ignore me as I went by, and I made it to the 'Vette without being surrounded and robbed. As I drove back to the freeway, the air came out of my lungs in a relieved whoosh.

I said to Sweaty Mathis, "Look, it's just for a few days. It won't be in your way, I guarantee you." I'd just hidden the carrying case, contents and all, in the bottom drawer of a vacant desk at the rear of Sweaty's office. One packet of bills—each wrapper contained ten thousand dollars, and there were fifty packages in all—was in the 'Vette's glove compartment. I didn't think that Jack would miss it.

Sweaty had a jeweler's magnifying glass squinched into his eye socket and was examining a diamond bracelet that someone had put up as collateral for bail. He wore a vest and tie. His tie was loosened and the collar of his white shirt was soiled. "Naw, it's okay," he said, "this ain't nothing but a hatcheck stand. So you're going to fuck off a few more days. Us po' folk got to work on Sunday." He removed the eyeglass and laid down the bracelet. "What about your buddy Breaux, why don't you leave whatever it is with him?"

I sat down in front of Sweaty's desk in a rickety leather swivel chair. The chair creaked. A spring poked my butt. I shifted my position. "I haven't seen Bodie in a while. Look, Sweat, I need to talk to you."

"What for? I ain't in the loan business." He picked up the bracelet and held it in his chubby fingers. "High quality, my ass. There's flaws here a blind man could spot."

"How much bond did you post with the bracelet as collateral?" I said. "Fifty bucks? Tell 'em to kick in a Piaget watch to boot and you'd make it a hundred? Come on, Sweat, I need to get down with you."

He set the eyepiece upright and cocked his head to one side. "You need a new gag writer, Bannion. The FBI was by here yesterday. That ain't funny."

So they'd already been here. There wasn't a thing Sweaty could tell them that would help as far as my relationship with Jack Brendy was concerned, but the feds would know that. They'd just come by to let Sweaty, along with anybody else that happened to know me, understand that they had me under investigation. I'd been through it before. "I guess I'm in trouble," I said.

"So what's new?" Sweaty said.

"That's what I want to talk to you about. Listen, I could get indicted any time for killing Jack Brendy. They've probably already got a warrant for me for burglarizing Jack's house. I've got to keep on the move, not stay where anybody can home in on me. The stuff in the case, well, it's pretty important. Nobody can know I've left it here except you."

Sweaty rubbed his face with his palms and watched me. He liked me a whole lot more than he let on. At least I hoped he did. Finally he said, "You do things ass-backwards. First you kill the guy, then you bust into his house. Ought to be the other way around. Listen, I don't want to know any more. You're a hot potato and I got no business fucking with you. You can leave the—I don't give a shit what it is. Anybody finds it here, I ain't never seen it before."

"You're a prince, Sweaty." I checked my watch: eight-thirty. Outside Sweaty's ground-floor office, dusk was turning to dark and lights were winking on. "And don't worry," I said. "Nothing comes back to you. You got my word on that, and you know me well enough to know I mean it. I'll be in touch. Tonight I think I'll take in a strip show, I need to blow off a little steam."

T W E L V E

I'd never been a titty-bar fan, and I'd never liked bars located far out in the country. I normally did my drinking in places where the girls weren't paid to be there, and where if there wasn't any action it was a short walk in any direction to the next watering hole. Baby Doll's was a titty-bar way out in the country, on Highway 157 in Grand Prairie, and it was a couple of miles down the road from the nearest civilization. Two strikes against the joint, as far as I was concerned.

Lorraine Daley had her name in lights, on a computerized marquee that ran the length of the white stucco building, and which alternated its flashing lights to spell out, "CONNIE SWARM," and then, "HOT TO TROT," a few seconds apart. The parking lot would hold about a hundred cars, and was three quarters full of Chryslers, Caddys, Chevys, and big super-cab pickups with gun racks across the back windows. It seemed there were a lot of folks who didn't care what I thought about titty-bars out in the country.

I let the 'Vette idle through the dusty gravel parking lot while I made up my mind where to park. The choice wasn't an easy one. If I stopped close to the highway, the car would be visible to passersby, and I didn't have any way of knowing if there was a warrant for me or if the highway patrol would be carrying a hot sheet on the 'Vette. But if I parked in close to the building, I was likely to be hemmed in if I had to leave in a hurry. Finally I chose the quick exit and stopped at the end of the nearest row of cars to the highway. I parked with the 'Vette's nose pointed away from the building, and didn't hesitate for a second about picking up the Smith & Wesson, checking to be sure it was loaded, and jamming it into my back pocket. So what if it was a felony to carry a firearm into a bar? The way the charges were piling up, what difference did one more make? The more the merrier. I got out and made my way toward the club entrance. The glow from the neon created a hazy film and blotted out the stars overhead.

A timid-looking, middle-aged balding guy came out of the front door and passed me going in the opposite direction. He shot me a hurried glance, did a double-take, and quickened his pace as he went to his car. I hadn't realized that I was glaring at the guy, but I had been. Probably some poor schnook on his way home to mama and hoping she didn't find out where he'd been, but to hell with it. From now on I was giving *everybody* the once-over.

I'd been so busy watching the scared little guy that I hadn't heard the gravel crunching underneath the tires of the vehicle that now blocked my path. It took a couple of seconds for it to dawn on me that the vehicle was a Jeep convertible with the top down, then a couple of more seconds for me to snap that it was Breaux's jeep. Sitting behind the wheel was Bodie himself. He was watching me from underneath the yellow bill of his cap, and he was scratching his chin.

We locked gazes. Bodie didn't smile.

I took a short, jogging step forward. "Bodie, I—"

He popped his clutch; the Jeep's rear tires spun on gravel. Small rocks banged painfully against my chest. The Jeep fishtailed out of the parking lot, straightened itself out, and disappeared over a hill. I stared after it, almost went back to the 'Vette to give chase, then shrugged my shoulders, and went inside. I wasn't that surprised to see Breaux: Baby Doll's was one of his regular hangouts. Nor could I worry over what he thought of me, since at the moment I had other things on my mind.

There was a two-dollar cover charge (another thing that bugged me about titty-bars) collected by a tall, rangy youngster with permed hair down to his shoulders and just enough peach fuzz on his upper lip to make the beginnings of a mustache. I thumbed through my dwindling bankroll—I hadn't dug into the ten thousand in the 'Vette's glove box as yet—located two singles, and gave them to him. He laid the money lengthwise in a change drawer, closed the drawer, and proceeded to ignore me.

I leaned over the counter toward him. "Listen," I said, "I need to speak to Connie Swarm."

He eyed me as though he'd rather take a nap than answer. "You and every other hard-dick," he said. He gestured toward the club's interior, where men sat at tables alone and in pairs and threesomes. Amid the hovering smoke, an occasional quick point of light from a cigarette glowed. "Look," he said, "when the girls are on break they have drinks with the customers. Tell the waitress. If you buy Connie a drink, maybe she'll sit a spell. A spell here and a spell there." This boy needed some etiquette lessons.

I glanced toward the stage, where a lanky brunette was doing a bored, hippy shuffle to the sounds of "Money Honey" pouring from the jukebox. She was wearing nothing but a G-string. I said to the doorman, "Well, it looks to me like Connie's having a break now, that's not her. She having a break?"

He blinked at me. "I don't know. Is she?" He sat down, picked up a paperback novel, and began to read by the single shaded lamp on the counter.

I resisted the urge to reach over and pull his hair. I tried another question. "Say, you know a guy comes in here named Bodie Breaux?"

He glanced up, dog-eared a corner of his book, closed it and set it aside, then stood. He had a couple of inches on me, or maybe the hair piled up on his head just made it appear that way. He beckoned with his index finger. I leaned closer. He said into my ear, "Look, man, I'm going to tell you one time. There ain't no Information sign on this here counter. Now, you want to talk to Connie Swarm, ask the waitress. You want to see Bodie Breaux, you put an ad in the paper. You want your two bucks back you can take a walk, I don't give a shit. You understand?"

My hand balled into a fist and had risen to waist level before I gained control of myself. I let my breath out slowly. Whatever he was dishing out, I was going to have to take. I simply couldn't afford trouble. I said from between clenched jaws, "Thanks. I'll keep it in mind." Then I went into the club, chalking the doorman up as another thing I didn't like about titty-bars. I found an unoccupied table close to the bar and about three yards from the stage and sat down.

The brunette was still doing her shuffle, her feet now on a level with my eyes. A spot bathed her in soft blue light as her hips gyrated and her small breasts quivered. I stifled a yawn. I've got nothing against watching young ladies take their clothes off; in private I've even been known to like it on occasion. It was just that the atmosphere of the Baby Doll's of the world wasn't my cup of tea. Anonymous men with nothing in common, watching a girl undress; a girl who couldn't care less whether the men were there or not so long as her paycheck came on time. Maybe somebody's scene, but not for me.

A waitress approached. She was young, maybe even too young to be working in Baby Doll's. She had a cute button nose and would have been pretty even in daylight. She wore a thigh-length mini and spike heels. She shifted a cud of gum to one side of her mouth and said, "Kin ah hepya?"

I'd already made up my mind to drink, just about the time the kid at the door had made his first unfunny remark. I told the waitress I wanted Cutty neat, water back. She nodded, took a couple of jiggly steps in the direction of the bar, then came back to me. She leaned over so that I could look down her blouse. She had a lot of cleavage. She said, "Ah kin joinya if you buy me one."

I shook my head. Politely, I hoped. "No thanks, but you can do me a favor. Tell Connie Swarm that Bodie's friend is here to see her. There's a tip in it for you."

Her lips bunched into a pout. "Connie's the star, mister.

Everbody wants to sit with her. Ah kin give you more 'tention."

I mulled that one over, wondering how I could possibly have more tension than I already had, then got it. Oh, *attention*. I shook my head once more. "Listen, if I was looking for company you'd be it, but I got some business with Connie. Maybe later, huh? For now, just talk to Connie, okay?" I dropped a five-dollar bill on her tip tray, and it didn't make me wince near as much as the two bucks at the door had.

She tucked the five into her waistband, making sure the money was out of my reach before saying, "If you wait a minute, you can tell her yourself. Connie's up, soon as Sherry's finished." She gestured toward the brunette on stage, and appeared ready to run if I tried to make a grab for the five bucks.

The brunette was doing some bumps and grinds in front of a black guy. He was standing beside a table directly across from me and was practically drooling on the stage. He was stuffing dollar bills into her G-string, and I was bright enough to figure out that she was Sherry. I thanked the waitress and said that I'd wait. She brought my drink—the whiskey in a stubby rock glass and the water back in a tall tumbler—then went over and joined two men seated a couple of tables away. I hoped that they communicated with her better than I had.

The brunette on stage ended her act with a little wiggle and a squeal that sounded sort of relieved. She hurried around the perimeter of the stage, picking up a wispy bra, a pair of mesh hose with black garters still attached, and a flowered sheath dress. She clasped the wad of clothing to her bosom, bounced down the steps, and started across the floor. The black guy came after her, grabbed her arm, and whispered something in her ear. She nodded and hustled on her way, then went behind the bar and through a doorway. Judging from the number of half-dressed females coming and going from that direction, that was where the dressing room was located. The black guy went back to his table and sank slowly into his seat. Onstage, the footlights changed from blue to red.

Suddenly the overture from *2001—A Space Odyssey*

boomed over the speakers, and I halfway expected Elvis himself to charge into the arena. A tenor voice superimposed
itself over the music, and it was with a pretty stiff jolt that
I realized that the voice belonged to the smart-aleck kid at
the door. He was now hunched over a microphone on the
counter, and his broadcast voice wasn't bad at all. Amid
drumrolls and trumpets he said, "And now what you've been
waiting for. Baby Doll's proudly presents . . . back home
from her triumphant tour . . . Conneee . . . *Swarm!*" Just as
I wondered what tour Connie could've been on since I'd seen
her at the lake house, the music quickened its pace and
Connie herself came around the end of the bar and paraded
onstage.

Paraded was a pretty good word for it: shoulders back,
boobs out, tight fanny wiggling from side to side. She
stopped and bowed low at the table where my waitress sat
with the two guys. The waitress leaned over and whispered
something in Connie's ear. Connie nodded and moved on,
blowing kisses in all directions. There was applause, first
only a smattering, then loud and boistrous clapping accompanied by cheers and whistles by the time Connie reached
the foot of the steps. She showed a quick hip thrust to an
enraptured pimply-faced boy seated alone, and I thought he
was going to fall out of his chair. Then Connie hop-skipped
up the stairs to center stage. Jesus, I was clapping myself. I
hated to admit it, but Miss Connie Swarm was electric as
hell.

She was wearing a filmy summer dress in blended shades
of pink and gold. The dress had a pleated skirt that swirled
around her thighs, and her blond hair was in waist-length
pigtails with the front of her hair wanton and carefully tousled. The footlights accentuated her tan; she wore a bright
pink lip gloss. Her cheeks were flushed with excitement and
she wasn't faking it. I'd thought that Connie had sounded
pretty dumb the other night, and she hadn't been faking that,
either, but here in her element the girl was something else.
A hush fell over the audience as she stood at attention, arms
at her sides, her head bowed. Jumpy music sounded, "One
Mint Julep," an old, old oldie. She moved her hips from side
to side, slowly at first, then picking up the tempo, wanton,

jerky movements that didn't look jerky at all. I swigged a
mouthful of scotch and chased it with water.

Connie's act brought the house down. She didn't just strip;
she yanked her clothes off in a frenzy, and as she cast them
aside there was a lusty challenge on her lips and in her
eyes. It had to be an illusion, of course, but the temperature
actually seemed to rise a few degrees as she moved around
up there. Naked but for a sequined G-string, upturned
breasts proud, she writhed. She strutted. She did a bouncy
stroll. She was pure poison, I didn't have any doubts about
that, but she was poison packaged in a way that caused men
to stand in line for a taste of it. And for a few minutes there
I couldn't blame a single one of them.

She finished her performance the same way she'd started
it, with a flourish that had every man in the club—including
me by then—straining like leashed Dobermans catching the
scent of a bitch in heat. The finale was a blistering, writhing,
show-it-all strut done to "Love Is Strange," a fifties Mickey
and Sylvia number reincarnated on the sound track from
Dirty Dancing. Her dancing was dirty, all right, dirty and
seamy and earthy and enough to warrant a call to the fire
department. She finished standing on one bare tanned leg,
her other leg straight out in front and bent at the knee like
a show's pony's; her arms at her sides, her breasts thrusting
proudly forward, her eyes shut tightly, her lips parted long-
ingly. She held the pose for a full thirty seconds after the
song had ended, and during that time a pin dropping would
have sounded like a heavy footfall.

The dancer who had preceded Connie—Sherry, in case anyone in the place remembered her by now—had swept her
clothes up in a flurry of modesty and had left the stage with
the garments as a shield. Not so with Connie Swarm. She
did bother to pick up her things, probably in compliance
with a club rule against cluttering the stage, but there the
similarity ended. Connie tossed her dress and lacy bra over
one arm, suspended her high-heeled sandals from her fingers
by the ankle straps, and pranced away as though she was at
home alone and headed for the laundry room. One guy, a
man in his fifties or sixties with a snow-white goatee, blew
kisses at her with both hands as she passed by his table. She

interrupted her walk long enough to kiss the guy on his bald head and pinch his cheek. He said something to her that I couldn't hear over the claps and whistles. She hesitated, then with an elfin grin tossed him her bra. He put the cups on top of his head like rabbit ears and tilted the straps underneath his chin like a bonnet. Connie really seemed to get a kick out of that; she threw back her head and laughed, golden pigtails flying around her bare waist. Then she moved a few more steps toward the dressing room, did a sudden, bouncy column-left, and made a beeline for my table. She sat down across from me and tossed her clothes, minus bra, onto an empty chair. She crossed her shapely legs. She folded her arms. She smiled. Connie in the flesh.

"So, darlin'," she said, "nobody's getting choked in this place, what you doing here? I thought you only showed up to chase tough guys away."

Well, I'd asked for her. I just wasn't ready for Connie in the buff. I cleared my throat. "I need to talk to you. Would you like to, well, put some clothes on?" Men at nearby tables were gawking. I didn't blame them.

She cupped a dainty hand, covered her mouth, and giggled. The movement caused a tousled bang to rise, then fall softly back into place. "Why, the big, tough man is em-*bar*-rassed, folks. This is a strip show, darlin'. What do I need clothes for? I'm glad you came by, anyway, I got a bone to pick with you." Visible behind her, the bartender was squirting something from a liquor gun into a glass. A couple of men quit staring at us, swiveled on their stools, and faced the bar.

"A bone? What for?" I said.

"You made my chubby cherub disappear," she said. "Skeezix, what happened to him? I'm havin' to stay in that great big house all alone, and it's scare-ree." She tossed her head. Her pigtails wiggled. She didn't look scared at all.

I was having trouble picturing Skeezix as a cherub, halo suspended over his head, playing a harp. "You haven't heard from him at all?" I said. I'd intended to check up on Skeezix myself, but with everything else going on I hadn't gotten around to it.

"Not a lovin' word. I want to ask Bodie if he knows, but

I can't get ahold of him. What's goin' on?" She blinked at me with the same vacant expression she'd worn the other night, and it dawned on me that the exit Breaux and I had made with Skeezix probably had looked to Connie as though we were all the best of pals.

"Why can't you get in touch with him?" I said. "I just saw Bodie a few minutes ago, outside in the parking lot."

"Here at Baby Doll's? Well, he hadn' been in to see me." Connie paused as the pouty-lipped waitress approached and stood by expectantly. "Hey, no, Sandy, nothin' for me," Connie said. "This guy is a friend for real, he's not buyin' me anything." She was talking pretty loud, and guys at nearby tables shot surprised looks in my direction. Probably they'd all been buying drinks for Connie and had thought that they were friends for real as well. The waitress went on her way, and Connie said, "That's really funny that Bodie'd be right outside and not even come by to say hidy."

I thought that Breaux's behavior was pretty strange as well, and a tiny nagging began at the back of my mind. If he hadn't even gone inside the place, what in hell had Breaux been doing in the parking lot? Following *me*? Wouldn't make sense. I drank some scotch.

Connie said, "Rick. That's your name, huh? Rick."

I nodded.

She brightened as though she'd just scored high on a pop quiz. "I thought I remembered it right," she said. She adjusted her position, lifting one leg and clasping her hands over her knee. Her bare upper arms compressed her breasts together. She said, "So, Rick. Whatcha want?"

"I'm working a few things out that might help my old buddy Skeezix, as a matter of fact," I said. "It's some private stuff that we probably shouldn't discuss here."

She ran the tip of her little finger across her lower lip. "Well, I don't know. Say, you sure you're not just tryin' to get me off someplace alone?"

"Nothing like that, honest. Skeezix being out of town for a while, I'm looking after his interests. Your house, that's one thing I'm interested in." What I was telling her wasn't a lie, not a hundred percent lie. I did want to see the papers on her house, especially after what Donna had told me over the phone. Plus, it might help Skeezix if I could find out who had Jack killed—it might keep the little twerp alive. What I really wanted to visit with Connie about had to do with the pictures featuring her and Jack, but I didn't want to spring that on her as yet.

"Well, since you're bein' *honest* . . ." She favored me with a coquettish blink. "If you want to find out about my house, I guess the best place to do that is at my house. So, darlin', you want to follow me home?"

She'd thrown me a curve and the twinkle in her eye said that she'd intended to. No rocket scientist here, but not many men would be the favorite over Connie in the boy-versus-girl department. I said, "Your house . . . ? Now?"

"No time like the present," she said. She stood and gathered up her clothes, then bent over close to me with her nipples brushing the tabletop. "And close your mouth, darlin', you look like you're tryin' to catch some flies. Don't worry, I'll run back and get dressed before we go. I wouldn' want to embarrass you none."

Connie Swarm drove the same way she danced, as though the devil himself were in hot pursuit and she wasn't about to let him catch her, but at the same time she didn't want him to stop trying. As I followed the tail lamps of her Trans Am north on I-35, she zipped in and out in speeding traffic, changing lanes without signaling, and sometimes would whiz completely out of sight. But each time I'd thought I'd lost her for good, her brake lights would flash into view, then she'd stick her arm out the window and give me a come-on wave. Visible through the Trans Am's rear window, her pigtails flopped about in the car-generated wind. Once I glanced at my speedometer just as the needle hovered at ninety miles per. Visions of patrol cars—alternating with glimpses of Norman Aycock, county D.A. Pierson, and Detective Atchley—danced in my head. I swallowed the lump in my throat, took a firm grip on the steering wheel, and kept on truckin'.

She took the Hawley Road exit. Her car's rear end bobbed left and right, then the Trans Am lurched hard on its springs as she whipped left underneath the freeway, headed for the lake. Grimly, my teeth grinding together, I followed. The Quik Stop where I'd bought gas on my first trip to Connie's flashed by on my right, the gas pumps a string of lighted blurs. The mesquite trees were gray, gnarled phantoms on my left; farther away the lake was still as a picture, the trees and brush on the opposite shore showing upside-down reflections like toy electric train scenery on a mirrored table. Connie left a trail of flying dust as she wheeled into her driveway and threw on the brakes; I parked parallel in front of the yard. The windmill's arms stood unmoving.

Her porch light was on. Visible down at the shore, the Cris Craft rocked gently near the end of the dock. There'd been two more cars in the drive the other night, now there were none. Connie flounced out of the Trans Am. She had changed into a flimsy blue T-shirt and short white shorts. She stopped beside the low cedar bush, beckoned, then half jogged, half strutted across the yard and up onto the porch. I followed, walking up behind her as she fumbled with the key in the door. She bumped me with her hip, and I wondered whether it was an accident. The grin she flashed me as she opened the door said that she'd bumped me on purpose. "So, darlin'," she said, "here we are."

I avoided looking directly at her as I crossed the threshold, but still I saw her outline in the corner of my eye as I crossed the darkened living room and sat on the sofa. I had to get my head on straight. I'd been under some sort of goofy spell since I'd watched her dance, and the heady, roller-coaster ride to the lake had done nothing to break the enchantment. But playing around with Connie wasn't going to help me with the trouble I was in. I tried to shut her face and body out of my mind. What the hell, wasn't she strictly a play-for-pay girl? Not in the sense of cash in, sex out, maybe, but if you fooled with Connie you were going to pay one way or the other. And hadn't she once shot a guy—her husband, in fact—right in the balls? That thought made me cringe. I dug into my mind and came up with two mental pictures: one the porno shot of Connie and Jack I'd seen in Catfish's place, the other an image of Connie rolling in the hay with my old pal Skeezix. I think it was the idea of being Skeezix's competition that really put me in the right frame of mind.

Finally I called up an image of Donna, lovely Donna with the laughing eyes. Okay, now, spell broken. I peered through the dimness at Connie Swarm.

The yellowish glare from the porch silhouetted her in the doorway. She switched on the interior light; she suddenly was visible head to toe. She still was quite a number, but whatever I'd been building for her was gone. I wondered if she noticed the change in the way I was looking at her.

Evidently she didn't. With a smile playing on her lips she left the room, then returned in a moment with a baggie dangling from between her fingers. In the baggie was some three grams of off-white powder. Until today, I hadn't seen any cocaine in a long time; a few years earlier I could've told you the weight to the nearest milligram. In her other hand Connie carried a hand mirror and a rolled-up dollar bill. Party time. She threw me a wink and flowed onto the couch beside me.

"So, Mr. Rick. Ricky-Rick. Rick nobody, just like in *Casablanca*. I watch it every time it comes on. Rick's Cafe American. D'ja know he never had no last name, never in the whole show? So Ricky-Rick, you want to have a toot with me?"

"No, Connie," I said. "Let's get something straight, right now. I really need to ask you some things. It's not a front to get alone with you, make a pass, or anything." She was holding the mirror in her lap and scraping some of the powder into a line, using a razor blade she'd had in the baggie. Jesus, it had been a long time, but I really didn't want any. At least I was pretty sure I didn't. "Come on, we really need to talk," I said.

She wasn't listening. She snorted a little coke through the dollar bill. "Dynamite, Ricky," she said. "Come on, don't you want some?"

"Not me."

"Don't be a stick-in-the-mud, Ricky-Rick, you don't look like one. You married?"

"No," I said.

"No wifey-poo? If you're telling the truth, and I don't care if you are or not. Oooo, I'm getting a rushy-rush, Ricky-Rick." She sat up straight, rested her hands on her thighs, and inhaled. She held the breath for a few seconds, then let it out slowly. "Deep breathin' makes it last. Trust me, darlin', you don't know what you're missin'.""

This wasn't getting me anywhere. "Oh, I know what I'm missing," I said. "Listen, Connie, the house. Who do you make your payments to?" I was hoping she was just high enough to rattle off some answers without thinking.

She wasn't. She watched me with a doubtful arched eyebrow as she scraped together another line. "Are you sure you want to help Skeezix? You ought to know about the payments already, if you're really so friendly with him."

"Well, to tell you the truth," I said, "I'm supposed to make the payments for you while he's gone. I told him I'd take care of them—Jesus, he wrote down the name, who I'm supposed to pay. But I lost the piece of paper. I ought to have my butt kicked."

She doubled up her leg and sat on her foot. "Where's he gone, if you know so much? You been talking to him?"

Going to see Connie was beginning to look like a royal screwup. Not only was I not finding anything out, I was making her just curious enough to start asking around about me. And to start checking up on Skeezix as well. I tried a stab in the dark. "Well, sure, I talk to him most every day. Don't you know who I am?"

"Sure, you're Rick. Ricky-Rick, only you're not as fun as I thought." She did another line; the powder vanished from the surface of the mirror as if by magic. She sneezed.

I took a shallow breath and plunged ahead. "Hey, doll, I'm the guy that's handling the pictures. For Catfish. I'm the distributor." Bringing up the porno shots was either going to get me some information or the bum's rush. Maybe both.

Connie's reaction was the last thing I expected. Her hands fell limply into her lap. Her lower lip trembled. The cocaine brightness in her eyes dimmed as though someone had thrown a switch. Tears welled in her eyes. One ran down her cheek and streaked her makeup. In a shaky, childlike voice she said, "Where's Debbie?"

My mouth was probably agape. I didn't say anything.

She covered her face with her hands, her shoulders heaving with sobs. "I've done what you said, all of it. Where is she? Please."

I don't guess I could have been more surprised if snakes had started wriggling and writhing on top of her head, like on the Medusa. I'm pretty much of a softie when it comes to girls crying, even girls like Connie Swarm. It took all that I could muster to say, stone-faced, "Well, where did Catfish tell you that she was?"

"It's been *three months*. The last time you let me see her Skeezix promised I could play with her again in a couple of weeks. Catfish promised, too, he was right there with us. Now they tell me it's you that won't let me see her. I don't care what you think about me, it's not right for you to keep her away from her mommy. Not right! My little girl, she's all I've got." Between the cocaine and the grief—real grief, too, this girl wasn't capable of faking anything—Connie was close to hysteria.

I left her sobbing and hugging herself alone on the couch while I hustled into the converted dining room and rummaged through the wet bar. I found a big, smooth tumbler with "TEXAS TEA" decaled on its surface, and half filled it with tap water. I would have used whiskey if she hadn't been tooting the cocaine, but I'd seen some nasty results in my time from mixing the two. I carried the water back in to her. She took a big gulp and coughed a fine spray. The drink seemed to help—at least her shoulders weren't heaving quite so much. I sat back down beside her.

"Listen to me," I said. "I've been putting you on, because I thought I had to. I'm not in any porno ring, Connie, you've got me mixed up with somebody else. It's my fault that you do, because I was trying to fool you into telling me some things. I'm sorry for that, but now I'm telling you the truth. I'm a guy who's in trouble, and evidently you've got problems with the same group of folks that I do. If you'll help me, I'll do everything I can to bring your little girl to you. Any idea who's got her?"

The tears were still flowing, but at least she was listening. "You a cop?" she said.

"Just the opposite, I'm trying to get around the police. Did you know that Catfish is dead?"

I wasn't sure exactly what Connie's expression held, but

the grief was suddenly gone. Her voice was practically steady as she said, "You kill him?"

"No, but I got there right after somebody did. Trust me, Connie, he's gone."

Her upper lip curled. "The son of a bitch got himself killed. God, I wish I'd been there." She sank back against the cushions. "Nobody's got Debbie, not the way you're thinking. Just her asshole of a father, but he's got court orders to keep me from seeing her. Catfish and Skeezix had ways to get her out here to see me—they'd have Fred bring her once in a while if I was good. You know, darlin', if I'd make their pictures for them. That was bein' good."

"Fred?"

"He's a lawyer, Fred Cassel. I'm not sure what he had to do with it, but that's who they called when they'd let me see her."

I thought, Jesus Christ, old stand-up Fred. What in hell is going on? I said, "Are you sure? Little guy with a Hitler mustache, wears a lot of silk hankies in his breast pockets?"

"Sure, I know him. He used to be Skeezix's lawyer sometimes."

"When? When was he?" My temples were pounding.

"He was all the time until . . . just about, about a year ago Fred told Skeezix he couldn't be his lawyer no more, something about, what, a conflict? I don't understand it, but it was about the same time he started . . . hey, I didn't like it no better than anybody else."

"You're talking about when Skeezix started being a government informant?" I said.

"That's about it, about the time." Connie was wringing her hands in her lap.

I was going to need time to sort all this out, but right now I needed to accumulate what information I could, before Connie changed her mind about talking to me. Underneath the varnish, she was just another street-tough lady with a soft spot for her daughter, and she might decide to clam up at any moment. "Connie," I said, "think. Do you think Fred Cassel had anything to do with the porno business?"

"I couldn' say. He spent a lot of time at Baby Doll's, and out at the Bullrider Danceland, too, with Skeezix and Catfish. And Bodie Breaux, too. Him and Bodie did a lot of drinkin' together.''

"Naw. Fred Cassel and *Breaux*?"

"Sure, darlin','" Connie said. "Didn' you know that? I thought Bodie an' you were buddies.''

Sure, we were. My old buddy Breaux. Who just happened to know Fred Cassel, who just happened to forget to mention that he already knew Bodie when he hired me. Come to think about it, Cassel had told me he knew *of* Breaux, and had suggested that I get Bodie to help me get rid of Skeezix. Whom Cassel also knew, and who knew Bodie also. Jesus, the three of them must have died laughing every time my name came up.

"Connie," I began, then said, "Jesus Christ, what to ask." Then I cleared my throat and said, "Connie, really important this next one. Now, when I told you I was the porno distributor, you somehow thought you already knew about me. Does that mean that there is somebody else besides the people we've talked about? Like Jack Brendy maybe?"

She gave me a blank stare. "Who?" she said.

"Come on, Connie, don't start blowing smoke. Not now. I've already seen your picture with Jack. You know, the two of you doing it, over at Catfish's place."

She didn't show the slightest trace of embarrassment. Come to think about it, there wasn't any reason she should have. A modest woman Connie wasn't. She said, "Oh, that old guy. He's the one Fred brought over and Catfish took the pictures from the closet. They used some of those pictures to, you know, get people to do what they wanted. Like me with my little girl, they always wanted something on everybody. But no, no way that guy was part of the action. They were putting one over on him is all. I think he might've had something to do with dope. I remember they told me not to say nothing about Skeezix, that they didn' want him to know I knew him. I never asked why, I wasn't supposed to ask about anything. Just do. But there was somebody else they were all takin' orders from. They used to call him up."

Well, they had damn sure put one over on me. Easy as pie. Just set up Donna to have me over and . . . the thought of Donna being involved in it flashed through my mind, but

I quickly discarded the idea. Donna Sue Morley simply wouldn't do anything like that. But the others . . . well, they'd killed Catfish, or had it done, and probably Jack as well. And I was sitting here shooting the breeze with Connie Swarm, who had too much information about what was going on, in a house where Breaux knew right where to find us. I said, "Connie, I've got to get you out of here."

"No, no, I'm all right," she said. "Stayin' alone has been kind of different. Good for a change."

"You don't get it," I said. "We've got to go *now*. I'll put you up someplace. I doubt you've got time to pack even. If they haven't already, they're going to figure out that you're dangerous to them. They're not that worried about me—they'll let the state and the feds handle that one for them—but you're not safe where they can put their finger on you."

I'd just thrown a lot at her, and wasn't sure whether Connie would buy it or not. By now I was pretty sure that the quicker she did buy my line, the better chance she had of staying alive. She said, realization dawning, "You mean right now?"

"Right this second, Connie. Yeah, now." I took her arm and helped her to stand.

She had a strange look, an innocent gaze that reminded me of how young she was. Which in Connie's case was awfully easy to forget. "Do you really think they'd—" she began, then said, "I need to get a couple of things."

She left me alone and retreated to the rear of the house. I sat on the sofa and watched the baggie of cocaine with a strange fascination. In a few minutes Connie returned. I'd say this much for her, she traveled light. Her belongings were stored in a small overnight bag. I took the bag and led her toward the door. She paused, went back over to the couch, and picked up the baggie, then looked at me questioningly. I shook my head. She nodded and left it there. We went outside, and I led the way down the steps into the yard.

I said, "I don't think my place is safe, either. We'd better go check into a—"

The *brrrt! brrrt!* of a machine gun shattered the stillness. From the street, somewhere in the vicinity of where I'd parked the 'Vette, short orange bursts of flame spat like dragon's breath. Sod flew nearby, the line of fire directed to my left and moving in my direction.

I had a sudden crystal-clear memory of a day in the country I'd once spent with Breaux. Bodie was a real gun freak, and on this particular day he'd been practicing with a WW II relic, a Schmeizer machine pistol, riddling rows of beer bottles, fence posts, and dried-up horse turds.

"Sumbitch kicks up and to the left," he'd said. "One pull on the trigger shoots five rounds. You want to waste a fucker, aim low and to his left. You can't miss."

It was this split-second memory that saved me. I dove to my right and hit the ground rolling, jarring and numbing my shoulder. I had a glimpse of a vehicle parked out there behind the 'Vette, a dim shape in the moonlight. I tasted Bermuda grass. The slugs whined overhead and moved on.

From behind me on the porch came a scream. I looked. Connie pitched backward, slammed against the door frame, hung suspended for an instant, then sagged, and slid limply to the concrete in a tangle of arms and lovely legs. I had about one second to feel sad for Connie before the machine gun chattered again.

I didn't remember digging the Smith & Wesson from my back pocket; the pistol was suddenly there, its grip firm against my palm. I snapped two shots off in the direction of the machine gun, not aiming, shooting wild. I focused on the vehicle behind the 'Vette, and of course I'd seen it before. Breaux's Jeep, top still down.

Suddenly I was calm. Bodie—his hat now came into focus, more pale green than yellow in the moonlight—was crouched by the Jeep's front bumper. The Schmeizer was cradled on his thigh, and he was reloading. My old buddy, who'd probably been the one who'd suggested to Cassel that old down-and-out Rick would make a good patsy to begin with. I steadied the S&W in both hands, drew a bead on the center of his chest, and pulled the trigger. I'd never shot anyone, but this was easy. The bullet streaked toward him, whanged off the Jeep's bumper, and ricocheted into the night.

Breaux dove sideways and disappeared behind the Jeep. I

got off one more shot, which banged into a fender, and the Jeep rocked on its springs.

Silence, followed by two metallic clicks.

Breaux's head and shoulders popped into view. The machine gun was braced in the hollow of his shoulder. Flame spurted, the Schmeizer barked, slugs dug up the yard. I hit the deck again. The bullets whined overhead and thudded into wood.

I scrambled up and ran for the corner of the house, feet thudding and lungs about to burst, dove headlong for cover as the machine gun's *brrrt!* sounded again. Splinters flew.

More silence. Far away, down near the lake, a frog croaked. Slowly, carefully, I inched forward and peered around the corner.

Bodie was standing upright behind the Jeep, the Schmeizer held loosely in the crook of his arm. He spotted me and crouched down out of view. He shouted, his voice even hoarser than normal, "If it ain't me, it's going to be somebody else. You're dead, Ricky-boy. You just walking around and don't know it yet. You can't call no cops, you got less chance with them than you got with us. Tell you what, you give me that key of Brendy's, I'll let you go for now. Kind of give you a sporting chance, or whatever the dumbfucks call it."

I ducked behind the corner and leaned against the wall. Prison makes for strange alliances; except for jail I never would have known Bodie to begin with. Since we'd been out, we'd been friendly, sure, but I'd never known what he was up to when he wasn't partying with me. Now I had a pretty good idea. I reached around the corner and snapped another shot off. "What key?" I said. I flattened against the wall and waited.

The Jeep's starter chugged. The engine coughed, then roared to life. I looked again as its tires burned rubber; the Jeep with Breaux at the wheel did a fishtailing U-turn and sped off into the night. I stepped from my hiding place, leveled the S&W at the retreating tail lights, then relaxed. It would be a waste of time, for the Jeep was far out of range. Bodie had figured the angles, just as he always did, and had decided that the time wasn't right. Hell, why shoot it out with me? He had plenty of time. The twin red lights disappeared from view over a hill. I walked slowly back up on the porch, leaned through the front door, and switched on the porch light.

Connie was stretched out on her back, legs splayed, arms limp at her sides, palms upward. Her head was propped against the wall at an odd angle, and one corner of her mouth was upturned in an eternally frozen grin. Dollar-sized splotches of blood were thickening on the porch and on the wall. Three bullets had struck Connie's chest in a upward diagonal pattern from left to right. The wounds had almost stopped bleeding. I touched her neck, found the carotid artery. There was one tiny pulse beat, then nothing.

I shook my head slowly, stood, and looked down on her for long moments while the crickets whirred and the frogs *chirruped* in the distance. Before I left, I rolled her body onto its side. She looked more comfortable that way.

I spent the night in a rundown motel on East Grand Avenue, near the fairgrounds, where an old black man with kinky gray hair asked for cash in advance and forgot to have me sign the register. A hooker was operating next door to me; I counted four customers who came, frantically creaked the bedsprings for a while, and left, before I finally went to sleep. The air-conditioning had broken down and the temperature in my room was near ninety degrees. Beneath a grimy white sheet, I was shivering and my teeth were chattering.

THIRTEEN

In the morning I found a 7-Eleven store a block from the motel, poked around until I found a toothbrush, a tube of Gleem, a can of Barbasol, and a Bic disposable razor, and went to stand in line at the register behind a black girl who was buying four cans of Ranch Style Beans. As I waited, I watched two black kids shoplift a box of Hershey bars and a *Hustler* magazine. I thought about tipping off the clerk, then forgot the idea. If I snitched on them, the kids might look me up when they got out of jail.

Back in my room, I showered and shaved. The pipes were rusty, and I let the shower run until the brown tint was gone from the water before stepping into the stall. The motel's idea of hot water was the temperature of day-old coffee.

Clean shaven and with a slight razor burn, I squeezed green, minty paste onto the brush and did my teeth, then rinsed my mouth with tap water that tasted of minerals. I was ready for another lovely day.

My red knit shirt was wilted and limp. I sniffed it. No sweaty locker room smell, just a musty dampness. I put on my sneakers and jeans and climbed shirtless into the 'Vette, drove up and down some narrow streets until I found a laundromat in a red brick building on the corner of Capitol and

Bryan. While my lonesome shirt swirled and tumbled in the washer, I used the pay phone to call Donna.

"Leave a candle burning in the window," I said. "Tie a yellow ribbon around the tree."

"You'll love it here." She sounded happy as a lark, and just listening to her improved my disposition. "There's a Delta from DFW at eleven this morning," she said.

The round clock hanging beside the phone showed eight-thirty. I said, "And an American at one, another Delta at four-thirty, and two or three night flights on puddle jumpers. I've got the schedules memorized. I'll be on one of them, after I do a couple of things."

She chuckled merrily, the first real laugh I'd heard from Donna since the day I'd talked to her beside her pool. She said, "Burn a candle? How about a searchlight, maybe a Coast Guard blinker in my window, flashing S.O.S. Jacqueline's driving me crazy, ding-donging to go back to the amusement park. I swear if I take the Peter Pan ride one more time, I'm going to turn into Tinker Bell."

I wanted to be with her so badly that a lump came up in my throat. I swallowed and said, "Okay. Listen, I'll get my own room. I don't know how it would affect Jacqueline if I stayed in the same room with you."

"Rick. That's my line, you prude. But you're right, it would be better. Hurry, don't take too long. I'm getting lonesome."

Funny, that was the word I'd just been thinking about to describe my own feeling. "You won't be for long," I said.

This go-around, I took my sweet time about entering Texas Bank Plaza, cruising the parking lot in search of Jeep convertibles, wandering through the morning crowd in the lobby with an eye out for yellow-billed caps. I'd done some thinking and, in my own mind at least, had at least one murder solved. Catfish's. Of course it had to be Bodie. That's what had taken him so long to reach the Bullrider Danceland. All the while I'd been having my little talk with Candy, Bodie had been standing in Catfish's bathroom, pumping bullets through the shower door. I'd thought it a little strange at the time when Bodie had showed up waving Snakey's .45 instead of one of his own guns—a Beretta, a

Browning 9mm., or a Llama .380. The bullets that had killed Catfish wouldn't match the .45, I'd bet on it, and Bodie had known he'd be carrying the .45 when he and I were arrested at the scene. Oh, yeah, he'd set that up as well, had called the police or had them called. The only fly in the ointment had been when I'd talked Atchley into letting us go. Otherwise, I'd still be in jail while good old stand-up Fred Cassel got Bodie free on bond, and probably got the charges against him dropped as well. So old Catfish would still be walking around if I hadn't called Breaux before I went to the Bullrider Danceland. Somehow I didn't feel guilty about that.

I sat by the fountain in the lobby for the better part of an hour, watching throngs of people come and go. I was certain that Bodie hadn't passed by. He might be in Cassel's office waiting for me, but that was a chance I'd have to take. I fished out two quarters, dropped them into the fountain, and made a wish. Then I rode the elevator up to Cassel's floor.

There were four people—a white-haired woman wearing a lot of jewelry and three men in suits who looked like salesmen—waiting in Cassel & Grimes's reception area. The receptionist wasn't the same girl I'd seen on my last visit, and since I didn't want to be recognized, that suited me fine. This one was a pleasantly plump redhead with big boobs straining against the front of a light-weight cotton sweater. A green-jacketed paperback novel lay by her elbow: *A Catskill Eagle* by Robert B. Parker. This girl was into my kind of reading. I stopped before her half-moon-shaped desk and stood first on one foot and then the other while she pressed buttons and routed calls. She kept her long red lashes down and barely glanced at my belt buckle.

I told her, "This is a personal call. Fred told me to come on in." Then I skirted her desk as though I knew what I was doing and headed for the inner offices, holding my breath and hoping that she didn't notice. The trick had worked a couple of times when I'd been searching for Sweaty's bond skips, and so far it hadn't landed me in jail. She gave me the same quick nod-and-smile that she probably reserved for deliverymen, then went on about her business. I went through the doorway and down the carpeted hallway to call on good old Fred.

His office was at the back of the suite, behind a door of heavier wood and more ornate design than the rest of the doors along the corridor, and which was marked "MR. CASSEL" in plain understated gold letters. Fred's private secretary was a tall blonde with bright green eyes and long, manicured nails that didn't look as though she did a lot of typing. She was buffing her nails with an emory board.

I said, "Hi. Old Fred around?"

Her gaze flicked at me, then darted over my shoulder down the hallway. Her full lips parted. Before she could ask how I sneaked by the receptionist, Cassel's doorknob clicked and turned and good old Fred himself came out.

He was carrying some typewritten pages in one hand and was wearing, as usual, a navy suit. His breast-pocket hanky was silver gray. He said, "Look, beautiful, take these over to—"

He spotted me. As he'd come through the door, he'd been ogling the blonde's rear end and looking pretty hungry about it, but now his face seemed to melt. He nearly dropped the papers he was carrying, but finally clutched them with both hands. Then he turned on his heel, made sort of a squawking sound, reentered his office, and closed the door. I thought that he could have handled the situation a little better.

Beautiful half smiled and shrugged. "Well, as you can see for yourself, old Fred isn't anywhere around." She batted her eyes.

There was a phone on her desk, a three-button rotary with a mother-of-pearl finish. One of its buttons flashed on. That would be Fred, back there in his office calling either Breaux or the police. For me, either choice would yield the same results.

I tried to look happy and tossed Beautiful a wink. "Just a private joke," I said. "Old Fred really kids around sometimes." I stepped quickly around her desk and opened Cassel's door. She tossed her mane, started to rise, then shrugged once again, and picked up her emory board. I went on in. Old Fred was sure a lot easier to get in to see than Muhammed Double-X.

Cassel was behind his desk with the receiver flattening his ear. The view from his window hadn't changed: still the smokestacks and office buildings along Harry Hines Boulevard. The rolling server, still holding the coffeepot, was in front of the window. Cassel's U of Oklahoma degree still hung on the wall. The only thing that was different was Fred himself; he didn't look near as confident as the last time I'd visited.

He banged the receiver into its cradle. "You've got a lot of nerve crashing in here. Now wait outside, I'll be with you in a minute."

I smiled at him. His look said that he couldn't see what I thought was so funny. I crossed the room, went around his desk, sat on the edge nearest him, and pulled the Smith & Wesson out of my back pocket. I stuck the barrel up his nostril. His chair rolled backward about six inches and thudded softly against his credenza. His body went rigid and only his eyes moved as he shifted his gaze from me down to the pistol and back again.

"So, Fred," I said, "let's chat."

He sounded as though he was choking as he said, "Jesus Christ, man, be careful with that thing. Look, I *can't* pay you any more money. It was Jack's money I was going to give you, not my own."

For just a second there he had me stumped. Oh. The thirty grand that had gotten me into this to begin with—money I hadn't seen or now ever expected to see. I damn near giggled in his face. I said, "You can think up something better than that. Hell, I know I'm not going to get any money from you. I've come to talk about a real estate deal, among other things. But first you're going to give Beautiful, or whatever her name is out there, a buzz and tell her we're going to be tied up a while."

He nodded. The motion caused the S&W to press harder against his nostril. He whimpered, "Please. Just take it out of my nose."

"I shouldn't, Fred. You and your buddies have been jamming it up my nose." I sat back some and returned the gun to waist level, keeping it trained on Cassel. "Call her," I said.

I stood aside to give him room, held the pistol inches from his ear as he pressed the intercom button. He was trying his best not to look at the gun, but as he talked to his secretary his gaze darted in that direction anyway. He told Beautiful that we weren't to be disturbed, and during the conversation I learned that her name was Virginia. He hung up and swiveled to face me. His face was the color of a black-and-white movie.

"I'm going to cooperate with you," he said. "Just don't get excited."

I waved him back and he rolled away from his desk. With one eye on Cassel and the pistol held ready, I used my free hand to do a quick search. "Sounds like you've been reading up," I said, "on how to handle a crazy man, huh?" His top drawer held only pencils, pens, and paper clips. I slammed it closed and moved on to the side drawers. "Above all, keep calm, right?" I said. "Don't let him know you're afraid, huh? Well, Fred, you can bet your sweet ass I'm crazy. I might've already been a little bit crazy before I met you, but I'm damn sure crazy now. So you'd better humor me because the slightest fuckup on your part might drive me right over the edge." I found a gun in his bottom right-hand drawer, a Walther PPK .380, a collector's item. I checked the miniature clip: three rounds. I jammed the Walther into my waistband, circled the desk, and sat down across from him in a visitor's chair. "So do yourself a favor," I said. "Tell me about Connie Swarm's house and what Jack Brendy's money had to do with buying it."

He licked his lips and said shakily, "Connie Swarm?"

I aired back the hammer, two soft clicks. I didn't say a word.

He tried one more time. "I don't think I've heard the name. Is she supposed to be a client, or a friend of Jack Brendy's? I didn't really know Jack on a social basis."

I extended the pistol, holding the barrel two feet from his face, grinned, and crossed my eyes.

He flinched, held his hand palm outward between the gun and his nose. "No, wait. Her name's Lorraine Daley."

"That's better, but I already knew that," I said. "And you knew that Skeezix was staying at her place before you hired me to get rid of him. And you know that Bodie killed her. So don't give me anything that's old hat. I want to know about a loan on Connie's house, backed by some of Jack's stock. I want to see your file, and don't bother bullshitting me that you don't have one. You've got five seconds, Fred. One . . ."

He nodded quickly. "It's over there, in the top drawer." He was indicating a dark wood four-drawer file cabinet beside the window.

I went to the cabinet, opened the drawer, looked at the alphabetical guide cards. "Under Swarm or under Daley?" I said.

"Under *L*. For Lorraine," he said. A quick flash of sunlight glinting from the glass covering his law degree caused me to blink.

I found it, a letter-sized manila folder with an inch-thick sheath of papers held in its two-pronged braid. "What's the deal on the loan?" I said. "And don't worry. I'll go through this file, and if you lie to me I'll shoot you. The word was that Skeezix paid cash for the house."

Cassel sighed, his gaze riveted on the pistol. "That's true. There never was any loan on the house; that's just what Jack told the bank he needed the money for. He told them he was posting the stock as collateral so the house could be lien-free. Also because he didn't want his wife to know where the money was going. Sixty-two thousand dollars."

"And I guess the money went to bankroll a drug deal. With Breaux, or did Bodie use Skeezix as a go-between?"

He nodded slowly. "Look, Bannion, ten years ago I wouldn't have gotten involved in this. Times have been hard."

"They damn sure have, you asshole, but not near as hard as they're going to get. What was it, cocaine? How much?"

"It was . . . yeah, it was coke. Three kilos it was supposed to be. Four, it turned out. And Skeezix wasn't involved. We, well, *they* made over half a million dollars on the deal, Bodie and Jack. But Jack was living too high. Hell, you know that, you've seen his house. Jack's deal with Skeezix came later, and you know that story. The feds and all." Cassel removed his I'm-smart glasses and suddenly didn't look so smart anymore.

As I carried the file over and sat across from him, I thought over what he'd said. It was beginning to jell. I didn't like it, but it was. I crossed my legs and opened the folder across my thigh, all the time holding the pistol pointed loosely in Cassel's direction. "I'm pretty dumb, Fred, guess I always have been. I've been thinking all along that somebody killed Jack so he wouldn't talk about his drug connects, nothing more. But there's a lot more to it. Hell, Jack didn't even have any drug connects, except for Skeezix and Breaux. And Skeezix is on the federal payroll; telling about him isn't going to scare anybody. It was a lot more than the dope, wasn't it? I'll bet the dirty-picture business is even better than the dope business. And the filthy-picture business is one where you can kill two birds with one stone. You can blackmail people and sell the pictures to boot. Where you sell 'em, on the playground? You're a real shit, Fred."

He'd been watching me with a sort of resigned expression on his face, but now he lifted his chin and said, "Now, wait a minute. Not me, I'm just a lawyer."

"Oh, Bodie's a shit, too. But he doesn't represent himself to be anything *but* a shit. You're different. Stay tuned, I'll get back to you." I thumbed through the papers in my lap, the copies of Jack's stock—IBM, Placid Oil, a few shares of Xerox—and found the loan application. The loan document itself was underneath the application in the folder. Beside Jack's scrawl, Donna's signature appeared even more round and feminine. I paused with the file open to the note from Jack and Donna to Northpark National Bank. "What the hell is Waterproof, Inc.?" I said. "That's the name the loan is under."

He shifted nervously. "Oh, it's just a corporation, to limit personal liability. You've been around enough to know how it works."

"Waterproof, Inc.," I said thoughtfully. "Hell, I know. That's Bodie's hometown, isn't it? Waterproof, Louisiana. You forget we were cellies. He kept a newspaper headline up at El Reno for laughs. It was from the New Orleans *Times-Picayune*, and it said, 'Three Waterproof Men Drown.' Ha, Ha. What's the matter, Fred? You're not laughing. Don't you get it?"

He shifted again and ran his index finger around underneath his starched collar. He put his glasses back on. "You're not going to be able to make anything out of it. That corporation's a legitimately registered entity."

I snorted. "Legitimate? Jesus Christ. Let's see, Jack was a pretty weak guy underneath all the bullshit. He might've gotten into a few dope deals, little stuff, but he never would've had the nerve to put together anything of the size you just told me. So that's why the picture of Jack diddling Connie Swarm. Gave you a hammer on him. If he doesn't post the stock as collateral for the loan, then Donna gets the pictures. How many different loans did he have to make? And now I see why Jack was making dope deals even though he had all that money stashed in the mini-warehouse. Hell, the money wasn't even Jack's. He was holding the money for you and Bodie, from the dirty-picture business. What else you into, Cassel? Pimping young boys, what?"

Cassel removed his glasses once again, this time cleaning them with a spotless white hanky from his back pocket. His confidence was returning; now he spoke directly and barely glanced at the Smith & Wesson. "So what are you going to do about it?" he said. "You can make yourself a pretty good finder's fee, Bannion, if you know where that money is. There's quite a bit of it."

"Yeah, I can make a fee. Or I can make all of it, if I don't give you any. You've set me up pretty good. Nobody's going to pay much attention to me with *my* record. But I might just have an out. Skeezix, though I hate to have to depend on that fat son of a bitch. But just maybe between me and him we know enough for some prosecutor to put a case together on you."

Cassel looked straight at me as though he was going to laugh. I suppose he'd made up his mind that I really wasn't going to shoot him, and that except for the gun I wasn't particularly dangerous. "Yeah, well, you just talk to Skeezix," he said. His eyes did a funny little dance in his head, and then he stopped watching me and looked out the window.

Suddenly I got it. Not anywhere near all of it, but enough to raise goose bumps along my spine the size of mothballs. I said, "Christ, how did y'all keep Skeezix's killing out of the papers? The little toad never got on any plane to Minneapolis. What'd Bodie do, tell him they just had enough time to go in the john and take a leak? Then pop old Skeezix while he was standing there with his dick hanging out, I'll bet. I've got Skeezix's brother's phone number in Minneapolis. What do you think, Fred? Think I ought to call him?"

Cassel put his elbows on the armrests and his fingertips together in front of his nose. Now he was actually crowing. "No, actually we were worried about the word getting out as soon as somebody found the body. But we had to chance it. Skeezix was simply too hot and knew too much. An attendant found him around three in the morning when he was cleaning out the crapper. No, all along I expected headlines, 'Government Witness Executed,' something like that. We didn't have any way to hush it up. Aycock did that for us. The egotistical old fart couldn't stand for anybody to know his witness went and got himself popped. He must have had about fifteen cases hanging fire that went out the window with Skeezix. Or in this case, under the toilet. How many witnesses do you think the feds would have if word got around how they protect their boys, huh? I've got a few spies down at the county, and Skeeze is still on ice down at the medical center. The coroner's under orders not to talk to anybody about him but Aycock. Jesus, the only difference between Aycock and the people he's prosecuting is where their money comes from."

It figured. So now the only guy with the answers, excluding the people mixed up in the deal, was me. Fresh from El Reno and a suspect myself. Hell, if I tried to take the story to County D.A. Pierson he'd have me committed, just as soon as he could stop laughing and get a grand jury together. Not against Cassel or Breaux, against me. I'd be a lot easier to convict. Hell, when Bodie had taken a shot at me over at Connie's—and come to think about it, she'd probably been his main target—he was probably hoping he'd miss. No way did these people want me dead. With me out of the way the law might start an investigation in another direction.

For want of anything better to do, I riffled absently through the rest of the file in my lap. The sheet that followed the loan document was a form with oak leaves printed around its margins and "PRUDENTIAL" in bold script across the top of the page. It was a key-personnel, decreasing-term

life policy, with the named insured as Jack Brendy. The beneficiary was Waterproof, Inc., and the face value was seven
hundred and fifty thousand dollars. I said, "You collect on
Jack's policy yet? Jesus, what a bloodsucker."

He shrugged. "It's in the works." He sounded a little proud
of himself.

His answer didn't even register. I'd turned to the final page
in the folder, and was gripping its edge. Another policy, identical to the first, same amount, same beneficiary. Only on
this one, the name insured was Donna.

Hands trembling, I raised the pistol. This time I was ready
to shoot him. Eager to, in fact. I said tonelessly, "Where's
Breaux now, you fuck?" I pictured the scene yesterday,
upstairs in Donna's bedroom, phone in my hand, as someone
downstairs hung up the extension. Bodie, or someone who
was going to report to him. Hell, I'd called the motel; the
operator had given the name of the place. And Donna had
told me her room number. "Where is he, Fred?" I said. "I'm
not fucking around with you."

His expression said that he knew I meant business. He
said, "I haven't . . . well, he could have gone out of town."

I got to my feet, let the file slide to the carpet, walked
firmly around the desk toward Cassel. His expression was
doubtful at first, then fearful. I put the barrel of the gun
against his forehead. He closed his eyes.

I said, "I'm not going to kill you right now, Fred. But if
anything happens to Donna, and I mean to one single hair
on her head, there aren't enough cops in Dallas to keep me
away from you. You'd better hope to fuck I get to her before
Bodie does. You'd damn sure better."

After I'd locked Cassel, along with Beautiful—thinking it
over, I decided I had to put her out of commission, and I
noticed as I closed the door that she looked a whole lot
unhappier about being locked in there with Cassel than he
did about being with her—into the supply room, I used Cassel's phone to call Donna. No answer. A call ten minutes
later from the building lobby yielded the same result; I
watched the fountain send glistening sprays of water into
the air, gripped the receiver until my knuckles whitened, and

let the phone ring six extra times while blood pounded in my temples. I was too late for the eleven o'clock Delta and was going to have to hump it to make the American flight at one.

As I steered the 'Vette out of Texas Bank Plaza parking lot and took the northbound access road alongside Stemmons Freeway, I briefly considered stopping by my place at Turtle Creek North and packing a bag. No way, I couldn't chance it. The time factor was one problem; another was the likelihood that someone—FBI, county cops, Dallas police department, or somebody on Cassel's payroll, you could pretty much take your pick—would have the place staked out. I switched on the radio, clutched the wheel, and gunned the 'Vette through the entry ramp and up onto the freeway. Immediately I eased across four lanes of traffic and jockeyed for position on the center rail; the left-hand curve leading from Stemmons onto Airport Freeway wasn't that far ahead.

As I watched the bulk of Texas Stadium grow larger over the hood, I mentally went over the airplane schedules. There had been one midnight flight last night, on Continental, and Breaux couldn't have made it. It was around midnight when he'd been spraying Connie Swarm's front yard with machine-gun bullets. The midnighter had been the last flight until the eleven A.M. Delta, which meant that if I *had* caught the Delta I would've stood a pretty good chance of running into Breaux. Assuming he'd caught the eleven o'clock, Bodie had a two-hour head start. If Donna and Jacqueline spent the day at the amusement park and I could somehow get to Ramada Inn Disney World before they returned, Breaux's head start wouldn't mean a thing. If, if, *if*. I gave it the gas and the 'Vette's speedometer inched past seventy-five.

As I passed by the MacArthur Boulevard exit, Irving Mall on my right and the Irving Bank Tower on my left, someone called my name. I looked around. Hell, it was the radio. My hand trembled slightly as I increased the volume.

A mellow-voiced female newscaster was saying, ". . . and Assistant District Attorney Tom Pierson offered no further comment. The indictments, returned shortly after nine o'clock this morning, name Bannion along with Donna Morley Brendy, the dead man's wife, as alleged conspirators in the murder. Both are still at large, bond having been set on the two at one million dollars each. Informed sources close to the DA's office told KVIL news that Bannion is also a suspect in two other slayings, the most recent the midnight killing of Lorraine Daley, also know as Connie Swarm, a local stripper. Miss Daley's bullet-riddled body was found by police around three this morning on the porch of her lakeside home. Bannion, who has served a federal prison sentence for cocaine trafficking, is best remembered as the Cowboy lineman who was called offside during—"

I turned the knob, and a pop from the speakers cut the newslady off in mid-sentence. So Pierson hadn't waited until Tuesday. I felt as though a bucket of ice water had just been dumped in my lap. My throat constricted, my spittle dried up. The traffic in front of me slowed without warning, and I barely had enough of my senses left to jam on the brakes. The traffic gradually picked up speed and I followed along as though in a trance.

As the initial surge of adrenaline cleared—what the hell, I thought, I've known the indictment was coming down sooner or later—I thought about Donna. I'd hidden it from her on purpose. What in hell was she going to think of me? Would she already know when I saw her—Jesus, if I could get to her before Breaux—or was I going to have to lay it out for her? And if I did have to spell it out, how was she going to take it? After what she'd been through, this just might set her off. And Jacqueline . . . Jesus Christ.

The midday lull had thinned the traffic quite a bit by the time I went through the ticket booths at the entrance to DFW. The machine spat a ticket at me; I took it through the window, gunned the 'Vette down the interior freeway and into American's covered terminal parking. One lone jet streaked away on takeoff as I drove underneath the steel and concrete awning. I parked and checked the time; I had forty-five minutes until takeoff. With the packet of hundred-dollar bills from the glove compartment jammed into my pocket, and with the Smith & Wesson along with Cassel's Walther locked in the 'Vette's trunk—I was going to need a gun, of course, but I couldn't fly with a piece and was going to have to figure a way to rearm in Orlando—I went inside the terminal. Just inside the door a young girl in a yellow dress handed me a lapel pin in the shape of a rose and told me that she was taking a survey. I said that I was in a hurry, gave the pin back to her, and hustled up to the ticket counter.

A skinny young guy behind the counter, wearing a pale blue shirt and navy tie, sold me a one-way ticket and asked if I had any luggage. I shook my head and counted out three crisp hundreds, then watched two men in the airport bar put the make on a slick-looking woman in a leopard dress while I waited for my change. Visible beyond the bar, past rows of waiting-room chairs and beyond a huge plate glass window, an American 707 stood ready at the boarding gate. I took my change and went through the metal detectors, fidgeted in the waiting area for what seemed an eternity, boarded the jet, and flew to Orlando. I sat in the smoking section, went through a half pack of Pall Malls, and landed with a taste in my mouth as though a bird had crapped in it.

In the Orlando terminal I dodged two panhandlers, another girl in a yellow dress who was handing out pins and taking a survey, and called Donna's room once more. Still no answer. I hailed a cab and told the driver to take me to Ramada Inn Disney World.

I hadn't ridden in a whole lot of taxis in my life, but it seemed to me that the same guy had been driving every single one of them. Guy around sixty who needed a shave, and who talked to me from the side of his mouth, over his shoulder, while a filterless cigarette waggled between his lips.

"This ain't the tourist season," he said. "That's in January and February. Summer business ain't for shit. Next year I'm taking the summer off if that old lady of mine can keep from charging every thing in the fucking store. You vacationin', or you got business?" High, leafy trees lined either side of the highway. A billboard featuring a cartoon drawing of a lion advertised Circus World; another sign showing a dolphin jumping through a hoop and clapping his fins touted Sea World. A hundred yards from the highway, two pink flamingos circled lazily, landed, and drank from a swampy pond. The sun was an orange ball sinking gradually below the horizon.

I said casually, "Oh, a little of both."

The cabbie plowed ahead. "Well, if you're of a mind to do some sightseeing, give me a call." He reached above the visor and handed me a business card over the seat back. He said, "Lotta ripoffs around here, lotta bullshit traps. You got to watch yourself. Take that fucking guy." He indicated a big sign on our left. The sign was pitch black with some really spooky ghosts and fanged monsters outlined against the backdrop in luminescent paint. House of Horrors, bold white script read. My cabbie said, "I'm going to guarantee you he spends more money on that billboard than he does on his whole fucking horror show. You ever . . . well, been to a March of Dimes haunted house, like on Halloween? Now I like 'em, don't get me wrong. The kids that run 'em got a lot of enthusiasm. But this fucking guy, the House of Horrors? He's got his old lady running around in the dark dressed up in one of those paper costumes like you buy in the grocery store and jumping out from behind doors and hollering boo at people. Only thing scary ever happened in that joint was when one of the kids over to Orlando Junior College reached up inside the costume and pinched his old lady on the tit." He threw back his head and cackled. "Took over an hour to get the broad to turn loose of the kid. Anyway, that's what you got to look out for around here, that kind of shit."

I noted that my driver's name was Pete, that he was the owner of Pete's Cab Service, and that his business card had a ketchup stain along the edges. I thanked him and put the card away. Then I leaned back against the cushions and watched through the window while we passed Wet 'n' Wild with its giant water slides and its concrete beach and pool with simulated rolling breakers. Strutting around inside were teenage girls in tiny French bikinis, muscular young guys in boxer swim trunks, and middle-aged women in one-piece jobs who held children by their hands. I said to Pete the cabbie, "Listen, is there anyplace a guy can buy a pistol this time of day?" I did my best to sound off-handed about it.

He threw on his brakes, swerved to avoid an old man who was driving a camper, shook his fist at the old guy. Then he turned around and squinted at me. "Look, you ain't no holdup man. I just dumped my money at the house before I picked you up, 'case you are."

"No, no way am I," I said. "You know, staying alone in a strange town I might feel better with some protection."

He adjusted his cap on his head and returned his attention to the road, swerving once more and this time nearly side-swiping a Dodge mini-van. "Tell you what, then, maybe I can help. There's a thirty-eight revolver, a Siebrig longnose. Son of a bitch is a hogleg, but it shoots. Cost you pretty good."

"Just how much is pretty good?" I said.

He cracked his window open and flipped his cigarette out-side, fished in the ashtray, found a soggy toothpick, and poked that into his mouth. "Well, I could let you have it, maybe, for four hundred." The sign on top of the Ramada Inn was now visible in the distance; the lights on the motel's roof winked on in the gathering dusk.

"Sold," I said.

Pete's chin moved slightly to one side. He removed the toothpick. "Say, bud, this here gun's registered in my name. It's be my ass if there's any trouble."

"There won't be, unless somebody besides me starts it. Protection, just like I told you."

He braked, then wheeled underneath the Ramada Inn awning. The motel was built in three sections, which were strung out to the north behind the lobby and restaurant. Just across the highway was a sign pointing to Disney World. Inside the lobby a girl in a black and gold clerk's uniform was helping an old woman sign the register. Pete slung an arm over the seat back and said to me, "Here we are, twenty-four eighty on the meter."

I dug in my pocket. "What about the gun?"

"It's right underneath my seat," he said. "You stand outside and hand me the money through the window, and I'll hand the pistol out to you. Then I'll throw in a box of shells, the gun's empty. I ain't handing no loaded gun to no stranger. Shit, I ain't a raving lunatic."

*   *   *

The Siebrig was a hogleg, all right, a real Dirty Harry weapon. I stood in the motel driveway, made certain the wall shielded me from the desk clerk's view, and looked the gun over.

I'd never heard the brand name before, but then I wasn't any kind of gun expert. I now decided that this was some sort of gimmick pistol. It was a huge revolver with an ornamental handle straight from the cowboy movies, and had a barrel that was at least eight inches long. The size of the gun made the .38-caliber bore appear tiny, like a piece of copper tubing encased in a foot diameter of concrete. Along with the gun had come an honest-to-goodness, Wyatt Earp quick-draw holster—only if Wyatt had tried to draw *this* gun on anybody, he would probably have wound up by shooting himself in the foot. I rolled the cylinder, *click-click-click*, then inserted five rounds in the chambers and left one empty. I glanced toward the lobby to make sure the clerk hadn't noticed me, then went about trying to hide the gun.

I tossed the holster into a nearby trash can and stuck the Siebrig into my pants pocket. The result was a joke; the barrel was doing its damnedest to poke a hole in the bottom of my pocket and the handle was on a level with my belt. Next I tried shoving the gun inside my waistband and covering the handle with my shirt. The result was even more comical; the knit fabric molded around the handle, and the barrel made an obscene bulge in the front of my pants. There was a news rack nearby, and finally in desperation I bought an *Orlando Sun* and folded the Siebrig inside the newspaper. Then, carrying my bundle under my arm, I took off in search of Donna's room.

I came to the first building, went through a breezeway, and entered a huge courtyard. Beads of sweat were on my forehead; I wiped them away with a handkerchief. I didn't think that it was any hotter, temperature wise, in Orlando than it was in Dallas, but this Florida humidity was something else. It was getting dark fast, but didn't seem to be cooling off. My shirt was sticking to my back.

The building was three stories high and surrounded the courtyard on all sides. Inside the courtyard fifty-foot palm trees grew around a swimming pool the size of a football field. Underwater lights in the pool made aqua shadows that danced on the exposed aggregate walks.

I stopped to check a first-floor room number: 1128. The room directly overhead had a balcony with an iron railing; I stepped back and looked at the second-floor. Donna's room, 3340, would be in the third building, on the third floor, and at the back. I left the courtyard, went through an iron gate, crossed a small parking lot, and walked through another breezeway.

The courtyard in Building Two was identical to the one I'd just left; here one palm tree had been cut down to a three-foot stump and stood out like a missing tooth. Two teenagers, a boy and a girl, were wrestling and giggling in the shallow end of the pool; as I passed by, the girl twisted in the boy's grasp and shrieked, "Stop it, Dickie. Stop it." The way she was laughing, if Dickie stopped it he was a fool. I left Dickie and the girl to their whatever and went on to Building Three.

This patio was different. The pool was small and in the shape of a parabola, and had no diving board. On the far bank, about twenty feet from the pool's edge, was a circular bar covered by a pointed bamboo roof. The bartender, a jolly-looking gent who must have weighed over three hundred pounds, and who wore a flowered Hawaiian shirt the size of a tent, was free-pouring light rum into a tall glass. He had one customer, a woman with long auburn hair who was a whole lot older than she was trying to look. She was wearing a French bikini and she didn't look very good in it, fleshy hips bulging at the sides and rolls of flab sticking out beneath the snug top. She was drinking a hurricane in a tall, bell-shaped glass and sitting unsteadily on a wooden stool. The bartender lifted his sirloin of a hand and waved at me. The woman lifted her glass in my direction in a toast. I nodded to both of them. An iron staircase ran up the side of the building in a zigzag pattern, and I climbed the stairs to the third floor. On the way up I passed a square-shouldered young man who was wearing red swim trunks and had a towel draped over his shoulder. He barely glanced at me. My Nikes made rubbery squeaking noises on the steps.

As I neared Donna's room I felt a chill of anticipation, accompanied by a nagging dread. She should be here by now, actually should have been in her room by the time I'd called from the Orlando airport. What if I'd been wrong? What if Bodie had somehow beaten me here? Jesus, what if . . . ? I reached inside the folded newspaper and touched the handle of the gun.

Using the third-floor walkway, I skirted around to the exterior of the building and found Room 3340. The door was painted a dull red and the numerals ran in a diagonal pattern. Far below and behind me, headlights moved in slow motion down the freeway. I steadied myself, took a deep breath, and knocked twice.

Silence, no sound from within, just the faraway rushing noise of freeway traffic. I shifted my weight from one foot to the other. Still nothing.

I knocked again, three quick raps with my knuckles.

A full minute went by. From inside the room, nothing. My spine was a row of prickly icicles. I tried the knob. It turned easily and the door swung inward with a feathery sliding noise over thick carpet. I went inside.

Donna had taken a suite. I was standing in a small sitting room, maybe ten by twenty, with a couch, two easy chairs, and a console TV. There was muted light from a small lamp beside the couch. On my right was a kitchenette complete with a miniature stove and a porcelain sink. Directly in front of me was an open doorway; through it the foot of a bed was visible. The bed was covered with a green quilted spread. Beyond the bed was a sliding glass door that led to the balcony overlooking the pool and patio.

I took two hesitant steps in the direction of the bedroom.

Donna stood up behind the couch and leveled a derringer at me. "Don't dare move," she said. The lamplight illuminated the creases of determination across her forehead.

My heart plummeted into my belly, and for just a second I thought I was going to be sick. *Not Donna. Sweet Jesus, not Donna, anyone but her.* I was looking down the pistol barrel, and right then I wouldn't have cared if she shot me. She was holding the little derringer in both hands, her arms extended, and even standing there holding a gun on me, an all-business air about her, the lady simply took my breath away. I opened my mouth, tried to speak. I couldn't.

Her features softened at once and she let the derringer hang loosely at her side. "Rick. Oh, Rick, I'm . . ."

She came around the sofa and buried her face in the hollow of my shoulder. She was shaking. I stood there like a store window dummy for a second, then let my bundle, Siebrig .38 and all, slide to the floor as I threw my arms around her and hugged.

She felt warm and alive and smelled of lilac. She was wearing a rose-patterned cotton shirt with pale blue shorts and white sandals. Her hair was soft and downy against my cheek as she moved her head and whimpered against me. I took her chin and lifted her face to mine, kissed her eyes, tasted her tears, placed my mouth on hers. Her lips yielded, pliant at first, then demanding as she darted her tongue between my teeth. She slid her arms around my neck. The derringer's handle pressed gently against my collar.

Donna withdrew her arms from around me, pushed against my chest, and stood back. Her lips were parted and her breathing was slowing. She said, "God, I thought you were . . ."

I took the derringer, laid it on the table beside the lamp, then sat on the couch, and held out my hands. "What is it? Who's been here?"

She took my hands and sank down beside me. "Nobody. Nobody's been here, it's these phone calls." She glanced toward the bedroom. "Shh. Jacqueline, in there." She lowered her voice to a whisper. "We came in from the park around four, and the phone was ringing. A man . . . he said, 'Mrs. Brendy?' I'm registered here as Donna Morley, just like we planned. God, I nearly dropped the phone."

I rubbed my forehead. "Guy with a husky voice, Cajun accent?"

Her eyes widened. "You know him? Who is he?"

I just didn't want to drop all of it on her at once. "Tell you in a minute," I said. "First you tell me. What'd he say?"

She pulled her legs up underneath her and sat on her ankles. "Something about a key. I don't know for sure, I was trying to get rid of him. I told him my name wasn't Brendy and hung up, I was so petrified."

"Hanging up wouldn't work with this guy. How long before he called again?"

"Not over five . . . hey, who is he?"

"Later," I said. "What'd he say the second time?"

"The key again. The key, that's what he called it, as though I'd know. He said that if I hung up on him again he'd come over here and he'd . . . God."

"He would, too," I said. "Whatever he told you." I pictured Breaux, a sneer on his lips as he talked to her. I marked the image down and filed it away.

"He said something about you," she said. "Said you wouldn't give it to him and he knew I must have it. I was shaking like a leaf and Jacqueline was standing there watching me with . . . as though she was going to cry. This trip's been so good for her, and then this creep. How do you know him?"

I thought about lying to her, I really did, even opened my mouth, then closed it. I finally said, "I celled with him for two years. Don't . . . he's a full-blood horse's ass, even more so than I thought. The key he was talking about is one Jack had hidden in your bookcase. It fits a storage locker where there was a lot of money. It's lucky that you didn't know about the key, because the fact that he thinks you might have it is probably the only reason he hasn't . . . done anything. But he won't wait much longer. Babe, you're going to have to trust what I say. I've got to get you out of here. Tonight, to another motel, and then tomorrow, well, I'm not sure. Donna, besides me, are you positive nobody knows where you are?"

A slight look of guilt crossed her face, then was gone. She said, "Mother. I know what we agreed on, but Mother? I had to let her know. If she didn't hear from me she'd panic. She was barely up to Jack's funeral, and I didn't want to give her any more to worry about."

I'd stayed far in the background at the funeral, on purpose. Funny, but I hadn't even looked for Mrs. Morley. I'd had too much else on my mind. I said, "That's okay, sure. She's still in Corpus, isn't she?"

Donna nodded.

I said, "What about Buddy?"

She looked down at her lap. "I never see him, and you know he's right there in Dallas? Two Christmases ago, I suppose. He seems to be doing well, in investments or something. I think Mom talks to him, but we've drifted pretty far apart. My own brother."

Once I thought about it, that wasn't really so surprising. Like most siblings, they hadn't gotten along really well. It's not like in the story books. I said, "Okay. Nobody else?"

She shook her head firmly.

I got up and crossed over to the kitchenette, looked around inside. There was a bottle of Johnnie Walker Red on the counter with the level of the whiskey an inch or two below the neck. Donna's nightcaps, that was about the extent of her drinking. From this angle I now could see Jacqueline, lying on her stomach on the bed. She wore loose green shorts and a matching T-shirt with one of the Care Bears— the green one with the half-moon sitting on a cloud as its logo, Bedtime Bear I think—in a grinning cartoon across the back. Jacqueline's face was turned to one side, her tiny thumb just inches from her mouth. She was breathing the gentle sleep breaths of children. I went back over and sat beside Donna.

"We're going to move, right now," I said. "You won't even check out of here, we'll just find another place and register under . . . I can't use my own name, but I'll think of something. You'll have to call your mother again, and tomorrow she's going to have to fly here from Corpus and pick up Jacqueline. You and I have some traveling to do, and we don't need to be putting a child through it. Your mother's going to have to keep mum about where we are, too, but unless she's changed a lot in the last twenty years or so, she won't have any problem with that."

Donna was watching me with a doubtful look in her eyes. I avoided meeting her gaze. She said, "I wish I knew more about what was going on."

I took her hands in mine. "You will. I'll fill you in on the whole bit, just as soon as . . . as we get the arrangements made, with your mother and all. Wake up Jacqueline, babe. Trust me."

I selected the Radisson because it was over in Orlando, pretty far removed from Disney World and away from the area where Bodie was likely to search for us. Donna had rented a car, a blue Ford Taurus. I thought briefly about ditching the rental car, then decided against it. Breaux wouldn't have any way of knowing what she was driving, and even if he did know, finding the car over in Orlando would be like finding a needle in a haystack. Besides, we were going to need transportation.

Waking Jacqueline was a job. The child had worn herself completely out at the amusement park and was sleeping as though drugged. Donna shook her, gently at first and then harder, but the only response Jacqueline gave was to curl up into a tight ball and murmur something about Mickey and Donald. Finally I told Donna to pack her things—which she did in a wink; thank whoever that she'd traveled light— while I carried Jacqueline to the car. As I slid her tenderly in the backseat of the Taurus, Jacqueline opened one eye and looked at me. "Daddy's friend," she said. Then she snuggled down among the cushions and was fast asleep once more. Donna carried her things down, I loaded them in the trunk, and away we went. I stayed well within the speed limit and drove with one eye on the road and the other on the rear view mirror. No one followed us and, surprisingly, I thought, no one shot at me.

The Radisson had seen better days. It was located on a four-lane thoroughfare along a row of tourist-trap T-shirt shops. Directly across the street from a shopping mall that had given up the ghost and apparently closed for good. The motel lawns needed mowing, and runners of grass had infested the sidewalks. The guests standing about the lobby and sitting inside the restaurant were families: men with executive paunches whose white legs showed that they didn't wear shorts too often, and harried-looking housewife types who chased unruly kids about the lobby or rescued squealing toddlers who were about to plunge headlong into the deep end of the swimming pool. I liked the idea. With Jacqueline in tow, Donna and I would fit right in.

I hesitated for a moment with the pen poised over the registration card, then filled in the blanks as Morris Tyler, Athens, Texas. It was the name on a phony driver's license that Sweaty had furnished me as a tool for chasing bail-bond skips. I paid cash in advance and didn't have to show the license after all.

We parked in a lot directly across from the deserted shopping mall, and with me carrying Jacqueline and Donna struggling along with the suitcase and overnight bag, we found our way down the sidewalk, through a maze of corridors, and located our room. It was a closet-sized arrangement with one king-size and a couch that converted into a double daybed. I hesitated, then placed Jacqueline on the king-size. "You can sleep with her," I said to Donna. A smile played on her lips as she turned down the covers. When she finished, she sat on the sofa, crossed her legs, and said, "Okay, double-oh-seven. What's the story?"

I'd known I was going to have to tell her sooner or later, but knowing it didn't make things any easier. I glanced at her luggage. "The scotch. I'm afraid you're going to need it."

She raised an eyebrow. "That bad?"

I picked up her suitcase, opened it on the foot of the bed, found the scotch, hefted it up. "Worse," I said.

I went down the hall, found an ice machine, filled a styrofoam bucket with ice cubes, and came back to the room. The two glass tumblers on a small stand didn't appear very clean, and I washed them out in the bathroom sink. I dropped in the ice, poured two fingers in both glasses, hesitated, and added another shot to one of the drinks. Then I added water and gave Donna the stronger of the two.

She sipped and made a face. "God, that's a real Cardinal Puff."

"Who?" I said.

"Oh, you know, Cardinal Puff. It's the old drinking game where everyone says a limerick and if you don't say it right you have to chugalug." She took another sip. "Mother still asks about you. When you didn't marry me, she was more disappointed than I was, I think."

Not as disappointed as she's going to be when she finds out what I've gotten you into, I thought. I swallowed some of my own drink, took a deep breath, and told her. All of it, the indictment, everything. She listened calmly, her expression a mask, her gaze level. She sipped from her glass occasionally, and once lit a Virginia Slim, took a couple of puffs, and stubbed the cigarette out in an ashtray. When I'd finished she said quietly, "I'll have to let it sink in for a while. Watch me, I may start screaming and kicking my feet."

"It's a lot to take at once," I said. "I'm sorry, babe. I wish I could've given it to you in smaller doses."

"And this Breaux person. He's supposed to be your friend and he—God, I thought there was supposed to be honor among thieves."

"That's a fairy story," I said. "The penitentiary's loaded with guys like Bodie Breaux. I put together a theory around my second year at El Reno: it's all self. All those guys are interested in is number one. They all give each other a line about how they're going to be friends for life, and once they get out a lot of them do hang around together. But that's mainly because nobody else will have anything to do with them, and believe me, if push comes to shove they'll stick a knife in their buddy in a minute. If I'd just remembered my own theory, then I wouldn't have trusted Bodie as far as I could throw him and we wouldn't be in this mess. Another thing you can mark up as being my fault. They used you, too, Donna."

Her expression changed, slightly inquisitive now, watching me calmly.

"To get me," I said. "They knew I was the perfect fall guy, in fact that's probably why Bodie kept in touch from time to time. He was keeping his finger on me so I'd be handy when he needed to screw me. They knew if you called I'd come running."

"How would they know that?" she said. "I don't think Jack would have told Fred Cassel or anyone else that I'd known you before—"

"Jack wouldn't have to tell anyone. Bodie already knew about you and me. This probably won't make you feel like Betty Grable on a World War II bomber, babe, but you were quite a hit up at El Reno. That picture of us, the one at Las Colinas? I had it in my cell, and Bodie saw you every day. He'd have recognized you from that photo. Don't worry, he saw Jack's wife even if you didn't know him. That would be taking care of business to Breaux. Even if I hadn't looked him up to help me with Skeezix, he'd have accidentally on purpose bumped into me in the next day or so."

She reached out and pushed a gray lock of hair away from my forehead. Her hand was cool and dry. She said, "You kept that picture? You're a mystery man if I ever. First you give me the gate, now you tell me you had my picture hanging up in your cell. Rick, you broke my heart half in two, and I think you knew it. I only started in with Jack to spite you. Not that I didn't care for him later. God, that's a shameful admission for a new widow to be making."

I stood and paced the room, forcing myself not to look at her. "Not now, Donna. We just don't have the time. We're going to have to stay loose and on the move. I guess you'd better call your mother." On the bed, Jacqueline stirred. She rolled from her back onto her side with a tiny sigh.

"Sure," Donna said, reaching for the telephone. "It's good there's an hour's difference. Mom turns in with the chickens these days."

I sat down and fidgeted, listened in a daze while Donna called her mother. Mrs. Morley used to sit Buddy and me down and give us lectures, and her chocolate chip cookies were so delicious that we always listened. Donna would sneak in to steal one of the cookies occasionally, and though we wouldn't tell Mrs. Morley on her, we always made it a point to give Donna hell afterward. Donna's phone conversation didn't take but a few minutes; Mrs. Morley was the kind of mom who would understand that her little girl needed her, and that would be all there was to it. I caught enough of the conversation to know that Mrs. Morley had heard about the indictments, and that she didn't believe a word of them. I felt pretty good about that.

Donna hung up, called and checked the airline schedules, then briefly talked to her mom again. When she hung up a second time, Donna said to me, "She's got to change planes in Dallas. The earliest she can get here is around two, on American. I think it's the same flight you came in on today."

I nodded. "It is. We'll have to watch ourselves until then."

From over within the bed, Jacqueline said, "Were you talking to Grandma?" She sat up and rubbed her eyes.

Donna and I glanced at each other. Finally Donna said, "Yes. You're going to stay with her a while."

Jacqueline sniffled. "I don't want to. I want to go to Disney World."

Donna went over and sat beside her, and anyone who didn't think that Donna was a first-rate mother, maternal instincts and all, just had to read the expression of concern on her lovely face. "You've been to Disney World, darling. Mommy has some things she has to do, and Grandma is going to take care of you. You know you like going to Grandma's house."

Jacqueline began to cry. "You promised me, Mommy. You promised."

I probably shouldn't have gotten involved, but watching little girls cry affects me even more than seeing big girls turn on the tears. Which is quite a bit. I said to Donna, "I suppose we could take her in the morning. The plane's not coming in until two."

Donna, cradling her daughter's head against her chest, gave me a sharp glance, then nodded. "How about that? You can go see Mickey Mouse in the morning and tell him good-bye, *and* get to go to Grandma's."

Jacqueline looked up and for just an instant a look of cunning crossed her face. If all—and I mean one hundred percent of all—children have anything in common, it's the ability to know when they've got adults by the throat and can get their way. Jacqueline said, "And can I watch TV right now?"

Donna rolled her eyes. "I suppose, for just a little while."

Jacqueline looked at me, now with a growing look of little-girl excitement. "And will you take me on the Space Mountain ride? Mommy's afraid to."

Donna looked to me, winked, and said, "Yeah, Mommy's a big chicken."

I shrugged. "Well . . . sure. Yeah, okay, I'll take you." I bent over and switched on the TV. The set made a tiny sizzling noise, then came on. And there I was, my picture in living color right there in the middle of the screen. I said quickly to Donna, "Get her."

Donna glanced at the picture, then snapped to. She bent her head to block Jacqueline's view in a hurry. "And for a really big treat, I think the man in the coffee shop has ice cream." Jacqueline squealed and clapped her hands. Donna picked her up and carried her quickly to the door, the little girl still in her shorts and Care Bear T-shirt. Donna scooped Jacqueline's shoes up in one hand, said quickly to me, "We'll be in the coffee shop," and left.

So we were now national news, Donna and I. I had to admit, the television pictures were about as much as I could have hoped for. The photo of me was a twelve-year-old football shot, with me in a silver and metallic blue uniform, wearing pads and about fifty pounds heavier than I was now. Also, my hair in the news release was merely salt-and-pepper instead of its current silver gray. They used Donna's picture from the wall alongside the staircase in her house: the semicheesecake photo taken on the deck of the yacht, with her posing with the marlin. Just sensational for the viewing audience, but I doubted whether anybody was going to recognize either of us from our TV pictures. I increased the volume and listened to the news blurb—there was really nothing new, just a rehash of the same things I'd heard earlier on the local Dallas radio broadcast—waited until our story was followed by a picture of Oliver North with Fawn Hall, his leggy secretary, in an insert photo in the upper right corner of the screen, then switched off the set, and went downstairs. Before I left, I stowed the Siebrig .38 in a drawer and tucked Donna's pearl-handled derringer into my back pocket. No way was I going unarmed again. I paused outside the suite, locked the door, and rattled the handle.

Outside, halfway around the hotel building in the direction of the coffee shop, I paused and looked around. A three-quarter moon was just above the horizon and the Little Dipper twinkled directly overhead. There was no one wandering around in the parking lot; on the main thoroughfare the traffic had thinned to practically nothing. Breaux couldn't

possibly know where we were. But he was out there somewhere, searching and waiting and watching. Sooner or later
I was going to see him. I patted the handle of the derringer
and went on my way.

The coffee shop had five customers besides us, a Mr.-Hobbs-
takes-a-vacation type along with a pudgy wife and two pudgy
kids, and an overweight woman in a wraparound flowered
dress who sat alone at the counter, drinking coffee. Jacqueline put away two chocolate sundaes—she asked for the second one rather coquettishly, and when the waitress set the
second mountain of whipped cream, crushed nuts, and mara-
schino cherries at her elbow Jacqueline's eyes got round as
saucers—while Donna and I had one scoop of vanilla apiece.
On the way back to the room, on the stairs leading up to
the second floor, Donna told Jacqueline that it was bedtime
and that she'd changed her mind about the TV watching.

"*Maaa*-um. You promised. Can't I just for a teeny bit? I'll
go see what's on." Jacqueline quickened her pace, leaving us
behind watching her cute knees moving like pistons and her
long mahogany hair wiggling from side to side as she
bounded out of sight up the stairs.

"Damn all that sugar," Donna said. "She's high as a tree,
no telling when I'll get her to sleep. And the TV won't help,
either."

"Well, she won't be turning it on just yet," I said. "I locked
the door when I left to meet you. Jesus, you do have your
key, don't you?" I was fumbling in my pockets, picturing my
own room key lying on top of the TV as I'd turned off the
set. We reached the top step and went down the second-
floor hallway toward our room.

"Yes, I've got it," she said. "But you really should be more
careful. You could lock yourself—" Donna halted in mid-
sentence and stopped in her tracks. Her jaw slackened.

Forty feet down the hall in front of us, Jacqueline stopped
in front of our room, turned the knob, banged open the door,
and charged on in.

Donna said, "Rick, I thought you said you locked the—"

I was already running, legs churning, hand digging into
my back pocket for the derringer, bringing it out, airing back

the hammer. My breath whistled between my teeth like a marathoner's breath as I ran into the room and stopped, pistol ready. Jacqueline was saying in her little-girl voice, "What are you doing?"

She was looking up at a frail woman in a maid's uniform who stood near the foot of the bed. Donna's purse was in her hand, and as she looked at me she dropped it. The purse fell on the bedspread, spilling change, car keys, and a round plastic compact. The woman held out her hands, palms out. Her tongue lolled to one side of her mouth. "Lord, mister, don't shoot me," she said.

I just stood there holding the gun. Donna came alongside me from out in the hall. She was breathing fast.

The woman sat on the edge of the bed and covered her face with her hands. "Please, sir, my baby's sick. I never do nothin' like this before, I swear."

Jacqueline stepped forward, reached up, and patted the maid on top of the head. "Poor lady," Jacqueline said. "I got some cookies, you want one?"

After the dumbfounded maid had become the first burglar in history to be rewarded by a twenty-dollar tip from the intended victim, she left. Then Jacqueline got her way. We turned on the TV and sat on the couch, Jacqueline in the middle and Donna and me on either side. The late show was in progress, and it was a great children's program. *The Exorcist*, starring Ellen Burstyn.

We'd tuned in on the scene where the demon-possessed child throws her mother to the floor and tries to crush her to death with a mammoth dresser. Donna and I stared at each other in horror. In between us, Jacqueline was giggling.

Donna came to me in the wee hours of the morning. She and Jacqueline had been sleeping in the king-size; I'd sat on the sofa until I'd heard their even breathing, then turned down the daybed, and crawled in myself. I was on my side, only half asleep when something bumped the edge of the bed. I opened one eye.

Donna was standing there in a filmy white nightgown that

tied at the throat and extended to just above her knee. In the dimness of the room, she smiled at me.

I said, "Why aren't you—?"

She reached out and covered my mouth. "Shh," she said. She undid the bow and slipped the gown over her head; the lacy thing fluttered to the carpet. She stood erect. Two white strips of flesh divided her smooth, even tan. My breath caught in my throat.

She folded back the covers and slid in beside me, bed springs creaking slightly, dark waves of hair spreading out on the pillow. She snuggled close, her arms about my waist, her firm bare thigh sliding between my legs, her lips inches from my chin. The scent of lilac mixed with the faint odor of tobacco.

"Take me," she said. "Now, dammit. Don't give me a chance to feel guilty about it."

We spoke in whispers.

"It's this act I'm putting on," Donna said. "Actually I'm petrified. You'll have to pardon me, I'm new at being on the lam."

I glanced toward the king-size, where Jacqueline continued to snore little snores. After what I'd just been through, I decided that the kid could sleep through a tornado. I said, "It won't be for long. First we get Jacqueline safe with your mother, then I put you where they can't find you. One thing at a time."

Donna's hands were clasped behind her head, her long, fine legs outstretched and crossed at the ankles, her firm breasts rising and falling as she breathed. The thin blanket was on the floor in a twisted heap, the sheets rumpled and damp in spots. "Sounds wonderful," she said. "Where is it that I'm going to hole up?"

I was beside her on my naked belly, raised up on my elbows. "I've got a friend in Tampa—I don't think that's over sixty or seventy miles from here. The guy's name is Tyson. Good Plates Tyson. I'm not sure about his real first name, but I've got his phone number. We keep in touch, he's somebody I can count on."

"Good Plates? What is he, a dishwasher?"

"Not exactly. He's a guy I knew in El Reno. They call him Good Plates because he makes good plates. You know, like in counterfeiting."

Her chin moved upward a bit. "I don't think I'm cut out for this."

"We're in trouble, Donna, you want me to call the FBI? Plates will take care of you while I try and get us out of this. I'm going to have to go to Dallas and see some people. I think I can clear this up if I can stay out of jail long enough. One guy I have to see is a cop. You'll be glad to hear that."

She snickered. "A crooked cop, I guess."

"Honest as the day. Detective Atchley, Dallas County. He'll want to arrest me on sight, but I think he'll listen to me. Unless I've got him completly wrong, he's pretty good at putting two and two together."

"Are you sure he won't listen to you *after* he's locked you up? And then agree with you while he's throwing away the key?"

"I'm . . . well, I just can't let that happen," I said. "I'll probably have to talk to him over the phone if I want to keep breathing the free." I avoided looking directly at her. I had some things in mind in connection with talking to Atchley, but Donna had enough to worry about.

"I wonder if this will ever end," she said. "All of it, it's like I should be waking up soon. God, not a month ago I was . . ."

She rolled onto her side, her supple body twisting. The lump in my throat wouldn't go down no matter how hard I tried to swallow it. I couldn't undo any of the things that had happened, but I made a silent promise to myself that Donna wasn't going to get hurt any more. Not while I had breath left in me.

I put my arm around her and she nestled against me. In seconds my shoulder was wet with her tears.

FOURTEEN

The jiggling and rocking of the bed woke me up, and for a crazy instant I thought I was in an earthquake. I rolled onto my back to watch Ernie and Bert—a cartoon of the two fighting over a big green toothbrush—go up and down, up and down on the front of Jacqueline's T-shirt. Her feet were bare and she was doing her damnedest to transform the daybed into a trampoline.

"Time to get *uh*-up," she said. "Space Mountain today. Spa-a-ace Mountain. You promised, you promised." Her chanting was a little too loud and a little too cheery and cute as the devil. I sat groggily up and looked around.

I had a sudden flash of panic and patted the mattress beside me. If her daughter discovered the two of us in bed together, Donna was going straight up the wall. But Donna was gone, leaving only rumpled sheets and a faint lilac scent to remember her by. I still was naked; with a slight flush of my cheeks I bunched the covers around my waist. Bright sunlight was filtering into the room around the edges of the closed drapes.

I said to Jacqueline, "You're one kid that never runs down. Where's your mother?"

She halted her bouncing, steadied herself on the mattress,

and wrinkled her nose at me. "She went out. She told me not to 'sturb you till you woke up."

"Well," I said, "is this your idea of not 'sturbing me?" Donna's derringer lay on the floor, where I'd placed it last night in arm's reach. I pushed it gently underneath the edge of the bed. Jacqueline didn't seem to notice.

She giggled like a munchkin. "I'm not 'sturbing you. I'm playing."

The hallway door rattled, a key turned, and Donna backed carefully in carrying a plastic shopping bag under each arm. She wore blue Jamaican shorts and a white sleeveless knit shirt along with blue sunglasses with big Elton John lenses perched above her forehead, riding a crest of mahogany hair. She said, "Jacqueline, I *told* you not to . . . Gosh, Rick, I'm so sorry. I guess I should've taken her along."

"No sweat," I said, sitting up straighter and holding the blanket around me. "I was already awake. I told her to show me some tricks, that's all."

Jacqueline beamed at me and resumed her bouncing.

"That's enough, I said." Donna plopped the bags on the foot of the bed. Jacqueline halted and filled her cheeks with air. Then Donna said, "Thirty-four, thirty-four?"

"Huh?" I said.

"What, Mom?" Jacqueline said, eyeing the packages as only children can.

Donna rummaged in one of the bags and came up with a pair of pale blue denim Levis. She gripped them at the waist, shook them, and let the legs dangle near the floor. "These," she said. "Thirty-four, thirty-four, the same size as you're wearing. They're preshrunk. I got you a couple of shirts, too. Improve your traveling wardrobe."

"Space Mountain today, Mom," Jacqueline said. "Spa-a-ace Mountain. I never got to go yet."

Donna smiled wistfully and put her arm around Jacqueline's shoulders. Side by side they were like child and grown-up photos of the same beautiful woman. Donna checked her watch. "It's nine-thirty, Rick. Do you think we have time?"

"You women get out of here and let me dress," I said. "We'll make time."

*   *   *

We rode the silver *L* from the entrance to Disney World to the gate leading to the Magic Kingdom, whizzing along high above acres of lawns like putting greens, bed after bed of sun-washed red and yellow and blue flowers, and ponds with still aqua surfaces like polished glass. There was a big, calm lake on our left; on the other side of the lake the rolling fairways of three championship golf courses. As far as the eye could see, the landscape was dotted with leafy hedges sculptured into perfect likenesses of Mickey, Goofy, Donald, and Dumbo. We rolled through a tunnel that bisected two hotels; on our right, six tanned and flat-bellied dancers shimmied in grass hula skirts. The train picked up speed and we went on our way.

The car in which we were riding was three-quarters full, families mostly, and one group of women in their seventies or eighties who gawked and rubbernecked and chatted like Well-I-Never. I was seated by the aisle with Donna on my right, and Jacqueline squeezed between her mother and the window. I'd chosen the yellow MacGregor Tournament knit that Donna had bought for me—the other shirt was a maroon polo—and the shirt and jeans felt good and smelled new.

At some point during the ride, Donna nudged me with her elbow. She gestured with her head toward Jacqueline, who was sitting on her knees with her nose pressed against the window. Donna's voice was soft and warm and barely audible over the noise of the train. "She could have been yours, you know," Donna said.

My vision blurred slightly and the derringer pressed into my backside. I nodded, shifted, and crossed my legs.

On the ramp leading down into the heart of Space Mountain, Jacqueline grabbed my hand and swung it back and fourth. "Goody toenails," she said. "Goody, goody, goody. This is *fuh*-un. Mommy's a scaredy-cat." She cupped her hands at her mouth and yelled over the handrail, "Scaredy-cat, Mom. Scaredy-cat, scaredy-cat."

We were in baking Florida sunshine, standing in line among men in Bermuda shorts, walking shorts, or jeans, women in everything from near-nothing sunsuits to floor-length casual summer dresses, and little boys and girls who giggled and jumped up and down and clamored for the line to move faster. The glassed-in entrance to the Space Mountain roller coaster—which was enclosed in a mammoth silver building in the shape of a rocket ship and the size of a convention center—was about forty yards in front of us. On my right, a square sign attached to the railing announced that the wait from this point was approximately a half hour.

"Scaredy-cat, Mom. Mom's a scaredy-cat." Now Jacqueline was waving her arms and shouting at the top of her lungs.

Donna was a good hundred yards away, standing behind a low railing that encircled Space Mountain's perimeter. Her big, round sunglasses covered her eyes, and she wore a floppy straw sun hat I'd bought her, a pale blue hat with "WALT DISNEY WORLD" stitched in gold across its forward brim. In her shorts and snug white knit top, and with her perfect legs the color of dark rum, she stood out in the crowd like a movie queen. She smiled, waved, and blew a kiss in our direction.

My gaze shifted beyond Donna, over the heads of the throng to the huge building across the way housing the General Motors ride into the future. To the right of that building was the arch that separated Tomorrowland from Fantasyland, with men, women, and children streaming back and forth underneath the arch. As I looked once again to Donna, a flash of yellow caught my eye. I squinted and zeroed in. It was a yellow hat, bobbing in the crowd and approaching Donna from the rear.

My breath caught in my throat. I stepped forward and put one hand on the railing, ready to vault over, my free hand traveling to my back pocket and touching the derringer through the cloth.

A grizzled, white-bearded man wearing a yellow baseball cap and holding onto a cluster of green and white and red helium-filled balloons touched Donna's arm and held out one balloon by the string. She smiled at him and shook her head.

I relaxed and backed away from the rail.

Jacqueline tugged the hem of my shirt. " 'S matter?" she said.

"Nothing," I said. I took her hand and moved up in line.

*   *   *

The roller coaster whipped around corners and dropped suddenly in stomach-churning dips, speeding along in nearly total darkness. The bottom dropped from underneath us; we raced down a long incline in the blackness. I tasted my breakfast.

Jacqueline dug her fingers into my arm. "I'm *sca-a-ared*. I'm *sca-ared*," she wailed.

Hell, so was I. I hugged her to me, squeezed my eyes tightly shut, and took a death grip on the safety bar.

At Orlando International Airport, I told Donna to take Jacqueline on a stroll past the ticket counters. I watched them go, Jacqueline's head on a level with Donna's waist, Jacqueline's round white overnight bag dangling from a strap held in Donna's hand. Donna had changed her daughter for the flight: Jacqueline wore a pleated navy dress that reached her knees. On the dress were rows of identical outlines, a pink bunny rabbit kissing a white bunny rabbit on the nose. Jacqueline was wearing turned-down white socks and patent leather sandals that she scraped along the floor. As they passed the Ozark ticket counter, a rosy-cheeked man in his sixties smiled down at Jacqueline and patted her head. I ducked into the gift shop.

I went past a glassed-in counter topped by a computerized cash register between displays of Spearmint and Doublemint gum, Life Savers, and every flavor of Certs known to man, nudged my way around an enormously fat lady who was blocking the aisle, and found a newspaper rack. Passing over the Orlando and Tampa papers, I selected a *Miami Herald*, unfolded the paper, and spread it open.

There it was on the front page, midway down from the top, the most prominent headline screaming, "Search Continues for Missing Beauty, Former Football Star." A crazy grin tugged at the corners of my mouth; all it took was a string of murders and some innovative reporters to transform the Offside Goat of the Decade into a star. I scanned a couple of lines of the story before side-by-side photos of Donna and me, positioned directly beneath the article, caught my eye.

These pictures were better than the ones I'd seen on TV.

Jesus, a whole lot better. My image was one that I'd seen over and over, so many times that I was sick of the thing. It was the mug shot taken on my release from Big Spring, the one stapled inside the front cover of my parole officer's file. They'd intentionally included the row of numbers across my chest; I knew them by heart, of course, 12959-077. My expression in the photo was a whole lot meaner than I really look—at least that's what I like to believe. My hair was quite a bit shorter—during my last year in prison I'd worn almost a burr—than it was now, but otherwise the likeness was pretty good.

I had a sudden sensation of someone watching me, and I looked around the gift shop. A gray-haired lady, a grand-motherly type complete with spectacles, was standing behind the cash register and facing in my direction. Her gaze wasn't directly at me; rather it was more behind me and over my head. Nonetheless, I shook the newspaper and held it higher, blocking my face from her view.

In Donna's picture, her hair was short and in bangs. I couldn't remember ever having seen her in such a hairstyle, so I assumed that the photo had been taken sometime while I was in prison, during the nine years while she was married to Jack and I was spending my nights dreaming about her. The picture was in color, the almost blue, almost gray eyes widened in a half question. Her features—the full lower lip, the straight, slim nose, the laugh crinkles at the corners of her eyes—were perfectly clear. The noose was tightening around us.

I folded the paper and returned it to the rack. As I left the gift shop, hands in my pockets and trying to appear casual, I felt the woman's gaze on me again.

As I stood off to one side and watched Mrs. Morley give Donna a motherly peck on the lips, then crouch down to hug Jacqueline in earnest, I was surprised at how youthful she appeared. In fact, she didn't look much different than when I'd been in high school; I would have recognized her anywhere. Her sandy hair had grayed and she wore gold wire-frame bifocals, but otherwise she was the same. Maybe a few extra wrinkles, but she'd strategically done her makeup to hide all that. She wore a tasteful summer cotton dress, charcoal gray, flesh-colored hose, and matching gray low-heeled shoes. Mrs. Morley had always been a stylish woman and would be until the day she died. Twenty years hadn't changed her much, and another twenty probably wouldn't do much more.

She let go of Jacqueline, avoided a skycap who rolled a baggage cart between us, came over, and properly hugged my neck. "You look well, Richard," she said. Her hug had been firm enough and her smile was for real, but the corners of her mouth were bunched in worry lines. Mrs. Morley and my mother were the only people in my life who'd ever called me by my given name. My folks had been gone for some time: fifteen years to be exact. They'd passed on together in an auto accident, on their way up to Dallas to watch me play for the Cowboys.

"Thanks, even if it isn't true," I said. "I hope you've got enough of a layover that we can visit. I'm sorry about the circumstances, Mrs. Morley, but—"

"Shh," she said, glancing cautiously toward Donna. She was busy with Jacqueline, checking the little girl's outfit, making sure that her daughter's face was presentable. Mrs. Morley said to me, "I have an hour until the return flight, and I do want to visit with you. Alone, at first. There are some things I wouldn't want little Jacqueline to hear."

I nodded, then went over, and whispered to Donna, "Take precious somewhere for a few minutes. Your mom wants to read me the riot act or something." I winked at her. Donna threw a sharp glance at her mother, who nodded.

Donna bent and said to Jacqueline, "I think I saw a couple of toys you might want to take with you. Back there, in the gift shop." Then she took her daughter by the hand and led her away, Jacqueline doing a happy little skip-step at her side. I escorted Mrs. Morley into the restaurant located just beyond the security checkpoint. We found a table, ordered two coffees, and eyed each other. I'd seen this same expression on Mrs. Morley years ago, when Buddy and I had been in one mess or another, and I didn't think I was going to like what was coming.

I broke the silence. "You don't know how much this

means, Mrs. Morley, to know there's still someone to count on."

Mrs. Morley sipped the coffee and set down her cup with a soft, glassy clink. Her lips were in a rigid line. "I didn't want to make a scene in front of Donna, Richard," she said, "and especially not in front of Jacqueline. But as far as counting on me goes, the only thing that my coming here proves is that blood is thicker than water. Buddy didn't want me to come at all."

"Buddy? You've talked to him?"

"Daily. He's worried sick about his little sister, just as I am. I'm not doing this for you, that you can count on. Didn't you do enough to Donna a few years ago? I wrote that off to you being a young man, but what you're into now certainly isn't kid stuff. You weren't such a bad boy, Richard, but I don't know what's happened to you in the past couple of decades. I don't think I want to know. I do think my baby girl is out of her mind for going along with you, but at least my grandchild is going to be safe. That much is a relief."

My mouth was hanging open. Of all people, I hadn't expected this from Mrs. Morley. The expression on her face reminded me of the look on a red-faced man who had stuck his nose just inches from mine in the federal courthouse hallway just moments after my conviction on the cocaine charges. "Fucking dope dealer," the guy had said. "They ought to put you away until your ass freezes." Now I swallowed hard and said to Mrs. Morley, "Now hold on, ma'am, I didn't—"

"Didn't what?" she said. "Don't tell me what you didn't do, I don't want to hear about it. Nobody says the kind of things they're saying about you unless there's something to it, so don't pretend to be lily-white, Richard."

I sipped some coffee, studied my knuckles. Finally I said, "I don't blame you for the way you feel, Mrs. Morley. Fifteen years ago I felt the same about people who'd been to prison as you do. But things happen, and everything you read in the paper or hear on the television isn't true. I didn't kill anyone, Mrs. Morley, and Donna didn't have anything to do with anyone dying, either. And I'll tell you something else. I love your little girl, Mrs. Morley, and I'm going to do everything I can to take care of her. I'm going to try to get her out of this mess, and I think I can. That's all I can promise, to try, and if you don't believe me, I can't do anything about that."

Mrs. Morley watched me in silence. Her jaw was firm. This was very much a lady, but she could be tough as well. After all, she was Buddy Morley's mom. She said, "I'm praying that you're telling the truth, Richard. For my little girl's sake, I'm getting on my knees and talking to God every night. I'll tell Buddy what you said. It might make him feel better about you."

The good-byes we said at the boarding gate were far too formal and far too strained. After she'd finished telling me how the cow ate the cabbage in the restaurant, Mrs. Morley had taken Donna aside. It had been my turn to entertain Jacqueline, which I'd done with an ice cream sundae. When we returned, Donna's gaze was averted from her mother, and Donna's mouth was twitching at the corners. Mrs. Morley had let Donna have it as well; maybe not with both barrels as she had with me, but enough so that Donna was more than a little shaken.

It was Jacqueline who broke the ice for all of us. She made it like a little trooper all the way to the doorway where the flight attendant was collecting the boarding passes. Then, without warning, she left her grandmother's side and ran back to Donna, patent leather sandals clicking on tile and her little pleated skirt swirling about her knees. She hugged Donna about the thighs and clung to her as though the world was ending.

"Oh, Mommy," she said between sobs, "let me stay with you. Please. Please, I'll be a good girl."

Suddenly I couldn't watch. I turned away and wiped tears from my eyes with the back of my hand. By the time I got ahold of myself and turned back to them, Mrs. Morley had joined Jacqueline. She was hugging Donna's neck, and her gaze met mine over Donna's shoulder. A tear rolled down Mrs. Morley's face and dropped from her chin.

She stepped around Donna and Jacqueline and hugged me

as well. She was crying as she said, "I do get carried away, Richard. Can you forgive me?"

"I already have," I said. "You just take care of Jacqueline. I can't promise how this will turn out, Mrs. Morley, but I can tell you a couple of things. I'm sure no saint, my track record shows that. I don't know if I can clear myself or not. I'm on the wrong side of some people who have a lot of clout. But I'm going to protect your daughter. That much you can count on."

We said our good-byes a second time, with a different meaning, and Jacqueline and Mrs. Morley boarded the plane. Jacqueline paused just before entering the gate, turned, and favored us with a tiny wave. Now she was smiling.

On the way back to the Radisson, it began to rain. The storm gathered in what seemed like seconds; one moment the clouds were white puffs in an ocean of blue, the next they had joined to blot out the sun and to send large drops plummeting down to slicken the pavement and muddy the windshield. I'd never before driven a Taurus, and it took a few seconds for me to locate the rental car's wiper switch. Finally the wipers rose hesitantly from their compartments and thunked monotonously back and forth.

As rain-silhouetted forests paraded by on both sides, Donna leaned back and crossed her legs, her knee close to the dash. She closed her eyes, then said, "Mother teased me to death about you."

"She didn't look to me like she was teasing," I said. "She looked pretty grim." I slowed the car, peered through rain-drops like a thousand falling pencils, recognized the intersection, and turned onto the thoroughfare leading to the Radisson.

She rolled her head on the seat back and looked at me from a slanted angle. "Oh, not back there at the airport, silly. Years ago, when we were kids. When I was a kid, you and Buddy always seemed like men to me. Mom teased me quite a bit, but it was really more Buddy's doing. I was ten and had this horrible crush on you, and Buddy found out. He told Mom. She pulled my chain a little, but Buddy was downright mean. Every day he'd threaten to tell you about it, and every time he did that I'd about die. You know how big brothers are. Can you remember the time your football letter jacket was missing from your locker?"

I had a tickling of memory, not a clear image. High school seemed a hundred years ago. "Seems like I recall something about it," I said.

"Well, if we ever get out of this," she said, closing her eyes and facing front, "I'll return your property to you. It's still somewhere at Mother's, I think."

I drooped my hand over the wheel, steering with my wrist. "You?"

"Guilty," she said. "I was in fourth grade and not even supposed to go near the high school. I asked one of the building janitors which locker was yours, told him I was your sister and I had to leave something for you. I rolled your jacket up and carried it under my arm. All the way home I expected to hear sirens. God, I was so petrified."

The Radisson was now a hazy outline through the sheets of rain. I braked and eased the Taurus across the slick pavement into the right-hand lane behind a forty-foot National Van Lines tractor trailer. "Well, at least I had a fan," I said.

"Oh, more than that. You went off to Texas A&I the same year Elvis came out of the army. Oh, I had a poster of Elvis along with everybody else in the world, but I'll bet I was the only teen queen in America who hung Elvis on the left, the Beatles on the right, and the Texas A&I Javelinas in the center. And when you made the Cowboys, wow. There wasn't anybody at Ray High School that didn't hear about it from me. Rick, I've got a confession to make."

"Sounds like you've already made one," I said.

She stroked my forearm with a perfectly formed hand. "Only a small one. This confession's a lot bigger."

I steered the Taurus into the right turn lane. The rain let up abruptly, as though someone had turned down the faucet. "I'll drop two counts and let you plead to one," I said.

"Let me . . . ?"

"Let you plead to one count if you make a confession. It's a plea bargain: the U.S. attorney lets you plead to one count if you won't take him to trial."

"Silly," she said.

"That's what I thought about the U.S. Attorney," I said. "What's your confession?"

"Well, you remember when I came to Dallas and took the job with Wilson Drilling? The one you lined up for me?"

Sure, I remembered. So had the county prosecutor and the FBI. I said, "Yeah. Buddy called me and asked if I could find work for his little sister. Tom Wilson had hit quite a few wells in a row and was a football groupie, always hanging around. It wasn't that big of deal. I just made one call."

"Maybe not to you, but it was a big deal to me," she said. "See, I already had a job lined up in Houston, as a secretary with Exxon. Only I hadn't told Mother and Dad about the Houston job, and when Buddy suggested that he might be able to get *Rick Bannion* to find me a job in Dallas, God, I like to have swooned. I was supposed to go to work in Houston on a Monday, but I called Exxon on Friday and told them I wasn't coming. Just on the chance I might get to see you. What do you think about that, buster?" She reached over and tickled my ribs.

If I could've rolled the clock back a dozen years I would have known how to answer, but now I wasn't sure. We were making the turn into the Radisson parking lot, the awning over the lobby entry on my right. We rolled through puddles that sent out fine sprays on both sides of the Taurus. The rain had stopped completely, the storm ending as quickly as it had come, the cloud bank thinning and showing patches of brilliant blue. I nosed the Taurus into a parking space near the sidewalk leading to the side entrance to the hotel. The wipers were making rubbery squeaking noises. I turned them off. I cut the engine and the Taurus gave a final shudder and was still. The motor ticked and cooled.

Donna sat up and put her hand on the door handle. "What now?"

My problem came back to me in a flood: the indictments, the warrants, our pictures in the paper, Connie Swarm's riddled body, all of these superimposed over a leering image of Bodie Breaux. I said, "I think we'd better start moving, babe. Get you out of this town and over to Tampa. I don't think we should chance another night here."

"You mean right now?" She nervously licked her lips.

"Now. Pronto. I'll breathe easier with you somewhere you can't be found, and the quicker we get this handled, the quicker I can go about trying to straighten this mess out."

She opened her door and put one foot on the ground. "Well, far be it from me to question you, sir. I'll go upstairs and pack, and you can go settle our bill. I do have time to pack, don't I?"

I hunched over the steering wheel and peered toward the side entrance to the hotel. A frail elderly woman wearing a pink sun bonnet and carrying an umbrella came out, looked upward and found that the rain had gone, and went back inside. I said to Donna, "I wish I could joke about this, and maybe someday I can. But right now I can't see anything funny about it. Bodie shouldn't have any way of knowing what hotel we're staying in, but I don't feel safe in the same town where he's looking for you. And call me paranoid or whatever, but I don't like the idea of you going up in that room alone. So tell you what. *You* settle the bill, and I'll go pack. I paid cash for the room, but there might be a service charge, phone calls—yeah, we made a couple." I reached in my pocket and gave her a hundred-dollar bill. "You can join me after I check everything out. And Donna. When you get to the room, knock loud. If I don't answer, you beat it out of there."

She took the money and watched me, and for just a second I thought she was going to cry. Then she snapped out of it, flashed me a pretty good imitation of a smile, and left in the direction of the lobby. She carefully avoided the puddles of standing water as she crossed the parking lot and disappeared around the corner of the building. I went in the side entrance and up to our room.

There was a tightness in my chest as I turned the key, brandished the derringer, and went inside. Everything looked shipshape: the freshly made bed, the couch and TV, the bottle of scotch, now half full, on the small table where I'd left it. I gasped at my reflection in the mirror as I entered the bathroom. Nothing there, either. I carefully folded my new shirt along with the clothes I'd worn on the plane and dropped them in Donna's suitcase, then got the Siebrig .38

from the dresser drawer, and packed it as well. Also in the dresser I found two summer dresses, a yellow bikini, three blouses with matching shorts, three bras, and three pairs of skimpy lace panties that I looked over carefully. Just as I was about to toss Donna's things on top of my own in the suitcase, I paused. There was a little warning bell going off somewhere inside me. Where was Donna? She should have been here by now. I went downstairs, stood outside the exit, and scanned the parking lot.

The cloud cover had completely dissipated, and it was steamy as a jungle. Flashes of sunlight reflected from the puddles on the asphalt and the roofs of the cars. I watched a small red pickup truck—a Nissan, probably, it was about the right size—mosey off the thoroughfare and cruise slowly into the parking lot. Deciding to go to the lobby and look for Donna, I took a step in that direction. As I did, she came into view around the building. Her hands were on her hips and she was shaking her head. A sigh of relief escaped me.

She saw me, stopped, smiled and waved. Then she cupped her hands at her mouth and shouted, "Their computer's got bats in its belfry, God, I thought they'd never get the balance right." Then she carefully picked her way around the standing water as she came toward me.

The little red pickup pulled alongside Donna and stopped. Its driver's side window was down and a hand was sticking out the window. Held in the hand was a . . . Jesus Christ, I thought, is that a potato? That's what it was, all right, someone was waving a potato at Donna. Only they weren't exactly waving it, they were pointing it, and burrowed into the heart of the potato was the barrel of a slim automatic pistol. A potato: the perfect, foolproof, untraceable silencer.

I was able to yell, "Donna!"

The potato exploded with a dull pop like the breaking of a balloon. Donna pitched sideways as though hit with a flying tackle, tried to right herself, then sprawled headlong into a big puddle of water. The water flew in droplets. Donna lay facedown and didn't move.

The pickup's gears meshed. It lurched, picked up speed, and wheeled out of the parking lot.

My feet were pounding on the sidewalk, my breath whis-
tling between my teeth. The pickup bounced up and down
as it careened onto the thoroughfare and straightened out;
the outline of a bald, square, hatless head was visible
through the rear window. It was Bodie, of course. But then,
I'd already known that.

I charged across the parking lot. With my second long
stride my foot landed square in a puddle; a sheet of flying
water soaked my pants and shoes. I'd forgotten about the
truck now, forgotten all about Bodie, about the hotel,
about where I was. All I could see was lovely Donna, facedown in muddy water. I thought, *God, Donna, don't die. Anything, anything at all, just please . . . Jesus, please, babe, hang
on.*

I knelt beside her, my knees inch deep in muddy water,
grasped her shoulder, and rolled her over. Her arms were
limp as towels, her soft lips parted. A bright red stain was
spreading around a hole in her blouse, over her heart. Her
eyes were open, vacant, and staring. One appeared blue, the
other gray.

I shielded my face with my arms and cried. My body
heaved with sobs, sobs of frustration mixed with grief and
hatred for myself. Loathing for myself. I'd failed. Failed
Donna. Failed.

A gravelly female voice behind me said, "Careful, he's got
a gun."

A man, also behind me, said. "Are you sure it's him?"

"Never surer, dearie," the woman said. "It's the same man,
just like in the picture. I thought there was something funny
about that guy."

The man raised his voice. He had an East Coast, northern
accent and his speech was loud and piercing. "Get on the
phone, Billy. Get on the phone and call the police."

I raised my head. Not fifteen feet away stood the same
overweight woman I'd seen the night before in the coffee
shop. She wore a strapless, backless tube dress that was too
small. A man stood beside her, a beer-bellied, gray-haired
man with fleshy white legs, wearing flowered Bermuda
shorts and rubber shower shoes. The man had a *Miami Her-*

ald spread open in front of him. He was alternating his gaze between me and my picture in the paper.

The man said, "Jesus Christ, Anna, it could be him."

I scanned the parking lot and the entrance to the hotel. Quite a crowd was gathering, people standing in twos and threes, groups clustered by the building and in the lot.

I stood numbly. I didn't remember drawing the pistol, but there it was in my hand, the derringer. I let it fall limply to my side.

The man backed away, slowly at first and then moved faster, finally turning and making a break for it. His fat tail waggled and his white legs churned. "Take cover. Take cover, everybody. Jesus Christ, he may start shooting any minute."

The woman let out a terrified yelp and thundered after him.

"I called them, Granddaddy." The peanut-whistle voice came from a kid of around twelve who had just run from the direction of the lobby. He was a towhead whose mother let him eat too much. Puffs of flab were visible around the armholes in his purple tank top. "They're coming, they're coming," he said.

From the side entrance, a man yelled, "Inside, sonny, Christ, get a move on."

Out on the thoroughfare, faintly at first and growing louder, a siren bellowed.

The fog inside my head began to clear. The keys to the rented Taurus were in my pocket; I dug them out and took a couple of steps in the direction of the car, then halted, turned, and looked toward Donna. For an instant I imagined her waking up from her nap, standing, holding out her hand, smiling at me. But it was over for her, she'd never stand again. Never smile again. Never . . . I thought, *Can you ever forgive me if I leave you like this? I'm not going because I want to. Please, babe, please understand.*

The siren howled louder, now only blocks away.

I forced myself to look away from her and ran to the Taurus, yanked open the door, climbed in, and turned the key. The motor chugged, almost flooded, and roared to life. I backed up, dropped the lever into forward gear, and wheeled out of the lot. I didn't really want to, but as I wheeled onto the thoroughfare I glanced in the side-view mirror. Donna lay where she'd fallen, and the crowd was gathering around her still form.

FIFTEEN

The suntanned guy was built like Popeye, complete with big, muscular forearms and an anchor tattoo. He wore a billed captain's hat and a red-and-white striped T-shirt, and he was seated two stools down from me. He said, "Idn it amazing?"

I squinted to gaze past him down the length of the bar, past the old-timey, dusty-slatted Venetian blinds, out the streaked and grimy window. In the distance a seagull made wide circles in the air, and finally landed on a piece of drift-wood bobbing among the waves. Onshore a toddler stood ankle deep in salt water, scooping sand with a toy shovel and loading it into a pail.

The muscular seafaring type said, "Hey, pal. I said, 'Idn it amazing?'"

The wooden bar top was scarred with carved initials. My rum and Coke was nearly empty; and melting ice had diluted the drink to the color of weak tea. I thought about draining the glass, but wasn't sure I could raise it all the way to my lips without dropping it. My tongue was thick as prime steak. Finally I said to the guy, "Beg pardon?"

"Hey, you deaf?" he said. "It's fuckin' amazing, that's what it is. You shave and take a bath, you look like this guy. But don't do it. Rum-dum that you are, you ain't as bad off as this fucking guy. They get him, they gonna fry his ass."

He was showing me my picture in the *Tampa Gazette*. I'd seen the photo before someplace, sometime. Oh, yeah. In a different paper just a couple of days—or was it weeks?—ago. I said, "What day is this?"

"What day . . . ?" The seaman bent for a closer look at me. He had a square jaw and a big nose over a droopy Fu Manchu. "Hey, Charley, what kind of rummies you serving in here? This fucker don't even know what day it is."

Charley, a wrinkled, jockey-sized little guy who held the butt of a cigar clenched between yellowed teeth—for some reason I'd been calling him Joe—approached us and leaned on his side of the counter. He unscrewed the lid from a gallon jar, dipped into the pepper juice with grimy fingers, and held up a pickled sausage. He grasped the link between a thumb and forefinger and shook the moisture back into the jar. He said, "Man pays his money, sits up at the bar, I fixes him a drink. Hell, H.E., man's twenty-one I don't know if he's drunk or not. Sometimes you don't walk too straight yourself." Charley bit a chunk of sausage off and made a face.

"Yeah, but goddamn, Charley. You smelled this guy? Jesus, he'll run ya business off." H.E. tilted back his hat and took a pull from his beer. "How 'bout that, rummy? You ought to take some of your whiskey money and getcha a bar of soap, you know that?"

I scratched my chin through a half-inch stubble. Hell, money wasn't the problem. I had a roll in my pocket. The problem was . . . what the hell, I wasn't sure. I tried to remember how long it had been since I'd left the rented Taurus at a parking meter in downtown Tampa, but that had been a lot of hours and a lot of bars ago. I pictured a cot with dirty sheets and a guy who farted and snored sleeping next to me. Was it one or two nights that I had spent at the Salvation Army? Didn't matter, did it? I said again, "What day is this?" I pushed my glass in Charley's direction. "And another, please," I said. Maybe one more would erase the image of lovely Donna facedown in muddy water. The hundred or so drinks I'd had in the past—how long was it?—

hadn't wiped out her image, but maybe this one would do the trick.

The only other customer was a woman seated a few stools down from H.E. She was more of a girl, really, in her late teens or early twenties, with a pretty, round face and coal black hair, and she weighed close to three hundred pounds. She was wearing a red tent dress, and her puffy rear stuck out over three sides of her barstool. She said, "Hey, Charley, I'll take him home wi' me. He'll find out what day it is over there, all right. His lucky day's what it'll be."

Charley cackled like a henhouse fox, then broke into a coughing spasm without bothering to cover his mouth. Neither H.E. nor the woman seemed to notice Charley's manners. Charley took another bite of sausage and washed it down with water. "Hey, now, that's an idea," Charley said. "Want to go home with Rosie, fella? Trouble is, Rosie likes to get on top. The last two fellas she suffocated."

H.E. really seemed to get a kick out of that one, howling gales of laughter and slapping his knee. Rosie pursed her lips and didn't seem to think that Charley was very funny. For some reason, neither did I.

Charley leaned over for a close look at me. He had a long, bony, crooked nose and his breath smelled of sausage. He said, "It's Thursday, pal. And H.E.'s right, I ain't serving you no more. Doin' you a favor though you don't know it. You'll wind up in a squad car takin' a ride downtown if you ain't careful. They don't fuck around with public drunks in this town."

Squad car? I wasn't sure exactly why, but for some reason I didn't want to see any cops. I said, "Call me a cab?"

Charley pointed at H.E. and said, "What you think he—"

"No way," H.E. said. "Not me, it'll take a week to air out the hack. 'Sides, what makes you think this here rummy can pay for a cab?"

I dug in my pocket, floundering, feeling dizzy, thinking for a second that I was going to fall off the stool. I found a wadded fifty-dollar bill and dropped it on the bar. "I got money," I said.

H.E. picked up the bill, smoothed it out, looked it over,

flipped it, examined the other side. "Hey, rummy," he said. "You smelling better every minute, you know that?"

The cab was an ancient Ford. There was cotton stuffing poking out through holes in the upholstery, and the Ford rattled like a buckboard. It pulled to the curb in a neighborhood of pre-war, grayish wood houses with patches of scrubby grass in the yards. The streets had been mended so many times that there was more asphalt on the surface than concrete. A row of thick oak trees with long, gnarled branches overhung the sidewalks and curbs. The sun was setting and the trees cast big, dark shadows.

H.E. draped a weightlifter's arm over the seat back and turned around. "This here's the address you gimme. It ain't no castle, but a damn sight better than where I expected the likes of you to be livin'." A short, uneven sidewalk led to a house with a porch swing and a black screen door.

The ride hadn't sobered me up much. I groped for the door handle, pulled on it, and the rusty back door creaked open. I put one foot on the curb, made it halfway to my feet, and flopped back down inside the cab.

H.E. got out and came around to me, looking suddenly concerned. "Poor rummy, you really had a rough time of it. Come on, let ole H.E. help you." He hoisted me to my feet, put his arm around my waist, and steered me up the sidewalk, one halting step at a time. The guy was strong as an ox; he probably would have been an even match for me even if I had been sober. As it was, he was handling me as though I was Raggedy Andy.

And I had to admit, I was glad for the help. I'd never been much of a boozer, even in the old days, and the past seventy-two hours was really taking its toll. I had just enough of my senses intact to realize that I'd wasted precious time if I was going to do the things I had planned, but was far too drunk to do anything about it. I had to get some sleep. Had to sober up, clean up. Had to . . .

H.E.'s hand was digging into my side pocket, where I kept my bankroll. He was steering me along, keeping up the sympathetic chatter, but the bastard was picking my pocket.

I planted my feet, tried to stop. He took a firmer hold and

pushed me along. We were scant feet from the porch now, and I was conscious of his after-shave—a musky scent, maybe Old Spice—and the faraway noise of running machinery. I grabbed H.E.'s wrist and tried to pull his hand from my pocket. He strengthened his grip and lifted me bodily onto the porch.

I yelled. It was probably more of a croak, but as far as I was concerned, I was bellowing at the top of my lungs. H.E. clamped his hand over my mouth. I bit him. He grunted, then punched me in the ribs. The pain razored through me, slightly clearing the whiskey fog.

The screen door sung open, and the noise of machinery increased in volume, a clanking, throbbing sound that I'd heard before but couldn't quite place. Good Plates Tyson came onto the porch. His bushy eyebrows were knitted in anger, and his thin red hair waved in the breeze like bug tendrils. In the crook of his arm he carried a sawed-off, double-barreled shotgun.

"The fuck is going on out here?" Plates said. "You come any closer, I'll blow your ass off."

H.E. let me go and stepped to one side. His hands were balled into fists and he was breathing hard.

I felt a sloppy-drunk relief. Right then the shotgun was pretty as a bouquet of roses. I managed to say, "Plates."

Plates leveled the shotgun at H.E. To me, he said, "Jesus Christ, all I need, the hottest fucker in America. You look terrible. You been hiding in a sewer?" Then, to H.E., "What's your story, bud?"

H.E. managed a frozen smile. "Just makin' a livin', drivin' this here gent around in my cab."

The three of us stood there for a second, then Plates said, "Yeah? Well, looks like you got him where he was going. Now disappear, I'll take care of this guy. I know him. Jesus, he smells like a dead fish."

"Lucky?" Plates said. "Hell, lucky ain't the word for it. You got a golden screw in your belly button. I got old A.B. Dick cranked up, spitting out the twenties, suddenly there's two guys in front of my house and they're ducking it. Yeah, you're lucky. You and the cabbie both ought to be pushing up daisies right now. Let you try and throw a shoulder block into a load of buckshot." He was holding up a twenty-dollar bill, gripping the corner with a pair of tweezers. Plates had positioned the twenty by a lamp so that the light shone through the paper, and he was squinting carefully at the bill. Satisfied, he suspended the twenty from a clothespin, where it dangled from a line alongside a row of identical bills running the length of the room. There must have been two thousand of them, hanging about four feet off the floor. "Solid perfect," Plates said. "Shit, if Alex Hamilton's old lady was looking at them pictures, her drawers would get wet."

My eyes were having trouble getting accustomed to the shadowy contrasts in the room. I'd slept for twelve solid hours, showered, shaved, wolfed down three eggs over easy and six or seven crisp slices of bacon, and taken a three-mile walk in clean air and morning sunshine. I felt human once more, though my head still throbbed. I was sitting in an easy chair with one leg draped over an arm. "You're still making twenties," I said. "Seems like it'd take all day to pass enough of 'em to keep you in pocket money."

The lamplight reflected from Plates's scalp through his thin hair. His hair was like red spun glass. "That's the idea," he said. "Fuck the fifties and hunnerds, everybody's on the lookout for them. Same thing the U.S. attorney wanted to know when I got busted the last time, how come I made all them tens and twenties. Know what I told him? 'Shit,' I told him, 'they make great tips.' Man, was he pissed. They're still spending tens out there that old Plates made fifteen years ago." He sat down on a wooden kitchen stool. He wore blue jogging shorts and he crossed his skinny white legs. "What you wanting to do, Ricky? Go to Belize, maybe one of them islands down there? Shit, you ought to. It's a miracle nobody's recognized you, much ink as you're getting."

I licked my lips and scratched the bridge of my nose. "I can't leave the country. I got something to do."

He caught something in my expression and suddenly was serious. "You got a big hard-on for somebody, ain't you? You're damn sure not using your head, staying within a million miles of cops."

"Well, maybe I'm not," I said. "I don't have much time to

waste. Sooner or later they'll be picking me up. Listen, Plates. When you go shopping . . . that's still what you call it, isn't it, when you're passing that funny money?" He nodded. I went on. "When you go out, how do you disguise yourself? You're not exactly a forgettable guy."

He shrugged his birdlike shoulders and spread his palms. "Makeup. Shit, don't you remember the minstrel show up at El Reno? Yeah, okay, the singing wasn't so hot, but them blackfaces was straight from vaudeville. I'm a pro at it— shoulda done it for a living and won me a coupla Oscars. Never show 'em the same guy twice, is what I always say. Shit, there's guys took three, four bills from me at different times and never knocked me off."

I ran my fingers through my silver-gray hair. "Think you could do a job on me? There'd be something in it for you."

He waved as though he was batting mosquitoes. "Shit, Ricky, I wouldn't want no real money. I wouldn't know which was which." He bent closer, his gaze roaming my face. "Tell you what, though. Yeah. Yeah, I guess I could fix you so's your momma wouldn't know you. I can even make you up to be a broad, if that was your bag. Shit, make your dick longer if you wanted me to." He grinned. "But that'd cost you, I did that."

The mustache wasn't bad. It was thick and brushy and dark blond, a shade lighter than brown. And it looked plenty real. The part of the false mustache glued to my upper lip was a flesh-colored panty-hose material so that the individual hairs seemed to sprout from my own skin. Yeah, the mustache was pretty good. The rest of the disguise was so perfect that it was incredible.

I'd naturally assumed that a beard was part of the standard disguise. But Plates had said no, that's what everyone would expect, for a man in hiding to wear a beard. So instead he had used a plastic filler—it was a thick, gooey paste going on, but had dried into a smooth surface that looked and felt like my own skin, fatty tissue and all—to reshape my chin. Where my chin had been square it was now round, almost cherubic. Cotton stuffing had flared my nostrils and puffed out my cheeks so that my entire face now had a round, scholarly look. Soft contact lenses—these had been a problem at first, but after fifteen minutes of wearing I couldn't feel them in my eyes—had turned my eyes from blue to dark brown.

What Plates had done to my hair was the crowning touch. It was the same dark blond as the mustache, hanging straight down on the sides to touch the tops of my ears. And now I was bald on top. Plates had taken the better part of two hours working on my hair, his jaw working nonstop, and what he'd done was an absolute miracle. He hadn't used a razor at all; he'd done the entire job with scissors, painstakingly clipping the hair in sections so that I appeared to have tiny tufts sprouting here and there. The natural bald look, complete with sparse tendrils to wave in the breeze. I bent and examined the top of my head in the mirror for about the twentieth time. Couldn't have been better.

As I turned my back to the mirror and examined my rearview side, Plates said, "Remember to shorten your stride in them shoes. You're two inches taller. The shorter steps'll feel funny to you, but to everybody else they'll look natural."

"Jesus," I said, "those fat pouches hanging out over the rear of my belt, well, they're just the ticket. What do you call that stuff?"

"Aw, it's only a silicone. Is pretty good, though, huh? I've tried two or three different kinds, I get that stuff from a guy in Atlanta. One thing sure, nobody's gonna spot you. Hell, if you *tell* 'em who you are, they're gonna think you're bullshitting them. The stuffing in your mouth and nose even changes your voice. You probably don't notice it, but you should hear yourself talk. Like I said, Ricky, your own momma."

I faced the mirror, lifted and dropped my shoulders. The fat pouches on my back and sides gave the illusion that my shoulders were rounded. Enter one soft, pudgy bald guy.

"I don't think she'd know me, either, Plates," I said. "Trouble is, it's not my mother I'm trying to fool. It's some other folks."

Plates had finally made some money off me, I was pretty sure of that. The navy blue suit, white shirt, and thin polka-dot tie I was wearing couldn't have cost a third of the five hundred bucks I'd paid him. Plates was like that. He'd never have let me give him anything, but selling me a fifty-dollar suit for five hundred, now that was something else again. Part of the game. When I'd tried to pay him for the use of his pad and the makeup job as he dropped me off at Tampa Airport, he refused. Now he'd be laughing all the way home about what a sucker I was for giving him five hundred for the suit. Spending time in prison with a man lets you get to know him pretty well.

Now as I stood at a pay phone in my third airport in as many days, Muhammed Double-X said over the line, "Yeah, I got your message. The fuck you want with me? From what I'm seeing on the TV, I'd be better off not getting your message. Come on, Bannion, you popped the broad? Brendy's old lady? Whadja do that for?"

The message he was referring to was one I'd left with Elmo, the bartender at the Green Parrot, giving Elmo the phone number of the pay station where I now stood. Muhammed had returned my call ten minutes later.

"I didn't kill her," I said, feeling an empty space in the pit of my stomach. "Nobody else, either. I need your help."

"Sho you didn't. Nobody kills nobody. Help *you*? Shit, I got trouble enough, honky cop trouble. They busting my guys one after another."

"I've got things to do, Muhammed. You'll be better off for helping me, if you'll think about it."

"So convince me. And don't give me no shit about leading me to no Skeezix. That fat honky snitch ain't no more."

That stunned me; how the hell had Muhammed known Skeezix was dead? Never mind, I knew. The FBI shooting its mouth off again. The word would be out all over town. They'd also be putting out the word that I was under investigation for still another murder, Skeezix's. Mentally I chalked off the main bargaining approach that I'd planned to use with Muhammed.

"How about money?" I said. A porter rolled a baggage cart by; farther away a Sean Penn type, sunglasses and all, strolled through the airport with a white cotton sports coat slung over his shoulder and a big-breasted blonde on his arm. I shifted the receiver from one ear to the other.

"What money?" Muhammed said. "Fuck."

"Some money I'm holding. I'll pay you to help me." I crossed my fingers and hoped that the money was still there in Sweaty's office. If it wasn't, there'd be hell to pay.

"It'll take some serious bread for me to chance fucking with you," Muhammed said.

"I'm *talking* serious money," I said.

There was a moment of silence and I listened to the long-distance static and watched a Delta flight attendant pull her luggage along on little metal rollers. Her hips swayed nicely under her straight green skirt.

Finally Muhammed said, "Okay, you got me curious. Honeybear going to meet your plane. And Bannion. You better not be shitting me about the bread. Just stand around the gate after you land, Bear, he be watching you. The cops don't pick you up, he do. And any funny shit you ain't gonna be around too long."

DFW Airport on Friday afternoon was a madhouse, mobs of businessmen coming home from a week on the road, harried-looking mothers with kids squealing and clapping and jumping up and down, anxious to see Daddy. My face had sweated quite a bit during the three-hour flight, and I had a mental picture of my false chin melting and my mustache floating off my upper lip. I shouldered my way into the men's room and checked my makeup in the mirror. It was still intact, and I guess I shouldn't have been surprised. Good Plates Tyson probably sweated quite a bit while he was passing the phony money, and his makeup job would have a built-in perspiration factor. I blended back into the throng in the terminal corridor and looked around for Honeybear. He wasn't hard to spot. They didn't make crowds big enough for Honeybear to hide in.

He was wearing mirror shades, probably one of Muhammed's discarded pair, and tight Levis that his bulging thighs were threatening to rip into shreds. His sleeveless mesh shirt was yellow and his hands were jammed into his pockets. As I approached, he yawned.

I stood before him, fished out a bent Pall Mall, and held it between my lips. "Got a light?" I said.

He didn't even notice me; he was too busy checking out the men in the crowd as they filed by. One man, hatless and coatless, wearing a white shirt and tie, hustled along toward the baggage claim, got a load of Honeybear lurking in his path, and made a six-foot detour.

I grabbed Honeybear's bicep and pulled him toward me—not hard, just enough to get his attention. His arm was a quarter-inch thickness of skin stretched taut over muscle and sinew. I said, "Hey, man, you listening to me or what? Got a light?"

His jaw was slack in amazement, and I don't suppose that many people had ever walked up and grabbed him in public. He used his middle finger to snug his glasses up on his face. "Naw, I got no light, I don't smoke. Say, cantcha see I'm waiting for somebody? How 'bout fucking off?" He turned his back and watched the crowd file by.

I couldn't believe it; he'd looked straight at me and really given me the once-over. Honeybear was no scholar, but recognizing people was a way of life with him. Part of the survival routine. A woman in a red pantsuit brushed me slightly as she walked by. I stepped up and clamped my hand onto Honeybear's wrist. "Hey," I said, "who you waiting for?" I was pretty sure he wouldn't lower the boom on me right here in the airport, but not sure enough to keep my stomach muscles from tightening on their own.

"Say, buddy," Honeybear said, "you got a screw loose or something? I toldja I don't smoke."

"Yeah, but I do." I pointed the tip of the cigarette, still holding it in my mouth, in his direction. "Come on, gimme a light," I said.

Now Honeybear was completely buffaloed. He put one hand on his hip and looked me over from head to toe while he rubbed the strip of hair between the shaved sides of his head. In the elevated shoes I was a couple of inches taller than he was, and I felt as though I was standing in front of a short refrigerator. He said, "Man, that smoking bad for your lungs. How 'bout if I poke one of them cigarettes up your ass where it won't do so much damage, huh?"

The tight leer of anticipation on his face changed my mind about whether he'd jump me here in the airport. I said quickly, "Honeybear, old buddy. Don't you know me?"

He moved his chin to one side. "Naw. Know who?"

"Me. Your old pal. The guy who sent you and Snakey and Muhammed on a nice little boat ride up at Connie Swarm's place."

"Bannion? Now you fucking magic, huh. Took over somebody else's body like one of them Martians on TV."

"It's only a disguise," I said.

He reached carefully over and rubbed the top of my head. "Fer real? I guess it is you. Nobody else ignorant enough to go around poking cigarettes in nobody's face. Well, come on, I'm taking you with me. But I ain't so dumb I ain't going to beat the shit out of you, I find out you taken somebody's body over."

SIXTEEN

I didn't think Honeybear looked particularly happy. On the other hand, he didn't look particularly unhappy, either. He just looked like Honeybear, eyes hidden behind mirrored shades, big body slouched down behind the wheel of Muhammed Double-X's Caddy limo, a toothpick dangling from the corner of his mouth. His window was down and his ear rested on the ledge. I was pretty sure he wasn't asleep, but he looked as though he might be. The rest of the limo's one-way black windows were closed, the silver antenna protruding from the trunk lid. The hood vibrated slightly as the Caddy idled. Beyond the idling limo was the jam-packed parking lot around Texas Bank Plaza, the cars' roofs shimmering in the afternoon sun. Farther away, the building's mammoth bulk blotted out the skyline. A low green hedge ran along the sidewalk between the Caddy and the phone booth in which I stood.

Fred Cassel's voice came to me over the line, slightly higher-pitched than normal. "I don't know what you think *I'm* going to do for you. I don't even know why you're calling here."

"No, I don't guess you do," I said. "I'd be the last person you'd expect to call. You might expect me to kill you someday, but not to call." I was trying to keep my voice calm, but a tremor crept into my tone. Just hearing Cassel's voice tightened my grip on the receiver.

After a few seconds' pause, Cassel said, "Well, for your information I'm protected from you. The best thing you can do for yourself, Mr. Bannion, is to keep the hell away from me. They'll slap on the cuffs if you come within a mile of me, I'm not fooling you."

"You're scaring me to death, Fred." I estimated the distance from where I stood to the Texas Bank Plaza's yawning entryway. Couple of hundred yards, give or take.

"Where are you calling from?" After the initial shock he was calming down.

"I might be in Chicago," I said. "On the other hand, I might be in the office right next to yours."

"Hold it, now you just hold it right there. I don't know what your game is, but you're not scaring me a bit. You understand that?" The edge crept back into his tone. I was scaring him, all right, and plenty.

"How about if I tell you in person what my game is?" I said.

"You wouldn't."

"No, I wouldn't, you're right about that. I hate your guts, Fred, but right now I need you. I've got something that belongs to you—you and Breaux and whoever else it is that's in with you. Maybe if you can get your hands on what I've got, you can figure out a way to screw the others out of their share. That's the way you guys do business, isn't it?"

I pictured Cassel sitting up straighter, adjusting his I'm-smart glasses. Briefly I wondered what color his silk breast pocket hanky was today. He said, "What? What belongs to me?"

"I'll let you guess. Even give you a clue. It's white and powdery and goes up your nose. Getting warmer?"

"What makes you think it's mine?" Cassel said.

"Oh, a tape recording that came with it. A little talk between you and Jack Brendy. You sound pretty good over the tape player, Fred. Maybe you should have gone into broadcasting."

"That's bullshit, Bannion. You don't have any tape of me."

No, I didn't, but Cassel couldn't possibly be sure of that. I said. "Maybe that's what the feds will think when I play it for them, that it couldn't be you talking."

There was a rustling noise on the line: a drawer opening, probably Cassel getting out a notepad and a pen. He said, "Well, let's say you do have such . . . merchandise. When can I see a sample?"

"You can't, not before you buy. Look, Fred, I need traveling money. I've got to find a way out of the country."

"I thought there was a lot of money hidden with the . . . whatever it is that you're talking about. At least that's what you told me at our last conference."

Cassel was speaking in code, probably because someone had just walked in on him. Maybe Beautiful. I briefly wondered how long Beautiful had stayed locked in the closet, in there with the Xerox and good old Fred himself. I said, "There isn't any money, that part *was* a bluff. But what I do have is for sale. Fifty thousand. Cash. You'll never hear from me again."

"It's Friday afternoon. I don't know if I can get that much at once. You know, the banks. Tell you what, Mr. Johnson"— I pictured Cassel's gaze darting quickly at whoever was in his office as he called me by the made-up name—"can you call me in the morning? I normally don't come in on Saturday, but I'll make a special trip if you'll call. Say around nine? Be sure, now."

"I'll be sure, Fred. And I've got to have it this weekend. Get on the stick. I can't afford to fuck around, and neither can you."

I hung up, hopped over the low hedge, and climbed into the front seat of the limo beside Honeybear. "There'll be a guy coming out that door any minute," I said, pointing toward the Texas Bank Plaza's entrance, toward the steps leading down with people hustling along and passing one another coming and going. "When he comes out, we're going to follow him."

Honeybear folded his massive arms and shifted the toothpick from one corner of his mouth to the other. "You getting to be a pain in the ass, you know?" he said. "Boss say haul you around, I haul you around. Don't make my ass feel any better, though."

Less than five minutes passed before Fred Cassel came out. He was in a big hurry, going down the steps in little jogging hops with one hand lightly on the bannister. His pale blue Mercedes four-door sedan was parked near the foot of the stairs in a numbered head-in slot. He fished for his keys, unlocked the door, and climbed in. The Mercedes backed up, reversed direction, and headed toward the entrance to Stemmons Freeway. Cassel was gripping the wheel in both hands, looking neither right nor left. That was good. The limo with Honeybear driving wasn't exactly inconspicuous. As Cassel rolled out of the parking lot and turned onto the freeway access road, I touched Honeybear's forearm. "That guy," I said. "Blue Mercedes."

Honeybear dropped the lever into gear and the Caddy moved smoothly into traffic, cutting in between a Mustang and a Mercury Sable and following along a couple of cars behind the Mercedes. Honeybear said, "Sho, massa, I'se followin'." Then he sang the opening lines to "Old Man River" in a deep basso, raising his voice when he got to the lines where the colored folk work for the white man boss. I threw him a sidelong glance. He shifted the toothpick in his mouth and sang even louder.

Cassel went north, exiting the freeway on Inwood Road, going past Harry Hines Boulevard and Lemmon Avenue, ducking down an alley behind the Lemonwood Motel, and finally emerging on Beverly Drive, winding along on Beverly into the heart of Highland Park. Soon we were driving between lawns the size of polo fields that fronted multi-storied homes built in the twenties and thirties for a king's ransom at any day's prices. If you had to ask how much, you couldn't live on Beverly Drive.

Cassel finally parked at the curb just beyond the point where Beverly Drive crossed the bridge over Turtle Creek. In late August and early September the creek was a bare trickle; in late fall and early spring it would become a raging torrent. Hundred-year-old trees lined both shores of the creek, their branches meeting overhead to form a natural roof above the grassy bed where the water flowed. Cassel had stopped in front of a house—more of a castle, really, with Gothic spires dotting its eaves—whose western wall rose from the creek bank. A man was in the front yard, throwing a Nerf ball back and forth with a little girl. The man was tall and stoop-shouldered. Cassel approached him. I told Honeybear to park a couple of houses down, which he did, then I craned my neck to watch what was going on.

Cassel stood off to one side with his hands in his pockets while the man played catch with the little girl. The man was wearing a white tennis outfit; the child was in yellow shorts with a pale blue top. Cassel and the man carried on a running conversation for a few moments, and as the man cocked his arm to toss the child a long one, I zeroed in on his face. My upper lip curled.

I guess I shouldn't have been surprised, but I was. My old buddy James. State Senator Louis P. James, home entertaining a child on his lawn. I wondered if he'd been getting high with Crystal lately. Whatever, along with Cassel, Breaux, and others he was responsible for Donna not being around anymore.

James made a bad throw; the little girl jumped as high as she could, but the ball floated over her fingertips. Giggling, she turned to retrieve it, and I got my first frontal glimpse of Debbie. No doubt about it. My breath caught in my throat.

The facial features were identical: same blond hair, same upturned nose, same saucy tilt to the chin, same wide eyes. As I realized I was looking at Connie Swarm's child a lot of things began to fit together. On top of the other little sidelines he was into, Senator James was using his own illegitimate daughter to coax her mother into posing for a few porno pics. Wonderful guy, the senator. I was suddenly sick to my stomach.

I said to Honeybear, "Let's go. I've seen enough of this crap for one day."

Honeybear pressed down on the accelerator, and we moved on down Beverly Drive. "I seen enough before I ever picked you up," Honeybear said. "So, yeah, we going, but we got one more thing to do. Boss say I supposed to take you someplace where you got some money. Then Boss say if you don't got no money, then I supposed to kill you." He favored me with a broad grin. "So, Massa White Man Boss. Which way you want me to turn?"

It was a peculiar feeling for me, standing on the public side of the counter in Sweaty Mathis's Bail Bond Company and pretending that I'd never been there before. There were the same familiar dusty tiles underfoot, the government-surplus gray metal desks that were dented and scarred and cluttered with stacks of forms, the same ancient ceiling fan clicking monotonously overhead while not creating much of a breeze. The collar of the white cotton dress shirt Plates had sold me was too tight. I loosened the collar and pulled my tie down. Close beside me, Honeybear's breathing was slow and even.

The skinny black kid working behind Sweaty's counter was a buddy of sorts. His name was Polymeus Jackson, a short, ebony-skinned youngster with close-cropped, kinky hair, big round eyes, and sunken cheeks like a vampire's. Polymeus was a burglar who'd never been caught in the act, but who had a record of misdemeanor drunk charges as long as a Tony Franklin field goal. Seemed that he couldn't stay away from the bottle once he'd made a burglary score. Right now he'd be helping Sweaty out around the office in exchange for one or more of his bail-bond fees.

After I'd watched Polymeus collect a small pile of money from a Mexican hooker in a thigh-length mini, then put all of the money in the cash drawer except for one ten-dollar bill he slipped into his pocket, I stepped up to the counter and said, "Mr. Mathis, please." Behind me, a bell tinkled as the hooker went out the front door and onto Jackson Street to tend to business.

Polymeus put one elbow on the counter and rested his chin on his closed fist, eyeing me with no recognition in his gaze. He was wearing a red-and-yellow flowered Hawaiian shirt. "Mister Sweaty ain't here," he said.

That didn't make any sense. Sweaty was never out, not while the jail was doing business and there was a buck to be made. Often Sweaty would sleep at his desk. I said, "You mean he went up the street, like for coffee or something?"

Polymeus glanced from me to Honeybear and back again. "No, man, I told you," Polymeus said. "Mr. Sweaty's gone, till Monday. He say he take his old lady fishin'."

Fishing. Jesus Christ, once in ten years. Suddenly Honeybear seemed a whole lot bigger and a whole lot meaner, which was saying quite a bit. I said, "Are you sure there's not a number where I can call him?"

"They got no numbers in the middle of Lake Tawakoni," Polymeus said. "You come back Monday." He closed the cash drawer, locked it, and retreated toward the rear of the office.

I was panicking. Hell, I couldn't wait until Monday, I couldn't even wait for another hour. Muhammed would . . . I glanced through the storefront window at Jackson Street; it was getting dark and traffic was sparse. Across the street, two uniformed Dallas County sheriff's deputies disappeared through swinging doors into the rear of the Dallas County Courthouse. I leaned over and whispered to Honeybear, "Stay loose." He grunted and folded his arms.

I said loudly, "Hey!" Polymeus halted in his tracks and turned back to me. I put both hands on the counter and vaulted over, my feet thudding to the floor, nearly falling in the two-inch elevator shoes. I righted myself.

Polymeus said, "Hey, you crazy or something?"

I moved quickly over to Sweaty's desk and opened the top drawer: Sweaty's 9mm Browning automatic was there. I picked up the gun. It would be loaded, Sweaty kept it that way.

Polymeus held out both hands, palms toward me, his eyes as round as Stepin Fetchit's. "Man, I got no stake in this. Take whatcha want. Here, you want the cash drawer key?"

I ignored him and went over to the vacant desk where I'd stashed the Samsonite carrying case nearly a week before. If the bag wasn't there I was going to have a real need for Sweaty's gun, to protect myself from Honeybear. As I opened the bottom drawer my breath caught in my chest, then whooshed out in a relieved sigh as I picked the bag up by the handle. I didn't have time to open the case, but the money and the cocaine would still be there. Sweaty would never have touched the bag.

I went back to the counter and out through the swinging gate, poking Sweaty's Browning into my pants pocket on my way. I gave Honeybear a come-on jerk with my head, then went out onto Jackson Street with him at my heels. As the door closed behind us, Polymeus Jackson said, "Hey, man, don't you want the fucking money? I split it with you. Mr. Sweaty, he don't know the difference."

"I'm going to need a car tonight," I said. "Then tomorrow night some backup. About tomorrow night . . . well, I think somebody's going to get shot. I hope it's not me and whoever goes with me, but it might be. How much money we talking?" I folded my hands on top of the Samsonite carrying case, which I was holding in my lap.

Muhammed Double-X was drinking grapefruit juice over ice, seated behind his polished skating rink of a desk. The aerial photo of Dallas hung to his left. Tonight Muhammed wore an iridescent chartreuse suit with matching tie and diamond cuff links. A full six inches of cuff was visible below his coat sleeves. And, of course, he was wearing mirrored shades. I was seated in an easy chair across from him with Honeybear standing to my right and a little behind me.

Muhammed said, "Bear, how many times I tell you not to wear those fucking glasses when I'm around? You look like you trying to scare the shit out of somebody."

Honeybear reached up and took off his mirrored shades, then folded over the earpieces and stuck them in his pocket, blinking his eyes and looking sort of sheepish.

To me, Muhammed said, "You one mothafuckah I don't understand. You ought to be hauling ass out of the country and you wanting to have meetings with people. Who? Bodie Breaux, I guess, and that lawyer asshole Fred Cassel. Those two mothafuckahs done made a jackass out of you, boy."

"How'd you know about them?" I said.

"I keep up with shit. You ask about that Catfish, next thing I know Catfish ain't walkin' around. Couple of girls, they sell they pussy down on Hatcher Street, they say Catfish taken them over someplace to make some pictures. They say Bodie Breaux come by while they double-teamin' this guy, say Bodie Breaux got this lawyer with him. I think that funny,

Bodie Breaux goin' around with you and hangin' out with Catfish same time. You know there's another dude, don't you? Another man doin' them things with Bodie Breaux and Fred Cassel. Guy nobody knows about."

"That senator," I said. "Louis P. James."

"Shit, no, not that funky mothafuckah. Louis P. James ain't even no big deal, he jus' a pussy freak. Them guys, Bodie Breaux and them, they just use what they know about that politician fucking around Connie Swarm to make him do things for 'em. But there's somebody's else."

I blinked. "I know that, and I think whoever that somebody else is will be along tomorrow night. I've got something they want quite a bit, and those kind of guys, they're not going to trust each other enough to let one of them meet me without the others coming along. That's what I'm figuring on."

Muhammed rubbed his chin with his knuckles. "They pretty secret about that somebody else. Bodie Breaux, Fred Cassel, that Louis P. James, I can find out about them. But the other guy I got nothing on, and when there's something *I* can't find out about, that means nobody know nothing. You got any idea who that other mothafuckah?"

"I might have," I said. "How much my backup going to cost me?"

"You not talking no hit? Just go along for the ride, shoot a few guys if we have to. Jesus, you don't even *look* like no Bannion. You sure you the right mothafuckah?"

I told Muhammed I was the right mothafuckah, and that no, I wasn't talking a hit. Like he said, just maybe shooting a few guys. His eyes were hidden behind the shades, but the expression on his lips told me he liked the idea.

"How many dudes you talking about?" Muhammed said.

"Two besides myself will do it. I think they'll have three, and they'll be expecting me alone."

Muhammed swirled his grapefruit juice around and listened to the ice tinkle. Finally he said, "Bear, you wait outside."

Honeybear lumbered out into the room containing the wet bar, the room where Honeybear had punched me in the stomach a few nights ago. "Fifty thousand," Muhammed said. "I don't like putting my men where they might get shot; I got their safety to think about. Besides, I got overhead, so don't give me no quibbling bullshit. Fifty, that what it take. And oh, the price strictly between you and me. Don't no Honeybear know what you paying. I take care of him and the other nigger."

I said, "Sold."

He paused with his glass partway to his mouth. "Bannion, you got as much as fifty thousand in that bag?" A ray of artificial light glinted from a diamond on his cuff.

I turned the case in my lap so that the latches faced me and opened them, then raised the lid about six inches and put my hands inside. With my fingertips I counted five packets of bills. I was operating strictly by feel—no way was I going to let Muhammed see that pile of money. I took the packets out and dropped them on Muhammed's desk. "Just barely," I said.

Muhammed took a drink and smacked his lips. "Well, you just bought yoself an African safari."

"And what about the car tonight?" I said. "Not your limo, by the way. It sticks out like a sore thumb."

"You can bet your ass you ain't getting my limo," Muhammed said. "Not for what you paying. But I got just the wheels. Honeybear's, it got some miles on it, but Bear keep it up pretty good. It what you honkies use to call a Congo wagon. But it run good. Get you where you going, mothafuckah."

For a 1951 Ford, Honeybear's car was a cream puff. It was tuned up like a Stradivarius and ran without a miss, and under the circumstances I couldn't have asked for better transportation. There were a few drawbacks, though.

One problem had to do with the three-speed stick shift, with the lever mounted on the steering column. It had been twenty years since I'd driven a car without an automatic transmission, and it took me a few warm-ups to get the hang of it. At first I was letting out the clutch too quickly; my initial standing starts from intersections were bucking, neck-popping maneuvers that reminded me of the bumper cars on the state fair midway. To make matters worse, the Ford's rear end was lowered a full eight inches, and the twin chrome exhaust extensions dragged the pavement on takeoff.

It was a tossup as to which stood out the most in traffic, Muhammed's limo or Honeybear's Ford. The Ford had a sparkling new pale green paint job, and black mud flaps with chrome lightning bolts covered the top portions of the rear gangster-wall tires. The hood ornament was a big chrome goose with its wings extended, and I had to sit up high in the seat in order to see over the silver bird. As a crowning touch Honeybear had installed Hollywood Glaspac twin mufflers; I hadn't heard the crackling, rumbling noise made by Glaspacs since the sixties, and I wondered where Honeybear had found the muffler shop that still carried the things. So I was off and running. But I was going to have a hard time sneaking up on anyone.

First I drove out to Redbird Shopping Mall and bought some more comfortable clothes. Plates Tyson's disguise was so good that I'd quit worrying about anyone recognizing me, so I strolled right on into the mall among throngs of shoppers—working women mostly, poking here and there among the dress shops and lingering around the paperback counter at B. Dalton's, checking out the week's supply of historical romance bodice-rippers—and went straight to the Gap. There I bought a pair of soft Levi preshrunk jeans—I was surprised to find that my artificial fat pouches had increased my waist size to a thirty-eight—along with a pale blue T-shirt with the Gap's logo across the front. From the Gap I moseyed on down to the Athlete's Foot, where a pimply teenager with braces sold me a pair of white Reebok low-quarter sneakers. I went into the fitting room and changed my clothes, discarding my suit, tie, and built-up shoes in a wastebasket, then walked casually out of the mall. From there I drove the rumbling old Ford out to Highland Park and cruised the neighborhood around Senator James's house.

Ever since I'd watched the good senator cavort on his lawn while he and Cassel discussed the best way to get rid of me for good, I'd been forming an idea. Whatever scores I had to settle with Breaux, Cassel, and Company were going to come to a head in the next twenty-four hours, but James was an entirely different proposition. Whatever else James was into—in spite of what Muhammed had told me about the senator being a pawn, I wasn't convinced that James was entirely clear of the dope and porno business—he had something coming for the way he'd treated his daughter. And no way was he coming to our party tomorrow night; he couldn't afford to take the chance. So for the good senator to get what was coming to him I was going to do a little framing.

First I cruised the alley running behind the houses on James's block. It was a waste of time. The rear of the senator's home was guarded by a high redwood fence with three wicked strands of barbed wire across the top; there were no hand- or footholds in the smooth redwood of the fence, so getting into James's yard from the rear would have been a pretty good trick even if it hadn't been for the wire. Just beyond the senator's fence the alley became a dead end that overlooked Turtle Creek. I backed up, turned around, drove around to Beverly Drive, and parked on the bridge as close as possible to the curb. Then I took the bags of cocaine from the Samsonite case, carried them to the end of the bridge and down the dirt bank to the creek bed. There I crept along ten feet below the western wall of James's Gothic home and looked for a good place to break in.

Clods of soft dirt broke up under my feet; once I tripped on a root and nearly fell, catching myself with one outstretched hand and nearly dropping the cocaine into the foot-wide trickle of water. On my right, something slithered along the bank and wriggled into the stream. Probably a cottonmouth on the prowl.

There was a waist-high, clipped hedge along the house, spanning beneath the six visible ground-floor windows. Lights shone in two of the windows: one with curtains drawn at the front of the house, and the drapeless, next-to-last window on my right. I gulped some moist creek-bed air and clambered up the bank to crouch beneath the lighted window with the drapes closed. There was a slit about an inch wide between the thick curtains, so I raised my head above the windowsill and peeked inside.

I was looking at a formal living room. James was seated on a loveseat drinking a tiny stemmed glass of liqueur, probably cognac, along with a woman. The senator wore the same tennis outfit I'd seen earlier in the day. The woman was a statuesque brunette of around forty, who had the kind of figure that she kept in shape with lots of massages and tennis at the club. She wore a flowing white nightdress belted at the waist, and a big white diamond sparkled on her marrying finger. As I watched, James leaned close and said something to her. Her big bosom shook with laughter and she squeezed his thigh. In addition to the loveseat where the senator and his lady fair were seated, the room held a long velvet divan, several easy chairs, and a concert grand piano. Several oil paintings hung on the walls, and I wondered if the portrait of James behind his desk at the capitol was a Dimitri Vail like the one of Donna, Jack, and the palomino that hung in the Brendy home. Hanging from the center of the ceiling was a crystal chandelier. I got back down on my haunches and half crawled, half duck-walked along the side of the house to the other lighted window, and rose up to see what I could see.

This room was a study. The walls were lined with floor-to-ceiling bookcases containing law books, four or five sets of encyclopedias, and a three-volume set of the current edition of *Books in Print* in addition to classic fiction and some current stuff: Stephen King, Tom Clancy, Anne Tyler, and Rosamunde Pilcher, to name a few. There was a small wood conference table, and on one end of it was a portable electric typewriter—either a Smith-Corona or a Burroughs, I couldn't make out the brand name—with a single sheet of paper rolled into the platen. I reached out and jiggled the window. It slid noiselessly open; Jesus, this was too easy. The hairs at the nape of my neck standing on end, I threw a leg over the sill and climbed inside.

I held my breath and waited for the roof to cave in. It didn't. Visible through the open doorway and across the hall was a darkened room with the foot of a twin bed in sight. Beside the bed sat a Pretty Pony rocking horse. I stood still a little longer. No one came running into the study to shoot me, so I began to move around.

I bent to look at the page in the typewriter. Centered at the top was the title, "To Kill a Vampire," and the second line of print identified the work as "A Novel by Cora James." So the lady of the house was a horror fiction writer, probably something to occupy her time while her husband got high with Crystal.

I went over to the bookcase and removed three volumes of the *Southwestern Reporter*. I was in luck; there was just enough space behind the books for me to hide the cocaine. So I did, carefully lining the cellophane bags along the wall and replacing the volumes. Climbing out the window, I closed it behind me, then stood, and listened for the sirens. Miraculously, I heard none. I retraced my path through the creek bed, climbed the bank up to Beverly Drive, and drove Honeybear's Ford away from there.

"Then I need his home number," I said. "It's important." I was seated on the bed, facing the window. Outside, lights illuminated a ragged, unkept patch of lawn, a white wood fence with chipped paint, and a faded sign in the shape of a sailing vessel with the title "ANCHOR MOTEL" done in blue script. Beyond the sign, a forty-foot tractor-trailer thundered by on Harry Hines Boulevard, braked, and pulled into Googie's Restaurant. Inside Googie's, truckers dawdled over thick coffee, stale doughnuts, and greasy cheeseburgers.

The tenor voice on the phone said to me, "We're not authorized to give out home numbers. Look, I'm Detective Green, I'm handling his caseload on the night shift. Why don't you just discuss whatever it is with me?"

I took a hot drag from a Pall Mall, then set the cigarette in an ashtray on the nightstand. "I've got to talk to Atchley personally," I said. "I've got some information about Rick Bannion."

"Everybody got information about Rick Bannion, friend. Why don't you come on down and fill out a form?"

All I needed, a funny guy. I said, "Listen, you dumbfuck. You're talking to Rick Bannion, and if you don't give me Atchley's number in five seconds, I'm hanging up and taking my most-wanted ass out of town."

"Yeah, Bannion. Come on down, I got a coffeepot on."

"One," I said. "Two."

"Hold it," the cop said. "Hold it, I'm getting the number."

He put me on hold, then came back on, and gave me the number while I wrote it on a motel message pad. The cop asked me which seasons I'd played for the Cowboys. I hung up on him and called Atchley. A sleepy female answered, listened, told me to wait. Finally Atchley's good-ole-boy voice said, "Yeah, Roy Atchley."

"When you got me out of the city lockup, I told you I'd deliver whoever killed Jack Brendy within forty-eight hours," I said. "Doesn't look like I've come through for you too well."

After a brief silence, he said, "Jesus Christ."

"I think I may be in a little trouble, Roy. But I do know who killed Jack. And Catfish, Donald Lund, plus Connie Swarm. Oh, yeah, and a fat federal snitch named Skeezix. And . . . Donna Brendy, too." The thought of Donna caused my vision to blur.

"Yeah," Atchley said. "Yeah, I think I know who killed 'em, too. I think I'm talking to him. Bannion, I'm not going to waste time asking you to turn yourself in, but I'll promise you that sooner or later we'll pick you up. Or somebody will."

"I'm not staying on the phone long enough for anybody to trace me, Roy, in case you're thinking of it. You won't waste time asking me to come in, I won't waste time telling you I didn't kill anybody. I didn't, but it's gone so far I'll never clear myself. It's going to take a manhunt to get me, buddy, and I'm going to take care of the people responsible for the killings myself. Or they might take care of me, I'm not sure." I held the receiver against my ear and lay back on the bed, looking now at the motel's cracked ceiling.

"Use your head for once, Bannion," Atchley said. "Where the hell are you?"

"No way will I tell you that, but I am going to give you a tip. You can call it an anonymous tip if you don't want people knowing it came from me. I don't give a shit anymore."

"A tip on what?" Atchley sounded as though he'd rather go back to sleep.

"A tip on Senator Louis P. James. About two pounds of cocaine hidden behind three volumes of the *Southwestern Reporter*. In the bookcase in James's study."

"Louis . . . now I'm convinced you're a nut. Hell, I couldn't get a warrant even if it was true. No judge is going to call a tip from you sufficient probable cause. What is it, you on peyote?"

"Oh, I think you can get a warrant, Roy," I said. "Dream up some probable cause. That's what you guys usually do."

"On a state senator?" Atchley said. "Good fucking luck."

"I'm going to give you two days, Roy," I said. "Then I'm going to give the information to Norman Aycock. I'll tell him you knew about James having the coke all along, but wouldn't do anything about it. Don't think for a minute I won't, Roy."

"Now, goddammit," Atchley said, "I didn't tell you I wasn't going to do anything. You keep the hell away from those federal fucks. Jesus, I just got rid of the bastards."

"Now, that's more like it, Roy," I said.

SEVENTEEN

I sat on the fender of Muhammed's limo as a pair of head-lights, low beams glowing a dull off-white, came through the tunnel underneath Stemmons Freeway and began the gentle, winding climb up Grauwyler Road in my direction. From the freeway to Loop 12 in Irving, Grauwyler is a two-lane blacktop country road. Crickets whirred in scrubby bushes and low mesquite trees on both sides. On my right were the bald greens and burnt-out fairways of a failed municipal golf course. Overhead, the early September moon appeared to have a halo around it as it beamed softly through the light Dallas smog.

I was wearing the same clothes I'd bought the night before at Redbird Mall. As the headlights came nearer, I climbed down, went around, and opened the driver's door of the limo. Two cellophane bags of baking soda lay in the seat beside a couple of blank tape cassettes I'd bought at Radio Shack. I patted my back pocket: Sweaty's Browning 9mm made more of a bulge than my Smith & Wesson had. I car-ried the tapes and the bags back up front, laid them on the hood, and climbed back up on the fender.

I said loudly, "It's them, it's got to be."

From fifty yards ahead in the bushes, Honeybear answered.

"You think me an' Snakey blind? Hurry up. These chiggers biting the shit out of me."

The headlights stopped twenty feet from the limo's nose. In the bushes, ahead and to my right, there was a slight rustling noise, and I pictured Honeybear and Snakey crouched side by side, ready for whatever was coming down. The grille of the car was a shadowy outline behind the beams; it was a Mercedes grille, of course, but I hadn't needed to see that. I'd known all along that it was Cassel.

Both front doors of the Mercedes opened as one, and there was the scrape of leather soles on asphalt as dark figures emerged on both sides of the car. Fred Cassel's voice, slightly higher-pitched than normal, said, "I don't know who you are, friend, but you're blocking the road."

I nearly laughed out loud. Then I reached up with both hands and peeled the false mustache from my lips, held it off to one side, and dropped it on the asphalt. I'd removed the bloating material from my cheeks earlier. I rubbed the top of my head. "It's me, Fred," I said. "I can't do anything about the hair, it'll have to grow back in on its own. But trust me, it's me."

"Do you have the things we talked about?" Cassel's tone was returning to normal; he was pretty sure he had me right where he wanted me, and I wasn't certain that he wasn't dead on the money.

I patted the bags and tapes on the limo's hood. "Right here, old buddy."

Bodie Breaux came around from the passenger side, outlined in the headlights, and pointed a pistol at me with both hands. The beam caught a flash of yellow on his hat. "Don't be cute, Ricky boy. Twice I could have popped you and didn't, but that don't mean I won't."

A third man materialized behind Breaux, came around him, and started toward me. This guy was wearing a ski mask and dark clothes. He was broad-shouldered and about my height.

Breaux said, "Turn around and put your hands on the hood."

I glanced at the bags and tapes, climbed down, spread my

hands, and leaned on the hood. They'd play the tapes and check out the dope before they did anything more. Then they were planning to kill me. I didn't see that they had any choice about that.

In a few seconds gloved hands touched my neck, searched under my collar. Then the hands moved underneath my armpits, rubbed me down. As the hands approached my waist I said, "That ski mask is pretty hot, isn't it, Buddy?"

There was a sharp intake of breath behind me, and then Buddy Morley stood back and said, "How did you know?"

Twenty years since I'd heard that voice, but it hadn't changed any, same slow South Texas drawl. I looked down between my extended arms at my shoes. There was a dull ache in my throat. "It couldn't be anybody else," I said. "No one but your mom knew we'd changed hotels, and there wasn't but one person that she'd tell about that. You knew Jack through Donna, and since your family all thought you were in some kind of investments I guess you got that idea from him, to cover up what you *were* doing. You fuck. You had your little sister murdered." My voice was shaking and there were tears in my eyes.

"Shut up," he hissed. "Just shut up, Rick. You just shut up and stand there."

"A world full of people," I said. "A world full of people and a world full of towns, and I've got to grow up with you. I guess it's that fucking dope, Buddy. That what turned you into an asshole?"

"You should know," Buddy said.

"I kicked my habit," I said. I raised my head and stared at the limo's windshield. "Finish what you're doing, you fuck. Just don't talk to me anymore."

Buddy came closer behind me, ran his gloved hands underneath my waistband. As he did, there was a loud, scuffling noise behind us, followed by Cassel's voice, excited, saying, "Jesus, they're—" Cassel's voice became a strangled croak. I didn't have to see to know what was going on back there. I'd watched Honeybear and Snakey go to work on Skeezix, and not too long ago.

With a startled grunt Buddy whirled toward the Mercedes.

It was all the opening I needed. I brought my arm up behind me and threw an elbow; the elbow slammed into Buddy's face through the ski mask with a satisfying crunch. I turned around, stuck my head between the numbers, and tackled him. As Buddy and I fell, twisting and grappling, onto the asphalt, two rapid gunshots sounded from the vicinity of the Mercedes. I hugged Buddy around the middle and rolled on top of him, straddled his chest, and pinned his arms with my knees. I grabbed the ski mask from the top, yanked it off, and cast it aside. Then I grabbed Buddy's ears and pounded his head on the road. He yelled in pain. I dug the Browning from my hip pocket, pointed it at his face, and aired back the hammer. For an instant we were still, our gazes locked.

Moonlight is kind: it doesn't show the wrinkles of age. Buddy's square face was exactly as I remembered it. His eyes narrowed into angry slits, then suddenly he grinned. "Fuck you, Rick," he said.

I shot him in the face. The Browning jerked in my hand; his body stiffened, then went limp. There was a gaping hole in his right cheek; a dark mass oozed onto the pavement and puddled behind his head. He was still grinning at me.

From twenty feet away, Honeybear said, "This mothafuckah dead."

As though in a daze, I climbed to my feet and walked to the Mercedes. The Browning hung limply by my hip. Honeybear stood by the passenger side, his massive head bent as he looked downward. I stepped up beside him. Breaux lay on the asphalt on his back, his yellow cap askew. There was a bullet wound in his chest, over the heart, and his eyes were wide and staring. I went around to the other side, where Snakey stood watch over Fred Cassel. Cassel was facedown, his neck bent at an odd angle. I touched his wrist, felt for a pulse. There wasn't any.

I didn't glance at Buddy Morley as I led Snakey and Honeybear back to the limo. As I climbed in behind the wheel, Honeybear hesitated, shrugged, and got in the backseat with Snakey. I turned the key and started the engine; the automatic sentinel turned the headlights on. Buddy's still form was illuminated in the beam, and I looked at him for a second. Suddenly I dropped the lever into gear, floor-boarded the accelerator, and ran over him. Then I backed up and ran over him again. Finally I backed up a second time, turned the Caddy around, and drove off.

E I G H T E E N

As I dropped the quarters in the slot, I looked down at the New Orleans *Times-Picayune* spread out on the shelf beneath the pay phone. Senator Louis P. James's arrest was big news even in Louisiana. The front-page A.P. story quoted James's administrative assistant as saying that the senator was cooperating one hundred percent. Cora James had better get her typewriter in gear, she was going to need the income.

I said to the operator, "That's four seventy-five, is it enough?"

She said that it was and the other line began to ring. I gazed across the width of Canal Street, past the concrete island at the sign atop the Maison-Blanche department store across the way. It was close to five o'clock and the downtown streets were teeming with pedestrians. A block away, a man and a woman crossed Canal at the light and strolled hand in hand toward the French Quarter. There was a click on the line and Donna's mother said hello.

"I failed everyone, Mrs. Morley," I said. "But I got the people responsible, I want you to know that."

I listened to her measured breathing. Finally she said, "I've lost a daughter and a son, Richard. Was it Mr. Cassel, the lawyer?"

"Yes, ma'am," I said. "Along with some other folks."

"I never trusted that man. I can tell about people. Oh, Richard, I'm trying to be so strong, but I . . ." There was the sound of her sobbing as I looked at my shoes. Then she said, "I can't fault you for taking Buddy along to help you. He wouldn't have been talked out of that, even if you'd tried."

I closed my eyes, shifted the receiver from one ear to the other. "Buddy was a headstrong guy, ma'am," I said. "How's Jacqueline?"

"She's all I have. I'm praying to live long enough to raise her."

"Do you think . . . well, could I talk to her?" I said.

"I don't suppose it could hurt. Oh. Federal Express delivered a package here, I suppose it was from you. I'm not going to ask where the money came from. I don't think I want to know."

"You're right, Mrs. Morley," I said. "You don't."

"Well, I'm setting up a trust for Jacqueline. I suppose the money should do someone some good. Where are you, Richard?"

Across the street, in front of the Maison-Blanche, a gray New Orleans police car pulled to the curb. Two uniformed officers got out, approached an old man who was staggering as he walked, and began to talk to him. I said, "It'll be better for you if you don't know, Mrs. Morley. But I promise to be in touch from time to time. Can you put Jacqueline on?"

"Why, she's right here. Just a minute."

I watched the two cops herd the old drunk over to the squad car and deposit him in the backseat. Then Jacqueline said, "Hello?" She sounded older than I remembered. In a few years she'd sound just like Donna.

"How's my brave girl?" I said. "Bravest little girl who ever rode Space Mountain."

"And I'd ride it again, I'm not scared to," Jacqueline said. "Is Mom in a better place? The preacher said she was."

I had to clear a lump from my throat. "Wherever she is, she's happy," I said. "Your mom's a happy person. Are you making new friends?"

"Sure. Grandmama lets me go to town with her, and I

meet lots of new people. I think she's going to get me a puppy. Or a kitty-cat, I can't make up my mind."

The squad car cruised up the end of the block, made a U-turn around the island, and crept alongside the curb headed in my direction. "My time's up on the phone, Jacqueline," I said. "Tell you what. I'll call you every week if you want."

"Goody. When can we go to Space Mountain again?"

I brushed a tear away. "Soon. You can count on it. Look, sweetheart, I've got to go. Tell Grandmama good-bye for me."

I hung up, left the phone, and hurried along on Canal toward Bourbon Street. No way should the two patrolmen be able to ID me on sight, but you never knew.

I hustled across Canal at the light and slowed my pace as I moved down Bourbon toward the heart of the Quarter. Centuries-old buildings lined the streets, the ornate iron railings on their balconies overhead. The narrow strip of pavement that was Bourbon Street stretched out before me into the distance. I had a promise to keep, the promise to Jacqueline that one day we'd see Disney World again. And I'd keep that promise, too. But for now I had to get moving.